BLACK HAWKE,

THE HIGHWAYMAN.

WITH NUMEROUS ILLUSTRATIONS.

LONDON:

NEWSAGENTS' PUBLISHING COMPANY, 147, FLEET STREET, E.C.

1866.

BLACK HAWKE,
THE HIGHWAYMAN.

THE ARRIVAL AT THE INN.

CHAPTER I.
THE CHEQUERS INN.

LATE one winter's evening, somewhat about two hundred years ago, a traveller on horseback drew rein in front of a comfortable-looking hostelrie, a few miles on the road to Chipping Norton, Oxfordshire.

He had evidently ridden hard, and had come some distance, for his steed, although a very fine sample of the most splendid breed, was foaming, and reeked with steam. She panted visibly, too, and snorted with something of gratification at the prospect of rest and provender.

The traveller having dismounted, patted the noble animal caressingly, and giving her to the care of the officious ostler, entered the inn.

Even externally the place had a cosy aspect, as it nestled

within the shelter of a semicircle of fine old trees, the snow lying like a white thatching upon its roof, and a cheerful light beaming from its old-fashioned windows; but the interior was eminently inviting, and as soon as the traveller crossed the threshold, the genial warmth and the cosy array within gave him a welcome that he seemed to feel, for, shaking the snow from his cloak and hat, he regarded the view before him with the complacent air of a man who had made up his mind to make the most of the good quarters he found himself in.

The hostess came forward with a smile, and while the chambermaid took his light valise, invited him to a room, where a bright fire glowed upon the hearth. Here with much ceremony she saw him comfortably seated, and having received his orders, brought him the refreshment he desired, and, lowly curtseying, left him to his reflections.

When the door was closed, the traveller poured himself out a full bumper of wine, and remained at the table for some time, drinking somewhat deeply, though he only sparingly partook of the viands placed before him.

After awhile, he leaned forward in his chair, and with his hands clasped together, sat abstractedly gazing into the fire. As he watched the ruddy embers, his face, lit up by their glow, took a saddened look, and presently he arose, and musingly summoning his thoughts, slowly paced the room.

"The old 'Chequers' is very little altered since I last left it. Dame Margery is not here, though. I wonder if she lives still? That was her daughter Minnette; I suppose she would not remember me. I have changed in form and features since I went away five years ago. I am not expected to come yet. I dare say I shall not be so welcome everywhere as the news of my death would be.

"I used to have a boyish fancy for the orginal of this," he continued, taking a miniature from his pocket, and gazing earnestly at the fair face the artist had limned there; "but I am not likely to be insane enough to drown myself in despair if she has proved as fickle as the rest of her kind. No, no, I have returned for something better than that; I intend to establish my claim to my paternal estates, and if I cannot get them, why some one will have to pay, that's all. I have contracted some few expensive tastes in addition to those I was born with, and if fortune deserts me I must be ripe for mischief."

He replaced the miniature in his breast, and refilling his tankard tossed off the contents at a draught, "pledging his own health," as he pithily remarked, as he cast the dregs to the rushen floor.

The fire glow shone ruddily on his face, and as he stood erect you could judge to advantage of his form and feature.

He was tall, well made, lithe of limb, but broad at the chest, and with his fine head set well back on his shoulders; his face was bronzed; the features were pleasingly but boldly shaped; his brow was broad, and his curling hair was massed back from his temples; his hands were small, and fair almost as a woman's, and his whole *physique* was expressive of immense power and matchless beauty.

He had thrown his cloak aside, and his attire, which was of the richest material, set off his elegant shape; he had a short rapier by his side, the sheath elaborately ornamented, the hilt glittering with roundly-polished jewels.

As he strode across the room, treading with the graceful step of an Adonis, he tapped the hilt of his rapier carelessly, as if in response to his thoughts, when he pondered upon the means of gratifying those tastes which he had acknowledged as expensive.

The step of the hostess approaching he sat down again at the table, and was leisurely quaffing the ruby wine when she entered, and demurely asked if he intended to remain for the night.

The stranger smiled as he answered,

"I' faith, yes; he would be a dolt who would go forth to-night from such social quarters as these. Not I; prepare me a chamber in which I can repose in comfort, and let my horse be well tended to; we have come a long way, and of the two I fancy she has had the worst of the journey."

"The best chamber in the house shall be placed at your service," replied the pretty-looking hostess, "and I will see that your horse is well cared for, though, as for the worst of the journey, I think, good sir, she is well repaid in carrying so goodly and handsome a gentleman."

This was said with a modest blush as she was about to leave the room.

The stranger rose, a glow of pleasure suffusing his countenance as he walked quickly towards her, and taking her by the hand prevented her departure.

"And who taught you to flatter, little one?" he asked, lightly. "It is usually the part of the gallant to return compliments; but for so pretty a speech I must even kiss the ripe lips of so blithe a lassie."

"Indeed, sir, no; I—pray, sir—nay——"

She struggled to get from him, but the stranger deftly brought his face to hers, and kissed her right gallantly.

As he disengaged her from his hold he laughed lightly at her dismay. Instantly a change came over the young damsel's face, and she looked curiously at him.

"Why, Minnette," he said, quickly, "have you forgotten—"

"Master Merlin!" cried the young hostess, with a little cry of pleasure.

"'Tis I, faith; but no names, little one; there be some I would not have know of my return; not yet, at least, so prithee keep thy counsel for awhile."

"Oh, Master Merlin—dear sir, to think of your coming back after all this time; and how you have grown—so tall and handsome. Oh! if Lady Florence could only have seen you looking so noble——"

A change came quickly over the stranger's countenance. He paled slightly, and his eyes beamed with a deep light.

"Lady Florence!" he exclaimed, huskily. "Oh, Minnette, what of her?"

"Do you not know? Indeed, if you don't, I cannot tell you; though, for my part, a lady that could so forget her promises, and—and——I—I only know I wouldn't have acted so if I had been in her place."

"Forgotten her promises?"—a shadow stole over Merlin's face—"'Tis woman like. But come, Minnette, let me hear all. Is she - a wife?"

"Indeed she is; she is married to——"

"Whom, little one?"

"Sir Andrew Greville."

"To him?"

The stranger reeled as if a bullet had stricken to his heart. For a few moments he seemed about to fall. His lips were white, his features darkened, and the light in his eyes grew more intense.

"To him?" he muttered, between his grating teeth. "The LIAR!—the THIEF! Why, I have seen her cower when her father mentioned his name! I have heard her with shivering lips and whispering voice say that the cold tombstones should lie above her breast before that recreant traitor should take her to his arms! And now——But why—why trouble for a bauble so worthless as a woman's love? No more of her; but for him! 'fore God, I came to fight him for my rights—this is a man's cause—though not for her. And when I meet him, God and *this*!"

He struck his rapier hilt violently, and strode across the room, his face purpling with anger, his eyes gleaming fiercely, his lips wreathing in scorn and passion.

He seemed to have forgotten the presence of Minnette, who, with a face as pale as a sheet, stood timidly watching him in this ebullition of fury.

All of a sudden he turned, and saw her white face, and then his looks changed as if by a miracle; the wildness passed away, and he softened down to comparative calmness.

"My poor little one," he said, taking her hands in his, "I have scared you."

"Oh, Master Merlin, you did frighten me. You looked so awful, and the veins on your temples were like what Granddam Margery used to say could be seen on your father's when he was in a passion."

"My father? He had enough to make his heart swell from his body! To be run to earth by these white wolves—to be falsely charged and persecuted—to have his home stripped from him, and to see his enemies lording it in the halls where his fathers had been like kings—and now one of these vampires adds this insult to my wrongs! My father's curse fall on me if I do not avenge him to the full!"

Again he strode across the room, and frowned darkly in his rage.

In a few moments he was again calm.

The tempest of passion had passed away, but a settled look of stern resolve was on his countenance.

"Do not let me make you shrink, Minnette," he said; "I am calm now. Do not regard my passion; but come, sit down, and tell me all that has happened since I left England. First of all, your father; does he live?"

"He does, sir."

"And Dame Margery?"

"She is at peace !"

"Died full of years and in content. Ah, how happy are they who are free from the turbulence of this world ! But to hear all : Sir Andrew Greville has married Lady Florence ; have they children ?"

"One babe—a litttle boy."

"Sir Andrew's brother Marmaduke ; where is he ?"

"At the Hall ; he lives with them."

"They are twins, but I know not which is the more wicked of the two. Stay, there was one Simeon Lazarus, a sallow-visaged, usurious Jew, a robber of the poor and defrauder of the wealthy. It was by his aid also my father lost his lands."

"He is still intimate with Sir Andrew and his brother."

"I would have sworn it, the white-livered devil ! His evil visage is the spawn of sin !"

"He is a bad man ; it was only last week he was the ruin of a whole family for arrears of rent."

"The dog ! But, to turn from him, how fares it with honest Hugh Marks, the miller ?"

"He is as happy as ever, and his daughter Nancy is the prettiest maid of the village."

"I know no more I care to ask after ; so, now, good Minnette, I will tax your patience no further."

"Indeed, sir, it is a pleasure to speak to you, and an honour. But I forgot to tell you something I think you would like to hear."

"Whom concerns it ?"

"Simeon Lazarus."

"Ha ! what of him ?"

"Only that I expect him here to-night."

"To-night ? With whom, Minnette ?"

Minnette stepped close to Merlin, and, in a low voice, said cautiously,

"Sir Andrew's brother has been here this evening ; he sent a private message for old Simeon, and ordered him to come here ; and indeed, sir, I have my doubts that they are about no good, and so——"

"I see it ; you suspect their villany. Place me where I can overhear them ; do this, good Minnette, and trust me, if there be means, I will thwart them."

"I can do it if you won't mind being cramped up in a very small place."

"Mind ? I would get inside a scabbard to overhear the villains."

"The place won't be so small as that," said Minnette, with a smile. "There is a secret corner here behind these hangings ; I can place you there, and when they come I will show them into this room and——"

"You are a clever girl, Minnette. Good, the idea of circumventing these villains is like new life to my blood. Put me into this cranny, and if I do not help them after a style they don't expect, may I never be let out again."

Promising to be back in time to place him in his hiding-place, Minnette left the room, and Merlin, reseating himself at the table, recommenced quaffing the liberal wine. His thoughts were of a varying nature as he sat there, for at times he frowned darkly and clutched his rapier hilt, at others he muttered an impatient "Pshaw !" and, bringing his hand forcibly down upon the table, replenished his glass, and drank again to the success of some scheme he was concocting.

CHAPTER II.

WHAT MERLIN HAWKE HEARD FROM HIS HIDING-PLACE.

MINNETTE came back after the lapse of half an hour, and informed Merlin Hawke that he must enter his place of concealment, as Marmaduke Greville was approaching, and, having rapidly cleared away all signs of the apartment having been occupied, she opened a sliding panel in one corner of the room, and disclosed a dim and dusty aperture of barely sufficient width for a man to ensconce himself.

It looked anything but inviting ; but this was no time to be scrupulous.

Merlin gathered up his hat and cloak, and enveloping himself in the latter squeezed himself into the cavity.

Minnette closed the sliding door upon him, and he was left to solitude and darkness.

He had been about thirty minutes in his cramped and uncomfortable position when he heard the door of the room open, and somebody of evident importance rushed in.

Lights appeared at the same moment, and a chink in the wood enabled him to see Marmaduke Greville enter, followed by the Jew.

The former came in with a haughty step ; the latter, cringing and debased, sneaked like a felon after him.

There was a great contrast between them ; but the look of the villain was apparent in both, though anything more horribly repulsive than the flabby, puckered, ashy-hued lineaments of the Jewish money-lender it was hard to conceive.

"Some wine, and see that we are not disturbed," said Marmaduke Greville, peremptorily.

Minnette obeyed, and the door was closed.

"Before we proceed to business let us just see that we are not overheard," was Marmaduke's observations as he drew his rapier, and, stepping on tiptoe round the room, probed every place likely to give concealment to a listener.

Satisfied that they were not overheard he sat down, and for the space of nearly an hour the two were in close conference.

Merlin found his hiding-place conveniently constructed for hearing what passed.

Scarcely a word escaped him, low as was their tone.

He learned from their converse that Marmaduke cherished designs against the happiness of his brother, and this meeting was to arrange for the disposal of the child of the marriage, who was to be carried off by an agent of the Jew's, and secretly murdered, Marmaduke designing after this to make away with his brother, and assume his rank, at the same time possessing himself of Lady Florence.

Merlin's blood boiled as he heard the terms in which she was spoken of.

"Understand," said Marmaduke, "I must see this brat's death. The man whom you employ must bring it to me that I may be certain it will never trouble me hereafter."

"It shall be done—it shall be done. Depend upon the service," returned the Jew, forcing a ghastly grin to his countenance, and rubbing his emaciated hands servilely together. "We shall not be squeamish."

"Enough. When you desire gold let me know. I shall now depart that I may be absent on this night ; but before dawn let the child be in my power."

A few more words relative to their compact passed between them, and then Marmaduke went from the room, the Jew remaining.

"It shall be done, it shall be done, dear Marmaduke. *Sir* Marmaduke, as you are to be by my making," muttered the Jew, his drivelling face shrivelling with malice, " we shall not be squeamish. Oh, dear no ; the brat shall be taken, but it shall not die. Oh, no ; it shall live to be something which I will make it. Oh ! God of my Fathers ! Then some fine day it shall know its mother's name, and its mother shall know the name of her child, when I have brought it to the *gibbet* !"

As the Jew spoke, his grisly face was convulsed with rage ; his blearish eyes started in their sockets ; his lips frothed.

"That is how she shall pay for insulting me," he cried, in a screeching whisper, "when she shall see her child—ah, her dear babe—die on the gibbet the death of a *highwayman* !"

"Oh ! oh !" thought Merlin, "that is your little plan, is it, my fine son of Abraham ? Stop a bit, stop a bit ! You may be stopped in your gallop, you rascally old dog."

The Jew put on his hat, and drawing his cloak about his decrepit form, was preparing to quit the room, when Merlin, who had conceived a sudden idea, divested himself of his cloak and hat, and sliding back the panel, noiselessly stepped from his hiding-place, and stood motionless behind him.

Simeon Lazarus was standing opposite to one of those old-fashioned looking-glasses, when he saw, reflected there, the life-like image of a man whom he had long since believed dead.

So great was the shock that his visage was convulsed with fright, his tongue clove to his mouth, a spasm benumbed his frame, and in horrible fear he closed his eyes.

When he opened them again, Merlin (who had taken advantage of the opportunity to glide back to his hiding-place) was gone; but the Jew still seemed to see the dreaded image. Then he turned his palsied glance from the mirror and tottered towards the door.

"God of my Fathers!" he muttered, "I did see that cursed boy with mine own eyes lie dead! drowned! when I had thrust him into the river—and—now—he does come there again. Oh, it is awful! it is awful!"

And with chattering teeth he crawled from the room.

Merlin, who had rather enjoyed the spectacle of his dismay, then came from his concealment.

"So, you old venom spitter, I have found a way to reach you at last? You are superstitious. You thought it was my ghost, eh? good! You never thought I should get out of that river into which you flung me, scum of the devil's brood. A pretty plot for that poor babe—a *highwayman!* I know not if I should care to interfere if it were not *her* child. I would leave the villains to their own venom; but, as it is, I will save the boy. A highwayman, too! You will have cause to be grateful, Florence; and as I think you are at present in very bad company, why I shall take the liberty to carry you off to-night, dear one, for if you're to be made a prize of, I may as well win you as any of those d—d rascals!"

"Poor little dove," he added, a moment afterwards, his recklessness leaving him. "It is hard to think of your being made the sport of these inborn devils. I would I had them at my blade's end! But that time will come, and then, good rapier, you shall go home to the very hilt!"

Minnette came in, looking very frightened, but her confidence returned when she saw Merlin.

"I heard the Jew muttering your name as he went out, and I thought that he had discovered you."

"Oh, no, little one, I merely gave the chicken-hearted scoundrel a fright—that's all. I think I've sent him off shaking in his boots. But now, Minnette, I shall want Fair Rosamond saddled, for I must not abide here to-night, though, to-morrow, I trust to do so. Perhaps I may bring some one else also."

Minnette was surprised at the announcement; but a few words from Merlin acquainted her with his intentions, and, after expressing many fears for his safety and hopes of his success, she calmly entered into his plans and went to give orders for Fair Rosamond to be got ready immediately.

"That's a sensible girl," said Merlin, musing, after she had gone; "worth her weight in gold! She can be trusted, too. I'll get her to lie in wait and take the child after I have taken it from the villain, for I shall not have much time to spare, and I may as well take Lady Florence to-night as any other time."

CHAPTER III.

MERLIN FINDS HIMSELF IN THE CHAMBER OF LADY FLORENCE—THE JEW TURNS UP AT AN UNEXPECTED JUNCTURE—A HOT PURSUIT IS BROUGHT TO AN UNEXPECTED CONCLUSION.

THE night was not very light, although the snow was on the ground; the air was not frosty either; all the better, as Merlin thought, since there would be less chance of his horse's hoofs betraying him in the event—a not unlikely one—of his being followed after the daring abduction of Lady Florence.

Fair Rosamond looked sleek and glossy even after her short rest; the magnificent creature seemed to know that adventure was in the wind, or she would not be taken out again that night; she pawed the ground proudly and reared her finely pointed head as Merlin softly called her by name and sprang lightly to the saddle.

He took her at an easy pace along the high road for some miles, and, arriving in front of a commodious residence, took up his position under the shadow of a grove of chestnuts, and waited silently for what was to come.

He had not long left the "Chequers Inn" when Minnette, muffled from head to foot in a large shawl, cautiously left the hostelrie, and, unseen by any one, made her way after him.

Merlin Hawke had remained in his position, as motionless as if himself and horse had been carved out of granite, for about twenty minutes, when a fellow, whose low-looking features could be distinguished as he drew near to the house, approached on a broad grey mare which he was leisurely riding.

That the plot upon which the Jew and his employer had conversed had been well matured was evident from the fact that the new comer admitted himself into the grounds leading to the house, and, leaving his grey mare by the gate, went to the rear part of the house; here a confederate admitted him, and, for the next ten minutes, Merlin sat amid profound silence.

It was broken at length by the low crunch of a man's foot upon the soft snow.

Two figures came up the pathway from the house; one a man—the one he had seen go in—the other a woman.

She held a muffled bundle in her arms, and, when the fellow had mounted his mare, she handed him the parcel carefully, and, with every show of caution, let him out and closed the gate after him.

"A female confederate," thought Merlin, as she went noiselessly into the mansion. "Well, my fine fellow, you are hurrying off, I must be after you presently."

Having waited till he thought all was safe in the house he whispered a word to Fair Rosamond, and the mettled charger, arching her graceful neck, was instantly off like the wind; but, fleetly as she went, her hoofs touched the earth with such wondrous lightness that they awoke no echo from the snow-covered ground.

When Merlin had ridden a mile or so along the road he slackened pace; the cumbrous form of the grey mare could be seen in advance of him.

Without appearing to hasten he soon got close to the fellow, who, hearing the sound of horse's hoofs, and beholding the stranger riding behind him, would fain have been somewhere else with his suspicious burthen.

But Merlin was presently up beside him, and in spite of his taciturn sullenness, would carry on a conversation with him.

"Are you not afraid," he asked, "to ride alone in so unfrequented a spot?"

"No, I be not afraid," replied the man. "I carry nothing to lose."

"Indeed! Then what have you under your cloak, good friend?"

"Nothing that you would wish to carry even if you were a highwayman."

"Are you sure of that? Come, let us see; your burthen seems heavy and I may as well relieve you of it."

The man turned to make some saucy reply, but found the barrel of a pistol looking him in the face, and although he was armed, the determined air of the stranger quite overcame any idea of resistance, and he hastened to explain that his burthen was only a child, hoping by the confession to escape.

But Merlin pinned the rascal immediately.

"I am a man of few words," he said. "Deliver the child or lose your brains!"

Too terrified to offer opposition, he delivered up the babe; but Merlin had not done with the rogue just yet. He bound him securely, with his face to the horse's tail, and setting the animal off at full gallop, bade him God speed on his journey.

There was light enough for him to look at the child's face, and with strange emotions he traced the likeness of his lost love, Lady Florence.

"I will be a better keeper to ye both, than those men would have been," he soliloquised; "and that is all I dare say, for with no fortune but my sword and name, and the last attaint with treason, I have but poor chance against those wolves of the devil. Nevertheless, if they come to demand of me, I will make a hole in some of their skins."

He covered up the fair face of the child.

"A highwayman, indeed," he mused. "The old rascal. By all that's holy it would be a precious good idea to make a highwayman of him, the skinny-faced old harpy; and I'll do it too. There are one or two of the band about this vicinity. I'll get this infernal blood-sucker on their scent, so that he may fall into a trap, and be taken, and perhaps the next execution may be for him. At any rate he will have to bear enough if the highwaymen take him captive."

The fellow whom he had bound to his mare was out of sight, when he stopped on seeing a cloaked figure crouching by the road-side.

It was Minnette waiting for him.

She received the child tenderly, and nestling it to her breast, covered it with her shawl.

"Return quickly, Minnette, and be on the alert. Within an hour or so, I shall return with the mother—dear Lady Florence."

Minnette was about to hurry away, when he stopped her.

"If anything should occur, Minnette, that I should not return to-night," he said, in a kindlier tone, "take charge of the child. Rear it tenderly, and only let it know its parentage when it is old enough to battle for its own rights."

He whispered to Fair Rosamond, and almost in a moment was out of sight.

Minnette turned sadly homewards.

Foreboding was at her heart that the dangerous enterprise upon which Merlin was bound would involve him in deadly peril.

As for Merlin, he thought nothing of the mournful presentiment which had called forth his last injunctions to her; it passed away the moment his noble steed took him on in swift career. The blood glowed in his veins as the cool air freshened his temples, and he only drew rein when he came again in sight of Lady Florence's house.

Any one with less of the devil-may-care carelessness of our hero might have been incited to melancholy regrets at the view of the mansion of his ancestors in the grasp of his enemies; but Merlin was a strange being. He would have given his life gladly for his father to have retained his estates; but those had long been taken away, and his father had died of grief at the loss, having first slain the father of Sir Andrew and Marmaduke Greville. Merlin had, nevertheless, made up his mind to gain the property, if possible; and, if not, to bring the present owners to account in deadly combat.

His present mission had, however, not to do with the mansion, but with its lovely mistress.

Lady Florence, the peerless love of his early days, his boyhood's dream, the queen of his heart's dearest hopes, wrested from him, and now to be taken by force as she had been gained by cunning!

It was a wild scheme he had formed; but he was famous for wild schemes, and as he was generally pretty successful he looked forward to similar fortune on the present occasion.

It was true that he was about to enter a house swarming with retainers; to enter it alone, and alone risk the meeting with any of its inmates—its haughty possessors even; but the fearless courage only glowed upon Merlin's cheeks, and his eyes flashed as he thought of an encounter with Sir Andrew Greville or his twin brother.

Thoroughly acquainted with the house and its grounds he went round to the shrubbery separated from the road by a wall.

Satisfied that no one was in sight he put Fair Rosamond to the leap and cleared the wall in capital style.

His preparations were now noiselessly made; in a few seconds Rosamond was securely hidden amongst the shrubs. Merlin knew she would not stir till he came back; patting her neck caressingly he made his way to the house, and by a means of ingress not generally used gained access within.

Though the hour was late many of the inmates were yet stirring. Unperceived by them Merlin passed along the grand corridor; he had left his hat and cloak in the shelter with his horse.

A light gleaming from a half-open door attracted him; he remembered the room, and his thoughts grew fiercer. It had been his mother's apartment.

He advanced and passed within.

The vision made his breath come short and rapidly; his breast dilated, his heart seemed to expand.

A lady sat in the apartment. She was reading by the light of a taper. A small black bound missal and a white crucifix were before her.

She was richly dressed. Jewels hung round her arms, and encircled her fairy throat. Her raiment dazzled the eyes.

She had her face turned towards the doorway. Such a face! Its exquisite loveliness was almost beyond mortal conception. A pensive look gently overshadowed the features; the eyelids were half closed over the beautiful orbs flashing beneath, and swimming, as it seemed, in tears; her throat was white and full; her robe exposed a bosom of ravishing tint and softness.

Merlin Hawke stood bedazed on the threshold.

The seraphic being before him was Lady Florence.

Not as he had left her; her beauties had more expanded their glowing charms; her form and countenance were more divinely perfect.

Merlin might have remained there in dumb entrancement till discovery came if he had not suddenly thought of the purpose which brought him there.

It was a difficult matter how to betray his presence without startling her.

He tapped gently at the door, uttered her name in the softest tones, and entered as she rose to see who dared to intrude upon the seclusion of her private chamber.

When their eyes met Lady Florence went pale as an image of wax. Her tongue refused utterance.

Merlin took advantage of the occasion, and softly closed the door.

Then she found voice, and in a dismayed tone of anguish, exclaimed,

"Merlin!"

"'Tis I, fair lady," he replied, concealing his real emotion under a semblance of levity; "returned, as you perceive, to visit the friends to whom I have been dead these last few years."

"Dead? Yes," Lady Florence replied, half abstractedly; "it was said that you were dead."

"And the report most readily believed."

"Not readily. Oh, Merlin——"

She paused, seemed about to say something sorrowfully, but the unseemly place of their meeting occurred to her.

"We dare not speak now," she cried hurriedly, listening lest any one approached. "This is no place for you to come to me."

"I know it, madam; it is your husband's chamber, or one to which he has the privilege of entering. Do not uplift your hands; I am not here to vex you with vain remonstrances. Even a woman cannot *forget* when she has loved, or professed to love. I have dreamed a boy's foolish dream in my absence, and you have been the theme. But I am cured of love, as you see."

"Oh, Merlin! Alas! alas!"

"Nay, be not sad; I would not have asked you to bind yourself to a beggar, nor should I have felt the bitterness if you had wedded some honourable peer. But to marry this robber who struts in my father's hall, and steals the homage that should be mine! Craven that I am to let him live an hour! Pardon me; my blood is hot when I think of the past. A truce to that now; I have more of import to say. Put on your hood and mantle, lady, and come with me."

Lady Florence advanced a step nearer to him, and gazed into his face with the most unequivocal amazement.

"Am I so fallen," she asked, huskily, "that I am to be bidden leave my husband's roof by the first who likes to act the part of thief?"

"Not at all, lady; but, as time is precious, and I am not safe here an instant, and also do not intend to quit the house without you, I may as well repeat my desire, with the addition of my intention to enforce the commands if not attended to."

Lady Florence retreated from him with frigid dignity.

"Leave me, sir!" she said, coldly. "How I have wronged myself in thinking that I ever loved you."

A genial glow suffused Merlin's features.

"Then she loves me yet," he thought. "It is hard to hear that and not risk the danger of a stolen embrace. But it must not be."

"Madam," he said, in a forced tone of composure, "I beg of you to lose no time. I have a horse in readiness; I can conduct you secretly from the house. If you do not choose that mode, I must attempt to carry you off."

"Merlin, are you mad? Do you know what will follow?"

"Yes; an alarm will be given. Retainers—your husband—will come to the rescue; he will find me, sword in hand, preparing to carve my way out of his house, with you on my arm. We shall fight, one of us will fall, and you will have the spectacle of either him or myself lying in our blood at your feet."

Lady Florence crept a little closer to him and faced him.

Her earnest gaze was fixed, her large, lustrous eyes dilated in wild wonderment.

She did not seem to comprehend the scene.

Merlin gallantly offered his arm.

Despite the pain of such a course, he felt that it was best for him to affect indifference.

"Were I to fall on my knees, and in tears of mad despair entreat you to listen to me, I might find cause for your mistrust; but as I come chiefly to take you to your child, to take you from these men who have removed it, I beseech you to come. Fear not; I shall not forget that though you are the wife of my enemy you are the child of my father's friend."

Lady Florence paid no heed to his closing words.

She heard only his allusion to her child.

An agonised look overspread her countenance; her voice died away in frozen whispers.

"My child?"

"Aye, lady, come. I will take you to it. Trust me, and listen while I relate the truth of your true position."

With a bewildered air Lady Florence heard him while he recounted the compact made between the Jew and her husband's brother.

She was more like a breathless corpse than a living mortal as she heard.

Merlin feared she was about to faint.

He hastily stepped forward to slip his arm round her waist, but she put him from her, and stepped sadly away.

"You see what a pretty set you are amongst?" he said. "Let me persuade you to listen to me; besides, Lady Florence, though I now appear unmoved as a stone, I am not insensible either to our former intimacy or your matchless loveliness. I still love you—not madly; but so dearly that I would lose a crown to gain you."

A strange look came over her as she heard him.

Her deathly paleness became more excessive.

She trembled visibly.

"I know you now," she said, in her sad, sweet tones. "Time has changed you, and left nothing of your former self; even the last trace of your honour has gone. Leave me. I will not listen to your deceit, nor would all your persuasions, backed by truth, induce me to accompany you."

"S'death! madam," broke out the impetuous youth, "in that case I must make a captive of you, and carry you off against your will. And, hark you, any foolish screaming brings death on the threshold of this house."

Lady Florence placed her hand upon a silver bell.

Before she had time to summons help by its aid Merlin's arm was flung round her and she was lifted off her feet.

Terrified and aggrieved at this outrage she uttered a startling cry.

Merlin might have prevented this by placing his hand over her lips, but he forbore to do so, at the same time the brave fellow knew that the mischief was done.

Unmistakable sounds convinced him that help was approaching.

His thin, bright rapier leapt from its sheath.

A voice had reached him.

Sir Andrew's!

"Your husband comes, madam," he muttered. "You have invoked the result."

"Quit me," she replied, faintly. "I will be surety that you are not harmed."

"Trust myself to those wolves? No. I know them too well; besides, it is against my conscience to relinquish my designs while I can wield my blade."

"Fearful man, there will be blood shed."

"Aye, and either you will be short of a husband, or they will carry my carcase out to the moat."

He had gained the corridor with her on one arm, and as he spoke, Sir Andrew, followed by half-a-dozen armed domestics, came hurriedly to the spot.

Sir Andrew, sword in hand, and breathless with haste and agitation, was petrified at the sight of the daring abduction.

"You here, traitor?" he cried, hoarsely. "And with my wife?"

"'Tis I indeed, in veritable flesh and blood!"

"Put down the lady, villain! Down with him, men!"

"Pardon me," said Merlin, coolly. "It is many years since we met, and I am about to leave you a remembrance of the visit."

"Dastard, I myself will slay you!" Sir Andrew cried, hoarse with passion.

Their blades crossed, and the domestics gathered round them as he spoke. Merlin lightly fencing, retreated to the wall. Lady Florence hung almost helplessly upon his shoulder.

A few rapid exchanges passed between them, Sir Andrew fencing warily for fear of injuring his wife, and his servitors keeping back from the same reason.

All at once, to his very great surprise, his rapier went whirling from his grasp, and he stood defenceless before the thrust of his enemy.

That moment would have been his last, for Merlin, too furious to spare him, was about to run him through the body, but Lady Florence, by a violent struggle, diverted his aim, and Sir Andrew received the thrust in his left arm.

Ghastly with rage and mortification, he sprang to pick up his sword, at the same time calling to his servants,

"Slay him! Slaughter them both rather than let him escape!"

Merlin stood undauntedly at bay as they pressed upon him; he had been edging his way along the wall; once or twice he turned his head, as if looking for some mark he expected to find.

Unquailingly warding off the attacks of his numerous assailants, he paused at length to parry a stroke which Sir Andrew aimed with deadly fury at his throat.

In the act his sword fell from his hand.

At the moment that his sword was down two of the domestics sprang upon him.

Lady Florence closed her eyes and shuddered.

His death seemed imminent. But there was a flash, a loud report, and the first of his assailants fell to the floor.

Quick as lightning Merlin regained his sword.

A defiant yet not unmusical laugh broke from his lips: he saw the swords and pistols of the rest presented at his breast, but before any one else could make their attack, he had touched a secret spring he had long been looking for, and before the smoke cleared away from before his assailants' eyes, they saw him vanish with Lady Florence through the wall.

Sir Andrew leaped like a madman to the spot, and tore at the concealed panel.

"Unearth this mystery!" he cried. "Hasten some of you below. If he attempts to escape that way bring him down as you would a dog."

(To be continued.)

THE GOBLIN DOG;
A TALE OF FUN AND WONDER.

EVERY person in the parish knows the purty knoll that rises above the Routing Burn, some few miles from the renowned town of Knockimdowny, which, as all the world must allow, wants only houses and inhabitants to be as big a place as the great town of Dublin itself.

At the foot of this hill, jist undher the shelter of a dacent pebble of a rock, something about the bulk of half a dozen churches, one would be apt to see—if they knew how to look sharp, otherwise they mightn't be able to make it out from the grey rock above it, except from the smoke that ris from the chimbley—Nancy Magennis's little cabin, snug and cosey, with its corrag, or ould man of branches, standing on the windy side of the door, to keep away the blast.

Upon my word, it was a dacent little residence in its own way, and so was Nancy herself, for that matther; for though a poor widdy, she was very punctwell in paying for Jack's schooling, as I often heard ould Terry M'Phaudeen say, who tould me the story.

Jack, indeed, grew up a fine slip; and, for hurling, foot-ball playing, and lepping, hadn't his likes in the five quarthers of the parish. It's he that knew how to handle a spade and a raping-hook, and what was better nor all that, he was kind and tindher to his poor ould mother, and would let her want for nothing. Before he'd go to his day's work in the morning, he'd be sure to bring home from the clear spring well that ran out of the other side of the rock a pitcher of water to serve her for the day; nor would he forget to bring in a good creel of turf from the snug little peat-stack that stood, thatched with rushes, before the door, and leave it in the corner, beside the fire; so that she had nothing to do but put over her hand, without rising off her sate, and put down a sod when she wanted it.

Nancy, on her part, kept Jack very clane and comfortable; his linen, though coarse, was always a good colour, his working clothes tidily mended at all times, and when he'd have occasion to put on his good coat to work in for the first time Nancy would sew on the fore part of each sleeve a stout patch of ould cloth to keep them from being worn by the spade, so that when she'd rip them off every Saturday night, they would look as new and fresh as if he hadn't been working in them at all, at all.

Then, when Jack came home in the winter nights, it would do your heart good to see Nancy sitting at her wheel, singing "Stachan Maragah," or "Peggy na Laveen," beside a purty clear fire, with a small pot of murphys boiling on it for their supper, or in a wooden dish, comfortably covered with a clane praskeen, on the well-swept hearth-stone, whilst the quiet dancing blaze might be seen blinking in the nice earthen plates and dishes, that stood over against the side wall of the house.

Just before the fire you might see Jack's stool waiting for him to come home, and, on the opposite side, the brown cat washing her face with her paws, or sitting beside the dog that lay asleep, quite happy and continted, purring her song, and now and then looking over at Nancy, with her eyes half shut, as much as to say, "catch a happier pair nor we are, Nancy, if ye can."

Sitting quietly on the roost above the door were Dicky the cock and half-a-dozen of hens that kept this honest pair in eggs and egg-milk for the best part of the year, besides enabling Nancy to sell two or three clutches of March birds every sason to help to buy wool for Jack's big coat, and her own grey-beard gown and striped red and blue petticoat.

To make a long story short, no two could be more comfortable considering everything.

But, indeed, Jack was always obsarved to have a dacent, ginteel turn with him, for he'd scorn to see a bad gown on his mother, or a broken Sunday coat on himself, and, instead of dhrinking his little earning in a shebeen house and then eating his praties dry, he'd take care to have something to kitchen them, so that he was not only snug and dacent of a Sunday, regarding wearables, but so well fed and rosy that the point of a rush would take a drop of blood out of his cheek.

Then he was the comeliest and best-looking young man in the parish, could tell lots of droll stories and sing scores of merry songs that would make ye split your sides with downright laughing; and when a wake or dance would happen to be in the neighbourhood may-be there would'nt be many a sly look-out from the purty girls for pleasant Jack Magennis.

In this way lived Jack and his mother, as happy and continted as two lords, except now and thin that Jack would feel a little consarn for not being able to lay past anything for the sore foot, or that might enable him to think of marrying—for he was beginning to look about him for a wife; and why not, to be sure? But he was prudent for all that, and didn't wish to bring a wife and a small family into poverty and hardship.

It was one fine, frosty, moonlight night—the sky was without a cloud, and the stars all blinking, that it would delight anybody's heart to look at them—when Jack was crossing a bog that lay a few fields beyant his own cabin.

He was just crooning the "Humours of Glynn" to himself, and thinking that it was a very hard case that he couldn't save anything at all, to help him to the wife, when, on coming down a bank in the middle of the bog, he saw a dark-looking man, leaning against a clamp of turf, and a black dog sitting at his ase beside him, with a pipe of tobacky in his mouth, and he smoking as sober as a judge.

Jack, however, had a stout heart, bekase his conscience was clear, and barring being a little daunted, he wasn't very much afraid.

"Who is this coming down to'ards us?" said the black-favoured man, as he saw Jack approaching them.

"It's Jack Magennis," says the dog, making answer, and taking the pipe out of his mouth with his right paw, and, after puffing away the smoke, and rubbing the end of it against his leit leg, exactly as a Christian (this day's Friday, the Lord stand betune us and harm) would do against his sleeve, giving it at the same time to his comrade. "It's Jack Magennis," says the dog, "honest widow Magennis's dacent son."

"The very man," says the other, back to him, "that I'd wish to sarve out of a thousand. Arrah! Jack Magennis, how is every tether-length of you?" says the ould fellow, putting the furrawn on him; "and how is every bone in your body, Jack, my darling? I'll hould a thousand guineas," says he, pointing to a great big bag that lay beside him, "and that's only the tenth part of what's in the bag, Jack, that you're just going to be in luck this very night."

"And may worse never happen you, Jack ma bouchal," says the dog, putting in his tongue, then wagging his tail, and holding out his paw to shake hands with Jack.

"Gintlemen," says Jack, never minding to give the dog his hand bekase he heard it wasn't safe to touch the likes of him; "gintlemen," says he, "yere sitting far from the fire this frosty night."

"Why, that's true, Jack," answers the ould fellow, "but if we're sitting far from the fire we're sitting very near the makins of it."

So, with this, he pulls the bag of goold over to him, that Jack might know by the jingle of the shiners what was in it.

"Jack," says dark-face, "there's some born with a silver ladle in their mouth, and others with a wooden spoon, and if you'll just sit down on the one end of this clamp with me, and take a hand at the five and ten," pulling out, as he spoke, a pack of cards, "you may be a made man for the remainder of your life."

"Sir," says Jack, "with submission, both yourself and this cur ——I mane," says he, not wishing to give the dog offince, "both yourself and this dacent gintleman with the tail and claws upon him, have the advantage of me in respect of knowing my name; for, if I don't mistake," says he, putting his hand to his hat, "I never had the pleasure of seeing either ot ye before."

"Never mind that," says the dog, taking back the pipe from the other, and clapping it in his mouth, "we're both your well-wishers, anyhow, and it's now your own fault if you're not a rich man."

Jack, by this time, was beginning to think that they might be after wishing to throw luck in his way, for he had often heard of men being made up entirely by the fairies, till there was no end to their wealth.

"Jack," says the black man, "you had better be sed by us for this bout; upon the honour of a gintleman we wish you well. Howsoever, if you don't choose to take the ball at the right hop another may, and you're welcome to toil all your life, and die a beggar after."

"Upon my reputation what he says is true, Jack," says the dog, in his turn; "the lucky minnit of your life is come; let it pass without doing what them that wishes your mother's son well desire you, and you'll die in a ditch."

"And what am I to do," says Jack, "that's to make me so rich all of a sudden?"

"Why, only to sit down and take a game of cards with myself," says black-brow, "that's all, and I'm sure it's not much."

"And what is it to be for?" Jack inquires, "for I have no money; tarenation to the rap itself's in my company."

"Well, you have yourself," says the dog, putting up his fore-claw along his nose, and winking at Jack, "you have yourself, man; don't be faint-hearted, he'll bet the contents of this bag," and with that the ould thief gave it another great big shake to make the ginneys jingle again. It's ten thousand ginneys in hard gould; if he wins you're to sarve him for a year and a day, and if he loses you're to have the bag."

"And the money that's in it?" says Jack, wishing, you see, to make a sure bargain, anyhow.

"Ev'ry penny," answered the ould chap, "if you win it; and there's fifty to one in your favour."

By this time the dog had got into a great fit of laughing at Jack's sharpness about the money.

"The money that's in it, Jack," says he, and he took the pipe out of his mouth, and laughed till he brought on a hard fit of coughing; "oh, by this and by that," says he, "but that bates Banagher! and you're to get it ev'ry penny, you thief of the world, if you win it."

But, for all that, he seemed to be laughing at something that Jack wasn't up to.

At any rate, surely, they palavered Jack betune them, until he sot down and consinted.

"Well," says he, scratching his head, "why worse nor lose I can't, so here goes for one trial at the shiners, anyhow!"

"Now," says the obscure jintleman, just whin the first card was in his hand, ready to be laid down, "you're to sarve me for a year and a day, if I win; and if I lose, you shall have all the money in the bag."

"Exactly," says Jack, and, just as he said the word, he saw the dog putting the pipe into his pocket, and turning his head away for fraid Jack would see him breaking his sides laughing.

At last, when he got his face sobered, he looks at Jack, and says,

"Surely, Jack, if you win, you must get all the money in the bag; and upon my reputation you may build castles in the air with it, you'll be so rich."

This plucked up Jack's courage a little, and to work they went; but how could it end otherwise than Jack to lose betune two such knowing schemers as they soon turned out to be?

For what do you think, but as Jack was beginning the game, the dog tips him a wink, laying his fore claw along his nose, as before, as much as to say, "watch me, and you'll win;" turning round at the same time, and showing Jack a nate little looking-glass that was set in his oxther, in which Jack saw, dark as it was, the spots of all the other fellow's cards, as he thought, so that he was cock sure of bating him.

But they were a pair of downright knaves, any how; for Jack, by playing to the cards he saw in the looking-glass instead of to them the other held in his hand, lost the game and the money.

In short, he saw that he was blarnied and cheated by them both; and when the game was up he plainly tould them as much.

"What, you scoundrel!" says the black fellow, starting up and catching him by the collar, "dare you go for to impache my honour?"

"Leather him if he says a word," says the dog, running over on his hind legs, and laying his shut paw upon Jack's nose, "say another word, you rascal," says he, "and I'll down you!"

With this the ould fellow gives him another shake.

"I don't blame you so much," says Jack, to him, "it was the looking-glass that desaved me."

"What looking-glass, you knave?" says dark face, giving him a fresh haul.

"Why, the one that I saw under the dog's oxther," replied Jack.

"Under my oxther, you swindling rascal?" replied the dog, giving him a pull by the other side of the collar. "Did ever any honest pair of jintlemen hear the like? But he only wants to break through the agreement; so let us turn him at once into an ass, and then he'll break no more bargains, nor strive to take in honest men and win their money."

So saying, the dark fellow drew his hands over Jack's jaws, an' in a twinklin' there was a pair of ass's ears growing up out of his ears.

When Jack found this he knew that he wasn't in good hands; so he thought it best to get himself out of the scrape as soon as possible.

"Jintlemen, be aisy," says he, "and let us understand one another. I'm willing to sarve you for a year and a day, but I've one requist to ax, and it's this; I've a helpless ould mother at home, and if I go with you now, she'll break her heart with grief first, and starve afterwards. Now, if your honour will give me a year to work hard, and lay in provision to support her while I'm away, I'll sarve you with all the veins of my heart—for a bargain's a bargain."

With that the dog gave his companion a pluck by the skirt, and, after some chat together that Jack didn't hear, they came back and said they would comply with his wishes that far.

"So, on to-morrow twelve-month, Jack," says the dark fellow,

"the dog here will come to your mother's, and, if you follow him, he'll bring you safe to my castle."

"Very well, your honour," says Jack; "bnt as dogs resemble one another so much, how will I know him when he comes?"

"Why," answers the other, "he'll have a green ribbon about his neck, and a pair of Wellington boots on his hind legs."

"That's enough, sir," says Jack; "I can't mistake him in that dress, so I'll be ready."

During that year Jack wrought night and day that he might be able to lave as much provision with his mother as would support her in his absence; and when the morning came that he was to bid her farewell, he went down on his two knees and got her blessing.

He then left her with tears in his eyes, and promised to come back the very minnit his time would be up.

"Mother," says he, "be kind to your little family here, and feed them well, as they're all you have to keep you company till you see me agin."

His mother then stuffed his pockets with bread till they stuck out behind him, and gave him a crooked sixpence for luck; after which, he got his staff, and was just ready to tramp, when, sure enough, he spies his ould friend, the dog, with a green ribbon about his neck and the Wellington boots upon his hind legs.

He didn't go in, but waited on the outside till Jack came out.

They then set off, but no one knows how far they travelled, till they reached the dark jintleman's castle, who appeared very glad to see Jack and gave him a hearty welcome.

The next day, in consequence of his long journey, he was axed to do nothing; but in the coorse of the evening the dark chap brought him into a long, frightful room, where there were three hundred and sixty-five hooks sticking out of the wall, and on every hook but one, a man's head.

When Jack saw this agreeable sight, his dinner began to quake within him; but he felt himself still worse when his master pointed to the empty hook, saying,

"Now, Jack, your business to-morrow is to clane out a stable that wasn't claned for the last seven years, and if you don't have it finished before dusk—do you see that hook?"

"Ye—yes," replied Jack, hardly able to spake.

"Well, if you don't have finished before dusk, your head will be hanging on that hook as the sun sets."

"Very well, your honour," replied Jack, scarcely knowing what he said, or he wouldn't have said "very well" to such an evil-minded intention, any how. "Very well," says he, "I'll do my best, and all the world knows the best can do no more."

While this discourse was passing betune them, Jack happened to look to the upper end of the room, and there he saw one of the beautifullest faces that ever was seen on a woman, looking at him through a little panel that was in the wall.

She had a white, snowy forehead, such eyes, and cheeks, and teeth that there's no coming up to them, and the clusters of dark hair that hung about her beautiful temples—by the laws, I'm afeard of falling in love with her myself, so I'll say no more about her, only that she would charm the heart of a miser.

At any rate, in spite of all the ould fellow could say—heads, and hooks, and all—Jack couldn't help throwing an eye now an' then to the pannel; and, to tell the truth, if he had been born to riches and honour, it would be hard to follow him for a good face and a good figure.

"Now, Jack," says his master, "go and get your supper, and I hope you'll be able to perform your task."

But before breakfast time he lost all heart; and little wonder he should, poor fellow, bekase for every one shovelfull that he'd throw out, there would come three more in: so that, instead of making his task less according as he got on, it became greater.

He was now in the greatest dilemmy, and didn't know how to manage, so he was driven at last to such an amplush that he had no other shift for employment, only to sing *Paddeen O'Rafferty* out of meer vexation, and dance the hornpipe trebling step to it, cracking his fingers, half mad, through the stable.

Just in the middle of his tantrum, who comes to the door to call him to his breakfast but the beautiful crathur he saw the evening before peeping at him through the panel.

At this minnit Jack had so hated himself by the dancing that his handsome face was in a fine glow, entirely.

"I think," said she, to Jack, with one of her own sweet smiles, "that this is an odd way of performing your task."

"Och, thin, 'tis you that may say that," replies Jack; "but it's myself that's willing to have my head hung up any day just for one sight of you, you darling."

"Where did you come from?" asked the lady, with another smile, that bate the first all to nothing.

"Where did I come from, is it?" answered Jack. "Why, death alive! did you never hear of ould Ireland, my jewel?—hem! I mane, plase your ledyship's honour."

(To be continued.)

BLACK HAWKE, THE HIGHWAYMAN.

THE TREACHEROUS OSTLER.—*See Page* 14.

CHAPTER IV.

THE DARK PASSAGE AND A LOVE SCENE—HOW FAIR ROSA-
MOND SERVED HER CAPTOR—THE LEAP INTO THE
MIDST OF THE ENEMY—THE JEW COMES ON THE TRACK
BUT DOES NOT COME OFF IN TRIUMPH.

WHILE Sir Andrew Greville and his party were vainly endeavouring to find the secret panel, and those who, in
obedience to his orders, made their way to the front of the
house, were looking for the daring abductor of their mistress,
Merlin Hawke, bearing the drooping form of the fainting
Lady Florence in his arms, proceeded quickly along the
hidden passage to the exit, to which, from early acquaintance
in his boyhood, he knew it conducted.

He was in total darkness, and the descent of a few steps
here and there had to be accomplished with exceeding care ;
at times he fancied he heard a sound near him, but on pausing
to listen, he could detect only the quick breathing of Lady
Florence.

He still carried his sword in one hand, and whenever he
heard a suspicious noise, he probed the gloom with it in the

charitable hope of spitting somebody. Hitherto Lady
Florence had remained silent and half-unconscious.

Merlin found his burthen no inconvenience ; indeed, he
rather liked the pressure of the palpitating form as her bosom
rested on his breast.

Notwithstanding the danger he was still in, he could not
refrain from a reckless laugh at the audacious manner in which
he had partly accomplished his mad design. A little while
ago he stood in solitary dudgeon, a lonely adventurer at the
roadside inn, gloomily regarding the miniature of his early
love, while she was in the midst of security in her husband's
home ; and now he held her encircled by his arm in a dark
passage, having taken her by his sword from her husband and
his host of armed servants.

As I have said, he laughed lightly at his own successful
daring.

Lady Florence heard the laugh. She lifted her head and
said faintly,

" Why do you exult, fearful man ?"

" Fearful man ? It was dear Merlin once," returned he
" No matter, we shall be better friends by and bye."

"Then you still think you can carry me from my husband's home?"

" Right, merrily, I' faith. Have I not taken you from his very sword?"

"You forget the jeopardy you are in."

" In what? In having you in my arms? Truly, dear Lady Florence, that is jeopardy indeed."

Lady Florence blushed.

"I did not mean that," she replied, hastily ; " but my husband—his men, they will overtake you presently, and then you will be killed."

" So that I die with your lovely eyes looking on me I shall not fear a hundred deaths. Ah, Florence, I thought I could forget you when I heard you were married ; but the love of other days is not easily extinguished. I have perilled my life to see you, and I would yield my blood drop by drop to have your heart throbbing to mine, to gain a smile from your rich lips, to read but one glance of love in your thrilling eyes."

Lady Florence sighed ; a little of the "old love" was returning to her breast. She contrasted his ardent words, his daring, with the cold haughtiness of her husband. Then had she not wronged him by marrying another?

She was thinking somewhat in this fashion when Merlin's arm tightened round her waist, and he drew her soft, yielding form to his breast.

"Florence, dear Florence," he said, tenderly, " will you kiss me?"

"I cannot ; do not ask me, Merlin."

"Just one kiss from those dear lips."

"Merlin, you will make me angry if you ask."

It struck him that the tones were not very angry.

" In a few minutes," he said, " I shall have to face the whole of your husband's servants ; I may be killed."

"Oh! no, no! Heaven forbid!"

"You would then regret not having granted me this dear favour, the last I might ever ask. Dear Florence, will you consent?"

He was drawing her closer to him ; she did not seem to struggle to get away.

" I daren't kiss you," she said, in a faint whisper.

"That means I may kiss you," thought Merlin.

"Dearest," he said, aloud, " forgive me if I offend you. Come, it may be for the last time."

She held her warm beating bosom to his ; her face touched his as he raised her head ; the soft contact thrilled through his veins. A little closer, then their lips met in one long, clinging kiss that, spite of herself, thrilled through Lady Florence's frame, while, as for Merlin, he was nearly mad with the intoxicating ecstasy of the moment.

He could have held her there for ever, forgetful of the place or of his danger, had not a sudden gleam flashed upon them.

Lady Florence started from his embrace, and, in a frightened whisper—thoughts for his safety prevented her screaming—exclaimed,

"We are discovered! My husband and his men! Oh! Merlin, if you are killed!"

"I shall have gained Paradise before death," he answered, loyally snatching another kiss, and lifting her in his arms as a second and more powerful gleam shone upon them.

"They are there! Shoot them down!" an angry voice cried, and he saw through the gloom the forms of Sir Andrew and his followers.

"They will have to fight who come first," he muttered, as they rushed towards him like a pack of wolves.

The light of the lamps enabled him to see the locality of that part of the secret passage ; it was very narrow, and turned an abrupt angle a few yards off.

Merlin whispered softly to Florence,

" Speak when you wish me to be slain!"

She trembled as he spoke, and Merlin thought she clung to him ; but it might have been fancy, and he was too much engrossed with the preservation of his life to take heed then.

A few steps took him to the end where the passage turned ; he was still in advance of his pursuers. At this point only one could pass at a time, and he could, without much trouble, have passed his sword through every one that came singly. There was, however, a chance of a shower of bullets finding him out, and he had another way of escape.

There were several windings of the secret way, and if those behind him were ignorant of the true passage they might give him time to get away.

Whispering to Lady Florence to be silent, he hurried to the secret door, by which he could make his way into the shrubbery. He could hear the sounds of those following him, but they came no nearer. In a few instants he reached the place where he knew the door ought to be.

Lady Florence trembled violently ; she knew that she was doing wrong in tacitly allowing him to carry her off ; but her woman's nature would not allow her to betray him and be the cause of his death. So without any distinct idea of the probable consequences, she let him lead her from the corridor.

Merlin could not at first find the spring. He began to grow impatient. Lady Florence broke out in a cold sweat. Suddenly the spring clicked, and the door came open.

The cool air rushed in refreshingly ; the faint starlight just made things perceptible. Merlin breathed more freely ; the fresh air gave new vigour to his limbs.

Lady Florence thought she ought to make a protest against the abduction.

"You must let me leave you, now," she murmured, in a very soft whisper.

"Leave you, dear charmer?" Merlin answered. "Not while I have life to defend you, and sense to value the possession of so much loveliness."

" I dare not come with you."

" Then I must take you," he replied, lifting her from the ground.

At this moment a gleam of light, not proceeding from the stars, flashed behind them. Merlin knew his danger on the instant. The open door had revealed them.

He was about to hurry forth with his burthen, when a report echoed behind him, and a pistol flash lit up the passage.

Lady Florence uttered a little scream, and placed her hands to her side.

Merlin turned fiercely round ; his fine features were swarthy with deadly passion. He could see the figure of the man who had fired ; he was yet holding the pistol in his hand.

Tenderly placing Florence against the wall, Merlin, with the bound of a young lion, leapt upon the man.

A moment his sword glittered in the air, then gleamed out red with a dripping stain.

And the man who had fired at Lady Florence fell to the ground—dead!

Merlin's blade had cut its way through his heart.

This sudden and bold deed was witnessed by the others, and with a rush they came upon the daring youth. But they were too careful of their lives to come upon him singly, and Merlin, retiring as quickly as he had advanced, lifted Lady Florence's drooping form in his arms, and gliding through the narrow aperture, closed the door behind him.

He heard the furious shouts of his baffled pursuers, and congratulated himself that he had escaped them ; but he heard also other sounds, which convinced him that he had foes to meet in front.

The rest of the domestics, attracted by the report of firearms, came hurrying to the spot.

It was still rather dark.

Merlin crept along under the shadow of the wall. He was as yet unperceived, though he could see the others coming with weapons and lights.

"If I can reach Fair Rosamond unseen," he thought, "I will wish them a fair good-night."

Lady Florence had fainted in his arms.

Supporting her tenderly, he stole noiselessly towards the shrubbery where he had left his horse.

He had almost gained his object when a cry in his rear quickened his pace.

"There he is! there he goes!" he heard a voice exclaim.

At the same time a fellow rushed right before him, and seized the bridle of Fair Rosamond.

"Catch him! catch the thief!" he cried. "I've got his horse."

Merlin had well trained his steed. She had stood immovable during his absence. At the sound of fire-arms her ears had pricked up, but when the fellow came towards her, her graceful neck was arched quickly, and her ears lay flat to her head.

No other motion was visible till the man put out his hand to seize her bridle.

He thought he had got it.

So he had.

But not what he expected.

Darting out her glossy head swift and sure as the stroke of a serpent, she caught the man with her teeth in his chest, and closing her mouth, lifted him up, and then bore him backwards to the ground.

With a terrific cry, the man tried to get free, but almost fainting from the agony of his lacerated chest, he went slowly backwards, doubled up by the pressure the well-trained horse put out with the slow movement of her beautiful neck.

"You have got it, have you?" said Merlin. "More than you like, you varlet. You'll carry those marks to the grave!"

At the sound of his voice the horse set her ears erect and shook her flowing mane; then she unloosed her grip, and let the man fall at her master's feet, where he lay groaning and writhing in agony.

There was no time now for Merlin to pause; the garden was filling with his enemies.

Lights flashed in all directions; armed men came from all quarters.

Setting one foot in the stirrup, he tightened the grip of his arm round Lady Florence's waist, and lifting her with him, sprang into the saddle.

Seated on his favourite steed, he circled his weapon in the air, and defiantly turned towards his foes.

"Follow now, who dare!" he cried. "Your mistress is mine, and if your master seeks his death, let him stand before my sword!"

He seated himself well in the saddle, and passed them like a meteor.

Several pistols flashed, but he was by too swiftly to be touched.

Then came a fresh cry of rage. The secret door had been opened. Sir Andrew, foaming with rage, saw his young and beautiful wife borne away on the saddle of the daring horseman.

"Bring the robber down!" he cried, hoarsely. "A thousand pounds for him that brings him down!"

Merlin laughed a wild, "Ha, ha!" Then, stooping low to the neck of his horse, his sword swooped amongst those who came in his way, and two fell gashed to the earth.

Then, with the bound of a chamois, Fair Rosamond cleared the shrubbery wall.

Gathering herself to speed away, the faithful animal put her ears erect, and shook her splendid mane.

Merlin knew the signal. Foes were before him.

He was not long in doubt. The Jew, Sir Andrew's brother, and three officers, with the man whom he had tied to the horse, were in his path.

The man had told his tale to the Jew, and the latter had brought the officers to capture Merlin.

Merlin met them silently; he knew that they anticipated an easy victory.

Holding Florence tightly to his breast, he faced them with his gleaming sword, its point darting like the tongue of a snake.

"Look out, there!" cried Marmaduke Greville. "Have at him, fellows! Bring him down!"

"I'll do that," said one of the officers.

He came right in Merlin's way, a pistol in his hand, which he pointed at his horse.

Before he had time to fire Merlin wheeled aside, and slashed him across the face and forehead with his sword.

The officer, blinded with blood and pain, dropped his hand as his pistol exploded.

The bullet lodged in the skull of his own horse, and both went to the ground.

Gracefully putting forth her fore-legs, Fair Rosamond cleared the obstacle, and Merlin stood in the midst of the rest.

In that leap his cloak became disarranged, and as his hat fell slightly aside a broad plume, like the wing of a black eagle, fluttered from the brim.

One of the officers had his pistol almost at Merlin's throat, but when he saw that ominous plume, he exclaimed suddenly, while his arm dropped from its aim,

"It is Hawke—BLACK HAWKE, the Highwayman!"

Lady Florence, awakening from her insensibility, uttered a cry of anguish, and tried to drop to the ground; but Merlin's arm yet held her.

The cry that had so startled her, so far from ensuring Merlin's immediate death or capture, caused a totally different result.

The men who had been crowding to take him opened out as he came, and, with a leap, he went through their midst.

Only the Jew remained before him, cringing on his horse, his teeth grating, his eyes set in a deadly glare of savage spite and fury.

Merlin might easily then have run him through, but he disdained the cold-blooded action.

Passing his sword from his right hand to his left, he seized the hateful old usurer by the withered beard, and plucking him by it from his horse, let him fall heavily face downwards to the ground.

Then, with a rush like the wind, Fair Rosamond flew along the snow-covered road.

It was only then that the remainder of the party were startled to action; many of the members of Sir Andrew's household were now armed and mounted, and rode hurriedly up, as the Jew, foaming and gnashing his teeth, was lifted from the ground. As soon as he was placed on his horse, the whole body turned their horses' heads after Merlin.

But many a cheek blanched as they heard that the name of him they pursued was Black Hawke the Highwayman.

CHAPTER V.

THE RIDE FOR LIFE—THE SNOW RAVINE—THE MILL AND THE MILLER'S DAUGHTER.

THE whole party thundered on in pursuit. Merlin heard them close upon his heels, and had his horse been less fleet, he must speedily have been in their power.

But Fair Rosamond passed along the road with the stride of a race-horse.

He had sheathed his sword, and his arm held Florence tenderly to his breast; he had discovered where the bullet had struck her, and in their swift flight he bandaged the wound.

He would have kissed away the blood but for a noble delicacy.

Lady Florence was pure to him, as unsullied as the fallen snow.

"The ruffian's hand had nearly taken away your sweet life," he murmured, as he pressed his lips to hers! "and could I have slain him a thousand times, it would not have expiated such a foul deed. And for me, too, to die for me!" he continued, a glow of rapture on his face, and his voice tender in its rich melody. "Dear Florence, I could have lived only to avenge you, and then shed my own blood."

Florence shuddered. She was thinking of the terrible words which had fallen from the officer's lips.

When Merlin no longer heard any sound of pursuit, he slackened rein; he did not wish to breathe his faithful steed.

He looked at Lady Florence's pale face, and then at the white snow around him ; and then befell to musing, and after that his glance wandered to the solitary star still visible in the sapphire sky.

If he had cherished any impure thought, that bright star, shining so chastely, was enough to drive it from his mind.

"I must place this poor dove in safety," he mused ; "but to take her to the inn where her child is would be madness. My pursuers would be certain to go there, and I am mistrustful of pretty Minnette's father. Ha ! I have it. I will hie to the miller's house ; he has a staunch heart, and Florence will be safe with him till her child is brought to her."

The miller's house lay to the right ; the way across a snow field, and down a steep, rather dangerous at the present time on account of the snow drift. To attempt to pass while the officers were following him would have been madness, as they could have seen him from the road. He therefore selected a convenient spot, and having gone to and fro to make fresh footmarks, leapt from the centre of the road into the field on his right. There was a deep ditch on the other side ; he walked his horse into this, and having come to a point where the hedge was of great height, he waited there for the pursuing party to pass.

They came in the course of a few minutes' riding as hard as they could.

Merlin gently caressed his horse's neck and spoke a few words, when, to the surprise of Florence, the docile animal went down upon its haunches and lay perfectly still while the whole party thundered by.

Sir Andrew, the Jew, and Marmaduke were riding side by side.

Merlin heard them mention the name of the roadside inn as they passed, and, as he saw the villanous face of the Jew, he almost felt inclined to pity Sir Andrew in the hands of such a man as him and Marmaduke his brother.

The last of the party went by, and Merlin suffered Rosamond to rise.

Satisfied that he could not be seen he cantered her gently over the white field.

"Does your wound pain you ?" Merlin tenderly asked of Lady Florence.

"My heart pains me more acutely," she replied, with a slight shiver.

"Is it on my account, dear Florence ?"

"Oh, Merlin, I heard the name they called you by !"

"The name ?"

"Yes ; Black Hawke, the Highwayman !"

She tried to rise, and fell sobbing in his arms.

Merlin's careless laugh broke on her ears.

"Alas !" she said, "can you be so fearful a man ?"

"What is Black Hawke that his name should frighten you ?"

"A dreadful, merciless man ; a man of blood ; the terror of strong men ; the slayer of helpless babes !"

"You give him a strong character."

"I have shuddered at the recital of his barbarity. Seven nobleman, all young and scions of illustrious houses, fell by his hand, all murdered on the same spot ! I have even heard that he pierced his sword to the hilt in the heart of a young wife."

"I too have heard ; but the story is that, being wronged by the house you allude to, he challenged all the males to mortal combat, met them singly, and singly slew them, in each case piercing them through the heart. For the lady, I have heard that story ; she deceived him, cheated him, dishonoured him, and he slew her too."

Lady Florence shivered again, as he continued,

"The name of Black Hawke is terrible, indeed ; he is merciless, and when he fights a demon seems on his side. He is cruel, too, and never spares one who affronts him ; his hand is red with blood, his eyes are inflamed with bloody passion ; his brow, they say, is awful to look upon ! Look at me, Florence ; is mine the countenance of a fiend ?—is this hand the bloody hand of an assassin ?"

Lady Florence looked sadly up in his face, and then at the small, soft, white hand he held before her.

"Your heart was gentle once, yet I have seen to-night how swiftly you can slay. Still I dare not believe you are he."

His cold, careless laugh seemed to freeze her blood.

"What I am and what I may be," he said, solemnly, "I ask you to remember this—I never yet struck an unarmed enemy, but never yet did I spare one ! He who once does me a deadly injury makes prompt reparation, or dies. The passion is in our blood : your husband's father despoiled my father, and for that my father took his life. Your husband has despoiled me, and for that, sooner or later, I will sheath my sword in his breast !"

Lady Florence put up her small white hands in dismay.

"Oh, no, no !" she cried ; "he is my husband !" and her head bowed to her breast.

"And even for that I will not spare him !"

The swarthy glow rushed to Merlin's face, and Lady Florence shrank from the look of his passion-lit eyes. He had removed or concealed the ominous black feather, but a thrill of terror went to her heart as the fear stole upon her that he was indeed the terrible highwayman, Black Hawke the Merciless.

They rode on in silence for some time ; Lady Florence was too much awed to speak, her companion was engrossed by his own thoughts.

She ventured presently to ask timidly where her child was, and when she should see it.

"When I have placed you in safety I will fetch it," he replied, quickening the pace of his steed.

The most perilous part of their journey had yet to be performed, as they had to cross a deep ravine piled thickly with snow ; but Rosamond was sure of foot as a gazelle ; the descent was made in safety ; they reached the other side, and, in a few minutes, were at the entrance to the mill.

There was no sign of life within visible from the outside of the mill ; the windows were closed to keep out the snow which had filled in all crevices and lodged on the roof and on the idle sails.

Merlin tapped at the door with the butt of a pistol, and, stroking Rosamond, she gave a low whinney and commenced pawing on the hard stones.

Lady Florence waited with anxious face the coming of some one to admit them. She dreaded the coming of their pursuers—dreaded, for her own sake, for her husband could be brutal at times, and was mistrustful of his wife—dreaded for the sake of the desperate but handsome and gallant youth whose daring had brought her there, whom she half feared because of the apprehensive and terrible suspicion of his real character, yet whom she half loved because she had loved him in early days and knew that he loved her ardently still.

They heard the low sound of bolts being quietly withdrawn, then the door opened, and a large, red, round face, surmounted by a white nightcap, which looked as if it had been recently dipped amongst the flour, appeared.

"Hilloa, Hugh !" cried Merlin, in a cheery voice. Come, unbolt and unbar ; and, harkee, summon the mistress and the maid, for I've one here whom I would fain commit to her charge—a lady, bleeding and wounded."

The big face of the miller drew down till it was as long as a fiddle, his lips pursed up to a silent whistle, and he peered curiously out at the young cavalier and the lady.

"What, Master Merlin ! A lady, too ! God's will, but this is most unusual. But enter, enter ; be welcome, welcome to the house of old Hugh Marks."

"Enter, indeed ! Do you think Fair Rosamond can go through the eye of a needle ? Open wide, good friend, for the night air is keen, and you may have a fit of tooth-ache while you are keeping me waiting."

"A horse, too ! Gads ! I have visitors," quoth the good-tempered miller, as he opened the door.

Merlin stooped low, and Rosamond bore them safely inside, when the miller, who was but scantily clothed, and had indeed tumbled hastily out of bed, closed the door, and giving a furtive glance at the face of the lady, hobbled away, leaving his visitors to dismount and enter his cosy parlour while he went to summon his wife and daughter.

Fair Rosamond stood perfectly quiet, while Merlin led Lady Florence into the parlour.

His manner charmed her by its respectful deference.

The old man had left the lamp after he had opened the room door, and Merlin led Lady Florence to a seat, and, taking her hand, said, sadly,

"Florence, if I have offended you in what I have done, I humbly beseech your forgiveness. Do not reproach me or hold me in mistrust. I have completed my vow—you are safe from the power of those who threatened your future happiness and your honour. With me the latter, if not the former, is safe. I will leave you now. I go to bring you your child; when I have restored that to your arms I shall leave you—for ever if you wish it. You may remain here until you see fit to depart; but beware of both your husband and his brother!"

Lady Florence sighed deeply; her beautiful bosom rose tremblingly; a tear slid slowly down her cheek; she tried to speak harshly, but she could not. In spite of herself she could not but feel a love for him.

"Do not peril yourself," she said, timidly; "there are many foes lying in wait for you. If you should be killed——"

She paused, her large eyes swimming in tears.

"You would be sorry?" Merlin interrupted. "Dear lady, I could dare anything to know that you would care a little for me. Farewell, dear Florence."

He pressed her hand to his lips.

"You will guard yourself?" she said, softly.

"Say, for your sake?"

She cast down her eyes and softly spoke again,

"For my sake, Merlin."

He drew her rapturously to his breast, her neck and face suffused with blushes; but she did not resist, and when Merlin had stolen several kisses—the sweetest, so he thought, that could ever be given—he let her sink gently to the rough couch, while he led Fair Rosamond out, and went forth with the delicious sensation of her kisses still clinging, like the sweetness of Paradise, round his lips.

Meanwhile, the old miller had been lustily arousing his wife and daughter.

"Come, wife; come, Nancy; here be that scapegrace Master Merlin—he, he!—and—ha, ha!—a young lady—hum, hum!—ho, ho!—ha, ha! Come, wife; come, my girl; the dashing gentleman won't have the lady wait."

The elderly dame whom he styled wife, and his daughter Nancy, a spruce little maid, soon came down and hastened to their visitors, while old Hugh Marks stole off to another part of the mill, and taking out from a cupboard a black bottle, poured himself out a spanking draught, drank it off slowly, and with great relish, smacking his lips the while, and muttering, glumly,

"Ha, ha!—come again—ho, ho!—a lady, too—bleeding—wounded—hum—pistols, fire, and swords—we shall have warm work if Master Merlin be at his tricks again."

When Dame Marks and her daughter entered the parlour, they found Lady Florence sitting with her face buried in her hands. She looked up as they came in, and tried to hide the traces of her tears.

Dame Marks, a querulous old party, with a dry, semicomical visage, capable of being screwed up into any shape or expression, came bustling forward, holding up her hands in evident dismay when she saw the stains of blood on the handkerchief Merlin had bound over the wound.

"Gracious me!" she exclaimed; "my dear lady is bleeding; and how pale. Run, Nancy, and make up a good fire in your bed-room, while I see to the hurt myself."

Lady Florence languidly allowed her to divest her of her upper clothing, talking all the while in the utmost concern.

"We must be quiet until we get the bullet out, and then some liniment and a little of my famous ointment, that cures anything, and as my wretch of a husband says, 'would grow a new leg on if one had it cut off——'"

"The bullet is not there, it fell out as I was lifted on the horse," Lady Florence returned, with a faint smile; "and that, you know, proves it's not very deep."

Dame Marks was a plucky old woman herself, and she admired Florence's fortitude, for although the wound was not very deep, still, dressing it was rather a painful operation; but the young wife bore all without a murmur.

Nancy tripped lightly into the room.

"The fire is burning brightly," she said; "would my lady like to go now to the room?"

Lady Florence thought of her child.

"No," she answered; "I would prefer to remain here."

"Oh, then, we must put the place tidy," cried the old dame. "And, Nancy, make up the fire here, the night is cold, and my lady will be shivering; and run and fetch a warm coverlet, and bring some hot water that I may make her a drop of something nice."

Nancy departed on her various errands; and everything being satisfactorily accomplished, the talkative old dame went to look after her husband and get him to bed, while Florence was left, by her desire, alone.

Sitting there alone Lady Florence awaited in considerable anxiety Merlin's return. He had gone on a mission of extreme peril to serve her, to bring her the child that had been abducted from her care.

Would he return in safety? What if he were to fall?

The thought was one of extreme pain. Another thought forced itself upon her.

Was all that he had said the truth, or was it merely an invention to serve his purpose? and had he merely inveigled her there that he might have her in his power?

Did that terrible name she had heard spoken apply to him? Was he that most hunted of outcasts, a highwayman, and the fearful being known as Black Hawke?

It was hard to believe that he was playing her false; he had always seemed so noble; he was so brave, and his manners towards her were so tender, so tinged with the devotion of love.

All these reflections troubled her as she sat there alone. An hour passed, then another; it was time for him to return. Would he come, or was he slain?

Were these people in the house his friends? and would they befriend him if he arrived there pursued by the officers of justice?

Yet upon the latter she resolved to satisfy herself. She rose for the purpose of seeking Nancy to speak to her, and question her closely; but in place of leaving the room she walked to the little window, now perfectly closed by the shutters outside.

Was it fancy, or, as she stood there, could she hear the distant cries of men?

She placed her ear to the window and listened.

There was nothing but what sounded like the moaning of the wind.

Hark! was that the wind?

It was more like a cry of distress. She listened again intently, eagerly, misgivingly.

Yes, it came again, that wailing cry!

It was human; another sound succeeded it.

A loud shout, then another; sounds like the clattering of horses' hoofs, the cries of furious strife. Her heart beats wildly. If it should be he, the daring youth who had taken her from her husband, but who had taken possession of her heart!

The sounds come nearer, more distinct; a laugh, a freezing hollow, desperate laugh, awful to hear.

It was like his laugh, and she shivered with agony. The suspense was too great to bear; she flew wildly to the door; but before her hurried fingers could grasp the handle the report of a pistol arrested her as swiftly as though the bullet had gone to her heart.

It is he!" she cried, wildly. "They have killed him and my child! Oh, help! help! help!"

She tottered back, screaming, fainting.

Hasty steps came outside her door.

The tension of her feelings was too much for her to bear and a piercing scream broke from her lips as Nancy, pale as a corpse, and wild in her looks, rushed into the room.

Before either could speak, a second chorus of shouts filled the air, and in the thickest of the cries a second pistol was discharged with loud report.

Lady Florence's hands went swiftly to her breast.

Her distracted gaze was turned towards the window, as if

she would have torn away the blinds that kept her from seeing the deadly fray outside.

Her lips moved as she tried to speak, but her voice was refused utterance.

A ghastly pallor overspread her features, and she sank shuddering into Nancy's arms.

And then, as if in triumph over her, arose anew the fierce tumult from outside, and the cries of pursuing men came nearer and nearer, as they seemed to be hunting down to the death one who was fighting his way to the shelter of the miller's abode.

CHAPTER VI.

THE RETURN TO THE INN—MERLIN CONFRONTED BY SIR ANDREW—THE MILL SURROUNDED—AN HOUR OF PERIL AND DESPAIR.

MERLIN encountered no one on his way, and when he arrived at the inn, he was admitted by Minnette, who had been filled with anxiety on his account.

He did not see a pair of evil eyes glaring at him from behind as he entered the house.

Those eyes were owned by Red Dick, the ostler.

This fellow was secretly in the service of the Jew—who had sent him word during Merlin's arrival—to watch if such a horseman came to the door.

This fellow, as soon as he had watched him enter the house, hastened to where he knew a party of the horsemen were waiting.

Sir Andrew and his brother, with the old Jew and two officers, were confering moodily, when the spy arrived. Overjoyed at the news, they hurried back to surround the inn, the ostler returning with them, but quitting the party when he came near the house.

Red Dick was one of those low-bred ruffians who would sell their own father for gold.

He had been promised the heavy sum of fifty pounds if he betrayed Merlin, and he already imagined that he fingered the tempting gold.

Merlin came from the inn in a few minutes after the ostler had returned.

He had the child under his cloak. His pistols were ready to hand.

He had a prescience of his danger, for he knew who were on his track.

Sir Andrew, with his brother, and the Jew, saw him coming from the house by the side door in the yard.

Minnette was with him, and he stopped to kiss the pretty little hostess before he called for his horse.

"Aye, my fine fellow," muttered Sir Andrew, "play the gallant, we shall see you dancing soon on nothing."

"Dick," said Merlin.

The ostler, trying to conceal his treachery, came forward, cringing and smirking in his coarse way.

"Quick! my horse," Merlin exclaimed.

"All ready, sir," Red Dick rejoined, turning away to hide his grinning face.

In half a minute he returned leading Fair Rosamond by the bridle.

"Good bye, Minnette," Merlin cried, as he put foot in the stirrups.

In another moment he was in the saddle, and, waving his hand to the young girl, pushed his horse forward.

With all the low passions of his coarse nature aroused Red Dick had watched him spring into the saddle.

That was the moment he thought he might disable the gallant steed, and ensure the rider's capture.

With this purpose he seized a large stable fork, and, creeping behind Fair Rosomond, was about to plunge it into the noble animal's haunches, when Minnette, who saw the cowardly act, cried out,

"Merlin! you are betrayed! See!—Red Dick!"

Swift as lightning Merlin turned.

He saw the dastard aiming the cowardly blow.

Bending over in his saddle, he with one blow of his clenched hand sent the ostler reeling, and before he could

recover himself he had stooped down, and snatched the pitchfork from his grasp.

Red Dick cowered to the ground in terror.

"Help! help!" he cried to Sir Andrew's party. "Here he is!—murder!—I am killed!"

He was nearly so.

At the first cry Merlin made a lunge at him with the fork, and drove the prongs into his side, literally pinning him to the ground.

Then holding the child close to his breast he drew his pistols, and turned to face the foes whom he felt certain to meet.

They showed themselves as his horse sprang towards the gate.

Sir Andrew, white with passion; his brother, swarthy with rage; the Jew's shrivelled and loathsome visage peering from the rear, as he hung back out of the reach of possible danger.

There were the faces of the armed servants, too, and the officers whom Merlin had before encountered.

No small host against one man.

But our horseman felt no fear.

To rush in amongst them would have ensured a swift passage through their midst, unless some fatal bullet stayed his course; but he had another way to elude them.

A large haystack stood in the yard of the inn, behind this was a high wall, and on the other side the road.

Waving his cap at his foes, Merlin gracefully wheeled round, and in an instant he was behind the haystack.

Before the astonished party could follow, his gallant steed had taken the leap, and was the other side of the wall.

Then the armed party came thundering forward; but Merlin had got the start of them, and he laughed as their badly-aimed bullets whistled past his ears.

Taken thus by surprise, even the coolest hands are prone to act incautiously, and the very daring of Merlin's act gave him the start in safety, for before the others could clear the wall, he was speeding along the snow-clad highway.

It was almost an hour before he again had tidings of his pursuers, and then he had gained the valley leading to the mill.

He was in excellent spirits, for his sharp ride had exhilarated him. He had expected at nearly every gloomy spot to find his foes lurking in ambush, but, having got so far, he began to believe he had given them the slip.

He was mistaken. The cunning of the Jew was on a par with the rage of Sir Andrew; the old Israelite surmised that Merlin would come that way, and the whole party had taken up their ground at different positions.

Merlin, unknowingly, was walking right into the trap. He had been seen coming, and Sir Andrew appeased his fury when he saw him leisurely approaching.

There was a cluster of trees far down in the valley. Merlin was almost upon them when Fair Rosamond pricked up her ears, gave a sudden snort, and arching her graceful neck, pawed the ground.

"Ho, ho!" exclaimed our hero. "Danger nigh! Thanks, good steed, for this."

The words were hardly out of his mouth when Sir Andrew, followed by the rest, came from their hiding-place.

"Hold, villain! no further," he cried, hoarsely. "Yield, or my followers shall riddle you with bullets!"

Merlin drew rein immediately; his *sang froid* was wonderful. Rearing his elegant figure to its full height, he surveyed the party with calm self-possession, and said carelessly,

"Why so, gentlemen? The challenge is somewhat rude. Is it usual to stop the king's travellers in so unceremonious a way?"

"Dismount, robber!" yelled Sir Andrew, "before your brains are blown to the air!"

"The first condition I am not disposed to comply with, gentlemen.; the second I shall take especial care to prevent your doing.'

"White-livered scoundrel!" cried the baronet, "dare you parley with us? Where is the wife you have stolen from me? Reveal, or, by Heaven, you shall die like a dog!"

Merlin's glance swept proudly past the line of foes till it rested keenly on the baronet's face.

"The lady is safe enough, Sir Andrew, where you will not be likely to find her, or, if you did, would not take her away."

Sir Andrew turned yellow with passion.

"Down with him !" he cried. "Spare him no longer ! take him alive that he may adorn a gibbet ! If he resist send a dozen bullets through his skull !"

"Thank you," Merlin exclaimed, "I shall remember your kindness. Meanwhile, as I do not intend to be taken, nor to make my head a bullet case, I warn your fellows to stand out of my way, or, Sir Andrew, you will be the first to try the effect of carrying an ounce or so of lead in your brain."

For an instant Sir Andrew shrank back ; the fierce glance of the speaker, with the proximity of the small iron tube unpleasantly directed towards his skull, cowed him ; but in another moment his furious rage returned, and, in a voice, trembling with devilish hatred, he ordered them to cut the fearless horseman down.

It is hard to say what would have been the result had his orders then been carried out. At the first moment Merlin was ready to shoot him through the skull, while on the other side a dozen pistols were raised to bring down the daring rider ; but at that critical juncture Merlin was befriended by a strange circumstance.

A few flakes of snow had been falling all the night ; but now, just as ready fingers were about to press the triggers and discharge the missiles of death, the falling snow suddenly fell in a heavy shower, and the wind rising at the same time whirled the drifts from the earth, and instantaneously Merlin and his foes were enveloped in a blinding sheet.

It was impossible to see through this white cloud. Sir Andrew, imprecating fiercely, tried to shake the drift from his eyes, while the armed men, fearful to fire lest they should shoot each other, and, indeed, anticipating every moment receiving a bullet either from Merlin or one of their comrade's pistols, cowered down behind their horses, and anxiously awaited till the storm passed away.

This violent drift only lasted for a minute or so. As suddenly as it had begun there was a partial cessation, and through the haze of falling flakes they looked upon each other, but looked in vain for Merlin.

He was not there ; but, in the twinkling of an eye, an apparition, dreaded of all, came down upon them, came thundering swiftly into their very midst, scaring them like doves harried by an eagle.

A black horseman, tall, powerful and graceful, bestriding a steed that looked like breathing ebony, it was so black and glossy. The horseman was clad in complete sable, his habiliments were all of one hue, and a sable cloak swung grandly from his shoulders.

Upon his right arm was represented a monstrous black hawk in the act of pouncing on its prey, another with wings outspread was on his breast, a third formed the rich plume in his slouched hat.

Silently, swiftly, and with deadly force he rode them down, the broad chest of his steed swelling, and its eyes gleaming like coals. Silently, swiftly as a spectre, he passed through their ranks ; he singled out the cowering form of the Jew, who, with bleached features and palsied frame, sat shivering on his horse ; he singled him out, and darting into his quailing eyes a look that scathed his soul, raised his hand, clothed in a black gauntlet, and struck him between the temples.

When that blow fell it sounded as if a box had been driven in ; the trembling Jew collapsed, and tumbled in a quivering heap to the earth, where he lay huddled and supine.

For an instant the dread horseman regarded him ; then, with a laugh that made the blood of his listener curdle, he drew his finger across Sir Andrew's brow, and bounded from amongst them.

Sir Andrew shook as if stricken with death. That finger had passed across his brow like a burning steel, and a red mark revealed its blighting track ; he was palsied to a stupor, but his brother roused the others to action.

"Fire !" he cried, in a loud tone, "it is Black Hawke, the Horseman of Death !"

(*To be continued.*)

THE GOBLIN DOG;

A TALE OF FUN AND WONDER.

(*Continued from page 8.*)

"No," she answered ; "where is that country ?"

"Och ! by the honour of an Irishman," says Jack, "that takes the shine ! Not heard of green Erin—the Imerald Isle—the Jim of the Ocean—where all the men are brave and honourable, and all the women—hem ! I mane the ladies—chaste and beautiful ?"

"No," said she, "not a word ; but if I stay longer I may get you to blame. Come in to your breakfast, and I am sorry to find that you have done so little to your task. Your master's a man that always acts up to what he threatens, and if you have not this stable cleared out before dusk, your head will be taken off your shoulders this night."

"Why, then," says Jack, "my beautiful darl—plase, your honour's ladyship—if he hangs it up, will you do me the favour, a-cushla machree, to turn my head toardst that same panel where I saw a sartin fair face that I won't mintion ; and if you do, may I never——"

"What means cushla machree ?" inquired the lady, as she turned away.

"It manes that you're the pulse of my heart, avourneen, plase you're ledyship's reverence," says Jack.

"Well," says the lovely craythur, "any time you can speak to me in future, I would rather you would omit terms of honour, and just call me after the manner of your own country. Instead, for instance, of calling me your ladyship, I would be better pleased if you call me cushla—something—"

"Cushla machree, mavourneen—the pulse of my heart, my darling," said Jack, consthruin it (the thief) for her, for fraid she wouldn't know it well enough.

"Yes," she replied ; "cushla machree. Well, as I can pronounce it, cushla ma chree, will you come into your breakfast ?" said the darling, giving Jack a smile that would be enough any day to do up the heart of an Irishman.

Jack accordingly went after her, thinking of nothing except herself ; but on going in he could see no sign of her, so he sat down to his breakfast, though a single ounce the poor fellow couldn't ate at that bout for thinking of her.

Well, he went agin to his work, and thought he'd have better luck. But it was still the ould game—three shovelfulls would come in for every one he'd throw out ; and how he began in earnest to feel something about his heart that he didn't like, bekase he couldn't for the life of him help thinking of the three hundred and sixty-four heads and the empty hook.'

At last he gave up the work altogether, and took it into his head to make himself scarce from about the ould fellow's castle altogether ; and, without more to do, he sets off, never saying as much as "good bye" to his master.

But he hadn't got as far as the lower end of the yard, when his ould friend, the dog, steps out of a kennel, and meets him full butt in the teeth.

"So, Jack," says he, "you're going to give us leg bail, I see ; but walk back with yourself, you spalpeen, this minnit, and join your work, or if you don't," says he, "it'll be worse for your health. I'm not so much your enemy now as I was, bekase you have a friend in coort that you know nothing about ; so just do whatever you're bid, and keep never minding."

Jack went back with a heavy heart as you may be sure, knowing that whenever the black cur began to blarney him there was no good to come in his way.

He accordingly went into the stable, but consuming to the hand's turn he did, knowing it would be only useless, for, instead of clearing it out, he'd be only filling it.

It was now near dinner time, and Jack was very sad and sorrowful—as how could he be otherwise, poor fellow, with such a desperate ould chap to dale with?—when up comes the darling of the world again, to call him to his dinner.

"Well, Jack," says she, with her white arms so beautiful, and her dark clusters tossed about by the motion of the walk, "how are you coming on at your task?"

"How am I coming on, is it? Och, thin," says Jack, giving a good-humoured smile through the frown that was on his face, "plase your lady—*a cushla machree*—it's all over with me, for I've still the same story to tell, and off goes my head, as sure as it's on my shoulders, this blessed night."

"That would be a pity, Jack," says she, "for there are worse heads on worse shoulders; but will you give *me* the shovel?"

"Will I give you the shovel, is it? Och, thin, wouldn't I be a right big baste to do the likes of that any how?" says he. "What, *avourneen dheelish*, to stand up with myself, and let this hard shovel into them beautiful, soft, white hands of your own? Faith, my jewel, if you knew but all, my mother's son's not the man to do such a disgraceful turn as to let a lady like you take the shovel out of his hand, and he standing with his mouth under his nose, looking at you. Not myself, *avourneen*. We have no such unginteel manners as that in our country."

"Take my advice, Jack," says she, pleased in her heart at what Jack said, for all she didn't purtend it, "give me the shovel, and depend upon it I'll do more in a short time to clear the stable than you would for years."

"Why, then, *avourneen*, it goes to my heart to refuse you; but, for all that, may I never see yesterday, if a taste of it will go into your purty white fingers," says the thief, praising her to her face all the time. "My head may go off any day, and welcome, but death before dishonour. Say no more, my darling, but tell your father I'll be into my dinner immediately."

Notwithstanding all this, by jingo the lady would not be put off; like a ra-al woman, she'd have her way; so on telling Jack that she didn't intend to work with the shovel, at all at all, but only to take it for a minute in her hand, at long last he gave it to her; when she struck it three times on the threshel of the door, and, giving it back into his hand, tould him to try what he could do.

Well, sure enough, now there was a change; for instead of three shovelfuls coming in, as before, when he threw one out, there went nine more along with it.

Jack, in coorse, couldn't do less than thank the lovely crathur for her assistance; but, when he raised his head to spake to her, she was gone.

I needn't say, howsomever, that he went into his dinner with a light heart, and when the ould fellow axed him how he was coming on, Jack tould him that he was doing gloriously.

"Remember the empty hook, Jack," said he.

"Never fear, your honour," answered Jack, "if I don't finish my task, you may bob my head off any time."

Jack now went out, and was a short time getting through his job, for, before the sun set it was finished, and he came into the kitchen, ate his supper, and, sitting down before the fire, sung, "Love among the roses," and the "Black Joke," to vex the ould fellow.

This was one task over, and his head was safe for this bout; but that night, before he went to bed, his master called him up stairs, brought him into the bone-room, and gave him his orders for the next day.

"Jack," says he, "I have a wild filly that has never been caught, and you must go to my demesne to-morrow, and catch her, or if you don't—look there," says the big blackguard, "on that hook it hangs, before to-morrow, if you havn't her before sunset in the stable that you claned yesterday."

"Very well, your honour," says Jack, "I'll do every thing in my power, and if I fail, I can't help it."

The next morning Jack was out with his bridle in his hand, going to catch the filly. As soon as he got into the demesne, sure enough there she was in the middle of a green field, gazing quite at her ase.

When Jack saw this, he went over to'ards her, houlding out his hat, as if it was full of oats; but he kept the hand that had the bridle in it behind his back, for fraid she'd see it and make off.

Well my dear, on he went till he was almost within grip of her, cock sure that he had nothing more to do than to slip the bridle over her neck and secure her; but he made a bit of a mistake in his reckoning, for though she smelt and snoaked about him, just as if she didn't care a feed of oats whether he caught her or not, yet when he boulted over to hould her fast, she was off like a shot, with her tail cocked, to the far end of the demesne, and Jack had to set off hot foot after her.

All, however, was to no purpose; he couldn't come next or near

her for the rest of the day, and there she kept coorsing him about, from one field to another, till he hadn't a blast of breath in his body.

In this state was Jack, when the beautiful crathur came out to call him home to his breakfast, walking with the pretty small foot and light steps of her own, upon the green fields, so bright and beautiful, scarcely bending the grass and flowers as she went along, the darling.

"Jack," says she, "I fear you have as difficult a task to-day as you had yesterday?"

"Why, an' it's you that may say that with your own purty mouth," says Jack, says he; for out of breath and all as he was, he could'nt help giving her a bit of blarney, the rogue.

"Well, Jack," says she, "take my advice, and don't tire yourself any longer by attempting to catch her; truth's best—I tell you, you could never do it: come home to your breakfast, and when you return again, just amuse yourself as well as you can until dinner time."

"Och, och," says Jack, striving to look, the sly thief, as if she had promised to help him—"I only wish I was a king, and, by the powers, I know who would be my queen, any how; for it's your own sweet lady—*savourneen dheelish*—I say, amn't I bound to you for a year and a day longer, for promising to give me a lift as well for what you done yesterday?"

"Take care, Jack," says she, smiling, however, at his ingenuity in striving to trap her into a promise, "I don't think I made any promise of assistance."

"You didn't?" says Jack, wiping his face with the skirt of his coat, 'cause why?—you see pocket handkerchiefs weren't invinted in thim times; "why, then, may I never live to see yesterday, if there's not as much ra-al beauty in that smile that's divarting itself them sweet breathing lips of yours, and in them two eyes of light that's breaking both their hearts laughing at me, this minnit, as would encourage any poor fellow to expect a good turn from you—that is, when you could do it, without hurting or harming yourself, for it's he that would be the right rascal that could take it, if it would injure a silken hair of your head."

"Well," said the lady, with another roguish smile, "I shall call you home to dinner at all events."

When Jack went back from his breakfast, he didn't slave himself after the filly any more, but walked about to view the demense, and the avenue, and the green walks, and nice temples, and fishponds, and rookeries, and every thing, in short, that was worth seeing.

Towards dinner time, however, he began to have an eye to the way the sweet crathur was to come, and sure enough it's she that wasn't one minute late.

"Well, Jack," says she, "I'll keep you no longer in doubt," for the tender hearted crathur saw that Jack, although he didn't wish to let an to her, was fretting every now and then about the old hook and the bone-room.

"Jack," says she, "although I didn't promise, yet I'll perform;" and with that she pulled a small ivory whistle out of her pocket, and gave three blasts on it that brought the wild filly up to her very hand, as quick as the wind. She then took the bridle, and threw it over the baste's neck, giving her up, at the same time, to Jack.

"You need't fear now, Jack," says she, "you will find her as quiet as a lamb, and as tame as you wish; as a proof of it, just walk before her, and you'll see she'll follow you to any part of the field."

Jack, you may be sure, paid her as many and as sweet compliments as he could, and never heed one from his country for being able to say something toothsome to the ladies. At any rate, if he laid it on thick the day before, he gave her two or three additional coats this time, and the innocent soul went away, smiling as usual.

When Jack brought the filly home, the dark fellow, his master, if dark before, was a perfect tunder cloud this night: bedad, he was nothing less than near bursting with vexation, bakase the thieving ould sinner intended to have Jack's head upon the hook, but he fell short in his reckoning now as well as before.

Jack sung, "Love among the Roses," and the "Black Joke," to help him into better temper.

"Jack," said he, striving to make himself speak pleasant to him, "you've got two difficulty tasks over you; but you know the third time's the charm—take care of the next."

"No matter about that," says Jack, speaking up to him stiff and stout, bekase, as the dog tould him, he knew he had a friend in coort. "Let us hear what it is, anyhow."

"To-morrow, then," says the other, "you are to rob a crane's nest, on the top of a beech tree which grows in the middle of the lake that you saw, yesterday, in my demesne; you're to have neither boat nor oar, nor any kind of conveyance, but just as you stand; and if you fail to bring me the eggs, or if you break one of them—look there!" says he, again pointing to the odd hook, for all this took place in the bone-room.

(To be continued.)

BLACK HAWKE, THE HIGHWAYMAN.

"TWENTY SWORDS AND BAYONETS PIERCED THE PANELS."—*See Page* 31.

CHAPTER VI.—(*continued.*)

Impelling his own horse forward he fired.

The crash rang on the night air, but the wind again swept the drift in a cloud like the spray of the sea, and Sir Andrew's followers dispersed at the corner and fired at each other as they saw shadowy figures dimly through the hazy cloud, and fancied each other the foe they pursued.

This lasted for a few minutes, and then the mist cleared partially away again, and the glimmering light of the night revealed the scene.

The old Jew, lying heaped on the ground; three of their own party wounded or dead, lying trampled by the horses; Sir Andrew, ghastly as death, reeling in his saddle.

In the distance, speeding through the falling snowflakes,

they saw—not Black Hawke the Horseman of Death, that dread visitant was nowhere to be seen—but him they had first pursued, and whom they seemed never destined to capture, Merlin the abductor of Sir Andrew's beautiful wife !

He turned even as they looked at him, and gracefully waved his hat in defiance.

This spectacle aroused the drooping energy of Sir Andrew.

With violent gestures he blasphemously bade his followers stop the fugitive, promising large rewards to any who could bring him down.

The men, thus encouraged, swept on over the snow-clad vale, discharging their pistols incessantly at the gallant horseman.

For some time he rode on unharmed by this fusillade; but

before he could get out of distance a ball struck his horse in the flank, and brought her to her haunches.

At this success a loud shout rose from the pursuers.

Merlin's brow flushed; fortune seemed to desert him.

He prepared for a desperate resistance; but, to his joy, his brave steed rose again almost instantaneously, and once more bore him from his foes.

Merlin's eyes beamed with pleasure, though he found that the gallant animal rapidly flagged, and would be overtaken ultimately unless the speed of his pursuers slackened.

"I must shoot the horse of the foremost rider," he muttered. "Another of those friendly snow-storms would enable me to get shelter at the mill; but if I wait for that I may find myself in difficulties."

The brother of Sir Andrew was the foremost rider.

He made an imperative gesture for Merlin to stop, and aimed a pistol at him.

An instant after there was a flash, and a bullet sped through the air; but it came from Merlin's pistol, and the horse of Marmaduke fell to the ground dead—shot through the skull.

This had delayed Merlin a little, and now his horse perceptibly flagged.

Sir Andrew's brother was not long before he was in the saddle of one of the fallen men's horses.

He saw with delight that they were rapidly gaining upon their fugitive.

"If you fire, only wound him," he said; "we can take him alive."

"Can you?" said Merlin, who overheard the order. "I should advise you not to come too close in trying it."

They did come close, however, for a few minutes' chase brought them upon him.

His case seemed hopeless, and his dark eyes gleamed fiercely as he saw his enemies advancing.

"Sword and pistol to the work," he muttered; "he will find it warm who comes first."

"Taken at last!" Sir Andrew cried. "Yield, fellow, to save your brains!"

"Oh, they are safe enough for the present," a voice answered, and from behind a line of bushes, as from the earth, rose a party of horsemen, whom the darkness of the night had hitherto concealed.

A handsome looking fellow—their leader, evidently—was in front, and, as his followers interposed between Merlin and the others, he caught the young horseman's hand, and said,

"Away, your steed is failing; my lads and self will keep these hounds at bay."

At this interruption to his revenge at the very moment when Merlin seemed in his power, Sir Andrew, with livid features and husky voice, cried,

"Fire! he will escape! Shoot him! Down with the ruffian! A thousand crowns if he is slain!"

The leader of the horsemen smiled as he exclaimed,

"Not so fast. Your fellows, unless they would have a taste of steel, had better keep their weapons as they are."

Sir Andrew made an attempt to pass.

"Out of my way!" he shouted. "Who are you who dare aid that villain?"

The stranger lifted his hat.

"My name is Will Merry, gentleman of the king's highway; these are my comrades, the Golden Farmer, a very worthy one; Mulled Jack, a rare fellow, too, with his bottle; this gentleman we call Bill Nevison, and that long rascal, the Shadow. There are others of our band, but, as you will have the honour of a closer acquaintance, I will reserve the introduction."

"Aside, highwaymen! there are gibbets enough for you all."

"Doubtless," responded Will Merry, drily; "but for the present we do not intend to adorn them: and, as I perceive certain signs of restlessness amongst you, and some of your fellows are foolishly fingering their weapons, I may as well inform you that if there is any resistance to my designs I shall string you up to the tree and leave you there to realise what the gibbet is like."

"What do you mean, ruffian?"

"Why, firstly, I require your purses, you being on our domains; secondly, I want your persons, Will Merry being too polite a gentleman to part with noblemen at so slight acquaintance; thirdly, I shall suffer you to depart on condition that you leave me some handsome sum as a keepsake in remembrance of our pleasant meeting."

Sir Andrew foamed at the mouth.

"You would plunder, take prisoner, and ransom us?"

"That is my intention."

"Highway thief! I would be slain rather than surrender."

"No, you will not," replied Will, calmly; "not that your life is much of an object to me; but, for the sake of the ransom, I will make you prisoner."

He lifted his hand, and instantly Sir Andrew and his party were covered each by a pistol.

"You see, if I only whisper the word, you will all of you travel without brains; therefore, be wise, and submit, when your only alternative is death, and remember, Sir Andrew, the tree has a stout branch."

The baronet was boiling over with rage; but resistance was useless.

Will Merry and his band quietly disarmed and made the prisoners, the baronet and his brother, with the officers, being bound to their horses and led away captive after they had been plundered of every valuable they possessed.

The servants, after being bound in pairs, and deprived of their horses, were suffered to depart, the highwaymen taking the rest to their rendezvous.

While this was taking place, Merlin had safely reached the mill, and his faithful horse being taken in charge by the miller, Merlin was conducted by the miller's daughter to the inner room, and received in the arms of Lady Florence.

Yes, husband, duty, the past, the dread uncertainty of Merlin's profession, were all forgotten when she saw him return safely from danger, to restore to her the child for whose possession he had incurred such deadly peril.

She did not refuse him the kiss he claimed when he strained her to his breast; she repaid him for the recovery of her child—at least, so she said to herself—and if there was another feeling that prompted her to suffer his lips to rest against her cheeks, she may be pardoned the weakness.

At all events Merlin was too noble to take advantage of it.

* * * * * * *

There is one individual whom we have almost overlooked. The usurious Jew. He had been left stunned on the ground where he was felled by the Black Horseman.

He had not been killed.

When his senses returned he crawled along in the direction whence the sounds of fighting came. He thought and hoped that Merlin was taken, and his chagrin was extreme when he saw the means by which he had escaped.

While the highwaymen were making sure of their prisoners, he lay flat to the ground, but afterwards he crawled near enough to see Merlin make his way to the miller's abode.

When he had seen this, and thought himself safe, he stole cautiously back, his visage puckered up in wrinkles of devilish triumph.

"I will have him now," he muttered, "before this night is over. The house shall be surrounded by the king's officers. I will prove him a highwayman, and for that he shall die on the gallows! The cursed brat! to think he did not die, but lives to haunt me—lives to claim his father's property! God of my fathers! he shall die on the gibbet like a dog!"

CHAPTER VII.

THE MILLER RESOLVES UPON A JOLLIFICATION—THE STRANGE GUEST—THE JEW FINDS HIMSELF IN THE MILL AND WISHES HE WAS SAFE OUT AGAIN—SOME ACCOUNT OF THE MANNER IN WHICH HE GETS OUT AGAIN.

THE miller's daughter conducted Lady Florence to the best chamber in the miller's house, and left her there to endeavour to gain repose for the few remaining hours of the night while she took charge of her child.

Lady Florence was some time before the events of the night would suffer her to go to sleep, but at length she fell into a light slumber, and slept the troubled sleep of a disturbed mind.

When she awoke in the morning the light of day was streaming through the narrow windows of her chamber; the mill was at work, and from every side she could hear the bustle of men at their labour.

Her first thought was of her child, and, for the moment, a pang shot through her breast as the fear crossed her mind that she might again have lost it; but, remembering that the miller's daughter had it under her care, she composed herself, after she had rung the bell to summon the damsel to her presence.

Strange to say, her next thought, after she had satisfied herself respecting her child, was not for her husband, but of the man who had taken her from him. She sighed as she thought of his handsome looks and nobility of mind; and as she sat there, with the pale light streaming upon her sad white face, many troubled emotions took possession of her soul.

Nancy came in with her babe, and Florence timidly enquired after Merlin.

She was told that he was still 'in the house, the old miller not permitting him to go forth while so many of his foes were lurking about in hopes of capturing him.

Lady Florence questioned Nancy to discover, if possible, whether her worst fears respecting her admirer's mode of life were well founded; but Nancy, if she knew, answered so discreetly that she could gain no satisfaction, and she was left to her own conjectures.

A hundred times the fearful idea presented itself that he was the terrible being—the dreaded Black Hawke; and yet, as she called to memory his gallant bearing, his gentleness, and his frank bravery, she found it difficult to believe that he was the dreaded shedder of his fellow creatures' blood.

"It is impossible," she involuntarily exclaimed.

"What, my lady?" asked Nancy.

"That he can be the terrible Black Hawke, the highwayman."

"Who, my lady?"

"Merlin."

Nancy gave a little scream.

"He that notorious highwayman and night assassin? Why, my lady, you never heard of what Black Hawke can do: he would think nothing of cutting your child's throat, even as it lay on your breast. Ugh! you make me shiver at the idea! Master Merlin is a brave and honest gentleman, too true-hearted to betray a friend, too noble and generous to harm even an enemy, unless he have good cause. Were Black Hawke to stay one night in this house, all our heads would be cut off before morning."

From the fact of Merlin's being still in safety at the mill, it will be seen that the Jew had not carried out his treacherous intentions. This was not from any lack of inclination, but because he had not been able to mature his measures before daybreak, and knew that unless the place were approached under concealment of darkness, Merlin would be spirited away long before an entrance could be made.

So he had deferred the prosecution of his scheme until the succeeding night, when he intended to get admitted to the miller's house under a disguise, so that when all was ripe he might give the signal to admit the king's officers.

Merlin had slept soundly after once getting the opportunity of repose—a brief review of the incidents of the day, a last sweet thought of his beautiful mistress Lady Florence, and he cast himself upon the hard couch whereon he was to recline, and slept till the miller aroused him to breakfast.

Hugh Marks, the miller, was one of those dry old fellows, fond of a convivial glass, and ever ready to applaud acts of reckless bravery.

He was much attached to Merlin, who had frequently given proofs of his incontestible and reckless daring, and prouder still when he had the chance of giving him shelter.

Had his young friend been pursued to the house by the officers they would have found it no light task to take their prisoner. There were some stout fellows at the mill, and Marks himself was not one to be trifled with; when he once got a man in his powerful hug, he might as well have been in the clutches of a bear.

Old Lazarus, the Jew, then had some amount of courage to be willing to venture into such a lair.

There was some embarrassment between the pair when Merlin and Lady Florence met. The latter was in an equivocal position; her duty prompted her to return to her husband, and yet she hesitated. She did not know how he would receive her, unless by accusations of the most taunting nature. Besides, he would use every artifice to make her tell him where Merlin was concealed.

Then, for her to remain there, especially at Merlin's solicitations, was to countenance the daring abduction of which he had been guilty.

As for Merlin, now that he had time for reflection, he began to feel in something of a quandary.

To plan and execute the carrying off of a lady were simple things; but what to do with the lady after he had carried her off was another matter.

He could not very well marry her, seeing that she was already a wife. True, he might get over the difficulty by killing her husband; but the success of that venture was rather dubious. Neither could he ask her to live with him, as that would have been a dishonor he could never have stooped to.

The old miller, who observed their awkward meeting, went about the house, muttering to himself, and draining off no end of tumblers of strong spirits.

"A pretty pair of birds," he would say, with a chuckle. "Ho! ho! they're shy of each other now, but they'll come together some of these fine days, I'll warrant.

Here he was about to pour the contents of a huge tumbler down his throat, when Dame Marks, who had come behind him, caught the vessel, and took it away just as he got the first sip.

"Prithee, dame," said the old fellow, turning quickly round, "'tis the first sip I've taken to-day."

"Gramercy; you've emptied three bottles already."

"Well, well, never mind, there'll be more when they're gone; prithee, let me have the drain?"

"No more, on my life. If I were not as small a drinker as you are a great one, there would be fine doings, gadzooks."

"Ha, ha! dame," muttered the old fellow, with a chuckle, "an' I had a crown piece for every drain thou drinkest; but, there, peace to all. What of the young doves in our house?"

"They're well enow together; but I have news to tell. The dreadful Highwayman, Black Hawke, has been seen again in our neighbourhood. Gramercy, an' he come so far, we shall get up some fine morning and find ourselves murdered!"

The old miller laughed his dry chuckle.

"That be news, indeed," he said, "news, indeed, it be."

"More than that; Will Merry and his band have been at work."

"Eh? What have they done now?"

"Took Sir Andrew and his brother, robbed them, and made them pay a handsome sum before they suffered them to return."

"Ho! ho!" laughed the miller. "That be pleasant news indeed, hey? They were after Master Merlin last night. 'Tis good; we will have a grand carouse to-night; the lasses shall come to the lads in the old mill, and Master Merlin shall foot it with his lady down our big room; and, marry, some of that fine old brand Joe the Smuggler got here shall be brought out to make them merry. Ho! ho! that was rare fun. Will Merry, thee'st a prime lad, and if ever my mill can give 'ee shelter, gadzooks, you shall have it."

The miller was as good as his word; he invited the lads employed there to bring their lasses, and at night he broached his favourite cask.

The merriment had scarcely begun when a summons was made at the door. Lady Florence became pale with sudden fear lest it should be some one from her husband; but her alarm was dispelled when a faint trembling voice was heard inquiring the nearest way to the village.

Old Hugh went to see who it was; the croaking voice seemed to interest him, but more so the owner, a grotesque-looking old man, with a beard almost down to his waist, and great shaggy eye-brows bordering his uncouth forehead.

"Whither bound, old pilgrim?" he asked.

"To the village," was the reply, in a husky voice. "I have

come across the valley through the snow, and, seeing lights, thought I would make bold to knock and ask my way, for 'tis a cold night, and when one is faint——"

"Marry it is, and so, friend, you may even come in and take a draught with the lads. We are having a little merry-making, and no one, if I know it, shall be out in the cold."

This invite seemed to highly please the traveller, for he entered gladly; and the old miller, taking a survey of the wintry scene outside, just to see how cosy it looked afterwards within, as he said, ushered him to the room where the lads were assembled.

"Ho! ho!" he muttered, in his drawling way. "This is a poor wayfarer, and he shall have welcome, ho! ho! a fine welcome—a fine welcome."

But presently, meeting Dame Marks, he plucked her by the sleeve.

"Ho! ho! dame," he quoth, in his dry manner, "we have a strange guest, one Lazarus the Jew, the usurer. We will give him a welcome here."

"Lazarus?" cried the old dame, in alarm.

"Even so; but peace, dame. He comes to betray the boy. Ho! ho! we have him inside safe enow, safe enow. We will scratch his skin before he leaves; he shall take the miller's mark. Ho! ho! yes, yes."

With his usual quaint smile about his lips the old fellow went to the room. He found the Jew endeavouring to make himself at home, but not succeeding altogether to his satisfaction.

Now, the miller had quite made up his mind that the Jew's purpose there was to betray Merlin, and he had also made up his mind that he would make him pay the penalty of the intent.

So he went up to him, and, jocularly talking to him, plied him with glass after glass of his strong liquor, which Lazarus would fain have declined drinking, but Hugh was inflexible.

Having primed him against his will with more strong drink than was good for him, he next horrified the unfortunate Jew by forcing him to eat—much to his loathing—some very fine pork, which nothing but the fear of being suspected compelled Lazarus to swallow.

Neither Florence nor Merlin was there, but the latter came in soon after; he was elegantly dressed, and the long rapier by his side added much to the *eclat* of his appearance, except in the Jew's estimation, who felt that a lunge from that long thin weapon, given by such experienced hands as Merlin's, would be anything but pleasant if it happened to touch his shrunken old body.

When Lady Florence came in there was a general hush of admiration. She looked divinely beautiful.

A rich colour mantled her lovely cheeks, and her magnificent hair was arranged to its utmost advantage.

She was arrayed in a splendid robe, setting off her charming figure to the highest effect.

Merlin bowed lowly as she entered, and immediately afterwards went to her side.

"A dance is about to begin," he said, "may I have the pleasure of entreating your favour?"

Lady Florence sighed as she gave him her hand.

"I cannot pardon myself that I remain here," she said, in a sad, low tone, "yet I feel you would not dishonour me by a request."

"Lady, I should deserve to die were I to wrong you in thought, word or deed. Others have wronged you, but not I."

"You have been kind, indeed," she replied, blushing slightly, "but I cannot forget that I have a husband."

"I would I could make you forget it," murmured Merlin, "or make you remember it only to recognise that individual in me."

Lady Florence blushed again, and gently chided him for his speech, and then the musicians struck up and the dance began.

It was one of those famous old dances then so much in vogue.

Lady Florence and Merlin went gracefully through the steps, the old miller joining heartily in with the old dame, and giving the young couples sly nods and winks as he passed them by.

Certainly the old Jew had no cause to suspect that he was being watched by the miller as his malicious gaze fixed itself upon Merlin and his mistress.

But his every action was noted by the miller, who, while giving vent to the wildest glee, took care that nothing should escape his observation.

In one of the pauses at the conclusion of the dance he managed to get behind Lazarus unseen.

He had observed a bulky-looking paper in his pocket, and, while the Jew was glaring after the young pair, he dexterously took the paper forth.

No flush of anger deepened on his cheeks as he glanced over the document, but there was a roguish twinkle in his merry eye that betokened no good to the detected son of Abraham.

But as soon as the dance was over, and while Merlin was leading Florence to a seat, he stalked into the middle of the room, and in a loud, clear voice, proceeded to read—

"Warrant for the arrest of Merlin Hawke, the highwayman. Five hundred crowns reward for this notorious robber and assassin, now supposed to be concealed in the house of Hugh Marks, the miller."

The reading of this document produced the most abrupt confusion. Lady Florence turned deadly white, and clung to Merlin, who merely looked round with an interested air.

The miller's daughter gazed silently at her father, while the lads and their sweethearts, in the utmost wonderment, crowded round their host.

But on the usurer the effect was most palpable; his visage fell, and he began to tremble visibly in every limb.

Lady Florence was the first to speak.

"Oh, Merlin, what means this?"

"Dearest, I cannot say; Marks, perhaps, will tell."

Merlin spoke carelessly, but his eager glance went round the assembled faces, as if he would search out the suspected traitor.

He was not long in finding him out. His eye caught the slinking gaze of the Jew, and he instantly divined the state of affairs; but the miller's honest face, assuring him that all was right, he allowed matters to take their course.

Hugh Marks looked about as angry as it was possible for him to look.

"Lads," he said, addressing the millers, "you all know Master Merlin, a gentleman robbed of his estates. Some people, to get rid of him, have got this charge against him; now, what would you do to the scoundrel who tried to take him?"

"We'd show him," was the reply, and the looks that accompanied it made the Jew feel very nervous.

"Then," said the miller, walking straight up to Lazarus, and taking him by the collar, "here's the rascal, who not only makes this charge—ho, ho!—but comes here to betray him."

A general outcry saluted the Jew's ears, as the miller tore off his false beard, eyebrows, &c., and revealed his villanous face.

"There, look at him; the precious beauty! Take him, my lads, and do what you please with him."

The Jew's tongue clove to his mouth in his deadly terror; his eyeballs seemed starting from their sockets. He fell on his knees, and implored the miller to spare him; but the men were clamorous for justice on the traitor, and in the midst of his supplications he was carried away.

"They will not kill him?" Lady Florence said.

"Little loss, lady, if they did; but fear not, his worthless life is safe. I will not answer, though, for the terror he will suffer."

"Oh, Merlin, are you not fearful of danger? What terrible charge is this they bring against you?"

A strange expression settled on Merlin's features.

"I have no fear," he said, calmly, "and as for the rest, I beseech you ask nothing now; in a day you may learn too much respecting one who, when he dies, hopes it will be for you."

Meanwhile they had carried the old Jew along the passage to the lower part of the mill. So excited were they against him that his life did not appear worth one instant's purchase. Some were for lynching him on the spot with a stout rope, others for drowning him in the millstream, while some, again, were for securing him by the neck to the sails of the windmill and letting him beat to death.

The miller, however, would not have him put to death, and a more merciful arrangement was come to.

First they ducked him in the mill-pond until he thought his last gasp was come, then they nearly suffocated him with flour, he imploring all the time in the most abject manner for mercy. When they had finished with him in these ways his head was shaved and his beard plucked out, after which they let him go, a horrible spectacle, half dead with fear, and in awful torture through the treatment he had received.

The miller and his men returned to the inner room, and the Jew's punishment having been explained Hugh Marks and his dame set the example for a renewal of the evening's mirth by leading off in another dance.

Merlin with great difficulty prevailed upon Florence to join in again; it was only for his sake and to please the miller and his guests that she consented, for her heart was far from that scene. A dread foreboding threw its shadow over her mind, and, in spite of Merlin's gallantry, she could not assume a gaiety she did not feel.

In the midst of the dance there came a rude summons at the door.

The music ceased instantly, and the dancers, with paled cheeks, listened for what was to come.

The miller stalked calmly to the door.

"Who comes?" he asked, "and on what business?"

"The officers of justice," was the reply; "we come to arrest Merlin Hawke the Highwayman, and in the king's name command you to open the door."

CHAPTER VIII.

HOW THE OFFICERS TRIED TO GET AN ENTRY—WHAT THE MILLER GAVE ONE FOR HIS PAINS—THE ATTACK—BLOODSHED AND THE MILL ON FIRE.

LADY FLORENCE uttered a piercing shriek, and fell pale as alabaster on Merlin's breast. He, calm and undaunted, supported her trembling form, and, with one hand on the hilt of his sword, gazed round as if searching for his foes.

Then a loud, cold voice was heard on the outside bidding the officers force an entrance, and Florence shuddered as she recognised the tones of her husband.

The old miller went to the postern and put his head through.

The miller laughed at the mob without, and said,

"Well, lads, what are you making such a d—d row about?"

"Open the door!" shouted Sir Andrew, foaming with rage.

"Go to the devil!" Hugh replied, as he drew his head in.

"If you don't give up that highwayman and cut-throat," said Sir Andrew, again, "the mill shall be razed to the earth!"

"Don't tell lies!" growled the miller.

An officer seeing the opportunity put his head through the hole in the door. Had he known the reception he would receive, he would have left it to be filled by somebody else's head.

The miller saw him coming, and pulled him in by his ears as far as his shoulders would admit.

"Well, you ugly son of a thief, who told you to put your head into other people's places?"

Several of his brother officers who had wished to have the chance of doing something heroic, changed their minds as they saw their comrade's head come out much uglier than it went in.

Marmaduke and Sir Andrew were getting furious being kept outside so long, and they looked savagely at each other.

"Why didn't you shoot the villain?" Sir Andrew said, angrily, to his brother.

"Because you were closer to him than I was," answered Marmaduke. "It's your wife; therefore you had a greater right to shoot him than I had."

Sir Andrew turned away enraged, and swore at the officers because they did not knock the mill down.

He had abused the men till he had made himself tired, and finding that swearing at them did not make them work any better, he said,

"A hundred crowns for the first one that enters!"

That had an electric effect on them as they made a rush at the door.

The miller only laughed at their vain efforts, and putting his head out of the postern, he said,

"Sir Andrew, you seem very anxious to have an entry made, perhaps you will be the first to enter? Would you like to see your wife with her arms round another's neck, and her head resting on his chest?"

Sir Andrew could not stand the taunting words any longer; he fired a pistol at the miller, but the bullet struck a piece of iron and flattened.

Hugh Marks fastened the postern and double barred the door; he then returned to the merry-makers, and, ordering the music to strike up again, the dance was led off by the miller and the old dame.

Everything was gaiety and mirth; the merry laughter rang through the old mill, and the lads took the opportunity of kissing their fair companions as they danced round a shady part. Merlin had persuaded Florence to join in the merriment, and as they waltzed Florence looked lovingly into her companion's face.

"Bang! bang!" came at the door with tremendous force.

"Hullo!" said Merlin, "there's those ugly whelps hurting themselves!"

"Ha, ha, ha!" laughed the miller. "I say, lads, we will get ready to receive them."

The lads gave a shout of approval as their master went to get them sticks, broken swords, and other implements.

"It strikes me that somebody will get hurt to-night. I can smell a row brewing," Merlin said, playing with the hilt of his sword.

Lady Florence crept close to Merlin. She trembled violently.

Merlin watched her narrowly. Evidently many thoughts were coursing through his brain; he would smile, then the smile would pass away and a dark frown would come over his handsome face, and his hand would invariably wander to his sword and tighten on the hilt, then, as he caught her gaze fixed on him, he would gently smile again.

Lady Florence had watched his every movement.

"Merlin, they will break in," she said.

He laughed as he bent to kiss her, and answered,

"The first that enters will not get out alive."

Before Lady Florence had time to make any reply there came a tremendous crashing, and choruses of rough voices demanding admittance.

The miller walked towards the back of the mill, muttering, followed by his men.

"Open the door," shouted somebody, "or, by Heavens, you will rue it, Mr. Miller!"

"So will you," said Merlin, poking his sword through a crack in the door.

Somebody gave a howl of pain, and Merlin drew his sword back.

Its point was red!

"That fellow won't make a noise again in a hurry," Merlin said.

"In the king's name, open the door," somebody else shouted.

"See the king d——d first; and you will get a dig in the ribs that will stop your bawling if you keep using the king's name in vain," said Merlin, thrusting his sword through again.

The officers saw the point making its way through, and stood aside.

Merlin was greatly disappointed at not having had the pleasure of hearing another cry of agony.

The miller had armed his men, and was returning when he saw a crouching object crawling on all fours towards the window.

One of the officers had gone round the back in hopes of getting in unseen; he had imagined that, while his comrades were keeping a continual hammering at the door, Hugh Marks and the rest would be waiting for them to enter, and he thought that it would be a good opportunity for him to get in unseen.

"Ha, ha! my fine lad, you thought you had done it very cleverly," said Hugh Marks, laughing to himself. "Come in, I don't think you will get out again."

Under the window stood a large butt full of water, over which Hugh Marks carefully put a thin piece of canvas filled with flour and then waited for the unsuspecting officer.

He did not wait long.

The officer came stealthily creeping up the side of the window, and dexterously got a footing upon the window-sill and was about to enter when he received a tremendous blow from the miller's left in the wind which doubled him up and caused him to turn a somersault and fall head first into the barrel of water.

He floundered about like an eel, vainly trying to reach the edge, but, being head downwards, he had not room enough to turn.

The miller, thinking that he had been splashing about long enough, took hold of his feet, and ducked him up and down, till, getting tired of ducking him, he stood him on his feet.

The poor devil was half suffocated with the filth in the water, and as soon as he got breath, he spat and spluttered about as though he had got something nasty in his mouth.

"Here, lads," called the miller, "here's a spy; you know your duty."

The officer wished they had forgotten it as they came rushing upon him.

Their victim was dragged into a large shed where there were hundreds of sacks of flour.

He was thrown down and a sack of flour emptied on him, and then he was rolled over and kicked about like a foot-ball.

"For God's sake let me go!" asked the officer, in a feeble tone. "I'll take anything—help! mercy!"

"Open the door," shouted the leader of the officers, "or by h— the very foundation shall be torn up."

Hugh Marks laughed.

The hammering and shouting grew louder every minute; cries of defiance, and shouts as of welcome, and then they seemed to rush at the mill with renewed strength.

Hugh Marks went to the postern and peered out.

Then he discovered the cause of their welcome shouts.

A party of officers were coming, headed by the old Jew, who had crawled away, and meeting them on the road, led them to the mill.

They had provided themselves with huge hammers and crowbars.

The miller closed the postern, and going back to where he had left the officer, he beckoned his men to bring their victim with him to a dark, dirty shed.

The miller lifted up a stone trap, and taking hold of the officer, he pointed down a dark, deep, slimy, loathsome pit.

"Prepare," he said, "this is your resting-place. Once down there, you never come out again alive."

The man turned deadly pale, and pleaded for mercy; but the miller was deaf to him.

Taking the man up in his arms, he threw him down.

There was a sickening thud, not even a sound escaped the victim's lips. The fall had rendered him insensible or dead.

The trap was closed, and Hugh Marks went back to Merlin just as the door shook beneath a heavy blow.

"By heavens, the first that enters," said Merlin, his dark eyes glittering with a deadly purpose, "shall be made an example to the rest."

Lady Florence pleaded beseechingly to him not to hurt her husband.

"Fear not, my love," he said. "I will not harm him unless he dares to lay a finger on you."

Hugh Marks had been getting very excited during the time the officers kept up the battering at the door, and arming himself with a huge beam, he prepared to meet the enemy.

"Get thee selves ready, my lads," he said, "for a d—d good foight. Somebody will get hurt."

His men clustered round him like a lot of bees.

At that moment another tremendous crash came at the door, the panels began to split, and splinters flew about in all directions.

Merlin gave Lady Florence in the care of old Dame Marks, and then stood like a statue waiting the entry of his foes.

He did not wait long.

The door heaved to and fro, and the officers came on it with a rush.

The officers came dashing in, and in their hurry they did not see a thick rope that was tied across the doorway, and as the first came running in, he caught his foot in it and fell, the others came headlong in and fell on their comrades.

"He is there," said Sir Andrew, pointing at Merlin, "the robber that stole my wife."

Merlin regarded him with a defiant look, but said nothing.

One of the officers advanced, and fell pierced through the heart.

Merlin put his foot upon the bleeding body of the fallen officer.

"Down with him! Down with BLACK HAWKE THE HIGHWAYMAN!" exclaimed a stalwart fellow with a pair of huge pistols in his belt.

"I shall down with you if you make such a confounded row," said Merlin.

"Arrest him, men!" said Marmaduke Greville. "I know him; he tried to stop me on the road the other night."

Merlin had not moved; he had kept his foot on the lifeless body, and gazed steadily on the group that had come to take him.

"Hound!" said Merlin, in a voice of thunder, glaring at Marmaduke with deadly hate. "If you are no coward, come on and fight me singly—man to man."

Marmaduke didn't see it.

"Come, captain," said the big officer with the big pistols, "you had better come quietly; I know you well enough. Arrest him, men."

The men advanced; but came to a sudden halt.

Merlin stood confronting them, his sword between his teeth and a pistol in each hand.

Then putting one of the pistols away while he got his sword on his wrist, he kept the other levelled at one of the officers until he had got the other again.

"Now, men," he said, "if you have any respect for your lives you will go back."

They had respect for their lives, and obeyed his command.

"And now," continued Merlin, "if that cowardly cur, Marmaduke, does not come from behind you I will make a passage through you to get at him."

Levelling a pistol, he was about to fire, when his arms were caught from behind.

"For heaven's sake!" said Lady Florence, "do not shoot him, dear Merlin."

"My wife!" shouted Sir Andrew. "Secure her and kill him."

The whole gang rushed upon him before he had time to resist.

"Ha! ha! ha! my fine poy!" said the old Jew, rubbing his bony knuckles with glee. "So they have got you at last; you von't run avay with the ladies any more. No, no, no, my poy, you von't come to life any more ven you is hanged up by the neck, no, no."

His speech was rudely cut short by his receiving a tremendous clout on the head from the miller's beam, that floored him.

The excitement was growing intense.

The miller who had been leaning on a huge beam looking on, came to the rescue as soon as he saw Merlin penned in, and not liking to see the old Israelite in such good spirits over other people's misfortunes, gave him one for his nob.

His men followed him, and a sharp conflict ensued.

Lady Florence was deadly pale, and clasping her hands, hid her face on his shoulder, for she dearly loved the handsome reckless youth who was imperilling his life for her sake.

Merlin had once more got his hands free, and bearing Lady Florence on his left arm, cut his way to where Sir Andrew stood.

Sir Andrew turned pale as he saw the point of Merlin's sword coming close to his chest, and finding himself in immediate danger, cried,

"Do your duty, men! Take him, dead or alive."

"Sir Andrew," Merlin said, "I make a proposition to you as a brave man; but, as a coward, you order your servitors to do that which you could not do yourself."

"Coward!"

"Coward!"

Sir Andrew drew his sword.

Merlin put Lady Florence gently aside.

Sir Andrew put his sword back as he saw the determined look of hate on his opponent's face, and said,

"I should have enough to do were I to accept the challenge of every robber and foot-pad."

Merlin's passion grew terrible, and, leaping like a tiger on his foe, he said,

"Hound! fight with me foot to foot, or I will kill you where you stand!"

Their deadly weapons crossed.

"That's a brave stroke," said Merlin, guarding off a thrust.

Sir Andrew grew excited and less cautious; he had tried every cut and pass in the art of fencing, but his sword was caught coolly on the point of his adversary's.

Irritated and almost driven to madness, Sir Andrew made a terrific lunge; everybody thought that the weapon had gone through Merlin's body.

Merlin saw it, as quick as it was, and catching the point he wound the blade of his own weapon round that of his opponent, and with a sudden twist of his wrist he wrenched the sword from his grasp, and it fell broken in half.

Sir Andrew was now helpless, and at the mercy of his foe.

At that moment when, like a tiger, Merlin sprang at his throat, and in another instant would have buried his sword in his body, the old Jew, seeing the danger of Sir Andrew, fired a pistol at Merlin, the bullet entered his side, and he fell bleeding to the ground.

The officers rushed upon the fallen man as the miller came dashing in with his huge beam in a blaze.

"Cowards!" he shouted, "lay a finger upon him, or hurt a hair of his head, and I'll blow you all into the air.

"Fools!" said Sir Andrew, "secure your prisoner!"

"Fool!" repeated Hugh Marks, "in less than five minutes you will be surrounded by one mass of flame!"

As he spoke dense clouds of smoke came gushing through the boards, then the forked flames came darting through every crack and crevice.

They were all enveloped in one mass of fire!

The mill was on fire!

Sir Andrew, maddened at being baffled, caught hold of Lady Florence's white throat, and said,

"Wanton and traitress! see your lover bleeding and almost dead! Thus will I end your career!"

Tearing her dress open he put the point of his sword against her fair white breast.

"Lower your weapon," shouted Marks, "or by heavens I will fell you like an ox."

He raised the beam in a threatening manner, but the blow was arrested by his hearing his wife screaming.

Turning his head he saw her coming downstairs with a child in her arms.

The lower part of the staircase was in one mass of flame.

To venture down any further was impossible unless she wished to be burned alive.

Hugh Marks could not go to her assistance.

Should he move from Merlin's side the officers would take the opportunity and seize him.

"Look! look at your child for the last time," said Sir Andrew to Florence, mockingly. "Behold it, being scorched and burned to death!"

A wild cry came from Lady Florence's frozen lips. She put out her arms towards her child, but before she could move a step a shout of horror rose from the officers, and with Sir Andrew and Marmaduke they fell back.

A sullen, explosive sound shook the very building, a whitened sheet of flame shot into their midst; wells, floors, and roof rocked in a mighty throe, and with a deafening crash the burning mill fell in!

(*To be continued.*)

THE GOBLIN DOG;

A TALE OF FUN AND WONDER.

(*Continued from page* 16.)

"Good again," says Jack; "if I fail I know my doom."

"No you don't, you spalpeen," says the other, getting vexed with him entirely, "for I'll roast you till you are half dead, and ate my dinner off you after; and, what is more than that, you blackguard, you must sing the 'Black Joke' all the time."

"Divel fly away with you," thought Jack; "but you're fond of music, you vagabond."

The next morning Jack was going round and round the lake, trying about the edge of it, if he could find any place shallow enough to wade in; he might as well go for to wade the say, and, what was worst of all, if he attempted to swim, it would be like a tailor's goose,—straight to the bottom; so he kept himself safe on dry land, still expecting a visit from the "lovely crathur," but, bedad, his luck failed him for wanst; for, instead of seeing her coming over to him, so mild and sweet, who does he observe steering at a dog's trot, but his ould friend, the smoking cur.

"Confusion to that cur," says Jack to himself, "I know there's some bad fortune before me, or he wouldn't be coming acrass me."

"Come home to your breakfast, Jack," says the dog, walking up to him, "it's breakfast time."

"Aye," says Jack, scratching his head, "it's no great matter whether I do or not, for I bleeve my head's hardly worth a flat-dutch cabbage at the present speaking."

"Why, man, it was never worth so much," says the baste, pulling out his pipe and putting it in his mouth, when it lit at once.

"Take care of yourself," says Jack, quite desperate, for he thought he was near the end of his tether. "Take care of yourself, you dirty cur, or maybe I might take a gintleman's toe from the nape of your neck."

"You had better keep a straight tongue in your head," says four legs, "while it's on your shoulders, or I'll break every bone in your skin. Jack, you are a fool," says he, checking himself, and speaking kindly to him, "you are a fool; did not I tell you the other day to do what you were bid, and keep never minding?"

"Well," thought Jack to himself, "there's no use in making him any more my enemy than he is, particularly as I'm in such a hobble."

"You lie," says the dog, as if Jack had spoken *out* to him, wherein he only thought the words to himself, "you lie," says he, "I'm not, nor never was your enemy, if you knew but all."

"I beg your honour's pardon," answers Jack, "for being so smart with your honour; but, bedad, if you were in my case,—if you expected your master to roast you alive—eat his dinner off of your body—make you sing the 'Black Joke' by way of music for him; and, to crown all, knew that your head was to be stuck upon a hook after—maybe you would be a little short in your temper as well as your neighbours."

"Take heart, Jack," says the other, laying his foreclaw as knowingly as ever along his nose, and winking slyly at Jack. "Didn't I tell you that you have a friend in coort? The day's not past yet; so cheer up, who knows but there is luck before you still?"

"Why, thin," says Jack, getting a little cheerful, and wishing to crack a joke with him; "but your honour's very fond of the pipe!"

"Oh! don't you know, Jack," says he, "that that's the fashion at present among my tribe; sure all my brother puppies smoke now, and a man might as well be out of the world as out of the fashion, you know."

When they drew near home, they got quite thick entirely.

"Now," says Jack, in a good-humoured way, "if you can give me a lift in robbing the crane's nest, do; at any rate, I'm sure your honour won't be my enemy. I know you have too much good nature in your face to be one that wouldn't help a lame dog over the style—that is," says he, taking himself up for fear of offending the other—"I'm sure you'd be always inclined to help the weak side."

"Thank you for the compliment," says the dog; "but didn't I tell you that you have a friend in coort?"

When Jack went back to the lake, he could only sit and look sorrowfully at the tree, or walk about the edge of it, without being able to do anything else. He spent the whole day this way till dinner time, when what would you have of it, but he sees the "darling" coming out to him, as fair and as blooming as an angel. His heart, you may be sure, got up to his mouth, for he knew she would be apt to take him out of all his difficulties. When she came up.

"Now, Jack," says she, "there is not a minnit to be lost, for I am watched; and if it's discovered that I gave you any assistance we will be both destroyed."

"Oh, murther Sheery!" says Jack, "fly back, avourneen machree,—for rather than anything should happen you, I'd lose fifty lives."

"No," says she, "I think I'll be able to get you over this, as well as the rest; so have a good heart and be faithful."

"That's it," replied Jack, "that's it, a cushla—my own character to a shavin'."

She then pulled a small white wand out of her pocket, struck the lake, and there was the prettiest green ridge across it to the foot of the tree that ever eye beheld.

"Now," says she, turning her back to Jack, and stooping down to do something that he couldn't see, "take these, put them against the tree, and you will have steps to carry you to the top, but be sure not, for your life and mine, to forget any of them; if you do my life will be taken to-morrow morning, for your master puts on my slippers with his own hands."

Jack was now going to swear that he would give up the whole thing and surrender his head at once; but when he looked at her feet, and saw no appearance of blood, he went over without more to do and robbed the nest, taking down the eggs one by one that he mightn't break them.

There was no end to his joy as he secured the last egg.

He instantly took down the toes, one after another, save and except the little one of the left foot, which, in his joy and hurry, he forgot entirely.

He then returned by the green ridge to the shore, and according as he went along, it melted away into the water behind him.

"Jack," says the charmer, "I hope you forgot none of my toes."

"Is it me?" says Jack, quite sure that he had them all. "Arrah! catch any one from my country making a blunder of that kind."

"Well," says she, "let us see."

So, taking the toes, she placed them on again, just as if they had never been off.

But lo, and behold! on coming to the last of the left foot, it wasn't forthcoming.

"Oh! Jack! Jack!" says she, "you have destroyed me. To-morrow morning your master will notice the want of this toe, and that instant I'll be put to death."

"Lave that to me," says Jack. "By the powers you won't lose a drop of your darling blood for it. Have you a penknife about you, and I'll soon show you how you won't."

"What do you want with the knife?" she inquired.

"What do I want with it? Why to give you the best toe on both my feet, for the one I lost on you. Do you think I'd suffer you to want a toe, and I having ten thumping ones at your sarvice? Faith! I'm not the man for such a shabby trick as that comes to."

"But you forget," says the lady, who was a little cooler than Jack, "that none of yours would fit me."

"And must you die to morrow, a cushla?" asked Jack, in desperation.

"As sure as the sun rises," answered the lady, "for your master would know at once that it was by my toes that the nest was robbed."

"By the powers," observed Jack, "he's one of the greatest ould vag—I mane, isn't he a terrible man, out and out, for a father?"

"Father?" says the darling. "He's not my father, Jack; he only wishes to marry me, and if I'm not able to outdo him before three days more, it's decreed that he must have me."

When Jack heard this, surely the Irishman must come out.

There he stood, and began to wipe his eyes with the skirt of his coat, making as if he was crying, the thief of the world.

"What's the matter with you?" she axed.

"Ah!" says Jack, "you darling, I couldn't find it in my heart to desave you, for I have no way at home to keep a lady like you in proper style, at all, at all. I would only bring you into poverty, and since you wish to know what ails me, I'm vexed that I'm not rich for your sake; and next, that that thieving ould villain's to

have you; and, by the powers, I'm crying for both these misfortunes together."

The lady couldn't help being touched and plased with Jack's tinderness and generosity.

So, says she,

"Don't be cast down, Jack, come or go what will. I won't marry him—I'd die first. Do you go home, as usual; but take care and don't go to sleep at all this night. Saddle the wild filly, and meet me under the white-thorn bush at the end of the lawn, and we'll both leave him for ever. If you're willing to marry me, don't let poverty distress you, for I have more money than we'll know what to do with."

Jack's voice now began to tremble in earnest, with downright love and tinderness, as good right it had; so he promised to do everything just as she bid him, and then he went home to his supper.

You may be sure the ould fellow looked darker and grimmer than ever at Jack; but what could he do?

Jack had done his duty; so he sat before the fire, sung "Love among the Roses," and the "Black Joke," with a stouter and lighter heart than ever, whilst the black chap could have seen him skivered.

When midnight came, Jack, who kept a hawk's eye to the night was at the hawthorn with the wild filly, saddled and all—more betoken, she wasn't a bit wild then, but as tame as a dog.

Off they set, like Erin-go-bragh, Jack and the lady, and never pulled bridle till it was one o'clock next day, when they stopped at an inn and took some refreshment.

They then took to the road again, full speed.

However, they hadn't gone far, when they heard a great noise behind them, and the tramp of horses galloping like mad.

"Jack," says the darling, on hearing the hubbub, "look behind you, and see what's this."

"Och! by the elevens!" says Jack. "We're done at last! it's the dark fellow, and half the country after us."

"Put your hand," says she, "in the filly's right ear, and tell me what you find in it."

"Nothing at all, at all," says Jack, "but a weeshy bit of a dry stick."

"Throw it over your left shoulder," says she, "and see what will happen."

Jack, my dear, did so at once, and there was a great grove of thick trees growing so close to one another, that a dandy could scarcely get his arm betwixt them.

"Now," says she, "we are safe for another day."

"Well," says Jack, as he pushed on the filly, "you're the jewel of the world, sure enough; and, maybe, it's you that won't live happy when we get to Ireland."

As soon as dark-face saw what had happened, he was obliged to scour the country for hatchets and handsaws, and all kinds of sharp instruments, to hew himself and his men a passage through the grove.

As the saying goes, many hands make light work, and, sure enough, it wasn't long till they had cleared a way for themselves, thick as it was, and set off with double speed after Jack and the lady.

(*To be continued.*)

BLACK HAWKE, THE HIGHWAYMAN.

THE LEAP OVER THE BRIDGE.—*See No. 5.*

CHAPTER IX.

AN OUTCRY AND A ROBBERY—THE COACH—A BENEVOLENT OLD GENTLEMAN AND A PRETTY YOUNG LADY — THE STRANGER—HIGHWAYMEN AT THE CARRIAGE DOOR, AND GRAND CHARGE BY THE KING'S OFFICERS—HAL HUNTER FINDS HIMSELF IN A FIX.

"HELP! help! I'm robbed! Stop him! stop him! My emerald snuff-box! Officers! thieves! D——n you, why the devil don't you take him before he slips away like an eel?"

A crowd came rushing round the creator of this outcry—a testy-looking old admiral, who stood by the doors of the opera house, waving a heavy gold-headed stick above his head and gesticulating violently.

Two or three officers were in the throng, and they twirled about in all directions, looking vainly for the slippery thief.

The old admiral was in a high state of excitement.

"Why don't you take him, you lubberly incapables? Confound you, I could break your thick heads with my cane, I could, d——n you!"

No. 4.

"We don't see him, sir," an officer ventured to say; "which way did he run?"

"Which way? Why, under your blubber nose, you confounded numbskull? D——n you, is a king's admiral to be plundered in this way? Hulloo! hi! there he goes! Stop him! stop him!"

The officers leapt briskly round, nearly falling over the open-mouthed starers behind them. The individual pointed out by the irate admiral was a rollicking young fellow exceedingly well dressed and in sleek condition; he was almost on the outside of the crowd and was surveying the excited scene with the utmost unconcern when the admiral's stick singled him out from the rest.

The way the officers bundled towards him did not disturb him in the least, and it was only when the foremost of them, a red-faced, puffy gentleman, dexterously collared him that he appeared to be aware that he was the indicated culprit.

The admiral saw his capture from the distance, and bellowed out lustily,

"Hold him fast, the scoundrel! Rob me! I'll be there directly."

TALES OF HIGHWAYMEN.

"Gentlemen," said the accused, "you are, no doubt, a merry set of young fellows; your company is, doubtless, excessively agreeable, but the manner of your introduction is more abrupt than polite. Be good enough to take your hands off my collar lest the knuckle end of my fingers should suddenly brush the dust out of your eye."

This last remark was addressed to the one who held him by the collar, and who only clutched him more tightly by way of reply.

The two other officers had by this time arrived, and each took a wrist of the speaker with one hand, while with the other they proceeded to subject him to the ignominy of a search.

"Don't put your hands in my pockets, gentlemen," said he.

The officers laughed.

"You'll be sorry if you do."

"Sorry, you scoundrel?" roared the admiral. "Search the villain, search! Rob me, an admiral in the king's service!"

The officers had desisted when their prisoner spoke; now one of them eagerly thrust his hand into the nearest pocket.

"That's it," cried the admiral, "bring it out; my emerald snuff-box."

"I've got it," exclaimed the officer, diving deeper, "I've got it! Hullo! hi!—murder! Yow—ho—how!"

"Yo—how," mocked the admiral, "what are you howling like that for?—hang you."

"How—oh, oh!" the officer cried, as he dragged forth his hand as quickly as if he had found a red hot poker. "Oh, my fingers!—chopped off!—oh!"

He fell back howling in the greatest agony.

"I told you you'd be sorry," said the prisoner. "You needn't howl in that way though, you're not killed."

"My fingers are off."

"Oh no, they're merely pinched. That's a little contrivance I keep in my pocket in case any one should try to rob me. They never try twice—don't like the nip."

"You scoundrel!" roared the admiral, "to maim gentlemen with your infernal machine."

"Gentlemen don't pick pockets. And now, my friends, as I have stood here long enough to be gaped at by these people, I will, if you please, take my leave. Admiral, good evening, I hope you'll recover your valuable snuff-box."

"Recover?—hang you! Don't let him go."

"Who will stop me?"

"We will."

The officers looked valorous.

One of them even put himself in his way.

He went out of it.

The prisoner's arm went out like a lever.

The officer was doubled up on his back in the gutter, and lay trying to count the lights dancing before his eyes.

The other two had made a clutch at him; but the wipe each received over the bridge of the nose caused them to draw that sensitive member in a very speedy manner out of the reach of the long-armed young stranger, who, stalking through the crowd with easy grace, turned his back upon the admiral, and was lost to sight before that distinguished servant of the king's could bluster out more than a string of oaths, or the officers could sufficiently recover from their discomfiture to make up their minds whether or no they ought to insist upon the capture of their man.

Our hero's escape might not have been effected so easily if it had not been for the general belief that the admiral was mistaken in his identity.

But the gallant old salt was unshaken in his opinion; he abused the officers roundly for letting the thief escape, swore he would report their misconduct and ensure their punishment, and so terrified them by his threats that they made a desperate rush in the direction our hero had taken, the officer who had got his fingers pinched vowing agonised vengeance as he followed more slowly.

The officers were not mistaken in the direction; a glove dropped by the road assured them they were on his track; only a few people were about, but, as they took care to stop and question every one they met, they wasted a good deal of time.

Our hero, meanwhile, had imagined himself safe, and was sauntering leisurely along when he was tapped gently on the shoulder by a handsome-looking young fellow, who had walked quickly to overtake him.

"Take care of yourself, Hal," he said, as the other turned round, "the officers are dodging behind you."

"Thanks! I'll give them the slip."

"You can, easily. Old Judge Blenheim will be coming along the Kensington Road presently; we're going to stop him; his pretty young niece will be inside the coach with him; you can jump up behind, you know."

"If I ride anywhere it shall be inside," laughed Hal, lightly. "Au revoir! A wager—in half an hour you shall find me inside talking politics to him, and making love to his niece! What say you?"

"Well, if I find you outside after that challenge I'll rob you, by Jupiter!"

"Rob me? Of what?"

"Of Admiral Banjemore's emerald snuff-box! Good-bye, my boy! It's a prize, remember."

"I'll take care, never fear!" cried Hal, as, with a laugh, he went on his way.

Old Judge Blenheim was going home that night with his beautiful niece; they had been to the opera.

It was not often the old gentleman could get his niece to accompany him. She was his ward, and people did say that the judge's feelings were very warm indeed towards her, and that if they were a fair young girl of seventeen they would not have trusted themselves alone in a coach at night with him. But, then, certain people will say anything.

At all events here was the judge on this eventful evening seated opposite to his fair niece, Bella Claremont, in the old coach in which they were driving slowly home.

Bella certainly merited the repute she enjoyed; beautiful was a weak word by which to describe her charms. Her features were truly bewitching in their graceful loveliness; the voluptuous symmetry of her form was beyond compare.

As she sat leaning back amongst the cushions, her costly cloak drawn over her magnificent bust, but not altogether concealing her delicately tinted throat, the old judge's eyes feasted upon her with more than an uncle's warmth of gaze.

He had edged himself closer to her, too, than the ample width of the old vehicle necessitated, and strange thrills were coming through him as his knees rested in contact with the fair creature before him.

The fact was, rumour was, for once, correct; the old judge did entertain very unholy thoughts towards his niece, and at this precise moment he was thinking what he would give to be the possessor of such tempting loveliness, and gloating over the anticipated pleasures of getting her to yield to his highly improper passion, a passion of which the gentle Bella seemed wholly unconscious as she sat with half-closed eyes in bitter meditation.

The old judge had edged himself as close to her as he could without behaving rudely, and had rested one paw-like hand on her soft, round arms, preparatory to drawing her towards him in the pretended caress of a relative, when his amatory dreams and sinister thoughts were put to flight by a faint cry for help from the road.

Bella started up instantly.

"Some one in distress, dear uncle! Did you hear?"

"I heard nothing—nothing, my dear darling," mumbled the old rascal. "Nothing, my dear, dear girl."

The cry was repeated.

"Oh! I am sure some one requires our help. There again! Pray stop the coach, and let us see,"

"Stop the coach? There may be highwaymen about. No, no, my darling, no, no. Let us go on while we are safe."

The old judge did not at all relish the idea of picking up a passenger on the road.

A third party in the coach was not a welcome addition, and he would have had the man drive on if a further and most piteous call for help had not gone to Bella's heart.

She was too urgent to be resisted.

So, much against his will, he stopped the coach and looked out of window.

A young man came feebly up, and leaned against the door.

"I crave your pardon, sir. I have been attacked by highwaymen—plundered, wounded, and left by the road to die."

"Highwaymen!" cried the old judge, in well-feigned alarm. "God bless my soul, coachman, drive on ; they may be yet about."

He attempted to bang the window down ; but Bella prevented the act.

"Shall we desert a fellow-creature?" she asked.

The old judge felt ashamed of himself.

"How, sir?" he said. "Did you say robbed?—wounded, too?"

"Severely. Could I reach my house, which is some distance on the road, I should be grateful."

"Oh! uncle, dear, help him into our carriage. Here, he shall have a seat by me. Poor gentleman, he looks pale too."

The judge glared savagely at the comer ; but held his peace, and our hero got into the carriage, which once more drove slowly on.

The wounded man revived.

The bright eyes of Bella seemed to strengthen him.

He was able to tell them the story of his attack, and was much gratified by the sympathy his story excited from Bella.

Even the old judge was mollified when he incidentally mentioned that he was the nephew of Admiral Banjemore and warmly grasped his hand, saying,

"God bless my soul! his nephew?—an old friend of mine! How is my noble friend——"

The abrupt stoppage of the coach prevented a reply.

The window was let down with a bang, and the old judge, who had put his head out to see what was the matter, bobbed in again quickly, and fell back shivering with fear.

"Highwaymen!" he mumbled. "We shall be robbed and murdered! Oh!"

There, indeed, stood a veritable highwayman—a tall, thin figure mounted on a tall horse, a mask over his face, a pistol in his hand.

Bella Claremont shrank back, and the masked face peered into the carriage.

"One, two, *three!*" said a remarkably soft and agreeable voice. "Madam, pardon my rude approach. Gentlemen, your money, watches, &c., if you please."

"Villain!" cried Hal, "if I were armed I would shoot you down like a dog!"

"Fearless youth!" mumbled the old judge in admiring tones.

"Come, gentlemen ; no parley."

"Robber, there are officers on your track."

The highwayman laughed.

"Capital!" he said, in a dry tone. "Pardon me, you seem unable to deliver up your valuable possessions. I will take upon myself the trouble. Be good enough not to stir or cry out. Thank you, sir. Thank you, miss. Oh! some one has cleaned you out, my friend."

"Some of your gang, thief," Hal cried, affecting indignation.

"Do not be angry. If you had been riding outside I might have robbed you—of your wig. Good night, my dear judge ; a pleasant ride home to you all."

He withdrew from the window, which he let down with a bang. They heard him say a few words in an authoritative tone to the coachman, then there was the clatter of a horse's hoof, and he was gone.

Not till then did the old judge venture to look up.

"Atrocious," he cried, his jaw shaking as if he had the palsy, "to be robbed like this on the king's thoroughfare. Sir, I shall remember your courage ; I'll remember that rascal, too. He shall swing whenever he comes before me—yes, swing. I shall know him by his voice, the villain! My gold repeater and rings ; two hundred guineas, too, in my purse!"

"You should not carry so much about you," thought Hal, as the old judge sank back overwhelmed by his loss.

It was the loss of part of the collection of a life of villany. Judge Blenheim had spared no man, and many a prized family trinket had adorned his fat fingers until that night.

Hal gave his attentions now to Bella Claremont.

She had displayed singular courage during the scene.

Hal's arm had now stolen round her waist, and he was speaking assuring words that had a thrill of interest in them, when the old judge exclaimed,

"We'll have the scoundrel pursued. You, my dear young sir, shall come to my house ; your wound must be dressed. You can give evidence against this robber if we catch him. Drive on home, coachman, as quickly as you can go."

Hal fell into a reverie, and did not feel particularly anxious to go home with the judge.

True, he was deeply interested in the fair Bella, whose heaving bosom rested on his breast.

But it might be awkward to be found by the officers in the judge's house.

The admiral might be called in to see his nephew.

A doctor might be sent for, and, as his wound was only a fictitious one, things might go against him.

Besides, in examining for his wound, they might find the article in his breast pocket—

The admiral's emerald snuff box!

He was thinking how to effect a retreat when the carriage again pulled up.

"Highwaymen again!" yelled the old judge, in a fright, as the window was pulled down. "No, by G—d! saved!—the BOW STREET OFFICERS!"

Hal began to feel uneasy.

One of the officers, putting his ugly head in the carriage, said,

"Beg your pardon, sir, but you have got a robber in here."

The judge looked aghast.

Hal felt very uncomfortable.

The judge's pretty niece looked at Hal as though she didn't believe it.

"Uncle," said the young lady, "it's quite an absurd idea to have the carriage stopped on such a foolish pretext."

"Yes, my dear," he said. "What do you mean, you scoundrel, stopping my coach and——"

"Stole the admiral's snuff-box," said the officer.

"Don't interrupt me, you insolent scamp!"

"But——"

"Hold your tongue, I'll have you punished for this!"

"But I kn—o—"

"Silence, d—n you!" roared the judge, foaming with rage.

The judge had made himself quite exhausted, and now he leaned back to recover breath before he began again.

"Five minutes ago," he began, "my coach was stopped and a highwayman took from me a ring, my watch, and then took this lady's necklace, bracelets, and everything he could lay his hands on. Previously to that," he continued, "this gentleman was robbed and wounded, and left on the roadside to die."

The officer, without waiting to hear any more, begged the judge's pardon, and giving all a very doubtful look galloped in quest of the highwayman.

The coach once more rolled homewards, and Hal forgot about his wound as his arm stole gently round the slender waist of his fair companion, and her soft arm rested on his shoulder. The judge sat at the back of the carriage with his head buried in his hands. Had he raised his eyes he would have altered his opinion of the nice young man to whom he had been so benevolent.

The officer was riding down the road cursing the judge and swearing like a trooper, when he was brought to a stop by the admiral running up to him breathless.

"My snuff-box!" shouted the admiral. "Have you caught the robber?"

"No," shouted the officer, making the old sailor jump by the sharp reply. "Got me into trouble, d—n you!"

"You lubber, insult an admiral of his king's navy! You're connected with the robbery; I'll report you this instant."

That was more than his officership could stand to be told he was connected with the thief. Bending over in his saddle he hit the admiral between his eyes, and knocked him into a ditch, where he lay on his back counting the stars as they made their appearance through the horizon until some one was kind enough to assist him out, who took his watch for their trouble.

The old admiral, greatly disgusted with being knocked in the ditch, and getting very wet and slimy, made his way to the residence of the judge, swearing as only sailors can swear.

Hal heard the angry voice of the admiral.

"I wish the boards would open and let me through to the lower regions," he said to himself. "If that old fogey recognises me it will be all over with my love-making."

"Dam'me, sir," shouted the admiral, as he entered the room, "steal my emerald snuff-box; that's the robber."

As the admiral spoke the last words the judge's pretty niece turned very pale, and nestled closer to Hal. The judge looked at our hero as though he wished he were the thief so that he could have revenge on him for making love to his pretty charge, and our hero looked savagely at the admiral as though he would like to have revenge for interrupting him in his love-making.

"I knew him," began the infuriated old fellow again. "Search him. Robbed me on the highway; a king's admiral."

"I understood that he was a friend of yours," said the judge.

"A friend of mine? No, sir. Never saw him before; he stole my box."

"Then this was a trick to get in my carriage to escape?"

"To rob you."

"Somebody saved him the trouble."

"Dam'me, an accomplice."

"Not at all improbable. I took him in under the pretence that he had been wounded and robbed by highwaymen."

"Dam'me, let him show his wound."

Hal wished that he had got drowned when he was knocked in the ditch. He did not like the idea of leaving his companion so soon, yet he would have made some excuse to have got out of their way could he have thought of anything or have run the point of his sword in his side, so that he would be able to show a mark if they insisted upon seeing his hurt; but to do that would make a mess.

"You will allow me to see your hurt," said the judge, approaching him, "if it is no subterfuge."

"And if I will not let you see it?" said Hal, rising.

"You are what this gentleman said, and will be put under arrest as a highwayman and robber."

"Hands off!" said Hal, drawing his sword.

"Take him, men," said the judge, to four officers whom he had called in, "take him to the lock-up, and keep a double guard on."

Hal laughed a defiant laugh as the men advanced towards him.

"Stand back, men, if you value your lives!" he cried dashing forward. He clutched hold of the admiral's throat and flung him against the wall.

The judge had got his arm raised, and was about to shoot Hal, when the pistol was struck from his grasp by a tiny white hand. He turned with an oath on his tongue, but it died away as he saw his pretty niece trembling and white with fear.

"I am ashamed of you, uncle," she said, "I didn't think you would be so cowardly. I will not speak to you for another month."

"Bella, my dear," said the judge, "how dared he to tamper with your love? Seize him, men; give him no quarter; if he attempts to escape, shoot him."

The officers made a rush at Hal, but fell back as his glistening sword flashed before their eyes.

"Now, gentlemen," said Hal, standing erect, sword in hand, "the first one that bars my path will fall lanced."

None of the officers seemed to have a particular wish to be perforated, so kept back as wise men.

Hal, seeing that they didn't wish to stop him, made a quick retreat by the other door.

He had barely got outside when they made a rush after him, knocking each other over in their flight.

At that moment a masked horseman came galloping down the road, but stopped in front of the scene of confusion, and turning in his saddle, called out,

"Hal?"

Hal was coming down the steps backwards and fighting the officers in front. He started as he heard his name called out, and slipped down the rest of the steps, taking the bark off his shins in his descent.

"Hal, old boy, make haste," repeated the same voice "knock those fellows over."

Hal did so.

Running at the two foremost officers, he caught hold of them by the throat and threw them back; as they fell they knocked over the other two behind, and they all lay in a heap.

Hal then took the opportunity of running to his comrade, and getting on the horse's back. The noble animal galloped down the road with its double burden.

"I won my wager," said Hal.

"And I," said his friend, "got the old buffer's gold."

"And I still hold possession of the admiral's snuff-box, though I have had a hard fight to keep it."

"How was that? Did the old devil follow you?"

"No, but some officers did."

"You were making love, of course, to the pretty Bella?"

"Greatly to the annoyance of her wicked old uncle."

"Did he invite you in when the carriage arrived at his house?"

"No; his niece did before we got near, and I had just got in, and was sitting by her side, with my arm round her waist, making love as only gentlemen of our profession can make love——"

"When the judge put a stop to it?"

"No, but the admiral did. He said I had got his snuff-box."

"Which you strongly denied?"

"I did, but they wouldn't take my word, and wanted to search me, which I refused to let them do, and had to fight for it."

"Hulloa!"

"What's the matter?"

"Don't you see the dust rising in our rear!"

"I see a troop of those d——d bloodhounds after us!"

"Shall we stop and fight them?"

"No, let's wait till they pass."

So they did; the horse took a leap over the hedge, and landed on the other side, jerking Hal off his back.

They had hardly got concealed under some bushes before the officers came dashing down the road, shouting at some imaginary shadow in front of them which they mistook for the two daring highwaymen, who were laughing at their fruitless pursuit.

In another five minutes the highwaymen had stopped at the Chequers Inn, and giving their horse to the care of the ostler, they were conducted to a small room by Minnette.

"Well, my pretty lass," said Hal, taking the small white hand of the young hostess in his own palm, equally white, and almost as small, "and what travellers have you had this way lately?"

She blushed as she tried to disengage her hand, and replied,

"But few; none that you know, Master Hunter."

"How do you know?" Hal said, kindly, drawing her closer to him. "Did you know any of them?"

"Yes I did; we had Master Merlin here the other evening, whom we have not seen for some years, and I am sure you don't know him."

Hal and his friend laughed quietly.

"Bring us a bottle of your best wine, and some of your finest smokes," said Hal, kissing her before he let her go.

"There's two very rough-looking men just come in," she said, as she returned with the wine.

"Where are they?" enquired Hal.

"I have put them in the next room to this," she said, leaving them to themselves.

"Merton," said Hal, to his friend, "this is the finest drop of wine I have tasted for the last month."

"Very good," said Frank Merton, filling his glass for the sixth time.

"So it seems."

"We had better have another."

So they did, and drank it.

"What the devil are those rusty-throated blackguards making a noise about?" said Hal, throwing the end of his cigar across the table.

It stuck to Frank's finger, and took the skin off.

Frank threw the wine dregs in his companion's eye in the way of return.

They listened attentively to the conversation of their rusty-throated neighbours in the next compartment.

The partition being very thin enabled them to hear every word they said.

"Bill," said rusty throat No. 1, taking up a huge tankard that held about half a gallon, and taking a draught that would have made a horse snort and blow to get breath after, "I've got a job on to-night."

"Have yer?" said Bill, taking up the tankard, and looking at the contents very discontentedly. "Well, yer might have left a cove enough to wet his wisen."

"Ain't yer got enough there?"

"No," said the worthy Bill.

"Then call for another can full. I'll pay for it."

"Hal," said Frank, "if you don't mind, I will look at their ugly faces."

Hal gave Frank a dig in the wind with his elbow. Hal had been leaning half doubled up, looking through a crack in the partition while the conversation was going on between the two braves, and Frank had been leaning over his back, trying to get a glimpse of the interior of the chamber, but when Hal hit him just below the seventh rib, he doubled up, and lay on his back.

"Look here," said rusty throat No. 1, to his worthy companion Bill, "Lord Montague's carriage will come down the Hammersmith Road to-night, and he will have his only son and heir with him."

"Thank you for that information," said Frank. "I'll be there to take care of his jewels."

"You had the judge's?" said Hal.

"And you had his neice," replied Frank.

"Well, what of that?" growled Bill, as he took another swig at the malt liquor.

"I shall want you to be with me," replied his companion.

"What for?"

"To use your knife," he said, catching hold of his companion by the shoulder, and whispering in his ear. "They must *both* die."

"No they mustn't," said Hal, nudging Frank.

Frank tapped the hilt of his sword significantly.

"And what is I to have for the job?" asked ruffian Bill.

"Well, I is to have a thousand pounds if we do the work clean, and I shall act square with you."

Frank gave Hal a nudge, and said,

"We will settle accounts with them."

Hal answered in the affirmative by returning the nudge.

The ruffian Bill took a long-bladed knife out of his pocket, and, opening the blade, he stuck it in the table, and said,

"That'll settle 'em, and I'll leave it to you what to give me. I know you did act right with me, and I shan't grumble at a couple of hundred."

"All right," said his associate. "We will start in another hour, so that we can get a hole dug to hide all traces."

"Then we go in another hour?"

"Yes."

"So do we," said Hal to himself.

During the hour they had to spare Frank Morten and Hal Hunter were drinking of the finest branded wines, while the two braves were drinking can after can of the malt, and relished it with great gusto.

The murderous companions went out, and made their way towards their place of slaughter.

"Did you hear these d——d blackguards?" said Hal, swearing like the devil.

"Yes, the ugly whelps," replied Frank, "going to do murder. Ugh! we must stop it. Let us go."

"Not with one horse between two," said Frank.

"By Jove, no!" replied Hal; "you must get one from our host."

In less than ten minutes they were galloping on their road to rescue, and were soon snugly concealed in ambush.

Hal and his comrade hadn't been there a half-hour before the clattering of horses' hoofs was heard coming down the road.

Hal and Frank Merton drew in rein as they heard the approaching carriage as they thought, but soon altered their attitude as they saw at least a dozen officers dashing down the road towards them, headed by Judge Blenheim and Admiral Banjemore.

"By Jove!" exclaimed Frank, "here come your old friends."

"What the devil do they want?" said Hal, innocently.

"You, very likely."

"Or the admiral's snuff-box."

"We shall have to ride hard and give them the slip so that we can return here in time to save Lord Montague and his son from those murderous devils," said Frank.

"That's what I was thinking," replied Hal.

Before they had time to say more the officers dashed up to where they stood, and wedged them in.

The leader advanced towards them, and said,

"At last we have got two of Black Hawke's band of hawks."

"Have you?" said Frank.

"What an interesting individual you are," said Hal.

"Quite a study for an artist," put in his companion.

The officer looked savage, as he said,

"I want no more of your parley; resistance will be useless so you had better come quietly."

"As gentlemen," said Frank, "we never make a noise."

"And we are gentlemen," observed Hal.

"Then surrender!" shouted the officers, getting exasperated.

"Never," said Hal, dashing in their midst, and knocking them over on either side.

Frank followed his companion's mode of escape, and they both galloped in the same direction as the officers had come.

So quick was the act that the officers were quite staggered, but they soon recovered as the judge's anything but amiable voice thundered in their ears.

Then they sped away like the wind in pursuit of the dashing, reckless, young and handsome knights of his most gracious majesty's highway.

The sound of the horses' hoofs had hardly died away, and the dust barely settled when the noise of a rumbling coach could distinctly be heard coming down the road in an opposite direction to that which the officers had taken.

Then sneaked forth two ill-looking brutal ruffians, crawling from their place of concealment and standing under a shadowy part of the hedge, quietly regarding each other with murderous intent stamped on their brows.

They were the assassins waiting for their victims.

They did not wait long.

The carriage came rolling towards them when one pulled a pistol from under his cloak and fired.

The shot was effectual; the coachman fell from his box—dead!

The horses, finding they had the reins loose, plunged furiously.

The occupants of the carriage were greatly alarmed at the confusion and suddenly stopping of the coach, and Lord Montague, putting his head out of the window, shouted out, in a frantic tone,

"What is the meaning of this? If you are robbers, and want my money, come and take it!"

Without replying, the foremost ruffian dealt the nobleman a terrific blow on the back of his head, and flinging open the carriage door, jumped in.

Twice swiftly he buried a long keen knife in his victim's breast.

At the first attack the other occupant of the carriage thrust open the door on the other side, and leapt out.

He was not seen by the assassin's confederate.

The pair pulled the murdered man out of the coach, and dragging him over the hedge, they threw the corpse into a hole, and covering it over with earth, leaves, and pieces of sticks, so that there was no trace of the murder left, except for the blood in the carriage.

As the murderers returned to look for their other victim, a sound of shouting and the clatter of horses' feet startled them.

The guilty wretches turned deadly pale as they saw several officers advancing towards them.

CHAPTER X.

THE SCENE IN THE BURNING MILL—LADY FLORENCE IN THE POWER OF HER HUSBAND—FLIGHT OF MERLIN HAWKE—THE INN ATTACKED BY THE SOLDIERY.

THE partial blowing up of the mill was a ruse by which Hugh Marks hoped to be able to get Merlin and his fair mistress with her babe securely away.

In the midst of the general consternation when Merlin himself was staggered by the smoke and flames, he grasped him by the wrists, and drew him from the midst of the officers.

"Now," he said, huskily, "take your chance, Lady Florence is safe outside. A horse waits. Flee for your life."

A strange look deepened on Merlin's handsome face, his hand closed nervously on the hilt of his sword, and his eyes swept wanderingly round the scene.

He seemed loth to leave while so many of his foes remained unharmed.

Besides, he did not like the idea of leaving the miller to the fury of the gang.

But the staunch old fellow would take no denial.

He plucked him by the sleeve, and keeping the other hand on the hilt of Merlin's drawing sword, which appeared to have a desire of its own for running into the carcase of other people, he drew him from the room.

Sir Andrew Greville, with several of the officers, had been hurled to the floor when the explosion took place.

Many of them were severely injured by the falling fire-brands, and the whole party were so blinded by the smoke that they could see very little of what was taking place.

Merlin himself had been scathed by the sheeted flame, his hair was singed, and his skin felt blistered.

As for the helpers at the mill they lay in all directions howling with pain.

The old miller was so anxious to give the officers a strong dose, that he payed no heed to the danger of his cwn men.

He was one of those tough old fellows who do not stick at trifles.

He got outside the blazing room, and lifting a trap conducted Merlin down a flight of ricketty steps.

Presently he opened a door, and our hero found himself in the open air.

There was a horse standing all ready saddled, and, at a word from the miller, Merlin vaulted into the saddle.

Then half a dozen lads approached.

They bore in their arms an inanimate burthen, whom Merlin recognised as Lady Florence.

The miller took her in his brawny arms, and, lifting her as if she had been an infant, gave her to Merlin.

Then he handed up the babe.

"Now," he said, laughing quietly, "we have done them bravely. Away, and find shelter elsewhere, and mind—be careful of the lady; she is not your wife yet."

He went in quickly, and shut the door.

Merlin's arms tightened round the fair form of Lady Florence.

"Not mine yet," he murmured; "no, but soon to be, or destiny is false."

He raised his voice, and glanced up to the window of the burning room.

"Now," he cried, "come forth, Sir Andrew—come forth, to see your bride riding away with your foe. Follow who can. Hurrah!"

He gave a wild hurrah, and setting spurs to his horse, galloped swiftly from the mill.

The old miller heard his rash cry of exultation, and was petrified at his audacity.

"The headstrong, brainless boy!" he exclaimed. "If he won't have the whole lot of them at his heels I'm a Dutchman. They won't travel so fast, though, as they expect. Oh, dear no; not quite so fast."

Merlin's defiant challenge reached the ears of the party above as they were retreating from the burning room.

Sir Andrew, who believed that Merlin was either blown to pieces or a prisoner, leapt at the sound as if he had heard the voice of the dead.

In an instant, regardless of his danger, he rushed to the blazing window.

His livid features were dank with a clammy sweat, and he trembled from head to foot with passion.

Looking out into the darkness, he saw the shadowy form of the daring horseman riding fleetly away.

Riding hence with his guilty wife!

The sight maddened him.

Voiceless with deadly rage, he stood upon the charring heated timbers of the floor; stood there while the intense heat scorched his boots, and the red-hot sparks fell thick upon him; stood there till he had loaded his pistol, then, leaning half way out of the window, he took steady aim at Merlin, and fired.

"For you or her," he cried, hoarsely, "or both. Oh, that I might bring you to earth dying together."

The flash lighted up the darkness of the night.

The bullet sped whistling through the still air.

Watching, listening to see them fall, Sir Andrew, with every nerve straining, caught the sound of a swift scream of agony—his wife's.

He knew how well he had aimed, and laughed, expecting to see horse and riders tumble headlong down.

But there came back to him such a horribly cold and mocking laugh that his blood chilled as he heard it.

The horse paused in its mad career for a moment.

He saw the horseman rearing up in his stirrups, not the slim, elegant figure of Merlin, but the towering form of Black Hawke.

There he sat, plumed and cloaked, his sable form erect and majestic, and a living fire seemed leaping from his eyes as he turned his glance towards the baronet.

A streak of light flashed through the air; it was like a sword of lightning. Every drop of blood in Sir Andrew's veins crept icily as he gazed.

He thought he saw the pallid figure of Lady Florence hurled back and that glittering weapon driven through and through her breast.

A wilder and more demoniac laugh rang on his ears.

The horseman went from his sight.

With the foam gathering about his lips, Sir Andrew sprang upon the ledge of the window.

In a moment more he would have rolled headlong to the ground, but Marmaduke strode forward and held him back.

"What would you do, Andrew?" he cried.

"There!—there!" Sir Andrew whispered, "it is—the Evil One—the Fiend—from HELL!"

He fell back, babbling, in his brother's arms.

They dragged him away, and turned from the burning room.

The cadaverous face of the Jew met them outside.

"The miller hash done it—the miller hash done it," he cried. "I would tear hish housh down."

"True," Marmaduke answered; "every timber shall be torn down. We will leave the mill a blackened ruin."

Sir Andrew clutched his brother by the arm.

"Not now," he said, hoarsely. "After them first—pursue them to the death!—to the death!"

He shook as if stricken by the palsy.

The old miller made his appearance at the moment.

A cunning smile was on his honest face.

He lifted up his hands when he saw the ashy visage of Sir Andrew.

"Gad's mercy!" he cried, "this dreadful catastrophe! Is he much hurt? Alas! at least half my lads are shattered by the explosion."

"Out of the way, you lying old scoundrel!" Marmaduke exclaimed; "we'll have at you, when we've taken him, and, mark my words, this infernal old place shall be pulled to the ground about your ears."

"Yesh, yesh," chimed in the old Jew; "it ish a bad place, a very bad place; it ought all to be [pulled down about hish ears."

The miller gave him a glance that made the craven old villain shrink for safety behind Marmaduke.

The officers gave the old miller menacing looks; they were smarting from the effects of their burns and the hard knocks they had received, and would much rather have set to work pulling down the mill than have followed their mystic antagonist Merlin, who had such an unaccountable knack of escaping at the moment when he appeared to be in the most imminent peril.

As it was, the miller might have experienced rough treatment at their hands if it had not been for the half-score or so of stout armed lads behind the miller's back, ready on the shortest signal to use their cudgels, which had already made such good acquaintance with their shoulders.

So, muttering threats of what they intended to do when they returned, the officers, with Sir Andrew Marmaduke and the Jew, took their departure.

No sooner were they gone than the miller and his men set to work extinguishing the fire and putting the old place in a less dilapidated state.

A good deal of damage had been done, but the miller had succeeded in his object, and was too staunch a Briton to mind about having the piper to pay.

The officers had not got far on their road before they discovered the reason of the miller's chuckling farewell of them.

The straps and girths of their saddles had been so carefully cut as to hold till the riders got some distance from the mill, when they began to give way and one after another rolled under his horse's belly.

The first fellow who went down excited no little mirth amongst his comrades, but they had more lengthened faces as they experienced the same fate.

The more wary of them, taking example by the fate of their companions, dismounted and put their saddles to rights. This occasioned some considerable loss of time, during which Marmaduke cursed in the wildest manner, while Sir Andrew sat like one plague-stricken, incapable of word or movement.

When all were mounted again they started once more in pursuit.

Merlin had ridden some distance after the shot had been fired before he would release his lips from those of Lady Florence.

He thought she had been hit again, and, in a paroxysm of sorrow, he held her to his breast.

She spoke after awhile, and, looking into her white face by the pale moonlight, he saw a look in her eyes as if death were there.

Alarmed for her sake he reined in his steed and gently slid from the saddle.

Lifting her and her child tenderly down he raised her in his arms and kissed her clammy brow.

"Water! a drop of water!" she murmured faintly.

Merlin looked round; at some distance he could see a little streamlet flashing in the moonlight.

Tenderly pressing his lips to hers and bidding her be of good hope, for he would speedily return, he sprang on the back of his steed and rode off to the stream.

Lady Florence revived when he returned and gave her a draught of the refreshing fluid, and, once more mounting, he rode on till he reached the inn.

He placed Lady Florence in the care of Minnette, and, going to his own room, threw himself on a couch and fell into a sound sleep.

He seemed only to have dozed an hour or so when the fierce turmoil of an angry attack roused him.

Springing to his feet he ran to the door.

Then a well-known cry reached his ears.

The voice of Lady Florence pleading piteously for help, while Minnette screamed in accompaniment.

He heard, and the red flash swept to his brow, the cold cutting tones of Marmaduke, and the frenzied exultance of Sir Andrew.

Like lightning Merlin's sword leapt in the air.

With one bound he dashed at the door.

It was fastened.

With all his strength he forced against it.

"Hold there, devils!" he cried. "By door, window, or through the floor, I'll be with you."

"Ha! ha!" laughed a voice, "caged like a bird. Flutter your wings, we shall have you soon enough."

Merlin dashed heavily against the door.

He heard a sudden fall below.

Then a quick cry of anguish came from Lady Florence, and she shrieked aloud,

"Fly! Merlin, fly! Soldiers are here! Flee for your life!"

"Ha!" Merlin cried, and his hand went swiftly to his temple, "this is being caged, indeed—alone, too—with two of my brave band I could—no matter now—I am not taken yet. Cursed fate! that has put dear Lady Florence again in the power of her husband."

The scrambling of feet up the stairs was succeeded by furious bumping against the doors.

"Surrender!" a voice cried.

Merlin laughed.

"When I am taken," he said, lifting the point of his sword.

A word of command was given, and in an instant there was a fierce battering at the door. The wood began to split in all directions, and in a trice the points of twenty swords and bayonets darted through the yielding panels at his breast.

(*To be continued.*)

THE GOBLIN DOG;
A TALE OF FUN AND WONDER.
(*Continued from page 24.*)

The next day about one o'clock, he and she were after taking another refreshment, and pushing on, as before, when they heard the same tramping behind them, only it was ten times louder.

"Here they are again," says Jack. "I'm afeard they'll come up with us at last."

"If they do," says she, "they'll put us to death upon the spot; but we must try to stop him another way, if we can. Try the filly's right ear again, and see what you find in it."

Jack pulled out a little three-cornered pebble, telling her that it was all he got.

"Well," says she, "throw it over your left shoulder like the stick.

No sooner said than done; and there was a great chain of high sharp rocks right in the way of divel-face and all his clan.

"Now," says she, "we have gained another day."

"Tunder and ouns!" says Jack, "what's this for at all, at all?

But wait till I get you in Ireland for this, and if you don't enjoy happy days anyhow, why I'm not sitting here before you on this horse, by the same token that it's not a horse at all, but a filly though; if you don't get the hoith of good aiting and drinking—leshings of the best wine and whisky that the land can afford, my name's not Jack. We'll build a castle, and you'll have upstairs and downstairs, a coach and six to ride in, lots of servants to attind you, and full and plenty of every thing, not to mention—hem!—not to mention that you'll have a husband that the fairest lady in the land might be proud of," says he, stretching himself up in the saddle, and giving the filly a jay of the spurs to show off a bit, although the coaxing rogue knew that the money which was to do all this was her own.

At any rate, they spent the remainder of this day pleasantly enough, still moving on, though, as fast as they could; and Jack, every now and then would throw an eye behind him, as if to watch their pursuers, wherein, if the truth was known, it was to get a peep at the beautiful glowing face and warm lips that were breathing all kinds of fragrancies about him. I'll warrant he didn't envy the king upon his throne, when he felt the honey-suckle of her breath, like the smell of Father Ned's orchard there, of a May morning.

When the dark man found the great chain of rocks before him you may set it down that he was likely to blow up with vexation; but, for all that, the first thing that he blew up was the rocks—and that he might lose little or no time in doing it, he collected all the gunpowder, and crowbars, spades, and pick-axes that could be found for miles about him, working as if it was with inch of candle.

For half a day there was nothing but boring and splitting, and driving of iron wedges, and blowing up pieces of rock, as big as little houses, until, by hard labour, they made a passage for themselves sufficient to carry them over.

They then set off again full speed; and great advantage they had over the poor filly that Jack and the lady rode on, for their horses were well rested, and hadn't to carry double like Jack's.

The next day they spied Jack and his beautiful companion, just about a quarter of a mile before them.

"Now," says dark-brow, "I'll make any man's fortune for ever that will bring me them two, either living or dead, but, if possible, alive; so, spur on, for whoever secures them is a made man, but, above all things, make no noise."

It was now divel take the hindmost, among the whole pack—every spur was red with blood, and every horse smoking.

Jack and the lady were jogging on *acrass* a green field, not suspecting the rest was so near them, and talking over the pleasant days they would *spind* together in Ireland when they *hears* the hue-and-cry once more at their very heels.

"Quick as lightning, Jack," says she, "or we're lost—the right ear and the left shoulder, like thought—they're not three lengths of the filly from us!"

But Jack knew his business; for just as a long, grim-looking villain, with a great rusty rapier in his hand, was within a single leap of them, and quite sure of either killing or making prisoners of them both, Jack flings a little drop of green water that he got in the filly's ear, over his left shoulder, and in an instant there was a deep, dark gulf, filled with black, pitchy-looking water, between them.

The lady now desired Jack to pull up the filly a bit, till they would see what would become of the dark fellow; but just as they turned round, he set spurs to his horse, and, in a fit of desperation, plunged himself, horse and all, into the gulf, and was never seen or heard of more.

The rest that were with him went home, and began to quarrel about his wealth, and kept murdering and killing one another, until a single vagabond of them all wasn't left to enjoy it.

When Jack saw what happened, and that the blood-thirsty ould neger got what he deserved so richly, he was as happy as a prince, and ten times happier than the most of them, and she was every bit as delighted.

"We have nothing more to fear," said the darling that had put them all down so cleverly, seeing that she was but a woman; but, bedad, it's she that was the right sort of a woman. "Our dangers are now over, at least, all yours are; regarding myself," says she, "there is a trial before me yet, and that trial, Jack, depends upon your faithfulness and constancy."

"On me, is it? Och, then, murder! isn't it a poor case entirely that I have no way of showing you that you may depind your life upon me, only by telling you so?"

"I do depend upon you," says she; "and now, as you love me, do not, when the trial comes, forget her that saved you out of so many troubles, and made you such a great and wealthy man."

The foregoing part of this Jack could well understand, but the last part of it making *collusion* to the wealth, was a little dark, he thought, bekase he hadn't fingered any of it at the time; still, he knew she was truth to the backbone, and wouldn't *decave* him.

They hadn't travelled much further when Jack snaps his fingers,

with a "whoo! by the powers, there it is my darling—there it is at last!"

"There is what, Jack?" said she, surprised, as well she might, at his mirth and happiness. "There is what?" says she.

"Cheer up," says Jack, "there it is, my darling—the Shannon—as soon as we get to the other side of it we'll be in ould Ireland once more."

There was now no end to Jack's good humour, when he crassed the Shannon, and she was not a bit displased to see him so happy.

They had now no enemies to fear, were in a civilized country, and among green fields and well-bred people.

In this way they travelled at their ase till they came within a few miles of the town of Knockimdowny, near which Jack's mother lived.

"Now, Jack," says she, "I tould you that I would make you rich. You know the rock besides your mother's cabin? In the east side of that rock there is a loose stone, covered over with grey moss, just two feet below the cleft out of which the hanging rowan tree grows; pull that stone out, and you will find more goold than would make a duke. Neither speak to any person, nor let any living thing touch your lips till you come back to me, or you'll forget that you ever saw me, and I'll be left poor and friendless in a strange country."

"Why, then, my soul's within you," says Jack, "but the best way to guard against that is to touch your own sweet lips at the present time," says he, giving her a smack that you'd hear, of a calm evening, across a couple of fields.

Jack set off to touch the money with such speed that when he fell he scarcely waited to rise again. He was soon at the rock, any how, and without either doubt or disparagement, there was a cleft full of ra-al goolden guineas, as fresh as daisies.

The first thing that Jack did, after he had filled his pockets with the guineas, was to look if his mother's cabin was still to the fore; and there surely it was, as snug as ever, with the same dacent column of smoke rowling from the chimbley.

"Well," thought Jack, "I'll just stale over to the door-cheek, and peep in to get one sight of my poor mother; then I'll throw her in a handful of these guineas, and take to my scrapers."

Accordingly, he stole up at a half-bend at the door, and was just going to take a peep in, when out comes the little dog, Trig, and begins to leap and fawn upon him as if it would ate him.

The mother, too, came running out to see what was the matter, when the dog made another spring up about Jack's neck, and gave his lips the slightest lick in the world with his tongue, the crathur was so glad to see him.

The very moment that Jack's little dog Trig touched his master's lips for joy at his return, Jack *clane* forgot the lady who had saved him from so many dangers, and given him so much goold that he couldn't count in seven years of Sundays, and disremembered her as complately as if he had niver seen her at all at all.

But if he forgot her, catch him at forgetting the money—not he avick!—that stuck to him like pitch.

(To be continued.)

BLACK HAWKE, THE HIGHWAYMAN.

THE ORANGE GIRL.

CHAPTER XI.

THE OFFICERS DISCOVER THE LONE COACH—HAL HUNTER
AND HIS FRIEND RETURN TO THE INN—ALBION HALL—
MYSTERY—A VILLANOUS COUSIN—INTERVIEW WITH THE
ASSASSIN—ESCAPE OF MERLIN—MARMADUKE'S TRIUMPH
—THE APPARITION.

HAL HUNTER and his friend eluded the vigilance of the
officers by cutting through a lane that led to the main road
from which they started.

The leader of the officers was a crafty man, and knew every
turning, and where it led to.

A cunning grin spread over his swarthy visage, and turning
his horse's head, he, with the others, rode away as fast as their
clumsy steeds could take them to meet the young highwaymen.

As they came thundering down the road they suddenly
halted as they saw the carriage lying on its side, and the
form of the murdered coachman being trampled to hideous
shapelessness by the floundering horses.

Their faces lengthened as their gaze met the horrible spectacle, and they stared at each other aghast.

While they were looking so interestingly at one another,
Frank Morton and Hal arrived at the corner of the road,
but stopped in time to save themselves another ride, with
those unwelcome gentlemen trotting behind them, wasting
his majesty's ammunition, so useful for other purposes.

No. 5.

"There's a pretty lot of chumps on those ugly-looking
devils!" said Hal, in a tone of disgust. "If it had not been
through those meddling fools we might have prevented that
crime, and have got something for our trouble."

Frank made no reply to his companion as they rode towards the inn..

The sanguinary caitiffs stood looking at each other like the
two guilty wretches they were, until the officers approached
the coach.

Then they fell into the ditch with fright, and scrambling
through the hedge, made their way in different directions,
running as fast as their legs could take them, and never
stopping to look round to see if the officers of justice were
after them.

If they had they might have slackened their pace at seeing
they were not pursued.

The officers took the coach and the deceased servant to the
yard of the lock-up.

It had not been there long before enquiries were made
about it by Lord Montague's cousin, who pretended to be in
great agony of mind at the disaster, and ordered Judge Blenheim, with an air prerogative that he should send out a
force of officers to scour the country through, and bring to
justice the murderers of his servant, and discover the whereabouts of his absent relation.

When he left the judge a smile of satisfaction overspread
his handsome yet cunning face as he rode towards Albion Hall.

TALES OF HIGHWAYMEN.

Albion Hall was an immense estate that formed the great portion of Norton, Oxfordshire.

Lord Montague had always been very fond of travelling.

He had not long returned from Italy with his only son, Albert, who, at his father's death, would inherit the vast amount of property.

Should he not live, it would fall to the nearest of kin, Sir Thomas Brooke, Lord Montague's cousin, who had so long coveted it.

It was said that when his lordship left England for Italy he took his wife with him, a handsome, young, fair creature, of surpassing beauty, but he returned without her, and whenever her name was mentioned to him he would clasp his hands to his temples, and with a gloomy, desponding look on his countenance, would leave his guests, and shut himself in a room for hours, and not let a person approach him.

The unfortunate lord had always left everything to the management of his perfidious relation.

It would have been better had he given a little of his time to his own affairs and put less trust in his villanous cousin ; then, perhaps, that dreadful catastrophe might have been prevented.

The dark-souled Sir Thomas Brooke had carried out his villanous plans well.

He had hired the two bravoes to assassinate his own relation who had been so kind to him, never letting a thought cross his mind that seemed unjust towards the man whom he put all his trust in.

Yet Sir Thomas was covetous ; he had been living under his lordship's roof for years ; had the property been his own he could not have had things more his own way, but still he was not satisfied, he wanted to call them his, and had he to wade through a river of blood he would possess the estates.

He was in his own boudoir alone, and pacing up and down he muttered,

"Strange, only the coachman found ; if he has been playing any trickery I will blow his brains out."

That was alluding to the man he had hired, Crusher Bill.

He started as a tap came at his door.

A man entered, a brutal-looking ruffian encased in a huge cape, and a large slouched hat pulled half over his ugly visage.

He made a peculiar sort of scrape for a bow as he entered.

Sir Thomas looked at him searchingly, as though trying to read his thoughts, but his countenance was too deeply stamped with crime to be penetrated by a look.

"Be seated," said Sir Thomas.

The man obeyed, and sat opposite his master.

"What have you done with the occupants of the carriage ?" asked Sir Thomas, looking the fellow full in the face.

"Settled him first with the knife, and then buried him in the hedge," the bravo answered, readily.

"And the boy ?"

The fellow hesitated ere he answered.

"No lies," said Sir Thomas.

"Did the same with him," the Crusher replied.

"If I thought you were telling me a lie," said Sir Thomas, eyeing his man, "I would blow your brains out where you sit."

Crusher Bill laughed a loud, defiant laugh, and said,

"You hired me to put 'em out of the way, and me and my mate done it clean, and was just agoing to bury the coachy when the d——d officers came down the road and we had to bolt."

"'Tis well," said Sir Thomas, "if it is as you say ; but something seems to tell me the boy has escaped."

"Don't frighten yerself about him, I can answer for him being stiff enough !"

His countenance did not undergo the least change as he told that deliberate lie, but he looked his employer more steadily in the face.

Sir Thomas Brooke threw him a purse, and said,

"There is more than the sum agreed on."

The Crusher put it in his pocket, seemingly with great satisfaction, and chuckled as he left the room.

The heartless villain was alone once more.

"I am now master here," he said to himself, "there is nothing that stands in my way."

He suddenly stopped talking, and pressed his hand to his forehead, and looked as though he was thinking of something that troubled him very much.

As he sat the perspiration rolled down his cheeks.

Wiping his face with a beautiful silk kerchief he continued, in the same muttering voice,

"There's only one thing that I now fear, the mystery about Montague's wife. Strange he would never tell me where she was, or if she was dead. If she still lives, and should ever return !"

He paused again.

He laughed, a demoniac kind of laugh, and his eyes sparkled with some deadly intent, and again he resumed his self-communion.

"If she still lives, and should ever return, she must die !"

At that moment the light flickered.

It was was getting very late ; the domestics had all retired to rest.

He was the only one up in that large mansion.

Burying his face in his hands he fell into a deep reverie.

The fire burned slowly out, and the lights went gradually lower and lower, until the flickering wicks threw a dim, glimmering light over the room.

He suddenly started, as he heard a fluttering in the room.

Then his gaze wandered through the semi-darkness, and his eyes fixed upon some object at the end of the apartment.

What was that object that caused his eyes to start from their sockets, and him to turn so deadly pale ?

There stood a shadow.

Horrible !

The apparition of the murdered Lord Montague, standing, enveloped in a beautiful blue light, at the end of the room, facing the guilty stricken wretch.

His eyes were fixed upon the spectre with a frightful stare.

He opened his mouth to call for assistance, but his tongue clove to the roof.

He would have risen off his seat, but his legs refused, and every limb seemed paralyzed.

His hair slowly rose, and stood upright.

There he sat, unable to move or call.

The apparition raised one arm slowly, and pointed to the fear-striken brute.

It then seemed to sink through the floor.

It was gone !

Sir Thomas gave a terrific shriek, and fell to the floor senseless as the spectre vanished.

*   *   *   *   *   *

We will return to our hero at the "Chequer's Inn."

He staggered as the glistening blades were thrust through the door, then rushed to the window, sword in hand, but turned away with a dark frown.

To escape by the window would have been sudden death, as it was about twenty feet from the ground, and underneath stood a body of soldiers with fixed bayonets.

He was lost.

There was no way of exit only by the door, and that was guarded by soldiers ready to annihilate him should he be daring enough to venture that way.

The swords and bayonets were drawn from the door.

Then he heard the words,

"Present ! Fire !"

At the word "present," he stood against the wall by the side of the door.

Then came a volley of deadly messengers crashing through the door.

Splinters flew in all directions, and the bullets fell harmlessly against the opposite wall.

As the report died away, a low shriek caused him to start.

"Surely," he thought, "that voice was Lady Florence's, and so near it sounded ? Could any of those deadly bullets have struck her ?"

Such were the thoughts that rushed to his mind and maddened him.

He was staring round the apartment, abstractedly, when

he again started as he heard a click in the wall close to where he stood.

A panel slid aside, and there stood Minnette, pale and frightened.

It was she whom he had heard shriek.

She beckoned him to approach her, which he did in a very few steps.

He drew her tenderly to him, and kissed her gratefully, saying,

"Dear Minnette, how can I repay you for this kindness? It is not the first time you have saved my life."

"Hush!" said Minnette. "Every place is being ransacked by the soldiers, and should they hear us now you will be lost."

The panel had just glided back into its former position, and Merlin got through, when the soldiers charged the door with the butt ends of their muskets; with a crash it yielded, and the men rushed in, expecting to see the highwayman either wounded or dead.

Imagine their amazement when they found he had gone. Everything was pulled out of its place to see if he was concealed anywhere, but he was nowhere to be found.

"Some trickery," said the officer in command. "Search every place with fixed bayonets, and, if he attempts to resist, shoot him!"

While the soldiers were searching every room and corner, Minnette was leading Merlin through a long corridor in silence. She suddenly paused and listened, then put her finger on a spring in the wall, and they stood in an aperture, as something slid aside silently.

Merlin started as he beheld his mistress standing in the middle of a beautifully furnished apartment, looking pale and agitated. With a bound he was at her side, and in an instant they were locked in each other's arms.

"Are you hurt?" enquired Lady Florence, weeping with joy at having her lover once more at her side. "I feared that you had fallen when I heard the report of the musketry."

"I have escaped unhurt," he said, drawing her trembling form closer to him, "thanks to brave Minnette."

"You are still in danger," continued Lady Florence; "the house is surrounded with soldiers and officers."

"Let us escape while we are safe."

Before Merlin had time to finish his sentence, a body of soldiers rushed into the room, headed by Marmaduke Greville!

With a shout they seized Merlin and tore him away from Lady Florence.

She swooned as she saw the danger her lover was in.

Marmaduke took her in his arms, and, with a defiant yell, said,

"Your race is run. Look on your wanton mistress for the last time; she is in my power now!"

Merlin could not bear his taunting words.

Like a madman he tried to break from his captors.

"Hound!" shouted Merlin, in a voice of thunder, "you shall suffer for this."

Marmaduke laughed triumphantly, and said,

"You will hang at Tyburn ere long!"

"Liar!" said Merlin, his eyes darting fire at his tormentor, "BLACK HAWKE THE HIGHWAYMAN is not so easily taken!"

Marmaduke turned slightly pale as he heard that dreaded name, and, in an altered voice, said,

"Take him away, men."

Merlin turned his head as he was being led away, and, with a savage look at Marmaduke, said,

"Remember, hurt a hair of that lady's head, or try any of your vile intents on her, and I will chop you to pieces! We meet again before long!"

The soldiers looked at each other in surprise at his assurance in thinking that he would ever escape.

Marmaduke laughed a forced kind of laugh—one that plainly showed that Merlin's words had taken effect on him.

As the gallant captain was led off, Marmaduke took his brother's wife up in his arms and carried her away.

He vanished like a shadow with his lifeless burden when he got outside.

Sir Andrew had been rushing about like a maniac in search of his young wife, when he came in contact with Merlin, who was then the soldiers' prisoner.

"That's he!" shouted Sir Andrew, who was foaming with rage, "that's the villain that stole my wife! Shoot him! Shoot him!"

"That's more than they dare do," said Merlin, with a sneer.

"Then I will!" the infuriated Sir Andrew said, pointing a pistol at the brave young fellow's head.

"No, you won't," said a voice behind the nobleman, and a somebody struck the pistol from his hand.

Merlin fancied the voice familiar.

Looking round, he saw his two companions, Hal Hunter and Frank Morton!

They had been awaiting for an opportunity to occur when they could help their comrade.

Sir Andrew turned round with an oath, and drew his sword, but put it back in its scabbard.

Hal's weapon crossed it.

"Don't you feel strong enough in the wrist?" said Hal, as his opponent put his sword away.

"He don't feel strong enough in courage," remarked Frank, laughing.

Sir Andrew scowled darkly.

"Release our friend," said Hal, to the officer.

The officer looked at Hal in surprise.

"On what authority do you arrest him?" asked Frank.

"A warrant signed by the king for his apprehension," replied the young commander.

"Produce it," said Frank.

He did so.

Hal made a grab at it, but the officer was too quick.

"If you take my advice," said Hal, "you will release him."

"Not if I know it," the officer answered. "We had enough trouble to catch him."

"You won't let him go?" Frank said.

"No," was the officer's reply.

"Then I will," said Frank, giving one of the soldiers that held Merlin a chop on the knuckles.

The soldier let go his hold, and Merlin, finding he had got his arm free, twisted round and threw the other to the ground.

The two highwaymen shouted hurrah as Merlin bounded to their side.

"Secure the prisoners!" shouted the officer.

The soldiers advanced.

"Keep back!" thundered Merlin.

"Stand away," Frank said, in a very comical manner, brandishing his sword above his head. "You might get scratched if you come too close."

The soldiers advanced and wedged them in.

Like baffled lions that are driven in a corner, they gave a terrific leap in the midst of the soldiery, and scattered them on all sides.

A desperate conflict ensued.

They fought for life and liberty.

The officer had tried to take them by using as little force as possible, but, finding that no good, gave the word "Fix bayonets."

Step by step the trio were driven back with the cold, glistening steel levelled at their breasts. Back, back they gradually went, until they reached the wall, where they stood baffled, with the sharp points not an inch from their bodies.

To attempt an escape would have cost them their life.

"Be kind enough to turn the points another way," said Frank, in quite a cool, reserved tone. "They are not good for our digestion."

"You see, gentlemen, that further resistance is useless," said the officer, seeming not to take any notice of what Frank had said.

The three highwaymen bowed their heads in acknowledgment.

"You will be kind enough to give your swords up."

"No," said Hal. "Be content with taking us without wanting to deprive us of our weapons."

The officer was a good-hearted, brave soldier, and he admired the courage and recklessness of his prisoners.

"Keep your weapons," he said, "but you will have to give them up at the guard-room."

"You will have to get us there first," thought Merlin.

Again they were being marched away between the soldiers.

Sir Andrew clasped his hands in an ecstasy of delight, and capered about like a maniac at seeing Merlin marched off with two of his band between a strong body of soldiers.

They had just got outside the inn, and were marching along in silence, when a horseman galloped past elegantly dressed.

He made a sign with his hand, which the captives saw and understood, and a triumphant smile lit up their faces as the stranger galloped on.

Had the officer seen the faces of his prisoners when the horseman passed he might have altered his opinion on his successful capture and the grand reward he would receive for their apprehension.

They had not proceeded far down the road before there came a clatter of many horses' feet; nearing them there rang a shout through the air that made the officer and his men start.

A body of mounted men came swarming down the road like a regiment of cavalry; each man was mounted on a beautiful black steed, and streaming from each of their hats was a massive black plume.

The leader's uniform was one mass of gold and silver lace, and streaming over his head was the feathers of a raven.

The officer seemed paralyzed as he saw these handsome masked men swarming round his detachment. Were they highwaymen? he thought. That he soon found out.

The captain rode forward towards the officer in command of the soldiers as his band rode round them and stopped their progress.

"I am sorry to have to disappoint your expectations," said the captain, "but I require the liberation of these gentlemen."

"Who are you," inquired the officer, "that dares stop the KING's guard?"

"WILL MERRY, CAPTAIN OF THE BLACK HAWKS, which gentlemen you see here; and we require our president," he said, pointing to Merlin.

"Make ready!" cried the officer, "present!——"

Before he had time to say "Fire" the highwaymen put the reins in their mouths, and in an instant their swords were drawn, and in their left hands they held a pistol with which they covered the soldiers.

"There," said Will Merry, "you see you are all doomed men within three minutes unless those gentlemen are released."

The officer laughed defiantly, and said,

"Do you think SOLDIERS are frightened by the sight of a few cut-throats?"

"You have one minute more to live!", said Will Merry.

"Fire!" shouted the officer.

A deafening report followed his word.

A second report followed louder than the last.

Shrieks and cries of agony mingled with the echoes of the dying musket reports.

They were hidden from each other's sight by the white clouds of smoke that surrounded them.

CHAPTER XII.

PARTING BETWEEN THE SOLDIERY AND HIGHWAYMEN—THE FOUR CAPTAINS GO DIFFERENT ADVENTURES—THE OFFICERS MISCALCULATE—MERLIN AT ALBION HALL—THE LEAP FOR LIFE—THE HORSEMAN OF DEATH STOPS THE MAIL COACH—RESCUE OF LADY FLORENCE—SHOT FOR SHOT.

As the white mist cleared away the young officer saw about two of his men either dead or wounded to one of the highwaymen, and a look of remorse came over his countenance when he saw the men he had caused to lose their lives through his contumaciousness.

"This bloodshed might have been prevented," said Merlin, who had taken the opportunity of escaping with his two companions when their captors fell wounded, "had you released us before the conflict began."

The young officer said nothing in reply to what Merlin Hawke said; he was too depressed by the loss he had caused, although in the execution of his duty, and in a solemn tone ordered the remainder of his men to carry away their wounded and dead comrades.

A general greeting went round when the trio were free, and the band would have welcomed them with a shout of hurrah! but for the respect they held their dead companions in.

The four captains then rode away, leaving the band to return to the haunt, and take with them their fallen companions.

"I am sorry for that fellow," said Merlin, breaking the silence, "he is a brave soldier; he may get punished, but he did his duty."

"I am sorry, too," said Will Merry; "but it was his own fault."

Hal was about to speak, but was stopped by a volley of bullets flying past their heads.

"Can't the devils leave us alone?" said Frank. "Envious brutes, they have taken the feather out of my cap."

A chorus of voices rang through the air for the highwaymen to stop, but they laughed at the idea.

Will Merry turned in his saddle, and saw in their rear about twenty officers thundering towards them.

"We had better part here," said Merlin Hawke, "I have got an adventure in hand, and have not got any time to waste with these infernal fools!"

"Let's look at it," said Captain Will.

"At what?"

"The adventure you have in your hand."

A general laugh went round.

"I and Frank," said Hal, "are going to London for adventure.'"

"And I," said Captain Will, "am going love-seeking."

"Then we meet again at the haunt in three days hence," said Merlin.

"If all's well," put in Frank.

"Adieu," said Merlin, riding away on the horse of a fallen comrade.

Captain Will Merry took another direction.

Frank Morton and Hal Hunter rode towards London on two of their comrades' horses.

The officers had kept close behind until the four knights of the road dispersed in different directions, then they were utterly in a fix how to act, but broke into parties, and took different directions; fortunately for our heroes they had gone the wrong routes, and all met at one corner, where they swore at each other for being big blundering fools, and had to return without their intended captives.

Merlin rode towards Albion Hall in silence, evidently on some strange expedition.

His face wore a gloomy, thoughtful look that betokened it was something of not a very cheerful description.

He rode quietly through the grounds as he neared the estate, as though not wishing to cause any observation.

Approaching the grand entrance he dismounted, and knocked at the door—a large massive oaken structure.

His summons was answered by a handsome youth of about fifteen or sixteen winters; he was tall, and rather slight in statue; his complexion was fair, his hair brown, and hung in massive curls, and eyes of a beautiful bright brown.

Merlin looked at the boy with admiration at his handsome bearing, yet there was something depressed and sorrowful in the boy's looks that Merlin wondered at.

The boy was the first to speak, and his voice was soft and musical as a lady's, as he said,

"Do you wish to see his lordship?"

"Hush!" said Merlin. "I wish to see no one."

"Then, what is your business here?"

"Secrecy."

The boy looked at him in wonderment.

"I see," continued Merlin, "you do not understand me. You have heard of the murder——"

"Of the coachman?" said the boy, eagerly interrupting his

visitor. "But his lordship, and my young master, were they murdered ?"

"Lord Montague was assassinated, and his son——"

Merlin checked himself here.

"And his son, was he killed too ?" enquired the boy, anxiously.

"You shall know more soon," said Merlin.

The youth looked at Merlin gratefully, and clasped his hand in his own two, and squeezed it affectionately.

"Is Sir Thomas in ?" enquired Merlin.

"Yes ; but you cannot see him," said the boy. "He has just recovered from a fit."

"I don't wish to see him."

"He said he saw a ghost," said the boy, "the other evening, and ever since he has been having fits."

"I should not wonder were he haunted wherever he goes," said Merlin, significantly. "And it would serve him justly were he never to get out of the next fit."

"I have been wretched and lonely ever since that fatal night," said the boy, in a sorrowful voice, the tears streaming down his fair cheeks. "Whenever I meet Sir Thomas, I shrink away from him as though he were the murderer, and—and—"

He would have said more, but the last words seemed to choke him, and Merlin drew him affectionately towards him as though he had been his own brother.

"Be of good cheer," said Merlin, caressingly. "Do me a favour, and you shall not remain here."

"Anything at the hazard of my own life," the boy said, hardly knowing how to show his affection.

"Then show me the private-chamber of his late lordship."

"For heaven's sake, be cautious !" said the boy, leading Merlin towards the sacred room. "In the next apartment is Sir Thomas. If you should be discovered I shall be at hand."

"Thanks," said Merlin. "Take this in remembrance of me."

The youth took the proffered gift—a beautiful diamond ring—which he put on his finger, and a purse of gold, which he dropped in his pocket.

"My horse you will have at hand, in case of an emergency ?" Merlin said.

"I will," said the boy, leaving him.

In a minute Merlin had glided stealthily into the room, and was cautiously looking round by the aid of a taper that he held in his hand.

Assuring himself that he was alone, he approached a curious old-fashioned looking cabinet of peculiar shape.

He tried every possible means to force the doors open ; but their strong locks and superb springs resisted his every manœuvre.

He would not give in at that.

Taking a dagger out of his belt, he thrust it between the crevice, and tried to force it open ; but the implement severed in two.

With an oath he thrust the half he held through again, and by a sudden jerk the doors sprung open.

Then, putting his finger on a spring, a drawer flew out.

He had hardly time to take a roll of parchment out of the secret drawer when the room door was burst open, and Sir Thomas Brooke rushed in, looking white with fright and rage.

Another instant, and an alarm rang through the house.

In a trice retainers rushed upon the scene from all directions.

"Secure the intruder !" shouted Sir Thomas, in a husky voice. "He is the assassin of his lordship !"

"Stand back !" thundered Merlin, "or by heavens I will cut a way through you ! You, Sir Thomas Brooke, villain and plotter, shall suffer, and have to answer for the *murder* of his lordship !"

These last words caused Sir Thomas to stagger, and his knees knock together.

Standing opposite the scene of confusion was the boy who had admitted Merlin.

When our hero saw him he made a dash at the retainers, and broke through the file that were barring the door.

His young friend caught his hand as he got by his side, and took him through a long passage, where they had to walk behind one another.

The retainers were close behind them, but, fortunately, they could only come one at a time.

They were in total darkness, and Merlin knew not where he was going, but trusted to his young friend.

Suddenly his young leader turned down a narrower passage than the one they had turned out of, and pulled Merlin after him by the coat-sleeve.

As they groped their way through they had the pleasure of hearing their pursuers rushing past one after the other.

Emerging through a door at the end of the passage, the boy pointed to a clump of trees where Merlin's horse awaited him.

Our hero had barely time to thank the youth for his timely aid and vault in his saddle ere the retainers came rushing to the spot in pursuit of the fugitive.

Merlin Hawke gave a defiant laugh and dashed away.

The men rushed after him like a pack of wolves panting for his heart's blood, but they were soon outstripped.

Then rang through the night air a yell of triumph as Merlin's horse suddenly stopped.

The suddenness of that jerk would have sent many riders flying over their horses' heads, but Merlin kept his saddle firmly.

What it was that caused his noble animal to stop was the thought that rushed to his mind as he looked forward to see the cause.

In front of him was a stone bridge that parted the estate from the surrounding grounds.

From under the bridge gushed a strong current, that run either way under the wall.

To escape that way would be madness ; he would be smashed as he reached the ground.

"Surrender !" shouted the men, close behind him.

Merlin laughed scornfully at his pursuers, drew his horse back for a leap, and said,

"Follow, those who have courage !"

The men stood as though suddenly paralyzed by the sight of the daring act.

Their eyes seemed rivetted on him as his beautiful steed took a graceful bound over the bridge.

"A leap for liberty," cried Merlin, as he cleared the wall.

Every one thought horse and rider would fall into the moat a shapeless mass ; but the horse reached the ground with the lightness of a cat when they jump from a wall. In another minute he had dashed away, and was out of sight before his would-be captors could recover their senses.

Merlin had gained the high road, and letting the reins hang loose, he fell into a reverie ; and suddenly the horse paused as if by instinct, and pricking his ears forward, stood motionless as though listening.

Merlin knew what it meant, and leaning forward, he listened intently, but could not catch the sound that the keener susceptibility of his four-footed companion had heard.

In an instant horse and rider vanished like a shadow.

Had any one been near them at that moment they would have doubted the perception of their own eyesight.

The sounds drew nearer and more distinct, and a stage coach, evidently from London, came rumbling down the road, drawn by four horses, that flagged. They had eventually come a long distance. In spite of the coachman's long whip that curled round their flanks, they could not quicken their speed.

The passengers were in a state of excitement. They had heard horrible tales told of a hideous-looking horseman that stopped every one that passed down that road, robbed them of everything, and then murdered them.

Such were the rumours that were afloat, and filled every one's hearts with terror ; but rumour does not always speak the truth, as will be seen.

Suddenly the coach was brought to a standstill, and every one looked forth to see the cause.

Horror! There, in the centre of the road, stood a shadowy form, directly in front of the horses!

The passengers fell back terror-stricken.

In truth the spectacle caused the cheek to pale and send a chill to the very heart's core.

A form, sitting on a tall black steed, motionless—a form awful in its demoniac aspect.

Shaped like a human being, its limbs were like carved marble, so beautiful were they proportioned, dressed in an elegant black velvet jacket, with a silver star on the breast. The buckskin breeches were black, and fitted the limbs as though they were elastic; its form was lithe and graceful; its hands were small in size, but claw-like; they were black and covered with small glossy feathers, with the fingers thin; and in place of nails were strong claw-like talons; its hands represented the claw of a raven or a hawk.

But the head.

That was the most horrible of all.

Hideous and brutal—a monster of such a race unknown—but still may exist in some undiscovered island.

A face not human, though something of the shape—black, feathery in every lineament, and eyes of a glistening red.

A vivid red gleaming out like those of a fiend let loose upon the earth.

Such was the description of that monster who had stopped the coach and struck terror to the hearts of all who saw him.

With the horse there was some strange mystery.

None heard it approach the coach as the door was flung open.

"THE HORSEMAN OF DEATH!" gasped some inside.

"BLACK HAWKE!" echoed others in a whisper, "we are lost!"

"BLACK HAWKE, THE HORSEMAN OF DEATH."

This time the words were said in an unearthly voice that caused all who heard it to fall back in their seats and bury their heads in their hands.

Then came an exultant laugh of savage sarcasm as though he took a delight in the terror he caused.

"Your money," he said, in another mocking laugh.

With trembling hands some of the passengers held their purses out.

"Your jewels," he said, as he put the money in his pocket.

One by one the terrified people drew the rings from their fingers, and took their watches from their pockets.

Again that claw-like hand was put out.

Then turning to a man that sat in a corner, he said,

"Shall I assist you in getting the things out of your pocket?"

The man gave a dismal howl as he produced his valuables.

Again the things were dropped into the pocket of that mysterious being.

A young lady then drew a miniature from her bosom, and said, as she offered it.

"This is a sacred gift that my dead mother gave me, and I would not have parted with it for the world; but—bu——" her voice quivered, and she sunk back as she held out her hand.

"Keep it, fair lady," returned the monster, in a deep metallic voice, "Black Hawke would not deprive the fair of sacred gifts."

He bowed as he turned to ride away.

Like a spectre he vanished from their sight.

The coach then resumed its journey, greatly to the relief of the discomfited travellers.

Ten minutes later Merlin Hawke was riding down the road from which he had so suddenly disappeared.

Merlin seemed in a moody reverie as he rode carelessly along.

Several wayfarers passed him, but he was in too deep a meditation to notice them.

He started suddenly, and his face flushed as though something had suddenly flashed to his mind.

But that was not the cause.

"Help! help! help!"

That was what caused him so suddenly to arouse from his reverie.

A woman's voice it was that rang through the air, shrieking piteously for help.

The sound of that voice seemed to rend his very heart's cords, and cause his cheek to pale.

He looked round as though to ascertain where that cry came from.

Again that voice made him turn, and looking round he saw a woman leaning out of a window from a small cottage that lay back on his right, surrounded by a thick mass of trees.

The form and voice were those of Lady Florence.

She was in the grasp of Marmaduke Greville.

(*To be continued.*)

THE GOBLIN DOG;
A TALE OF FUN AND WONDER.
(*Concluded from page 32.*)

When the mother saw who it was, she flew to him, and clasping his arms about his neck, she hugged him till she wasn't worth three half-pence.

After Jack *sot* awhile, he made trial to let her know what had happened to him, but he *disremembered* it all, except having the money in the rock, so he up and tould her that, and a glad woman she was to hear of his good fortune. Still he kept the place where the goold was to himself, having been often forbid by his mother ever to trust a woman with a secret.

Everybody knows what changes the money makes, and Jack was no exception to this ould saying. In a few years he had built himself a fine castle, with three hundred and sixty-four *windys* in it, and he would have added another, to make one for every day in the year, only that would be equal to the number in the King's palace, and the Lord of the Black Rod would be sent to take his head off, it being high *trason* for a subject to have as many windys in his house as a King.

However, Jack at any rate had enough of them; and he that couldn't be happy with three hundred and sixty-four, wouldn't deserve to have three hundred and sixty-five.

Along with all this, he got coaches and carriages, and didn't get proud, like many an other beggarly upstart, but took especial good care of his mother, whom he dressed in silks and satins, and gave her nice nourishing food, that was fit for an ould woman in her condition.

He also got great tachers, men of deep larning, from Dublin, acquainted with all subjects; and, as his own abilities were very bright, he soon became a very great scholar, entirely, and was able, in the long run, to outdo all his tutherers.

In this way he lived for some years, was now a man of great larning himself, could spake the seven *langidges*, and it would delight your hearts to hear how high-flown and Englified he could talk.

All the world wondered where he got his wealth; but, as he was kind and charitable to every one that stood in need of assistance, the people said, that wherever he got it, it couldn't be in better hands.

At last he began to look about him for a wife, and the only one in that part of the country that was at all fit for him, was the Honourable Miss Bandbox, the daughter of a nobleman in the neighbourhood. She, indeed, flogged all the world for beauty; but it was said that she was proud and fond of wealth, though, God he knows, she had enough of that any how.

Jack, however, saw none of this; for she was cunning enough to smile and simper, and look pleasant, whenever he'd come to her father's.

Well, bedad, from one word, and one thing, to another, Jack thought it was better to make up to her at wanst, and try if she'd accept of him for a husband; accordingly, he put the word to her, like a man, and she, making as if she was blushing, put her fan before her face, and made no answer.

Jack, however, wasn't to be daunted; for he knew two things worth knowing when a man goes to look for a wife: the first is—that "faint heart never won fair lady," and the second—that "silence gives consint;" he, therefore, spoke up to her in fine

English, for it's he that knew how to spake now, and, after a little more fanning and blushing, by jingo, she consinted.

Jack then broke the matter to her father, who was as fond of money as the daughter, and only wanted to grab at him for the wealth.

When the match was a-making, says ould Bandbox to Jack, " Mr. Magennis," says he (for nobody called him Jack now but his mother)—" these two things you must comply with, if you marry my daughter, Miss Gripsy ; you must send away your mother from about you, and pull down the cabin in which you and she used to live. Gripsy says that they would jog her memory consarning your low birth and former poverty ; she's nervous and high spirited, Mr. Magennis, and declares upon her honour that she couldn't bear the thoughts of having the delicacy of her feeling offinded by these things."

" Good morning to you both,'" says Jack, like an honest fellow as he was, " if she doesn't marry me except on these conditions, give her my compliments, and tell her our courtship is at an end."

But it wasn't long till they soon came out with another story, for before another week passed they were very glad to get him on his own conditions.

Jack was now as happy as the day was long—all things appointed for the wedding, and nothing awanting to make every thing to his heart's content but the wife, and her he was to have in less than no time.

For a day or two before the wedding, there never was seen such grand preparations : bullocks, and hogs, and sheep were roasted whole ; kegs of whisky, both Koscrea and Innishowen barrels of ale and beer, were there in dozens. All descriptions of niceties, and wild-fowl, and fish from the say ; and the dearest wine that could be bought with money, was got from the gentry and grand folks. Fiddlers, and pipers, and harpers, in short all kinds of music and musicianers played in shoals.

Lords and ladies and squires of high degree ; and, to crown the thing, there was open house for all comers.

At length the wedding-day arrived ; there was nothing but roasting and boiling ; servants dressed in rich liveries ran about with joy and delight in their countenances, and white gloves and wedding favours in their hats and hands.

To make a long story short, they were all seated in Jack's castle at the wedding breakfast, ready for the priest to marry them when they'd be done : for in them times people were never married until they had laid in a good foundation to carry them through the ceremony.

Well, they were all seated round the table, the men dressed in the best of broad-cloth, and the ladies rustling in their silks and satins— their heads, necks, and arms hung round with jewels both rich and rare ; but of all that were there that day, there wasn't the likes of the bride and bridegroom.

As for him, nobody could think, at all at all, that he was ever any thing else than a born jintleman ; and what was more to his credit, he had his kind ould mother sitting beside the bride, to tache her that an honest person, though poorly born, is company for a king.

As soon as the breakfast was served up, they all set to, and maybe the various kinds of eatables did not pay for it ; and amongst all this cutting and thrusting, no doubt but it was remarked, that the bride herself was behind hand *wid* none of them—that she took her *dalin-trick* without flinching, and made nothing else than a right fog meal of it, and small blame to her for that same, you persave.

When the breakfast was over, up gets Father Flanagan, out with his book, and on with his stole to marry them.

The bride and the bridegroom went up to the end of the room, attended by their friends, and the rest of the company stood on each side of it, for you see they were too high-bred, and knew their manners too well to stand in a crowd like spalpeens.

For all that there was a sly look from the ladies to their bachelors, and many a titter among them, grand as they were ; for to tell the truth, the best of them, begad, likes to see fun in the way, particularly of that sort.

The priest himself was in as great a glee as any of them, only he kept it under, and well he might, for sure enough this marriage was nothing less than a ra-al wind-fall to him, and the parson that was to marry them after him—bekase you persave a Protestant and a Catholic must be married by both, otherwise it doesn't hould good in law.

The parson was as grave as a mustard pot, and Father Flanagan called the bride and bridegroom his chilther, which was a big bounce for him to say the likes of,—more, betoken, that neither of them was a drop's blood to him. However, he pulled out the book and was just beginning to buckle them, when in come's Jack's ould acquaintance, the smoking cur, as grave as ever.

The priest had just got through two or three words of Latin when the dog gives him a pluck by the sleeve.

Father Flanagan of coorse turned to see who it was that nudged him.

" Behave yourself," says the dog to him, just as he peeped over his shoulder ; " behave yourself," says he.

And with that he set him down on his hunkers, beside the priest, and pulling a cigar, instead of a pipe, out of his pocket, he put it in his mouth, and began to smoke for the bare life of him. And, by my own word, it's he that could smoke. At times he would shoot the smoke in a slender stream, like a knitting needle, with a round curl at the one end of it, ever so far out of the *right* side of his mouth ; then he would shoot it out of the *left*, and sometimes make it swirl out so beautifully from the middle of his lips—why, then, it's he that must have been the well-bred puppy all out, as far as smoking went.

" In the name of St. Anthony, and of that holy nun, Teresa," said his reverence to him, " who or what are you, after all ?"

" Never mind that," says the dog, taking the cigar for a minute between his claws, " but if you wish particularly to know, I'm the thirty-second cousin of your own, by the mother's side."

" I command you, in the name of all the saints," says Father Flanagan, " to disappear from amongst us, and never become visible to any one in this house again."

" The divel a budge at the present time will I budge," says the dog to him, " until I see all sides rightified, and the rogues disappointed."

Now one would be apt to think the appearance of a spaking dog might be after frightening the ladies ; but doesn't all the world know that spaking puppies are their greatest favourites ? Instead of that, you see, there was half-a-dozen of fierce-looking, whiskered fellows, and three or four half-pay officers, that were nearer making off than the ladies.

But, besides the cigar, the dog had, upon this occasion, a pair of green spectacles acrass his face, and through these, while he was spaking to Father Flanagan, he ogled all the ladies one after another, and when his eye would light upon any that plased him, he would kiss his paw to her, and wag his tail with the greatest politeness.

" John," said Father Flanagan to one of the servants, " bring me salt and water till I consecrate them to banish the devil, for he has appeared to us all during broad day-light in the shape of a dog."

" You had better behave yourself, I say again," said the dog, " or if you make me spake, by my honour as a jintleman, I'll expose you. I say you won't marry these two, neither this nor any other day, and I'll give you my rasons presently ; but I repeat it, Father Flanagan, if you compel me to spake, I'll make you look two ways at once."

" I defy you, Satan," says the priest, " and if you don't take yourself away before the holy wather's made, I'll send you off in a flame of fire."

" Yes, I am trimbling," said the dog. " Plenty of spirits you've laid in your day, but it was in a place nearer us than the Red Say you did it."

So he gets on his hind legs, puts his nose close to the priest's ear, and whispers something to him that none of the rest could hear, all before the priest had time to know where he was.

At any rate, whatever he said seemed to make his reverence look double—though faiks, that wasn't hard to do, for he was as big as two common men.

When the dog had done spaking, and had put his cigar in his mouth, the priest seemed thunderstruck, crossed himself, and was, no doubt of it, in great perplexity.

" I say it's false," says Father Flanagan, striving to pluck up courage. " But you know you're a liar, and the father of liars !"

" As true as gospel this bout, I tell you," says the dog, " and if it was all known, how you would feel ?"

" Wait till I make the holy wather," says the priest, " and if I don't cork you in a thumb bottle for this, I'm not here."

" You're better at uncorking," says the dog—" better at relasing spirits than confining them."

Just at this minnit the whole company sees a jintleman galloping for the bare life of him, up to the hall door, and he dressed like an officer.

In three jiffeys he was down off his horse, and in among the company.

The dog, as soon as he made his appearance, laid his claw, as usual, on his nose, and gave the bridegroom a wink, as much as to say,

" Watch what'll happen."

Now it was very odd that Jack, during all this time, remembered the dog very well, but could never once think of the darling that did so much for him.

As soon, however, as the officer made his appearance, the bride seemed as if she would sink outright, and when he went up to her, to ax what was the meaning of what he saw, why down she drops at once—fainted clane.

The jintleman then went up to Jack, and says,

"Sir, was this lady about to be married to you?"

"Sartinly," says Jack; "we were going to be yoked in the blessed and holy tackle of mathrimony"—or some high-flown words of that kind.

"Well, sir," says the other back to him, "I can only say that she is solemnly sworn never to marry another man but me. That oath she tuck when I was joining my regiment before it went abroad, and if the ceremony of your marriage be performed, you will sleep with a perjured bride."

Begad he did, plump before all their faces.

Jack, of coorse, was struck all of a hape at this, but as he'd the bride in his arms, giving her a little sup of whisky to bring her to, you persave, he couldn't make him an answer.

However, she soon came to herself, and on opening her eyes,

"Oh, hide me, hide me!" says she, "for I can't bear to look on him!"

"He says you are his sworn bride, my darling," says Jack.

"I am," says she, covering her eyes, and crying away at the rate of a wedding; "I cannot deny it, and by tare-an-ounty," says she, "I am unworthy to be either his wife or yours, for, unless I marry you both, I dunna how to settle this affair between you. Oh, murther, sherry! but I'm the unfortunate craythur entirely."

"Well," says Jack to the officer, "nobody can do more than be sorry for a wrong turn—small blame to her for taking a fancy to your humble servant, Mr. Officer"—and he stood as tall as possible to show off a bit. "You see the fair lady is sorryful for her folly, so, as it's not yet too late, as you came in the nick of time, in the name of Providence take my place, and let the marriage go on."

"No," says she, "never! I am unworthy of him, at all, at all. Tunder-an-ouns, but I'm the unlucky thief!"

While this was going forward, the officer looked closely at Jack, and seeing him such a fine handsome fellow, and having heard before of his riches, he began to think that, all things considered, she wasn't so much to be blempt.

Then, when he saw how sorry she was for having forgot him, he steps forrid.

"Well," says he, "I'm still willing to marry you, particularly as you feel conthrition for what you were going to do."

So with this they all gother about her, and, as the officer was a fine fellow himself, prevailed upon her to let the marrirge be performed, and they were accordingly spliced as fast as his reverence could make them.

"Now, Jack," says the dog, "I want to spake with you for a minnit; it's a word for your ear."

So up he stands on his two hind legs, and purtended to be whispering something to him. But what do you think? He gives him the slightest touch on the lips with his paw, and the instant Jack remimbered the lady and everything that happened betune them.

"Och, tundher-an-ages!" says Jack, "where is the darling, at all at all?"

Jack spoke finer than this, to be sure, but as I can't give his tall English, the sorrow one of me will bother myself striving to do it.

"Behave yourself," says the dog, "just say nothing, only follow me."

Accordingly Jack went out with the dog, and in a few minutes comes in again, leading on the one side the loveliest lady that ever eye beheld, along with him, and a beautiful illegant jintleman on the other.

"Now, Father Flanagan," says Jack, "you thought awhile ago you'd have no marriage; but, instead of that, you will have a brace of them:" up and telling the company at the same time all that happened to him, and how the beautiful crathur that he brought in with him had done so much for him.

When the jintlemen heard this, as they were all Irishmen, you may be sure there was nothing but huzzaing and throwing up of hats from them, and waving of handkerchiefs from the ladies.

Well, my dear, the wedding dinner was ate in great style; the nobleman proved himself no disgrace to his cloth at the trencher; and so, to make a long story short, such faisting and banqueteering was never seen since or before.

At last night came, and among ourselves not a doubt of it, but Jack found himself a happy man: and maybe, if all was known, the bride was much of the same opinion; be that as it may, night came—the bride, all blushing, beautiful, and modest as your own sweetheart, was getting tired after the dancing; Jack, too, though much stouter, wished for a trifle of repose, and many thought it was near time to throw the stocking, as is proper, of coorse, on every occasion of the kind.

Well, he was just going on his way up stairs, and had reached the first landing, when he hears a voice at his ear, shouting,

"Jack—Jack—Jack Magenis!"

Jack could have spittted a nybody for coming to disturb him at such a criticality.

"Jack Magennis," says the voice.

Jack looked about to see who it was that called him, and there he found himself lying on the green rath, a little above his mother's cabin, of a fine, calm, summer's evening in the month of June,

His mother was stooping over him with her mouth at his ear, striving to waken him, by shouting and shaking him out of his sleep.

"Tundher-an-age, mother," says Jack, "what did you waken me for?"

"Jack, a-vourneen," says the mother, "sure and you were lying grunting, and groaning, and snithering there, for all the world as if you had the colic, and I only nudged you for fraid you were in pain."

"I wouldn't for a thousand guinneys," said Jack, "that ever you wakened me at all at all; but whisht, mother, go into the house, and I'll be afther ye in less than no time."

The mother went in, and the first thing Jack did was to try the rock; and, sure enough, there he found as much money as made him the richest man that ever was in that country.

And, what was to his credit, when he did grow rich, he wouldn't let his cabin be thrown down, but built a fine house on a spot near it, to have it always under his eye.

BLACK HAWKE, THE HIGHWAYMAN.

THE ENCOUNTER BETWEEN MERLIN HAWKE AND CAPTAIN ASHBURNE.

CHAPTER XII.—(continued.)

With a bound Merlin was over the hedge and under the window in an instant, and standing in the stirrups he caught hold of an over-hanging bough, and swung himself up to the window.

The lady gave a cry of gladness as she beheld the face of her lover.

Her abductor gave a cry of savage hate when he saw Merlin, and rushing to the casement he closed it with a crash.

The suddenness of the shock caused Merlin to slip, and he would have fallen to the ground but he caught a branch of a tree, and coolly drew himself up again.

With his foot he smashed the window, and sprang into the room.

"Villain!" cried Merlin, catching hold of his foe by the throat and dashing him against the wall.

The profligate staggered to his feet, but reeled and fell again sick and weak.

"Lady Florence—dear Florence!" said Merlin, lifting her half inanimate form from the floor, "you are safe now."

She looked meekly into his face, and put both her soft pliant arms round his neck.

"Oh, Merlin, have you escaped these fearful men?" she said, affectionately, the tears trickling down her fair cheeks. "I never more expected to see you."

"And are you glad I have escaped?" he said, drawing her closer to him.

"How can you ask?" she said,

No. 6.

Merlin only replied by passing his arm round her lissom waist, and drawing her closer to him.

Her dress was torn open in front and greatly disordered through the desperate struggle she had had with her husband's treacherous brother in trying to keep him frcm his vile purpose, for which he had taken her there, and save her own honour.

To have had such a beautiful white bosom bare and palpitating would have made delirious with passion many a man less impassionable than Merlin.

As for him, he never let a thought wrong her ; he held her as sacredly to him as though she had been his own sister. Never before had he beheld such rare loveliness of form, so softly proportioned and dazzling white.

Thus they stood clasped in each other's arms, her breast heaving up against his.

Merlin had not noticed a new comer creep up behind him, until he felt a heavy hand grasp his collar.

"Hound, die !" cried a hoarse voice.

As Merlin turned a pistol glistened in his face, its deadly tube levelled point blank at his forehead, and he looked into the distorted countenance of Sir Andrew Greville.

"Not so fast," said Merlin, cooly pointing a like article in his opposer's face.

Each man looking at one another with a deadly interest in their eyes and a look of hate on their face.

Two deadly foes confronting each other with a pistol not an inch from either of their heads.

Each had his finger on the trigger ; a word or a movement on the part of either and they would both fall with their heads a shapeless mass and their brains scattered about the room.

Lady Florence shrank away terribly frightened and trembling in every limb to see the determined look on their faces. She did not fear alone for her husband ; her fear was for her lover, who had so timely saved her from a disgrace that nothing or any one could save her from when once perpetrated.

The door of the room was then quietly opened, and a grinning head, vicious and brutal in its expression, peeped round with a cunning leer.

The old hag who kept that house for deeds of crime to be committed had heard a noise and sneaked up to see what it was.

A sudden report and a scream caused the old hag to start.

A second report of a pistol and another shriek of pain followed it.

Then a heavy fall as though two men fell in a death grasp. Lady Florence screamed several times, then sank to the floor.

CHAPTER XIII.

THE TWO HIGHWAYMEN ON THEIR ROAD TO LONDON—THE ROOK'S NEST AND ITS VISITOR—HAL HUNTER AND FRANK HAVE AN ADVENTURE AT THE RUINED ABBEY—A SPY AT WORK—A LONG RIDE—THE OFFICERS ARE BAFFLED —THE HIDDEN TREASURE—THE TWO CAPTAINS ATTACKED BY THE GIPSIES.

HAL HUNTER and Frank had ridden some twenty or thirty miles on their journey, after leaving Merlin and their companions.

Evening had far advanced, and they were in a long, dreary, lonely road, where nothing surrounded them but the open expanse of country, with large, grim-looking, towering trees, and not at all a comfortable ditch on either side of the road where many a traveller had taken up his abode for the night, when they had been returning home rather too heavily laden with good liquor that had got in ther head, and caused them to slip and fall into the slimy stream where they lay quite passive until the morning.

Neither Hal nor Frank cared about making it their resting-place, though their horses were very jaded and went along at an extraordinary slow place for Knights of the Road.

They rode along for some time in silence ; not a light could they see from any distant habitation, nor even the reflection from the fire that the gipsies are wont to make on the roadside ; not even a caravan could they see, they were all gone. The two highwaymen thought it strange that the place should be thus deserted, even by those bronzed, sun-burnt people who so infested the country roads at that period.

"I'm blest if this ain't enough to give a fellow the hump," said Frank, arousing his friend from a deep reverie that he had fallen into by a smart smack on the back that brought water to his eyes through the pain.

"You might tell a fellow when you are going to knock him down," said Hal, half spitefully.

"Did you hear what I said ?"

"No. What was it ?"

"Don't you think this cheerful place enough to give a fellow the hump ?"

"Yes ; I have already got one."

"Have you got any smokes," inquired Frank.

"No," returned his companion, "I have not even got a piece of weed."

"Don't smoke such common stuff."

"You would be glad to get it now," said Hal.

"I am as dry as a salt herring that's been hanging in the sun for six months, and could polish off a couple of bottles of champagne."

"Will you stand it, I haven't got a coin left ?" asked his companion.

"And I am skinned out, too," said Frank, producing his moneyless pockets ; "but I am blessed if I don't stop the first person I come to, and shell him out of the last coin."

"Halloo !"

"What's the matter ?"

"Can't you hear the sound of approaching horses ?"

"No ; can you ?"

"Yes."

"Then I admire you for your keen hearing."

"Listen !"

Frank took the advice of his companion, and leaned his head on his horse's back, and said,

"We will make the acquaintance of the gentlemen. I like to see new faces, especially when the owners have got anything that might take my fancy."

"Get the barkers ready," said Hal.

"They are empty, but they will have the sme effect."

They drew in rein, and awaited the approach of the unsuspecting travellers.

They did not wait long ; their victims soon came in view, jogging along on horses that, by their appearance, were used for the plough.

One of the travellers was a jolly-looking farmer, with a couple of sacks of flour hanging across his horse's back, and the other was a thin, white, miserable-looking wretch, with a coat buttoned high up on the neck, and his hair plastered flat upon his head.

The latter was evidently a parson of a small village.

"Stop," said Frank, coming suddenly in front of them, and bringing them to a sudden standstill.

"Hand over, gentlemen," said Hal, coming from out of the shade where he had been concealed.

The wayfarers were so astounded at being confronted by two highwaymen that they stared at each other in utter amazement, their eyes almost darting from their sockets, and their mouths opened to such a frightful extent that Frank could not help exclaiming,

"If they keep on at that much longer, they will fall down each other's throats."

So thought Hal, and, to prevent that dreadful catastrophe, he hit the parson a smart smack under the chin, that caused him to shut his mouth with such suddenness that he almost took the tip of his tongue off.

"Now, then, old sanctified, hand over the coin," said Frank.

"Oh, what wicked men !" ejaculated the old hypocrite, in a long, whining tone, his eyes turned into his head until the whites were only visible, and his hands clasped together and pointed towards heaven.

"Stop that," said Frank, putting his hand in the pocket of the parson.

That soon caused the sanctimonious old coward to bring his eyes in their proper position, and his hands to the rescue of what he had in his pockets.

"Here's a fellow got the delirium tremens," cried Hal, alluding to the farmer, who shook like an aspen leaf.

"And my fellow," said Frank, "is trying to look through the back of his head."

"Desist, ill-minded man," began the parson again. "Where do you think thy wicked soul will go? Repent and——"

"Hold your prate," said Frank, giving him a tap across the mouth that stopped him short in his sermon preaching; "you will repent if you don't hand over."

"Oh, the wicked people that there are in this world!" he again began, thinking by his babbling he could escape and save his money, which he was loth to part with. "To think that a pious man, even as I am, should be stopped on his most gracious majesty's highway and robbed by wicked sinners!"

This was more than Frank could bear, and, pointing a pistol at the parson's forehead, said,

"Look here you confounded old hypocrite, if you don't give me your money without another word, I will blow your brains out."

These words had the effect of quieting him; but, nevertheless, he did not seem to be in any hurry to yield his money, and, looking more sanctified than ever, he said,

"Wicked-minded sinner, there is one above who sees and knows all, and you will some day be called to answer for all your sins. I pity you! Pray with me, and you shall be forgiven."

It was more than our adventurer could stand, to be talked to in this style when he held a pistol at the man's face.

Frank got in such a rage he did not know what to say, and in utter disgust he exclaimed,

"Go to the devil!"

Clasping his hands together and turning his head upwards like a dog before it commences to howl, he muttered, in a long wailing tone,

"The Lord have mercy on his wicked soul!"

"You sneaking old curse," said Frank, "I've had quite enough of your nonsense. Deliver every farthing, or I will deliver the contents of this in your skull!"

Had he delivered the contents it would not have hurt him, as it was empty, and they had forgotten to reload; however, the parson did not know that. As he felt the tube pressed against his temples a cold shiver ran through his frame, and he stammered out,

"My de-a-ar brother, I—I—have not got any money."

"That I must ascertain for myself."

He recovered his speech as he heard that, and rejoined,

"Thou darest not put thy sinful hand into the pocket of a holy man."

Hal Hunter had had a hard job with his captive to keep him from falling to pieces, he shook so violently.

He managed, however, quickly to abstract what money and valuables the farmer had about him.

He then left his victim, and went to the aid of Frank.

The parson was securely held, and Frank took a bag of gold, containing about a hundred pounds, an elegant gold watch, two or three rings set with the finest gems, and a beautiful gold snuff-box, inlaid with the rarest stones.

They plundered their captives of every valuable, then tied them to their horses, with their heads towards the tails of the animals, and emptying a sack of flour over the parson, they lashed the horses, and sent them galloping off with their frightened riders, the reverend gentleman swearing in a most unsaintly manner as his *fiery steed* dashed about just where its fancy liked to take it.

Frank and Hal were greatly delighted with their adventure, and were in ecstasies with pleasure at the fun and fortune they had met with.

"Here we are at last," said Hal.

"Where?" asked Frank.

"There: I can see a light that shows we are not far from a place of habitation."

"I think its an inn, by the light."

"If that's the case, I don't care how soon we get in."

A short ride soon brought them to a road-side inn, to which the lights belonged that Hal had seen glimmering through the trees.

"What are you looking for?" inquired Hal of his friend, who was looking up and down the front of the house, as though in search of something.

"For the sign," answered Frank, who always liked to know where he went. "Here it is—the 'Rook's Nest.'"

"I wonder whether any other kind of birds roost here?"

"There will be, when we are inside, two very uncommon kind of birds—*hawks!*"

Their horses were given to the care of the ostler, to be looked after till the morning.

The people that were lounging about looked at the two handsome, reckless young fellows with admiration as they entered.

Mine host of the "Rook's Nest" was a jovial-looking fellow, and treated his two new guests with great politeness, and showed them into a private parlour, which he specially kept for gentlemen.

A very comfortable apartment it was, with a cheerful fire burning.

Hal and his companion looked round with a very satisfied air, and threw themselves into a chair on each side of the fire.

"Bring us some of your best wine and cigars," said Frank, to a very pretty damsel, with her arms bare—a pair of beautifully-moulded limbs they were. "Come here; I must have a kiss from those enticing cherry lips of yours."

The girl did not resist as Frank drew her to him, but seemed as though she liked the idea of being caressed by such handsome gentlemen, and blushingly left them to bring the required articles.

The wine was brought, but not by her, though by one as pretty, and who proved as unresisting as Hal put his arm round her pliant waist, and served her in a like manner.

"Let us have something to eat," said Hal, "and you and your friend must sup with us."

Frank thought that a capital idea, and kicked the speaker approvingly.

The repast was soon got ready, and after their supper they had a song from each of the pretty damsels.

A chamber was got ready, and the highwaymen retired to rest.

They had not slept long before they were aroused by a mysterious tapping at the door.

"What do you want?" shouted Hal.

The tapping ceased for a short time; but he got no response.

Tap, tap, tap!

This time louder than before.

"Come in," roared Hal, sitting up in bed.

Again the noise stopped.

"Why the devil don't you come in?" shouted Frank, jumping out of bed, and opening the door.

Imagine his surprise at finding there was no one there. Everything was hushed in the sombre quietness of the dead of the night; every light was out, and he could not see anything through the darkness save for the moon that glimmered through a small sky-light, and threw an unearthly light dancing about his door.

Being quite satisfied that there was nothing outside, and very unsatisfied about the tapping, he returned to bed.

"Why don't the envious devils let a fellow go to sleep," said Hal, "if it is supernatural?"

Three distinct taps, as though in answer to his last word, interrupted him from saying any more.

"If you are of this world come in and we will fight you," Frank began, "and if you are a spirit of the other world, and can't rest, come in and let us look at you."

As he finished, the door was quietly opened, and a ghastly-looking figure, robed in white, entered noiselessly.

"Halloo," said Frank, gliding down the bed and clutching hold of Hal by the arm.

The spectre advanced to the bed side.

Frank and Hal gazed at it in breathless silence. They felt their hair rising upright and getting stiff, and their tongues clove to their mouth.

"Be not frightened," said the ghost, in a deep solemn voice, "I have not come to harm thee."

Neither of them made any answer, but rolled over each other with fright.

"A month to day—"

"You went away," said Frank, in a low voice.

"I wish he had kept away another month," Hal said, in a whisper.

The spectre waved its hand as though for them to be silent.

"Oh lor !" ejaculated Frank, as the shadowy hand waved about.

"I was murdered," continued the ghost, "and buried in the ruined abbey across the common."

Hal began to feel more composed as the ghost continued speaking.

"In what part ?" asked Frank, shivering.

"Under a stone in the subterranean passage, on the right," answered the spectre. "And twenty feet from where my body lies, there is another large stone, under which you will find an iron chest, containing thousands of pounds' worth of property which was buried there by one of the old barons that inhabited the place some years ago."

"We will attend to it the first thing in the morning," said Hal, summoning up courage to speak to their spectral visitor. "Where would you like your remains to be buried ?"

"In the village churchyard, about half a mile from the abbey ; and you will keep the treasure for your trouble."

Hal nodded in assent, as their unearthly visitor vanished into the air.

"I'm not frightened," said Frank, who could not keep his knees from knocking together, while the perspiration rolled down his back in big drops, "are you ?"

"No," answered Hal, diving his head under the bed-clothes, "only I don't care about making the acquaintance of any more to-night."

Frank followed his friend's example by pulling the clothes over his head.

He had pulled the covering from the feet, and their toes stuck out.

They both suddenly brought their feet up with a jerk.

One of Hal's knees struck Frank in the wind, and knocked him against the wall, where he lay doubled up, gasping, half for want of breath, and half with fright.

"Ugh !" said Hal, drawing a deep breath, "Did you feel that ?"

The only answer was a groan from his companion that made him shudder.

Hal thought he felt a cold hand tickling his feet, and drew them up so suddenly, that it frightened his friend, who by instinct brought his up at the same time.

They recovered from their terror, and tried to sleep, but each time they closed their eyes they fancied the gloomy phantom was dancing in front of them, fluttering the folds of its white robe.

The dreary night passed, and rising early in the morning, their horses were brought to them fresh and ready for another day's adventure.

A short ride brought them to the abbey, both looking anything but cheerful.

In silence they dismounted, and took their steeds inside, hiding them in a large cellar.

They proceeded on their solemn duty, their faces wearing a sad look of reverence as they searched for the stone that hid the murdered body.

"Here it is," said Frank, kicking against a stone.

"What ?"

"The stone."

"I thought you meant the body."

"Don't talk like that," Frank said, with a shiver ; "it makes a fellow feel uncomfortable."

"So I should think, by your appearance."

They were coarse men ; but such strange mysterious adventures seemed to sicken them at heart ; Frank was deadly pale, though he was no coward.

"How the devil can we get the stone up ?" enquired Hal.

"Lift it," replied Frank, not thinking by what means they could raise such a massive stone.

"Here is a friend that will aid us," Hal said, producing a crowbar. "I suppose this is what the fellows used for the same purpose that we want it."

After some exertion they got it under the stone, and raised it.

A horrible spectacle met their view as they moved the stone.

The still prone body of a young handsome fellow, about three or four and twenty.

The head was crushed in, and the blood was still moist on the pallid, rigid face.

On laying the corpse aside they replaced the stone.

"We have been successful so far," remarked Hal. "We will now look for the hidden treasure."

They counted the stones, and stopped at the one mentioned by the spectre, or whatever their nocturnal visitant was, and with the aid of the formidable implement succeeded in removing the covering of the vault.

"Here's something," Frank cried. "The ghost was very kind to put this in our way."

"A fine ghost, too," Hal replied ; "they tell such fibs sometimes ; but here's the chest, sure enough."

It was a large, heavy chest, bound with steel.

It took the pair a long time to remove it ; but at last the box was taken from its resting-place, and placed on firm land.

They had not much trouble in prising the lid open, the hinges over each were completely eaten away with rust.

Many years had it been hidden ; placed there, perhaps, by some avaricious old miser, who would rather have buried his last hoarded farthing than have given a penny to keep a poor person from starvation.

When the treasures contained within were revealed, the costly gems and diamonds glistened with a brilliancy that seemed to hold the young captains to the spot.

"This is worth seeing twenty ghosts for," said Hal.

"It's worth a dukedom," Frank replied.

"This will be enough to retire on. But how shall we get it away ?"

"We had better bury the body first, and then talk about this."

"That can't be done until night."

"Then we will put the treasure back, and return to-night to fulfil the promise we made to the dead, and then we can remove this chest."

Putting the gold chest back, they left the abbey, and were riding quietly down the road.

They were aroused by many voices shouting,

"Stop, in the king's name !"

"What the devil do they mean ?" asked Hal.

"They take us for some other individuals, very probably."

"Stand !" shouted a big officer, riding up to them, followed by twenty more of the same stamp.

"Stand !" he repeated.

"Anything you like," said Frank, coolly. "What will you drink ?"

"Nothing at your expense," growled the official.

"That is not at all courteous," remarked Frank.

"What do all these ugly-looking devils want ?" Hal said, in a tone of disgust.

"Surrender !"

"What the deuce do you mean ?" Frank asked, very innocently.

"It won't do, captain ; we know you."

"Indeed ?" said Captain Frank. "I can't say that I have ever had the pleasure of knowing you, nor do I remember any of those amiable-looking friends of yours."

"The game's up, cap'en ; last night's business done it."

"What do you mean, you infernal scamp ?" said Frank, seemingly very much annoyed.

"You don't remember stopping the parson last night, do you ?"

"No, my good fellow, I do not. What do you take us for ?"

"Highwaymen."

"An absurd idea," laughed Frank.

The officer looked at them very doubtingly.

The cool, deliberate way in which they both answered him took him completely off his guard; but he knew them too well, and was not to be baffled in that way.

"We know you; you may as well give in."

"You said that before," said Frank.

"Stand out of my path," Hal said, making a gesture with his hand.

"Don't let them pass men."

"The first that attempts to stop us dies," said Hal, with a determined look.

"I arrest you by a warrant signed by the king."

"Where is the warrant?" inquired Frank.

The man answered by putting his finger to his nose.

"Were you to arrest the first two gentleman you met?" Frank asked.

"We are to arrest you, two Captains of the Black Hawks."

"Then, you will have to catch us first," Hal said, defiantly, knocking two men down and dashing away.

Frank knocked two over and galloped after his companion.

The officers followed in their track like a pack of hounds.

Frank and Hal, heedless of the bullets that were flying about in all directions, galloped quickly forward.

"I will see if I can't pick this foremost fellow off his perch," said Hal, taking a pistol out of the holster.

A shriek followed the report, and the man rolled off his horse.

Getting at the end of the road they each took an opposite direction; the officers came to a sudden halt as they saw that artful manœuvre. They soon, however, decided how to act; breaking into three parties, one turned back, and the others followed the highwaymen.

"Hullo, stop!" shouted the pursuers, as they saw the two captains disappear in different routes.

"Hullo, Frank, have you slipped them?" asked Hal, as they met at the corner of a lane.

"Yes, d——n them, there's another troop close behind."

"We will give them a run."

As they did the officers uttered a most discordant yell as they saw them dart off again. The horses of the young captains were fresh after their night's rest and the attendance of a good ostler, and they sped along like the wind.

More than an hour they galloped without slackening their speed; the officers were soon left far behind at the start, and lost sight of their intended prisoners.

Frank, thinking that they had ridden an unnecessary distance slackened speed, and were cantering back when they were unexpectedly attacked by a lot of gipsies that swarmed from a cluster of trees.

"What do you want?" asked Frank, rather alarmed at the suddenness of the attack.

"Your money!" shouted the sunburnt scamps.

"You will get some bullets if you don't soon get out of our way," remarked Hal, insinuatingly.

"Pull 'em off the horses!" one proposed, in anything but an affectionate manner.

"Give 'em the knife!" said some others, pulling knives out of their pockets and holding them in a threatening way.

"Don't you do anything of the sort or you may get hurt," said Frank.

At a gesture from their leader the band of vagrants rushed upon Hal and Frank and pulled them from their horses; the attack was so quick that they had not time to get their pistols out of the holsters.

"What are you going to do?" Frank asked, as they were bearing him to the ground.

"We'll do for you!" said a gigantic fellow, with a huge stick.

"That's kind."

"Stand back, dogs!" cried Hal, leaping to his feet as he drew his sword.

"Come on!" shouted Frank, wrestling away from his captors and springing to his comrade's side sword in hand.

"How now, cowardly curs!" said Hal.

"Come on! I should like to give some of you a dig!" Frank said.

None of them seemed to like the idea of coming on as each highwaymen stood back to back with his weapon drawn, the point of which looked very sharp and not likely to suit their digestion.

The tawny-skinned brutes looked at each other savagely.

They had the inclination, but none of them liked to be first in the attack.

"How much longer are you thick-headed fools going to look at one another?" said a big, burly fellow, who appeared to be their leader.

Several fellows made a rush at them, but they kept their backs too firmly together.

One fellow ran against the point of Hal's sword, gave a howl, and fell—perforated.

"Number one," said Hal.

"Number two," said Frank, as another gipsy went down with a howl.

"Number three," said the big fellow, as he hit Frank across the head with a thick stick, that made him reel round his friend and settle in the same place.

"Number four," said Hal, giving the big bully a dig in retaliation for the clout he had given his companion.

"We had better make it a half-dozen," said Frank.

The gipsies appeared to be of a different opinion and got out of the way accordingly.

"They don't seem anxious for any more," remarked Hal.

"They have had enough, and so have I," said Frank.

Vaulting in their saddles they gave them a parting salute by firing a pistol each, the shot of which was not wasted, as two fellows rolled to the ground and lay by the side of their vagabond companions.

"This is the best sport we have had for a long time, being stopped by these dirty-looking brutes," Frank said.

"The audacity of them, stopping Gentlemen of the King's Highway!" was Hal's response, as they returned to the ruined abbey.

They thought it best to remain there out of sight till night came.

They did not perceive a form crouching in a corner of the underground passage when they entered.

When evening came on they emerged from their concealment and went about their work.

They laid the corpse on a large plank, and in solemn reverence they bore it to the churchyard and laid it in the grave that they dug.

Frank sprinkled a handful of earth on the lifeless body.

This task accomplished they returned to get their treasure, neither speaking a word, but riding side by side in a quiet, gloomy reverie.

They put their horses in the cellar where they had before hidden them, and proceeding down the passage they did not notice a figure emerge from the hall where they had hidden the chest, and conceal himself in a dark corner, watching their every action.

"This is strange," said Hal, approaching the spot where they had hidden the treasure.

"What is?" asked Frank.

"This stone has been moved."

"I can swear we laid it down."

"Some one must have been here."

"That's just my supposition," Frank said.

"I vote we explore this place."

"To find the intruder?"

"Exactly."

Hal went first, carrying a light in one hand and his sword in the other.

Frank kept close behind.

They were very near to the spy once or twice, but he crawled along on his hands and knees.

Frank suddenly uttered a yell as he was felled to the ground.

Hal, turning sharply, beheld the culprit crouched under the wall.

Frank soon regained his footing when he discovered it was nothing supernatural, and sprang upon his assailant.

He gave a frantic yell as Frank pierced him to the ground.

"A spy, Hal!" shouted Frank.

"I can hear it is."

"How ?"

"By the row he's making."

"I gave him something to make a row for."

"Give him something else to stop it."

The yelling spy was lugged out by his head, and stood against the wall with a pair of pistols glistening before his eyes.

The gunpowder smelt very unpleasant, and he put his head aside as far as he could get it.

"For what purpose did you seek this place ?" enquired Frank.

"Nuffin," answered the ruffian.

"Why did you lift that stone up ?"

"I didn't do it."

"Liar !" thundered Frank, in such a deep voice that it made the man tremble.

"What you know you must die for."

"Mercy ! mercy !"

"There is no mercy."

The man made a desperate effort to clutch one of the pistols, but he felt the cold tube pressed against his forehead ; he then kicked Frank in the stomach.

The report of two pistols was heard, and the man fell.

CHAPTER XIV.

HOW MERLIN HAWKE GOT OUT OF THE HOUSE—THE EN-COUNTER ON THE ROAD, AND A DUEL TO THE DEATH.

MERLIN HAWKE and Sir Andrew were wounded, not slain, when they fell to the floor of the old cottage.

They had taken deadly aim, and the bullets had well-nigh done their fatal work.

Merlin was hit on the right ride of the head, so close to the temple, that had it been the merest fraction nearer, the ball must have shattered his brain.

His own bullet had been discharged full at his opponent's heart.

But for an unexpected divergence of the leaden missile, caused by its striking against a small medallion in his vest pocket, Sir Andrew would have been a dead man.

As it was the ball cut through his flesh, and went so deep that he fainted from pain and loss of blood.

When Merlin staggered to his feet, and saw his adversary lying to all appearance dead, a momentary triumph inflated his breast.

But this feeling left him when his glance rested on the sad, terrified face of Lady Florence.

The report of their pistols had struck her dumb, as it were, with awe, and now she knelt beside her husband's form, her fair, soft arm bedabbled in his blood, as she tried to staunch the crimson stream.

This was the sight that chilled Merlin to the heart.

He took a step towards his prone enemy, but Lady Florence waved him back with a gesture of horror.

With all her tenderness towards him, he looked almost hateful as he stood before her imbrued in Sir Andrew's blood.

While Merlin was striving to speak, the noise of a party of new-comers dismounting at the door startled him and Lady Florence.

The latter understood his position in a moment.

"Fly !" she whispered, hoarsely. "The house is surrounded. If they find you here, you too must die !"

"Lady," Merlin answered, faintly, for he was yet half-stunned, "if for this deed I deserve to die, let my death come now."

Lady Florence outstretched her arm, and pointed to the window.

"Do I not bid you fly ?" she exclaimed, convulsively. "Escape while there is time. Let me not witness another deed like this."

During this excited colloquy, the old woman had shuffled to the cottage door, with the intention of admitting those outside.

As her hand was on the latch Merlin stood before her.

"I will admit all who enter here !" he cried, hurling her back, and flinging the door wide open. "Now, ye who seek admittance, come in. No sword bars your way. Your prisoner is here, when you are able to take him."

Pell-mell the new-comers rushed in at the door.

They were a party of officers, with some of Sir Andrew's servitors.

Without heeding Merlin, whose graceful form stood on the threshold, they crowded round Sir Andrew.

One of their number, a handsome young gallant in military costume, stepped up to Florence as she knelt beside her husband.

"Is he slain ?" he asked, hoarsely. "Answer me, sister, whom I now disown for ever, whose hand is steeped in his blood ; yours, minion, or your accursed paramour's ?"

"Henry !" Florence cried, and sank trembling back.

"Yes, girl, your unhappy brother, who returns to be present at his sister's shame. Leave us, girl, we have things to do that need no shivering guilty women as their witnesses."

He pushed her rudely away as she clung to his knees. She came again, and once more his arm was raised, but the hand of Merlin fell heavily on his shoulder, and twisted him half round.

"Answer to me, sir," Merlin exclaimed, haughtily. "I am here, a sword in my hand, a man's courage in my heart. Turn your rage on me, not on this defenceless girl."

"Villain and dastard !" the young soldier cried, "though it stain my blade, I will let out your heart's vile blood ! You know me of old ; think, then, whether I shall quail from you, as all these have done."

"Captain Henry Ashburne," Merlin replied, "I know of old, as a brave, headstrong boy, as little given to brook insults as myself, I had hoped to have met you as a friend ; but come you as a friend, or come you as a foe, as either, Merlin Hawke knows how to meet you. You have polluted your sister's name with vile accusations, and for that, if for no other cause, I am your deadly enemy, and though I seek not your blood, nor blood of her kin, yet for this will I wage battle to the death, and on this floor I swear to leave the dark stains of your living blood !"

"Draw, then," young Ashburne cried, "and let this encounter teach you that a sister's wrongs can be avenged !"

Their two weapons flashed brightly in the air ; but, as they crossed, Lady Florence, at imminent risk to her own life, came between them.

First forcing down her brother's blade she thrust Merlin back step by step till he was outside the cottage porch, when she closed the door in his face, and thrust her slender arms into the staple to keep it fast.

"Fly now," she shrieked, "there shall be no more murder here !"

Henry Ashburne leaped to the window.

"This way," he cried, excitedly, "by the window, men. The dastard will escape ! Tear her from the door !"

"Hold !"

It was Merlin's voice that came in at the window like a thunderbolt.

"Let one of you lay but a finger on Lady Florence and I will shoot you where you stand. Henry Ashburne, henceforth, then, we are mortal foes ; meet when we will it shall be to death. I give you this challenge, and will not keep from your way when you are eager to wipe it away."

He dealt young Ashburne a swift blow on the temple, and went from the window

They heard the sudden clatter of a horse's hoofs, and then a laugh of fearful triumph came on the air.

Lady Florence flew to the window, and gave utterance to a wild scream.

"He has escaped !" she cried ; "safe—safe—safe !"

Before her brother could rush by her to the door, she fell tottering back in a deathly swoon.

Sir Andrew was placed on a litter, and conveyed, with Lady Florence, to her own house.

The hot-headed young captain, Lady Florence's brother, mounted his horse, and rode in fierce pursuit after Merlin Hawke.

Merlin Hawke had ridden many miles, and was slackening pace, when he heard the sound of a horse following at a terrific pace.

Rousing from his meditations, he sat back in his saddle, and listened.

The horseman was evidently on his track, and the blood rushed to Merlin's temples as the thought crossed him who the coming rider was, and what was his purpose.

He allowed his own horse to proceed at an easy canter, and had not got much further on his way when a voice, hurling its tones of anger after him, electrified his every nerve, and brought the hot blood to his heart.

"Merlin Hawke," the voice cried, and in the passionate, tremulous tones Merlin recognised the voice of Captain Henry Ashburne, "if you are not wholly the dastard and traitor I deem you, halt, and make one stand for your worthless life."

The clatter of the horse's hoofs followed the challenge, and Merlin's hand closed on his rapier hilt, as he sat almost immovable in his saddle.

After a minute's pause, the voice rang out again,

"Merlin Hawke, highwayman and robber, liar and cheat, coward and cur, if you have one spark of manhood left in your craven breast, halt and face me! Halt, unless you fear the point of a soldier's sword! halt, white-livered runaway, assassin and poltroon!"

The fine features of Merlin Hawke purpled as he listened to the insulter's challenge.

The blood leaped wildly to his heart.

With one swift movement he reined in his impulsive steed.

"Captain Henry Ashburne!" he cried, his manly voice husky with haughty rage, "Merlin Hawke, who never yet turned his back on mortal foe, awaits here to answer you sword to sword, life for life. If your courage is not chilled, come on quickly. A sword's point waits you with defiance in the hilt, and death on its tip."

An eager, exultant cry came in response, and the steed of Captain Ashburne thundered into the lane.

Where, sitting his horse with princely grace, and with a deadly rage on his noble features, Merlin Hawke awaited the duel to the death!

(*To be continued.*)

THE PHANTOM'S WARNING;
A LEGEND OF THE TIME OF RICHARD THE THIRD.

CHAPTER I.

THE bell of Saint Helen's Priory was ringing for the evening vespers, when Lady Anne, with her attendants, reached the gloomy archway that led to the court-yard of Crosby Hall. The ponderous iron-studded gates were ajar, for Glo'ster had whispered to one of his followers to hurry on foremost, and have all in preparation for her reception. Two soldiers, who stood as guards, presented their halberts as the lady entered; menials were also ready, to take charge of the horses; and the sewer, with other officers, and serfs of the household, were drawn up in readiness to welcome the Lady Anne to her new home.

"Canst thou conduct me to a private room, worthy seneschal," said the lady, addressing an old man over whose brow threescore winters had passed, "for I am ill at ease, and would fain remain alone until his Grace's arrival?"

"I wot not, good lady, of any other than the great dining parlour, which is set apart for the guests of his royal Grace," replied the old man; "methinks that is most remote from the din of the hall, and might of a verity meet your will."

"It pleaseth me mightily, honest seneschal," answered the lady. "I would have thee conduct me thither."

The seneschal requested Bridget, a female who stood by, to accompany the lady; and they passed along the great hall, beyond the oriel window, by which a door was opened by a page in waiting, that led to the great dining-parlour.

"Nay, by our Lady, ye enter not here," said the page, confronting Tressel and Berkeley, who were preparing to follow their noble mistress; "none enter the western wing but by his Grace's permission."

"Out upon thee for an ill-natured churl," answered Berkeley; "hadst thou come to her lady's dwelling we would have given thee a cup of Malmsey ere we had made a stand at any door."

"By the mass," replied the page, "I thank thee for teaching me courtesy, though it belongs not to me to show his Grace's hospitality; but beshrew me, I will drink a cup with thee and thy fellow."

"Spoken like an honest page," said Tressel. "Go to now, why should we not make merry—marry, but this would be a fine place to troll a stave," proceeded Tressel, lifting up his eyes to the lofty roof: "by Saint Ann, there is no need to doff an helmet on entering."

"His Grace the Duke of Glo'ster hath a mind to give himself room enow to grow in," whispered Berkeley, who saw that the page had retired to order them refreshments. "I like not this sudden changing of our noble mistress' mind; methinks it bodes no good. Saw ye ever a woman wooed in such a plight good Tressel?"

"Never, by my faith! but there is no swearing for woman I trow; beside, he had a tongue might lure the devil to kneel and pray. She had a mind to use the sword, methought."

"So did I deem," answered Berkeley, "when that he said, 'twas I did kill your husband:' by my troth, this is a changing world—she, who did curse his wife, to consent for to become that wife which she so cursed—I like it not, 'tis enough to rouse the saints to work her woe."

"Marry, it matters not," replied Tressel; "but, for the sake of her dear master, whom we all did love, we will attend her well. I hate this humpbacked duke, who will as soon let a man's blood out as a cook will twist a capon. But see, the page beckons us to yonder table. By our Lady, this is a goodly hall, and well might vie with that at Westminster, in which we saw King Henry crowned."

The sun was now sinking in the west, and threw his last red beams upon the painted windows of the hall, scattering a dying glory over the rush-strewn floor, which floated from the rich tints of shields emblazoned on the quaint-wrought panes. Purple, and gold, and crimson, and azure, blazed from the fronts of stars, and the forms of rampant lions, glaring ruddily on the armorial bearings of barbaric heraldry; and saints shone dimly forth in twilight hues, darkened with excessive splendour, and grim warriors stood erect upon the oriel windows, clothed in scaly armour from head to foot, and flaming in various dyes, which the gaudy eye of the artist had fantastically given them. Boars' heads, and griffins, and green dragons and piled spears, and furled banners were all thereon enwrought, on which the crimson sunbeams burst, through every hue of the rainbow.

Around the hall hung suits of armour—below the high windows, corslets and helms, with vizors and drooping plumes, gauntlets and greaves, and cuishes, with grenoillerics and iron shoes, and triangular shields. Some of these bore the dints of battle, or were broken in the joints, showing where the heavy battle-axe or keen blade had pierced. Bows and arrows were also hung on high, and banners were suspended around, illuminated with rich bearings, which swayed to and fro as the breeze rushed in when the door was opened. Lamps were also suspended from the roof by long chains, which were let up and down by pulleys. The lamps were of an immense size, in the form of angels, all of iron; the flame issued from the tips of their wings when lighted, and as the wind swept through the apartment, they swung backward and forward with a creaking sound; the rushes on the floor were also swayed by the sudden gusts that at intervals entered, and made a rustling sound. At one end of the hall ran a long oaken gallery, richly carved after the manner of the period, in fir-cones and rude festoons, and the forms of cross-winged cherubs, with full-blown cheeks. In this gallery were the minstrels seated at festivals; behind it ran another division, broken into grotesque arches, and various openings, through which might be viewed the hall by those who wished not to mingle in the merriment; behind these were the private apartments for the guests or retainers of Glo'ster.

In the hall were various groups; some in armour pacing up and down, their swords and spurs clanking at every tread, as they walked in the centre, which was free from rushes. Others conversed in twos and threes, their numbers increasing or decreasing as fancy guided them; all were busy with the rumour of Glo'ster's conquest over the Lady Anne, for many of them had been out to witness the removal of the remains of King Henry from St. Paul's, and were present when the duke compelled the bearers to set down the royal corse. Some were seated at various tables, emptying the huge drinking horns, or attacking the immense barons of cold beef which stood piled in readiness for the attacks of every hungry follower who entered. Some helped themselves to large slices with their daggers, then washed down their repast with bumpers of old ale, leaving the unwiped foam upon their dark mustachios. Around the huge fire-place a group were collected, conversing in low tones, or laughing at the wit of the fool, who figured conspicuously amongst them, in his long ass's ears and bells, which jingled at every motion of his head. Two large dogs basked upon the hearth, and seemed to enjoy the cheerful blaze which issued from the wood-fire. A conversation was here carried on between the fool and a dark-looking man who kept occasionally stirring the fire with the point of his sword.

"Methinks thou art preparing for some hot work to-night, uncle," said the jester, addressing the dark warrior, who kept stirring the logs with his weapon.

"Peace, fool!" replied the other, "thou wilt never allow the thoughts in thy soft brains to cool."

"Marry, but thou art a cooling piece," persevered the fool, "and hast let out a deal of hot blood in thy day, at his Grace's bidding."

"Not so much," retorted the warrior, "as thou hast let out folly, when his Grace would have had thee silent."

"I know a thing, which if thou wast to let out, the Duke would not be silent," answered the jester.

"What is it?" inquired the warrior.

"Now out on thee for the veriest goose," replied the fool, "why, the lady thou didst let in."

"By my troth," answered the warrior, "neither wouldest thou, for it would deprive thee of wagging thy bells at the wedding feast."

"I'll tell thee how to woo Alice," said the jester, "if thou wilt be advised by a fool."

"Pr'ythee proceed then," said the warrior, "for I have a liking to the maiden."

"Hearken, then! Kill her brother!"

"Now, by St. Paul, thou provest thyself a greater fool; would that be the way to her heart?"

"Ask his Grace," replied the jester, "for so he won the Lady Anne, by killing her husband. Men do woo like cats now; who kill a mouse to win a spouse, and pur and pur, and shew what they have done. Trust me, 'tis a killing world. Wouldst have a large estate? kill the owner and take possession; for singing:

"For hipsy pipsy, high and high.
Oh marry, quoth my ladye,
For if two love, oh one must die,
So up and sharp thy bladey."

"Now, out upon thee for a hoarse raven. See the Duke enters, attended by his Grace of Buckingham."

As they approached, all who were in the hall drew towards the fire-place, leaving the two dukes to converse together at the south end, where they entered from under the balcony by a private door which communicated with the lesser apartments.

"I will marry her to-morrow," said Glo'ster, "in the meantime do thou muster a few of our friends to grace the feast, and speak to the Bishop betimes that we may have no delay. Hearken, I have a motive for so doing." Here he spoke in a low tone, "But I must console her, for by my soul this sudden transition from weeping to wooing will have affected her ladyship. Look I sad, my lord? for I must put on a woeful countenance, melancholy as those mutes who are trained to walk in mournful processions, who do moan and wail by the hour, not for the dead but for groats. Think not that I forget her curses; no, they shall return upon herself with ten-fold force. Thow knowest I would be king, but first there is much work to do, and some there are must sleep in Abraham's bosom."

"I will talk with your Grace to-morrow," replied Buckingham, "till then, adieu."

For a few moments Glo'ster stood alone at the end of the hall, biting his lip, and gazing upon the floor in deep meditation. At length he was aroused by the falling of the lamp-chains, which a menial had let down previous to lighting, for twilight was fast approaching, and the glare of the fire grew stronger as it flashed upon the deep bay window opposite, and the piled armour that glittered upon the walls, and the strong features of those who were assembled around it.

Turn we now to the great dining parlour, where the Lady Anne was seated in a high-backed oaken chair, gazing thoughtfully upon the sinking embers, which were only throwing out a fitful light, as some undecayed brand smouldered or blazed at intervals. Opposite to her, but at a respectful distance, sat Bridget Crosbie, whose father had built and given his name to the Hall. He had not long been dead, and Glo'ster had only hired the mansion for the term of seven years, after which Bridget was again to become the sole possessor.

(*To be continued.*)

BLACK HAWKE, THE HIGHWAYMAN.

THE ROBBERY ON THE BRIDGE.

CHAPTER XIV.—(continued.)

The fiery young captain came dashing towards Merlin like a madman.

"Hound, die !" he said, as he drew in rein, and made a terrific cut from his shoulder.

His sword was caught on the back of Merlin's. So quick was the act that it made their weapons quiver, and benumbed their hands.

The rattling of the steel caused their horses to start off in fright.

Then, turning the heads of their steeds, they galloped towards each other, at the same instant swinging their swords round their heads, and bringing them down with a quick cut.

A hundred sparks flew from the glistening steel as, with a clash, their weapons crossed.

Each thought their weapon would have severed the head off the other, with such terrific force they brought their swords down.

In amazement they looked at each other as their swords crossed.

The collision caused their steeds to prance and caper about. Then, wheeling them round, they confronted each other.

"This is a duel to the death," said Merlin Hawke, drawing his rein in tight, and sitting his noble animal like a statue.

No. 7.

"To the death, traitor and dastard !" cried Henry Ashburne, his eyes glistening with rage.

"Henry Ashburne," said Merlin, quietly, "I am sorry that we have met under such circumstances ; but since you called me a *coward* and traitor, I will prove to you that I am not afraid of meeting the point of a soldier's sword."

"Guard for your life !" cried the hot-headed young soldier, as he made a thrust at his opponent.

"A good cut," replied Merlin, guarding off the blow "Even such a *cur* as I will not brook an insult from an old friend as you are."

Every pass and cut the young captain tried, but each time his weapon was caught on the blade of Merlin's rapier.

Each man had the courage and strength of a lion, and, with untiring skill, they parried the cuts of each other's weapons.

They fought for the life of each other.

"In five minutes more you will be lying at your horse's feet," said Merlin, looking his foe earnestly in the face.

"Not while I have an arm to use a sword," said Henry Ashburne, cutting at Merlin on all sides. "You have dishonoured my sister, and for that wrong I have pursued you to avenge her shame. If I kill you my revenge will be satisfied."

"Liar !" cried Merlin, his voice tremulous with passion.

"Lady Florence, your sister, has been as sacred to me as an angel, and ever will be."

Henry Ashburne laughed scoffingly.

"Laugh," said Merlin, "it will be your last."

The weapon of Captain Ashburne came down with tremendous force for Merlin's head as he finished speaking, and, had he not caught the deadly blade, it would have cleft his skull in twain.

Merlin Hawke had drawn his sword back to lunge it through his foe's heart; another instant, and Henry Ashburne would have fallen from his horse, pierced, but Merlin's arm was caught in a grip like iron that stayed his weapon from drinking the life blood of Captain Ashburne.

"Hound! would you murder a man in cold blood?" said some one behind Merlin.

Merlin turned in his saddle to see the intruder who had so quietly interrupted the duel, not thinking of the danger he had put himself in by turning from his opponent; but Captain Henry was too noble to take such an advantage.

"Sir Andrew!" Merlin exclaimed.

"Yes, dastardly hound! 'tis I, and this is our last meeting."

He drew a pistol and pulled the trigger, but fortunately it missed fire.

Thus baffled he caught hold of it by the muzzle, and would have brained our hero, but, at the instant he raised his arm, and before he could put his savage purpose into execution, he was caught hold of by the throat and swung from his horse.

"Man to man, Sir Andrew Greville," said Captain Will Merry, for it was he who had so providentially come in time to save the life of his chief.

Again Merlin and Captain Henry commenced their deadly conflict while Captain Will had got Sir Andrew down by the throat, doing his best to strangle him with his own neck-tie.

Clash, clash, went their swords as they guarded off each other's cuts.

Merlin Hawke was getting tired of the fight; the young captain had tried his every pass and thrust, and still he kept on though he saw that his adversary only guarded his cuts. Still he would not give in; he fought to kill, and would not be content until one had fallen. Merlin saw this, and said,

"Henry Ashburne, we have been fighting for some considerable time, and you have used your science in every way; I have only been guarding; if I had chosen I could have killed you long ago, but I have only been trying your skill, which does not compete in any degree with my own swordsmanship. Your wrist is as strong as iron, but to stay here any longer wasting time is quite absurd. If you like to lower your point I will not strike, and we will part either as friends or foes."

"I fight to the death!" replied the young captain.

"Let it be so," said Merlin, looking at his antagonist regretfully. "I am sorry that you are so headstrong, but your blood be upon your own head."

Again their weapons crossed for the last time.

In an instant Merlin's rapier curled round the blade of his antagonist's, and it flew from the grasp of Captain Ashburne.

A sharp cry of pain escaped his lips, as Merlin's weapon entered his side, and he rolled from his steed, his life's blood oozing out from the wound.

Will Merry released his prisoner as the prone body of Henry Ashburne fell bleeding by his side.

"I am sorry that I had to do this," said Merlin, to his friend. "No one I ever loved more than I did Henry Ashburne. We were constant companions in our boyhood, and were expected to meet in quite a different way to this after his long absence; but it was his own fault."

"You have not mortally wounded him?" said Will Merry, sympathizingly.

"I fear such is the case."

They rode away, leaving Sir Andrew bending over the collapsed form of his stricken relative.

CHAPTER XV.

HAL HUNTER AND FRANK DISCOVER A NEW HIDING-PLACE FOR THEIR TREASURE—A NIGHT AT AN OPERA-HOUSE—HOW A LORD MAKES LOVE TO AN ORANGE-GIRL—THE WAY IN WHICH HE IS TAKEN IN BY A HIGHWAYMAN—TWELVE HAWKS IN LONDON—TWO CAPTAINS DOOMED TO DEATH.

"THAT'S settled him," Hal said, as the man fell, his skull shattered.

"Let us put the poor devil in a resting place," said Frank. "He ought not to have been so fast. If he had not kicked me in the ventricle of digestion, he might have kept those two pieces of lead out of his thick head."

They dropped the body in the hole, and put the stone over it that had hidden the body they had so recently buried.

Completing their task, Frank approached the iron chest that contained the treasure.

"I can tell you what it is, old boy," he said; "we shan't be able to get this away from here by ourselves."

"Shan't go away without it, Frank."

"Then you will have to stay here, Hal."

"I don't mind that, if I can have plenty of wine and cigars."

"And spirits?"

"No, they are too strong for me, and all shadowless visitors can keep away."

"You have no particular wish to remain here, I presume?"

"None."

"Then we will hide the chest," said Frank.

"Perhaps you will find a hiding place for it," returned Hal.

"We had better both look, and what one don't see the other will."

"If there are any more spectres walking about seeking some one to bury their bodies, I hope I shan't see them."

"All right, old boy. Come on," said Frank, leading the way through a long hall in the mansion. Going through several long passages they came to a door or rather a panel in the wall that represented a door.

It was movable; but they could not discover the way to open it.

Click!—click!—click!

Frank had been rubbing his hand up and down the panel, when a small part sunk in under the pressure of his fingers, then three distinct clicks were heard, and the secret door glided aside and presented to their view a spacious vault at the bottom of a deep flight of stone steps, that had evidently not been trodden on for many years.

"This is a cheerful-looking place. I vote we toss to see who's to be leader," said Frank.

"You can if you like," Hal said, readily.

"Thank you; but I don't like."

They tossed, and Frank lost, consequently he had to lead the way, which he did; but not too heroically.

He took particular precaution not to knock his shins against anything as he descended.

He had got his own sword, and his friend's besides, drawn, with the blades at arm's length in front of him.

They had reached the bottom, and the darkness was so intense that they could not see their hand in front of them.

Hal managed to kindle a light by the aid of a flint and steel, and they commenced to explore that underground dwelling, for such it was or had been occupied not long before the young knights of the road discovered the place.

"I wonder whether this den is inhabited by natural or supernatural occupants," said Hal.

"Anyway," replied Frank, "they have an idea of making themselves pretty jolly."

So it appeared; there had been a large fire made in one

corner of the vault, which was still smouldering, and in front of the fire was drawn a huge, roughly-made table, and round that were several rough-looking forms and stools ; goblets and empty bottles were lying about in all directions. The place in itself was very extensive, and built of one mass of stone, and in several parts of the wall was a kind of arch that sunk back, which did not escape the notice of Frank.

"Hal," he shouted, "I've discovered something."

"What a wonder."

Hal went to see what his friend had discovered ; to his surprise, one of the recesses in the wall was piled half way up with bottles of beautiful crusted old wines, from which they largely partook.

"They are a jolly lot of ghosts that live here ; I should not mind staying with them if they always keep such a stock of wine," said Hal.

"It's very good stuff," said Frank, approvingly smacking his lips, and opening the third bottle.

"If we stay here much longer I shan't wonder if we do see ghosts."

"Do you think it will be safe to hide the treasure here ?" enquired Frank.

"If this place is occupied by a band of robbers, as I dare say it is, it would be hardly safe."

"Yet we might hide it here," said Frank, pointing to one of the arches that went further back than the rest, and was half full of old sacking, wood, and all kinds of lumber. "We might hide it under that rubbish."

"We might lose it when we come to look for it."

"We will chance that ; it will not be long before some of our comrades come to take it to the haunt."

They returned for the chest containing the treasure, and hid it under the before-mentioned spot, and leaving the place after several searches to see if any one was concealed anywhere, sent a dispatch to their captain for him to send twelve of the band to them as soon as possible.

"Suppose we go to the opera house to-night ?" asked Hal.

"Anything on particular ?"

"Yes, a grand night."

"Is there anything to be made ?"

"I should think so ; all the nobs of town will be there."

"Then we will go."

"Agreed."

They soon reached London, and made their way to the opera house, where all the fashionable carriages were driving up to the door of the Royal Opera House.

The cheeks of the highwaymen flushed, and their hearts beat wildly as they caught a glimpse of the beautifully-moulded ankles as the fair damsels stepped from the carriages.

As the two friends entered their eyes were completely dazzled by the fashionable splendour that presented itself to the gazers.

The lamps threw not a too clear and steady light on the scene, but the sparkling diamonds and gems that entwined the slender wrists and lay on the white, beautiful heaving bosoms of the fair sex made many a spectator's gaze wander from the performance to their beautiful forms. Such rare loveliness was not seen every day, and the brilliant, lustrous light that sparkled from the precious jewels that were glistening from all parts would have made a casual observer's eyes grow dim, and his mind wander to some unholy thoughts.

But such was not the case with our young adventurers ; they only looked on with admiration.

There was an old gentleman in particular whose gaze had been kept on the exposed parts of the fair spectators.

"What a wicked-looking old devil," said Frank, addressing his companion.

"To whom are you alluding ?" inquired Hal.

"To that sinful old fellow in that box with the eyeglass ; he has not taken his eyes off those ladies since he has been in."

"If I were behind him I should drop my fist over his head

on to the tip of his probocis ; that would make him alter the direction of his optics."

"Serve him right ; the blackguard's been looking at the same lady that I had pointed out for myself."

"The one in the orange-coloured dress ?" said Hal, pointing to a most superb creature.

"That's the one I intend to conduct to her carriage," said Frank, in surprise.

"I am sorry for you, old boy," said Hal, "but that was exactly my intentions."

"Look here, I'll fight you for her."

"Can't fight here."

"Then you'll have to resign all ideas of the lady."

"I'll see you——"

"What ?"

"Stand on your head and go mad screeching first."

"The lady has been looking at me several times this evening."

"At me," said Hal.

"Very well, if you think so ; only I don't think she would take the trouble to look at your ugly face."

"She would rather look at mine than yours."

"That we will discover," Frank said, in complete disgust. "The one that she looks at next time will be victor."

Hal agreed to that, and patted his chest as though to insinuate that he would be the favoured one.

They both waited eagerly.

The lady turned her head towards them, and as she caught Frank's handsome eyes beaming on her with expectant pleasure, she smiled archly at him that caused his heart to beat with joy.

"There, did you see that ?" said Frank.

"No, nor did not want to," replied Hal, very crest-fallen, though he had been looking all the time.

"That proves what I said was right."

"I don't care, there are plenty more," Hal said, spitefully.

Frank waited patiently for the lady to retire.

He had not waited long before the lady rose to go.

Frank rose too, so did the gentleman with the eye-glass.

Frank Morton had just got down to the door where the gentleman with the eye-glass was standing at the other side of the entrance.

The lady came tripping down the stairs, and Frank raised his gold-laced trimmed hat as she approached, and by mutual consent he conducted her to the carriage.

The old gentleman fell back in astonishment as he saw Frank do the gallant. He had evidently made up his mind to be the lady's escort, but was greatly disappointed.

Frank whispered something to the lady, and his face flushed with pleasure as she said something in return.

He stood transfixed to the spot and his gaze was fixed upon the retreating carriage.

The old gentleman paused to listen suddenly, as a voice, clear and silvery, came ringing close to him,

"Oranges, sweet oranges !"

"Sweet indeed, if they are like the voice," muttered the gentleman.

He turned, and saw a girl standing close to him, a basket of oranges held gracefully in front of her, and her attitude and dress as pretty as the wearer.

She was fair, with hair as light and bright as the golden rays of the sun, and hung around her beautifully-sculptured shoulders in massive clusters of curls, while her eyes shone out from under the golden fringe a beautiful, soft, melting blue.

She was elegantly formed. Her hands and feet were small and delicate, her arms moulded to a turn, and her legs left bare by her dress, that came just below her knees, that were faultless in size or shape.

The girl blushed deeply as the searching eyes of the titled gentleman wandered over her beautiful limbs.

"They must be sweet indeed, if they are like the owner," said Lord Cavendish, for such was his name.

"Have one and judge for yourself," said the girl, picking one out of her basket and offering it to his lordship.

He took the orange and the little hand at the same time.

"You are too pretty to sell oranges," he said, putting his hand caressingly on her golden tresses.

"I do not find it so," she answered. "I would rather sell my oranges for what few pence I may chance make, than bartering the truth and purity of my womanhood for the temptor's gold."

Lord Cavendish blushed at this unexpected reply, and fell back two or three steps.

"Would it not be better for you," he said, recovering his shame, "to live in a place of beauty, where servants wait on you at every movement?"

"No," said the girl, drawing herself up proudly, "not to be a wanton toy for any profligate villain who would tempt me with their gold."

"No, no, such is not my intention," answered the lord, hurriedly. "I merely wish to keep you from such a life of wretched poverty."

"Better that than what I have just said."

After a little more conversation the girl seemed to yield more to what he said.

He bought some oranges, and gave her a handful of gold.

Frank extracted a silk handkerchief that hung half way out of his coat tail pocket as he left the girl, seemingly satisfied with his transactions.

"What did that wicked old sinner want of you?" enquired Frank of the orange girl.

The girl looked enquiringly at Frank before she answered, but seeing his handsome face, she told him all that Lord Cavendish had said to her.

"So he wants to meet you to-morrow, does he?" said Frank.

"Yes," she said, "and alone."

"So he shall," Frank said, significantly. "Do you know his purpose?"

"He said he would put me in a large house, and let me have servants to wait upon me, because he said he thought it a shame that I should be obliged to get my living by selling oranges."

"I dare say he would put you in a large house—an infirmary, after he had used you for his own vile purpose."

The girl shuddered as Frank spoke.

"He said he did not intend anything of the sort."

"He would say so to get you in his power."

"Then I won't go," said the girl.

"But I will," said Frank Morton.

"You can't."

"Why not?"

"Because he would know that I should not dress up in a cavalier's dress."

"But he would not know me if I were to dress in your clothes."

The girl looked at the speaker in utter amazement.

"I see," said Frank, taking the girl's hand, "you do not understand me. Listen! bring me a dress, shawl, and the rest of the things, and to-morrow evening I will meet him, and extort money from him."

The girl agreed readily to his proposition, and Frank, giving her about fifty pounds, she made her way home with a lighter and gayer heart than she would have done the following day if she had not have met with Frank, who saved the girl's honour, and kept her from shame and disgrace.

Frank and Hal made their way to the inn, where they remained until the following day, when he was going on his strange adventure.

"I'll give the dirty old wretch something for wanting to ruin the poor girl," said Frank, to his companion, when he had related how he meant to take Lord Cavendish in.

"Why don't he try his filthy passions on those to whom it is a business?"

"I'll ask him when I meet him."

"I think you are envious, Frank, and want to get her for yourself."

"You wrong me by saying that," said Frank, reproachfully.

"I know, my comrade," said Hal, taking his friend's hand. "I said it only in jest, Frank; forgive me."

They shook hands, and Frank left his friend, to proceed in the disguise of the orange girl to meet the profligate Lord Cavendish.

The previous evening Frank had arranged with the fair vendor of fruit for her to leave him a disguise at a small inn close to where he had to meet his lordship, which she did, and he soon changed his attire.

In five minutes Frank had reached the appointed spot.

His lordship hurried to meet his victim as he thought.

"You have kept your promise," said Lord Cavendish.

"How could I do otherwise?" replied Frank, assuming the voice of a female.

"I knew you would consent to what I said," he said, putting his arm round her waist as he thought. He did not know the difference, as Frank's waist was quite as small as my lady's, and his features as regular and delicate.

"Your lordship forgets yourself," said Frank, playfully, pretending to disengage himself.

"Me, my sweet one, I do not forget myself," he said, the hot blood mounting to his cheeks, and a wicked glitter in his eyes as he tried to thrust his hand down the bosom of her dress.

"I shall forget myself," Frank muttered to himself, "and give him a topper if he keeps on at this game."

"Is this what you have brought me here for to outrage me in a lone part like this?" said Frank, the supposed orange girl.

His only reply was a defiant laugh from the old villain as he fried on his fell purpose.

"Then this is what you decoyed me here for?" said Frank, in a low tremulous voice, as though frightened at his captor's purpose.

"What, my darling?" he said, his heart throbbing wildly at the thought of the lovely limbs he had beheld the previous night.

"To destroy my purity and make me a thing to be despised by every one. No, I will not yield to you," she cried.

"You can't do otherwise," he said; "look, I will give you this diamond ring."

"Tempt me not with your jewels; let me pass or I will call for assistance."

"Fool!" he said. "Do you think that I would be thwarted in my plans by a woman?"

"Hound!" she said, her voice getting rather louder than a woman's; but that on account of her rage, "if you don't take your hands off me, I will call for help. My lungs are strong, and would soon bring assistance to me."

"Fool that thou art. Dost thou think that I will be played with by a woman after daring so much?"

"No, villain!" thundered Frank, quite forgetting his female voice, and throwing off his disguise, "you thought you were going to ruin a poor virtuous girl that gets her livelihood honestly, not by being wantons to such old sinners as you."

"Fiends of hell!" muttered his lordship, as he staggered backwards. "This is a trick!"

"A trick that tricked you," replied Frank, looking at him, disgusted.

Lord Cavendish turned to walk away with a dark frown; but Captain Frank stood in front of him with a pair of pistols presented full at his head.

"Your lordship will be kind enough to give me that ring."

His lordship did not see it; he gave a howl and put his hand in his pocket.

"I must be under the painful necessity of taking what I want, since you will not give them quietly."

"Stand off, highwayman and robber!" shouted Lord Cavendish, foaming with rage, "or, by h—, I will make you answer for this."

"You shameless old wretch, if you say another word I'll crush the craven life out of your wicked old body."

Frank advanced to him and caught hold of his throat to throw him down.

His lordship grinned maliciously as he drew a stiletto from his vest.

"That's your game is it?" felling him with the butt of his pistol, and the dagger cut the flesh of his arm.

Lord Cavendish lay quite senseless while Frank rifled his person of everything he had about him.

"He will not try the seduction of another in a hurry," muttered the young knight of the road, "and there is something that will always make him remember to-night's adventure."

As he spoke he drew his finger across his victim's forehead, and in an instant a bright blood-red cross came on it.

"That's the cross of the Black Hawks," said Frank, in satisfaction. "He is a marked man for life, and whenever any of the band see him, his life will always be in danger."

His lordship slowly returned to consciousness when Frank had gone, and, rising to his feet, he clasped both his hands, and said, in a loud wailing voice,

"Great heavens! what is this burning pain on my head?" and he looked round as though he expected to get an answer from out of the surrounding wilderness.

But nothing came in reply, save the rustling of the trees, the twitter of the birds, or the hiss of some insects that prowled along the ground.

"Can it be the avenging cross of that terrible being Black Hawke the Horseman of Death?"

He shuddered as he thought of it, and with pale cheeks and trembling limbs he retraced his steps homewards.

"Hullo, old boy!" shouted Hal, by way of greeting his friend as he entered. "How have you got on?"

"I frightened the senses out of the old sinner," said Frank, eyeing the wine. "I am jolly dry; love-making is not so pleasant as you might imagine."

"I never made love in my life," said Hal, laughing.

"I mean when you take the female part."

"That is the easiest part, because they only listen and shake their heads accordingly, while we poor devils are pleading on our knees, wearing holes in our trousers to get a word or look from them."

"That may be, but you have not experienced the trials and temptations a female has to go through; it must be hard to resist sometimes."

"You could not do otherwise than resist," said Hal.

They both laughed.

"Our twelve comrades have arrived," said Hal, turning the subject.

"Where do they await?"

"Here."

"I don't see them."

"They are in the large room enjoying themselves."

"Let them remain there while we do the same."

They sat drinking wine until they thought they were going round the room on their heads.

Frank thought it quite time to make a move, and summoned the landlord.

"Tell those gentlemen to attend here at once, and have their horses brought round."

The landlord looked at the young captains curiously, and muttered something as he retired.

Their twelve companions attended, and Frank instructed them how they were to proceed.

Five minutes later they were all mounted, and, the twelve breaking into threes, went different ways to the old abbey, so that they should not attract attention, while the two captains rode together.

A short ride soon brought them to the place of appointment.

"I'm blowed if I can find the spring," said Frank, rubbing his hand up and down the panels, causing the skin to peel off his hand by the friction.

Click, click, click, and the panel flew aside.

"How clever," ejaculated Hal.

"Follow me, men," shouted Frank, brandishing his sword over his head.

"Don't be so fast," said Hal, lugging his comrade back by the collar. "Follow me, men."

Frank inserted the point of his rapier just under the tail of his friend's coat.

Hal started forward and missed the top step; he slid to the bottom, taking the skin off his back in his descent.

"What are you sitting here for?" asked Frank, laughing at the peculiar face his friend was making.

Hal could not answer, he had suddenly sat upon a sharp stone that caused him a peculiar sort of pain that causes you to laugh and cry at the same time.

When he had properly got his features in their former shape he got up and helped his comrade to divide the treasure into equal portions for the men to convey to the haunt.

"Hillo!" shouted Hal, turning round.

"What's the matter?" inquired Frank.

"We are in it."

"Take my advice and get out of it again as soon as possible; they are the ghosts, that inhabit this place," said Frank, alluding to a troop of about twenty rough, brutal-looking men that emerged through one of the archways.

"Hold!" roared the leader of the new comers.

"I don't intend to leave it go," said Frank, alluding to the jewels.

"Who dares enter the den of the Night Slayers?" said the same intelligent-looking fellow, in a voice of thunder.

"Two captains of the Black Hawks," said Hal, defiantly.

"Oh! oh! oh! ha! ha! ha!" laughed the fellow with savage glee. "Captains of the Black Hawks; our greatest enemies. Secure them, men, there is no quarter; you know your duty."

As he spoke twenty men rushed upon the young captains and bound their hands and feet with cords.

Then they were each conveyed to a different archway, where stood a man robed in a long black gown, and his face covered by a thick black mask that hid his features.

Each man stood at the entrance of the archways like a statue leaning on a ponderous axe, and at their feet stood a gloomy-looking block, which had seen the head of many a poor victim severed from the body.

The cravats were roughly torn from the throats of our heroes, and their heads placed upon the blocks.

Frank looked up at his savage murderer, and said,

"You cannot kill us; even if the axe falls we shall not die!"

The chief of the Night Slayers laughed at the idea, and beckoned for the executioners to do their work.

The ponderous axes were clutched by both hands, and raised above the executioners' heads.

Another minute and the heads that lay on the block would be rolling about reeking in their own blood.

Hal shudders as he thinks of his fate; he can feel that the massive weapon that is to do the bloody work is descending.

His eyes grow dim, his brain seems to whirl, a thrill runs through him.

A moment more and his head would have rolled from the block.

Frank has been more courageous; he has not moved, though breathlessly he awaits the fearful moment.

He begins to grow sick at heart; all hope of rescue had fled; he knows the axe must soon do its work; he shudders, and a cold chill runs through his body like electricity as he fancies the sharp, cold edge cleaving through his neck.

A shout stayed the arms of the executioners from letting the bloody weapon descend.

A rush of feet told their prisoners they were saved as the twelve highwaymen rushed in the midst of the bloodthirsty crew.

CHAPTER XVI.

THE CONSTERNATION OF SIR THOMAS BROOKE—STRANGE VOICES—THE INVISIBLE HANDS PUT THE LIGHTS OUT—SEARCH FOR THE INTRUDER——A HIGHWAYMAN AND SIR THOMAS MEET—THE YOUNG KNIGHT DISCLOSES A SECRET.

ALBION HALL had looked sombre and melancholy since that fatal night the peer and his son had so strangely disappeared. Rumours were afloat that made people shudder to hear when the gossipers congregated together and whispered to one another of horrible crimes that had taken place at the Montague estate since his lordship's disappearance.

A dark cloud seemed hovering over and around that beautiful mansion that gave it a gloomy aspect. The domestics walked about in silent dread, looking mysteriously at one another, and shuddered at the sound of their own foot-fall.

The time rolled on, and still no one came to bar the villain's way.

Sir Thomas Brooke cared little for what people said; he was now master of Albion Hall; he heeded not the rumour that had spread so fast over the country.

Though he was shunned, he had invitations sent from all parts.

He was young, and the possessor of the Montague estates, and many of the nobility had daughters, for whom they sought suitors with fortunes, and thought that Albion Hall would not be a bad speculation.

Sir Thomas had received an invitation to a grand ball given by the Duke of Cleveland, in honor of his only daughter's birthday, thinking, through the many aristocracy that would present themselves at the grand festival, he might find a suitor who would suit his daughter. He had heard of the disaster that had taken place at the above-mentioned mansion, and thought that Sir Thomas Brooke would be a likely person for him to wed his daughter to, consequently he sent a pressing invite, which the subtle villain accepted greedily.

Sir Thomas sat in his library contemplating over his fell work that had as yet proved so successful.

" Nothing now to bar my way," he muttered.

" Don't be too sure," whispered a voice, close behind him.

He shuddered, and his visage turned pale at the sound of that mysterious voice.

" Fool that I am to start at the sound of my own voice," he said, resuming his former position. " Why should I fear; there is nothing in my way now ?"

" Yes, there is," repeated the same voice.

Again he started, and said,

" It must be my fancy."

" No, it ain't," the same mysterious sound said, as though mocking what he said.

" H—l and furies ! what can it be ?" he exclaimed, excitedly; starting from his seat, and listening intently.

(*To be continued.*)

THE PHANTOM'S WARNING;

A LEGEND OF THE TIME OF RICHARD THE THIRD.

(*Continued from page 48.*)

" Then thou dost not belong to his Grace's household, fair maiden," inquired Anne.

" No, my lady," answered Bridget ; " it was rumoured that you was coming hither, and the Prioress of St. Helen's, with whom I bide at times, said it would be well for me to welcome you to the home of my fathers, as there were none but rude men-at-arms, who know more of the tug of war than the courtesy which should be shown a lady, and one of gentle blood, whom it behoves all to hold in high esteem."

" Saint Helen bless her," ejaculated Anne. " I had intended to be alone, for I have more of sorrow than I hope will befall thy lot, and it does grieve me much that I did hither come ; but by thy presence, much that does oppress me has been soothed. Comest thou often here ?"

" It was my wont," replied Bridget, " until his Grace did put aside the old dark portraits which hung in the large hall. My mother's and my father's pictures were amongst them, and I did love to come and gaze on them for hours, when none beside were with me. But his noble Grace made plaint that they did not stir up the minds of his followers to mighty deeds, and so resolved to hang those gloomy arms and armour in their places, which have cased so many goodly youths who all are dead. So he did move them to another room adjoining this, and I have power to come whenever it fits me best, to gaze upon them ; but they look now as if they never were owners of this Hall, so closely are they forced together in the small ante-room, which I will show your ladyship anon."

While Bridget was conversing, the Duke had entered by a private door, which was concealed by the wainscoting, and stood gazing upon the lady Anne unperceived. His face for the moment had lost its fierce demoniacal expression, his brow was unfurrowed, as if its dark workings had ceased at the sight of one so lovely. For Anne was clad in a rich mourning robe of black velvet, with her long raven curls unbound ; and her beautiful countenance rendered more interesting by sorrow, with an unusual paleness upon her cheeks, her face seemed to wear in the dim twilight more of the repose of a habitant of heaven than one that belonged to this earth. As Glo'ster gazed upon her for a few moments his harsh features became unrelaxed ; but when he thought how he had won her, even in the presence of the " bleeding witness of her hatred," and after having murdered her husband, his haughty brow gradually darkened, and his proud lip curled in all its accustomed contempt, and ambition again reined his thoughts; but this was not for long, for forcing his features into repose, he stepped forth into the apartment, and extending his hand to Lady Anne, bade her " good even."

A slight shuddering pervaded the lady as she arose, and her head seemed to shrink by impulse from the salute he imprinted upon her cheek. After requesting Bridget Crosbie not to depart, he sat down for several minutes, and carried on a playful conversation, in which the ladies took a part, charmed by his wit and enamoured of his discourse, for never did Satan when tempting our first mother in Eden talk more eloquently, or show greater powers of fascination. He then arose, stating that as the king was ill at ease much of the business of the state devolved upon him, and under pretence of reading his despatches, he retired by the private door; and ascending the staircase, entered the apartment above, and there awaited the return of the ruffians whom he had appointed to murder his brother Clarence.

The room in which Glo'ster was seated had an entrance from the pleasure garden (the site of which is still retained in the old ground plans of the Hall, marked as " the void piece of land or pleasaunce,") by means of an external staircase, from which the great dining parlour was also entered by a private door, at which the Duke had gained access to the Lady Anne. But the apartment in which he now sat for a long time retained the name of the throne-room, as it is supposed to have been here where the crown was offered him, it is at present known as the council-chamber. The apartment was hung round with rich arras of crimson, on which was enwrought a stag-hunt in golden tissue; horsemen and hounds glittered upon the drooping tapestry, and huntsmen lifted the bugle-horn to their lips, and, by their swelling cheeks, appeared to blow lustily; hills and heavy trees were thrown into rude perspective, and the dogs wore strange forms, some of them with heads like lions, for war was more cultivated than the arts. The beautiful ceiling was enriched with carved work, bunches of knot-grass, and festoons, and fir cones, and delicate trefoiled tracery. A splendid bay window looked into the courtyard. Along the centre of the room ran a long oaken table; this was covered with cloth of gold, on which were laid innumerable piles of paper, plans of battles which had been fought, and of murders that had yet to be executed. The floor was covered with rushes, not scattered loosely as in the hall, but woven slightly together, after the manner of our rush door-mats; several heavy oaken chairs also stood in the room.

In one of these sat Glo'ster, fronting the fire, busied in the perusal of a long sheet of parchment, which was written in a close cramped hand. An iron lamp in the form of a dolphin hung above his head, suspended from the ceiling, throwing its light upon an unsheathed sword which lay on the table. His brows were closely knit, and, while he read, his hand twice grasped, as if involuntarily, the hilt of a dagger which was stuck in his belt.

At length a page entered, splendidly dressed, and doffing his velvet cap, while the long white plumes swept the floor as he held it in his hand, he bowed his head, and said,

"There is one without impatient to speak with your grace."

"But one?" replied Glo'ster, "by Saint Paul! there should be two of them! Admit him."

The page retired, and a fierce-looking ruffian entered, clad in armour; he neither doffed his iron helmet, nor yet bowed, but striding up to within a few paces of the duke, exclaimed, in a deep, hollow voice,

"Clarence is murdered!"

"What have you done with the body?" said Glo'ster.

"Left it in a vault," replied the ruffian, "until your grace gives order for its being entombed."

"And your companion," said the duke, "comes he not for the reward?"

"He gave me no assistance," answered the murderer, "and did sorely grieve that he had undertaken to be there, and fain would have persuaded me to have left the deed undone."

"Why did you not stab him to the heart?" exclaimed Glo'ster, rising from the chair as he spoke. "Have you left him to escape?"

"He left me like a coward, as he is," replied the murderer, "and escaped; but he bid the duke to look behind him, while I stabbed him in the back, then plunged him into the Malmsey butt head foremost, to make security more firm."

"Thou hast done well," answered Glo'ster; "I would that thou had'st cut thy comrade's throat; but, as thou sayest, he was accessory to the deed, and dare not divulge. Died the duke bravely?"

"No, your grace," replied the murderer; "he did beseech us to return to you, and said you would reward us, if we spared his life."

"Poor shallow fool," said Glo'ster, and laughed loudly a horrid, fiendish laugh that echoed through the arched chamber, and even startled himself at its sound; then, looking full in the ruffian's face, he said,

"What is thy name?"

"Forest, your grace," replied the murderer.

"And if thou wouldst resolve to do me further service in this line, my good Forest, I would keep thee about my person, and see to it that thou fared'st well," said Glo'ster.

"I am at your grace's service," replied Forest, "and shall be glad to do your bidding."

"Then here is thy reward," said the duke, and lifting up the lid of a heavily iron-bound chest, he took out a handful of gold pieces, letting fall several upon the oaken floor, as he presented them to Forest. "In a day or two I will hold further converse with thee; in the meantime, I will add thee to the number of my retainers."

Then, striking the table with the hilt of his dagger, as a summons for the page, he gave orders that Forest should be attended to as one of his followers, and they quitted the apartment, leaving Glo'ster alone to his own dark thoughts.

The duke again resumed his seat, and sat for several moments with his face buried in his hands, in profound thought. At length the heavy arras moved upon the wall, making a rustling sound, which started him from his reverie, while gusts of wind continued at intervals to moan down the wide chimney. At length he arose from his seat, and began to pace to and fro in the apartment with rapid strides, muttering to himself, in a low tone at first, but which gradually arose as his passion increased.

"I fain would spare their lives, but, curse the brats, they stand between me and the throne. I have shed blood enough to appease an enraged lion; but more must yet be shed ere I attain the crown I grasp at. Clarence's death sits heavy on my soul just now. Poor, weak, confiding Clarence! But why should I let thoughts like these unman me?—he might have died by other hands, and I shed not his blood; 'tis the base world that finds these instruments to do such damned work. And Forest! yes, he shall murder the princes when they do arrive. To-night, I hear, they sleep at Northampton; a few more nights and they shall sleep, where?—what matter, though it be where I shall never go? This world was made for me to stir in: I will be king, if it be alone that I may have these lofty-headed lords kneel at my feet that I may spurn them. But I was born with teeth, and made to bite. Surely my sire was a wolf, and from his nature I did draw this love of prey. And what are a few drops of blood?—all must die, and those I murder might do many crimes. No, I am no villain; but one who hurries souls from out this wicked world to find a better place. Hark! methinks I'm like a child who sees wild faces moving on the wall!—again! what sound is that? 'tis like a dying groan, for so King Henry moaned when I stabbed him in the Tower, where but to night my brother died!"

Glo'ster strained his eyes through the dull gleams of the room, for the iron lamp burned dimly, and shed but an imperfect haze around. Sometimes the wind swept in fitful gusts from the wide chimney, and waved the faint flame aside, leaving that part where he stood in shadowy light. But soon a sound, as of a dying man, seemed to break through the door of the adjoining apartment, which was the duke's sleeping room, and at length the heavy door swung wide open upon its grating hinges, and a dim, blue, ghastly light issued from it, which gradually filled the place in which he stood.

Big drops oozed from his brow, and he placed his hand upon the table to support himself, for his knees knocked together with fear, as a shrill scream rang through the mansion.

At length Glo'ster snatched up his sword, and struck the table, but no page appeared; and again another sound arose, a horrid burst of fiendish laughter, chilling his very blood by its mockery. He tried to shout, but his tongue clove to the roof of his mouth, like one who attempts to call for help in a dream.

Then rose a shadowy form from the lurid haze, and stood full in the centre of the open door, growing in darker relief as the horrid light increased, and pointing its bleeding hand to the duke ; and then a low, sepulchral voice, terrible even by its hollow solemn tone, exclaimed, without moving a pallid lip, for the sound seemed to issue from the earth,

"Glo'ster! Glo'ster! Glo'ster! behold thy murdered brother!"

Then came a silence more frightful than the sound, for even the wind seemed at that moment to hold its breath. Glo'ster attempted in vain to rally himself ; the sword fell unconsciously from his grasp, and he made faint passes with his arm, as though he still held the weapon, uttering in husky accents, which seemed to choke themselves as they arose,

"Avaunt, d——d spirit ! or come in the shape of some tiger or devil—any—any, but thine own—I did not the deed—'twas—'twas——"

"By thy command, false Glo'ster," answered the phantom ; "again will I visit thee—then thou shalt know that thy hour is at hand."

The spirit then vanished, as though it sank through the floor, and the room was again enveloped in gloom, saving the faint ray which gleamed from the dying lamp, as it shot up its feeble flame fitfully. But the duke had fallen, and lay like one dead, among the scattered rushes ; not a sound reigned in the apartment.

CHAPTER II.

MORNING again arose, and the bright beams of a summer sun fell full upon the deep-dyed windows of Crosby Hall. The menials had all arisen ; some were busied in looking after the steeds, others in preparing for the marriage which was to take place on that day between the Duke of Glo'ster and the Lady Anne. Several had been engaged all night in cooking huge barons of beef, and sheep and hogs were roasted whole, which, when cold, were to be placed before the numerous retainers of the duke, at the lower end of the hall. Game of almost every description lay dead in the out-houses ready for dressing, fawns and fallow-deer, and boars'-heads, for they paid but little regard as to what was in season. Heath and wood, and mountain and river, had been compelled to give up their inhabitants to furnish forth the marriage-feast at Crosby Hall ; for, as Glo'ster intended at once to sieze upon the crown, he deemed it prudent to collect as many followers around his table as could possibly be seated. Tables stood in readiness for the guests, extending the whole length of the hall, with the exception of a passage left at each end for the servants in waiting to pass to and fro. Under the minstrel gallery was placed the orsille, or high table, elevated above the rest ; this was set apart for the nobles, and the line of division was also marked by a huge silver salt-cellar ; the cloth, too, that covered it was distinguished from the others, being bordered with flowers of gold. Below the salt-cellar was placed another table, a little elevated from that adjoining, beneath ; this was set apart for the knights, each being seated according to his rank, and was also covered with a cloth of less value. The others were strong oaken tables, wholly uncovered, and reaching down beyond the large fire-place. On the upper table, or orsille, stood drinking vessels of gold and silver. A rich throne covered with crimson velvet was also fixed at the head of it, which was the seat appointed for the duke and his consort. Green branches were suspended from various parts of the hall ; flowers were also strewn upon the floor. Dishes of silver, gold, brass, and pewter glittered upon the upper tables, while on the uncovered oaken ones were seen long rows of wooden trenchers. The royal banner of England hung over the crimson canopy, making a deep shadow where its heavy silken folds drooped, while the emblazoned arms were reflected on the burnished vessels beneath. It was placed there by Glo'ster's command, he being the protector during the minority of the Prince of Wales, and had been removed for that purpose from the Tower during the night. The duke's banner also was suspended from the minstrel's gallery, hanging high above the royal flag of England.

(To be continued.)

BLACK HAWKE, THE HIGHWAYMAN.

THE SIGNING OF THE BOND.

CHAPTER XVI.—(continued.)

The sound responded to his exclamation, and again he sat down.

"Idiot that I must be," he continued, getting a little cool, and looking round to ascertain himself that he was *alone*, "why should I fear? Yet that strange dread feeling seems to cling to me. I know not why there has been no one to come forward to denounce me. My cousin must be dead, or he would have returned, and his son——"

"Still lives."

"What was that I heard?" he said, starting as these two words were whispered in his ear. "Fool I must be to start at my own thoughts, though something seems to tell me that he still lives; but that cannot be; the men did their work."

"No, they did not," repeated some strange being.

"Fiend from hell, or whatever thou art, I will see," said he, the perspiration rolling down his sullen-looking face, and his eyes starting out of his head with fear, while his knees played a tune together.

"No you won't."

It was the page who had been playing with his master, the young preserver of Merlin Hawke, who had aided him in his mysterious visit. Herbert was the name by which he went under; no one ever knew his proper names; that mattered little. He was the favourite of the whole house, even

No. 8.

the villanous Sir Thomas Brooke had a liking to him, and would not let him go when he had given warning. Every means he had tried to gain a little affection from the boy, but to no purpose. Herbert shunned him whenever they met, but on this occasion he had entered the library and concealed himself for the purpose of gaining what information he could that some day might prove useful, and for another purpose, to frighten the villanous, wicked wretch.

Sir Thomas drew his rapier, and glared savagely about for the intruder.

"If thou art human," he said, "by heavens you shall suffer dearly for this playing with me, and if thou art supernatural——"

"You would have a fit through fright," said Herbert, in the same low voice, at the same time extinguishing the wax candle that stood on the table, and smacking the conscience-stricken, wicked wretch in the mouth with it.

The hot wax stuck to his mouth and he uttered a yell of fright, as he made a clutch at an imaginary shadow that stood in front of him making most hideous faces, as he thought. His foot came in contact with the leg of the table, and he fell sprawling over a heavy oaken chair, and lay on his face, groaning.

He howled miserably as he felt a hand clutch hold of the seat of his breeches.

TALES OF HIGHWAYMEN.

Herbert raised him up by his seat of honour.

Sir Thomas was in a very undignified position; his hands and feet were on the ground, and his body raised up, forming an arch.

His breeches fitted him very tight, and Herbert could not resist the temptation.

A shriek of agony followed the mischievous page as he vanished out of the apartment.

He had inserted the rapier in the most tender part of Sir Thomas's person and left it sticking there.

By the time he had extracted the weapon and staggered to his feet, Herbert had gained his room, and was in ecstacies of delight at the success of his "little game" that he had had at his master's expense.

Trembling in every limb, Sir Thomas reached the door and called his page.

Herbert ran to his master's assistance, looking as cool and innocent as though nothing had happened.

"There is somebody in the house," stammered the guilty wretch, quaking with fear, hardly able to keep his footing, his legs trembled so violently.

"Yes, sir," answered the boy, "there are many."

"Of whom do you speak?"

"The servants."

"No, no," said Sir Thomas, "I mean in my library. Some one extinguished the light, and then tried to assassinate me."

"Indeed," replied Herbert, making a very serious face, and speaking greatly alarmed; "we will seek for the intruder."

"We will," replied Sir Thomas.

So they did, but in vain.

Everything was removed, still there was no signs of the intruder.

Herbert took the opportunity of making all kinds of peculiar grimaces every time his master's back was turned towards him, and once or twice gave him a push when he was stooping to look into any remote corner, and so caused him to fall forward; consequently, a thick head and a hard wall came in collision.

"You must have been mistaken, sir," said the page.

"Me mistake, Herbert? I am positive there was some one here."

"There are none here now, evidently."

"Where have you been all the evening?" enquired Sir Thomas.

"In my room reading," replied the boy, earnestly. "If there has been any one here they have escaped."

"They could not, I have not been out of the room."

"Then, Sir Thomas, you must have been dreaming."

Sir Thomas shook his head very doubtfully, and pointed to the injured part, from which the red current streamed down his white stockings, leaving the red trail as it ran into his shoes.

Herbert could not repress a laugh when he saw the conspicuous sight of his master.

Sir Thomas was very dissatisfied with the search, and went out for a ride, to drown his gloomy thoughts in the surrounding beauties of the country.

He asked his page to accompany him; but Herbert kindly refused his offer, with many thanks. He preferred his room to his company, and always felt safer when they were apart.

It was a beautiful moonlight night; the heavens were one clear blue mass, with the stars glimmering like so many thousands of diamonds; the moon cast a soft, subdued light over the vast expanse of country; the glow-worms were glistening in the road like so many dazzling gems.

Everything seemed wrapped in peace and quietude.

Not even a breath of air disturbed the leaves of the gigantic trees that hung over the road, and met in the middle, forming an arch that shaded the road by day from the hot, burning sun.

Sir Thomas had fallen into a deep reverie through the solitary aspect of the place, and was riding leisurely down the road, never thinking of the men who infested the highroads.

He was suddenly brought to a halt.

A handsome youth sat on the back of an Arabian steed, motionless and quiet.

But a minute before the road was deserted, save for Sir Thomas, and the next instant horse and rider stood in his path like a shadow.

So mysteriously and strangely did the horseman appear on the road that Sir Thomas began to quake again with fear.

Everywhere he went some dark shadow seemed to follow in his track; when at home he is haunted by some invisible fiends, who mock and taunt him in every way; when in bed, where he seeks repose to shut out the thoughts of horrible crimes that he had caused, his vision is haunted by spectres that appear to dance about in mockery of his fears, and make most hideous faces, that often caused him to have convulsions through fright.

"Stop that shivering, you craven-hearted hound!" said the young horseman, "and answer to me by your sword for your many crimes."

Sir Thomas could not answer by his mouth through being attacked so abruptly.

"Who are you and how dare you stop me on the king's highway?" said Sir Thomas, recovering his speech by degrees.

"Who I am I would quickly show you by my sword if thou wert not such a dastardly cur!"

"Hound!" said the enraged baronet; "I will blow thy cursed brains out!"

"No, you won't, bounceable cur, villain, and subterfuge!" said the young horseman, striking the pistol from his hand; "if you have one spark of manhood or courage in your villanous breast, cross swords with me and fight for your vile life."

"Bah! I should have enough to do were I to fight every vagrant who chose to stop me."

"Base, shaking hound, you shall suffer before long; give me every coin you have about you, every piece of jewellery and trinkets, and even the gold buckles off your boots, breeches and gaiters."

Sir Thomas looked at him savagely and would have refused, but he saw the determined look on his opposer's face.

"But—but——"

"No buts; hand them over."

He produced his money and jewels, all but a magnificent diamond ring that sent its glistening rays on every side like some magic light.

He thought he had given enough.

The young knight of the road thought different as he remarked,

"Sir Thomas Brooke, you see I know who you are and all your plans. However, that's nothing to do with what I was going to say. I perceive, if my eyes do not deceive me, that you are wearing one of his late lordship's rings; you will be kind enough to give it me. Thank you."

Sir Thomas gave a howl as he drew it off; he would have refused, but a long-barrelled pistol held close to his nose made him alter his mind, and he gave it up with the greatest courtesy imaginable.

"This," he said, holding the ring up to Sir Thomas, "I shall wear to-morrow evening, when we shall meet again."

"No, we shan't."

"But I say we shall."

"Don't want to," muttered Sir Thomas, turning his horse's head to ride away.

"Stop!" shouted the highwayman.

Sir Thomas did so.

"Give me all those buckles."

"But not off my gaiters."

"Off everywhere."

"But I can't get them off."

"Then I will," said the boy highwayman, cutting them off one at the time with his sword.

Again Sir Thomas turned his steed's head and rode towards the Hall, wishing that he had not come out.

"He has never been so cleaned out in his life before," said the boy, pleased at the way he had served the cowardly wretch.

As he rode on his gaze fell on the glistening diamond, his head bowed to his chest, a look of sorrow settled on his handsome countenance, and the tears rolled down his cheeks, as he soliloquized,

"The hand that wore this ring before the villain I have just taken it from has often caressed me tenderly and with love, that I shall never experience again."

As he finished his self-communion he buried his face in his hands and wept bitterly.

"Why should I give way like this?" he continued. "No, no, I will not ; but I can't controul my feelings when I think how foully my only parent was murdered ; the only person for whom I lived and loved. But now I will live to avenge his death though I have to kill hundreds."

He rode on with a determined look on his face, evidently brooding over some plan by which he could carry out his vow.

During this time Sir Thomas reached Albion Hall and was admitted by his page, who said, as his master entered,

"You have lost the buckles off your breeches, boots, stock——"

"Stop—stop your mouth !" shouted Sir Thomas.

He did not want to be reminded of his misfortune.

"But they are gone," insisted the page, who knew it would annoy him by remarking that he had lost anything.

"Stopped by a highwayman, who took everything from me, and would have blown by brains out, only I took the weapon from his hand and threw it at him. It exploded, and the bullet stuck in his horse's flanks ; the animal reared up, and dashed off at a headlong speed, and so he escaped my vengeance."

"Whom—the horse or the rider?" said Herbert, who did not believe the lies Sir Thomas had been telling him.

He ground his teeth, and looked savagely at the page.

Sir Thomas knew it was no good to argue, so retired to his own room, telling Herbert to take him up a cup of coffee.

Herbert did, and put a drop of lamp oil in it which had the effect of making his master dreadfully sick and ill.

CHAPTER XVII.

A DEADLY CONFLICT FOR THE TREASURE—THE EXECU-
TIONERS EXECUTED—HAL HUNTER AND FRANK'S VICTORY
—THE FOUR CAPTAINS MEET AT THE BALL — LADY
CLEVELAND AND ALBERT MONTAGUE—THE RECOGNITION
—A SHOT—A DUEL—AND CAPTURE OF HIGHWAYMEN.

THE twelve men of the Black Hawks rushed into the vault, knocking over the savage-looking brutes on all sides.

Ere the executioners had time to bring down the axes they were dashed to the earth.

The two prisoners were released from their bonds by their noble comrades.

"Shoot them down !" shouted the enraged leader of the bloodthirsty band. "Let not one escape, or by h— you shall all swing for it."

"That's wise, my friend," said Frank, who felt himself quite cool and collected as soon as he was released from those cutting cords. "You see there are fourteen of us, and each one man owns two very large pistols, which hold very large bullets. Your number is twenty-five ; that will be a bullet each for you, and one extra each for those black-looking brutes that were standing over us just now with a very threatening weapon, and an extra one for yourself."

The leader of the Night Slayers, as they called themselves, dashed at Frank with a huge scimitar.

Frank saw his danger, and stepped aside.

Behind him stood a burly-looking brute, about to thrust a dagger into the young captain's back, and as Frank moved aside, the blow that was dealt for him the fellow received, and he fell with his head shattered.

This inspired their blood-thirsty natures, and they rushed upon the highwaymen like a tribe of savages.

They were met by the points of their swords.

A deadly conflict ensued.

The men thought not of their lives.

Their place of resort had been discovered by their deadly foes, and they fought for the lives of the enemy.

About half of them had fell wounded or dead, when Frank's voice rang out.

"Cease that useless slaughter," he said. "Secure the executioners and their leader !"

In a trice the trio were secured.

Frank motioned to his men to put the executioners on blocks.

Resistance was useless.

The miserable wretches were forced to their knees, and their heads laid on the blocks.

Two of the highwaymen were then blindfolded, and stood by the side of the miserable, crime-stained men.

The highwaymen stood with the axes upraised, waiting for the signal.

Another minute, and then a sickening sound.

The axes have descended.

The heads of the unhappy men roll along the stones, the bodies quiver, and fall prone to the ground.

Every nerve seems to work, the hands draw in and out, and the body shakes convulsively.

The sight has made Frank and Hal sick and faint, and they turn away with pale cheeks.

The merciless leader struggled terribly to get away from his captors, vowing vengeance on the whole of the Black Hawke Band.

"You see," said Hal, addressing their prisoner, "that you have lost your victory, and we will."

"Hell's curses on you ! but I'll have you yet."

"No, you won't."

"By Heavens, I will."

"By the Lord Harry, I don't think you will have the chance."

"What do you mean?" he asked, turning a ghastly hue.

"Exactly the same as you would have done to us," replied Hal.

"By G—d! you shall never say you or any one else killed me," he said, disengaging one of his hands.

Hal saw what he was going to do, and tried to secure his arm, but he was too late.

He thrust his hand under the breast of his coat and drew forth a dagger.

The next instant there was a dull thud, and he had buried it up to the hilt in his own heart !

He drew one long, deep breath and fell from Hal's arms.

"He has saved us the trouble of making a mess," said Frank.

"I am glad he has," said Hal. "Now, comrades, take the gold and jewels."

Each man took a portion and left the ruined abbey.

Frank and Hal rode away together towards London.

Night was fast drawing in as the two captains reached their destination.

This was the grand night of the festival at the Duke of Cleveland's.

The sweet, low sounds of music swept upwards to-night and sounded like a charm to the ear as it floated on the air and was borne away with a gentle breeze.

The warm, fragrant air was rich with a dazzling mist, and the softened beauty of the light gently hovered over a scene of gorgeous revelry.

Such forms of grace and faces of rare loveliness were there as might be imagined that only peopled the land of fairies.

The gallant figures of the cavaliers strode about with chivalric dignity, who kept each to his chosen love or fair companion for the night.

The time was all for gladness and mirth—a daze of thought like the spell of a delicious dream.

On this evening was a masquerade ball—a grand gathering of fashion and beauty.

The loveliness of the mustered throng seemed to thrill the heart to gaze upon, and wrapped the senses in delight.

The revelry was at its height when there entered two handsomely-dressed cavaliers, upon whom much attention was bestowed.

Tall and well-built; dressed exquisitely; stately, with grace and dignity they made their way through the festive throng.

Many a fair masquerader's gentle breast quickened with a thrill of admiration as they gazed round as though in search of a companion.

They seemed difficult to please, for though there were many fair damsels disengaged they gave no heed to them but passed through the assembly.

"All's well," said two more cavaliers, as they passed the two who had previously entered.

"Stay," said one of the first cavaliers.

The two latter ones returned.

"Captain Hawke and Will Merry," said Frank, for it was he and Hal who had passed and given the signal word.

"Have you seen them?" asked Merlin, of Frank.

"Of whom do you speak?"

"Sir Thomas and Lady Cleveland.

"I believe he has been with the duke all day."

"Then the confounded fellow has kept Lady Cleveland away from the festival?"

"No, he has not," said Albert Montague, the highwayman who had stopped Sir Thomas on the road the previous evening; "I have her here."

As he spoke he drew a most lovely creature to his side, as fair and gentle as an angel.

"By Jove!" said Will Merry, "there will be a fight to-night, I am thinking."

"How is it that you have managed to beguile Sir Thomas's promised *bride* away?" inquired Merlin.

The young nobleman laughed and shrugged his shoulders.

"I shall put a blight to his hopes this evening," he said, a cloud as dark as thunder spreading over his handsome features. "Ha, ha, ha! I am master of Albion Hall! He thought he had accomplished his murderous plans well. Yes, I will put a curse on his hopes; he shall be driven from place to place like a mad dog, and when I think he has had enough of that he shall adorn a gibbet! I will revenge my father's death!"

The young lady clung to the arm of Montague; and trembled with fear at the determined tone of his voice.

The four captains looked at each other in surprise; they had never before heard one so young pledge a vow of vengeance as he did.

A boy came running towards them and caught hold of Merlin Hawke's hand; he did not notice his young master and companion as he approached.

"Forgive me," he said, "if I have interrupted you, but I saw you and could not let the opportunity pass without speaking to you."

Merlin looked wonderingly at the boy.

"Do you not know me?" asked the boy.

"I have a slight recollection of you somewhere," Merlin said.

"Do you remember this?" the boy said, showing the ring he had given him.

Merlin's face lit with pleasure when he saw his gift, and he drew the boy affectionately towards him.

"The brave lad who saved my life," said Merlin, "why are you here?"

"I came with my villanous master. He has been with the duke all day trying to make a match with his fair daughter."

"I'm afraid it won't strike."

"No, strike me if it will. I saw her look at him as though he was something that infected the place."

"My friends have left," said Merlin, "and I must join them. We have business to attend to. I shall see you again in the course of the evning. Keep a good watch over Sir Thomas."

"I have something to tell you about him. Good bye, I must be off. We must meet again."

The boy disappeared in the dazzling throng, and Merlin strode after his companions who had so suddenly vanished.

Many a bright eye followed Merlin's elegant form with admiration as he sauntered through the clusters of the fair sex. He heeded none; his thoughts seemed pre-occupied, and standing against a marble pillar he watched his companions as they whirled round in the dance.

A man stood close to Merlin, watching a couple with a look of hatred as they brushed past him. He would have stayed them, but they passed in an instant.

"By gad," he muttered, as he watched them go through the figure of the dance with the grace and ease of fairies, "I'll make the proud beauty kneel at my feet before long; and as for that cursed whelp she is with, I could wring his infernal neck."

"My friend, Sir Thomas, is vicious about something," muttered Merlin, as he watched the malicious look of the stranger's face.

The young couple who had been watched so closely by the villanous Sir Thomas Brooke tripped lightly up to where Merlin stood.

The watcher availed himself of the opportunity; he walked up to the trio and laid his hand as gently as he could on the fair soft shoulder of the lady.

Albert, her companion, with whom she had just danced, turned sharply to the intruder; but seeing it was the affianced husband of the young Lady Cleveland, he did not make any comment, but anxiously awaited for him to speak.

"Come," said Sir Thomas, trying to take her hand which she held out of his reach, "your sire has sent me to seek you. I have been patiently waiting the termination of the last dance for the pleasure of having your hand in the next. "You, sir," he said, turning to Albert, "need not expect this lady's hand again."

The fair lady turned ghastly pale, and looked reproachfully at Albert, as Sir Thomas led her away; she knew she dared not refuse to go with him, as it was with her father's wish.

"Your pardon, sir," said Albert, stopping Sir Thomas as he was walking away in triumph with the fair creature, "the lady is engaged to me for the next dance."

"Since when?" asked Sir Thomas, indignantly, looking at him with disgust.

"That is not yours to ask."

"Then mine is a previous engagement, and I claim the lady by authority."

Albert displayed the ring that he had taken from Sir Thomas.

"The highwayman that robbed me the other evening!" said Sir Thomas, thinking that he would have him put under arrest.

"No, not a highwayman," said Albert, removing his mask, "but the heir of Albion Hall!"

"He still lives!" gasped the guilty wretch, shaking in every limb.

"Yes, villain, plotter, and murderer! I still live to claim that which belongs to me only."

Sir Thomas Brooke seemed to lose all power when he recognised the heir of Albion Hall still alive and standing in his path; he gasped for breath and fell senseless to the ground.

Few had witnessed what had taken place; but, as he fell, the revellers gathered around him.

"Fainted from over exhaustion," said one of the lookers on.

"The last dance was very fatiguing," said others.

And such were the remarks that were made.

He was conveyed to a chamber by the duke's command, and soon brought back to consciousness.

He gave information that there was a highwayman in the company. He had hit upon that, as he thought he would be able to get the right owner out of the way.

The duke sent for a body of officers.

Meanwhile, Frank and Hal had been going through all the dances with extremely pretty partners.

At the same time they had not been idle—the highwaymen, not the ladies. They had extracted several gold snuff-boxes and silk pocket-handkerchiefs.

Merlin had only watched one fair masquerader all the evening.

The coquetish richness of her attire was such as suited her bewitching figure.

Full, pliant, and slender—a realization of grace from head to foot—with a fair, swan-like throat, swelling out into smooth, round, and finely-moulded breasts; her shoulders bare, and leaving just enough of her magnificent bust exposed to the gaze to set the soul dreaming and tempt a man to love's rapture.

"Beautiful!" muttered our hero, as he approached her. "Something to set the heart dreaming and make the mind wander!"

So thinking, he was about to address her in his softest tones, when Will Merry stepped to her side at the same time, and took her hand, and was about to lead her in a dance.

"Then I must wait," said Merlin, "since my friend has the honour of a prior claim."

Will Merry gave his president a peculiar wink that he understood, and then whirled through the assembly.

Merlin watched them with admiration.

"She is not here," he soliloquized, as he stood there in a kind of reverie.

A sudden rush of feet, and a troop of officers rushed in, headed by the duke and the subtle Sir Thomas Brooke.

"What's the meaning of this?" said Merlin Hawke to himself. "Have any of my comrades been recognized?"

"This is Sir Thomas's work," said Frank, coming up to Merlin.

"Then he thinks by so doing he will be able to get Albert out of the way?"

"While he has four brave and noble comrades by his side he shall not be taken."

"Beware of the highwaymen!" shouted the officer in command.

Every fair damsel looked at her partner as though he were a highwaymen.

"Dam'me!—I—ah, yes, highwaymen stole my emerald snuff-box!"

This was the old admiral who shouted out about his snuff-box!

He had not forgotten being robbed by Hal Hunter.

Hal Hunter did not feel at all comfortable at hearing the voice of his old enemy, more especially as he was with the judge's niece, Bella.

Bella trembled violently with fear for the sake of her lover, and she nestled and clung to him fondly as she heard the angry voice of the old admiral approaching them.

"Here's that nasty old fellow that got you into trouble," said Bella, looking at Hal, fondly, and alluding to the night when they had first met. "If he recognises you he is sure to make an alarm."

"Fear not, my dear; he will not know me," Hal said, trying to quiet her fears.

"Stand off!" shouted Albert, as the officers were advancing towards him, "or by heavens I will slay the first that lays a hand on me!"

"Who dares to insult the heir of Albion Hall?" said Will Merry, coming to the spot at the time his friend was being accused.

He would have done better had he kept away.

"Captain Merry," said the chief of the officers, "captain of the band of Black Hawks, highwaymen and murderers!"

"Thank you," said the accused, coolly.

There was a marked sensation in the vast assembly.

Every face was turned towards the dashing, handsome fellow, as he stood with the lady of Merlin's admiration by his side.

"You are an intelligent gentleman," said Merlin to the officer, carelessly. "Perhaps you know me?"

"Black Hawke, the highwayman!" shouted out the worthy officer, in surprise.

Merlin removed his mask, and a shout was raised.

Some opened their mouths to shout, but were so astonished that their mouths stuck open for some time before they could close them.

"Captain Hawke," he said "at your service, ladies and gentlemen. Those who want me, take me."

As he finished speaking he drew himself erect, and unsheathing his sword, waited for the attack.

They did want him, but were afraid to try and capture him—his sword looked very sharp, and his eyes glittered dangerously.

"Black Hawke!" shouted a lot of the pleasure-seekers.

"Where is Black Hawke?" was the general cry.

"Secure this boy highwayman!" shouted Sir Thomas, foaming with rage and fear lest he might escape in the general row. "Secure him, men; he is one of the cursed band!"

"Liar!" thundered Albert, making a cut at his accuser; "you think by getting me in Newgate you will retain possession of my property. It is he who should be arrested; he is the murderer of my father, Lord Montague, and would have assassinated me had I not escaped."

A great portion of the people looked at the youth as though they believed him.

Sir Thomas turned deadly pale and trembled in every limb.

"It is for life or death," he thought, "and if I succeed the young hound will swing, and I then shall have nothing to fear."

Drawing his courage together he forced a defiant laugh, and said,

"A likely tale to take."

"A true one," said Albert.

"Who can prove it?"

"I can," said Hal, coming forward with Bella leaning on his arm.

"A d——d nice witness!" said old Admiral Banjemore. "Another of them! Stole my emerald snuff-box."

"Captain Hal Hunter, of the Black-Hawks," said the cunning officer, who seemed to know them all.

"At your service. I have given you many a hunt; how are you, old boy? My friend, Frank Morton."

Frank stepped forward and bowed as his comrade introduced him.

"I know all," said the officious officer; "there is a thousand pounds reward for each of the captains, and two thousand for their president, known as Black Hawke."

"Now is the time to make money," said Frank. "We are all here; that will make six thousand pounds."

The people started as another body of officers rushed in.

Everything grew into confusion.

People rushed against one another, and they fell heavily to the ground.

"Keep back," said Merlin Hawke. "We fight for liberty alone."

"Those who bar our way will get hurt," put in Will Merry.

"It's no good now, captain," said the leading officer. "Your time has come; you may as well come quietly."

"Fool," said Merlin, as he slew him with his sword, "to speak like that to me. Your time has come."

So it had.

The officer fell pierced through the heart.

His men recoiled for a minute, then dashed at the highwaymen like madmen, heeding nothing.

The excitement was growing intense.

The conflict was at its highest pitch.

Men were falling like reeds before the wind.

The highwaymen were fighting like tigers.

The men suddenly start.

Somebody has fired, a shriek follows the report, and Albert falls bleeding. Lady Cleveland shrieks, swoons, and falls by his side, his life blood saturating her elegant garments and dyeing her white delicate hand a bright purple.

"Cowardly hound!" said Frank, grasping Sir Thomas by the throat until his nails entered his flesh.

Frank had seen him fire, though he had got in a secluded part away from the excited revellers to carry out his murderous plans, and as soon as he had discharged the deadly weapon he glided from his place of concealment, and was hastening to the aid of Lady Cleveland; his craven heart sunk within him as she fell; he thought the bullet had entered them both.

"Who dares lay a hand on me?" said Sir Thomas.

"I do," said Frank, holding him tightly by the throat.

"For what cause?"

"For that dastardly act," Frank said, pointing to the still bleeding form of his companion.

"You mistake, man."

"Sneaking hound! here's the weapon still smoking," Frank said, taking the pistol from him.

When he had fired he put the pistol in his breast pocket, and when Frank took it from him the smoke was still curling from it.

Frank had forced him back, and had got his weapon's point at his throat.

In another instant it would have gone through his crime-stained flesh, but Frank was felled suddenly from behind like an ox.

One of the officers had seen Frank draw his sword back for a thrust, and crept behind him, and dealt him a blow with the butt-end of a big pistol just in time to stay the highwayman's weapon from doing its bloody work.

That officer did not strike another.

Merlin's sword swept through his body like a flash of lightning.

Before the rest of the highwaymen had time to come to the assistance of their friends the officers rushed upon them, and secured the two helpless men.

The three captains fought gallantly for their fallen comrades.

The odds were awful to contend against.

Shots were flying in all directions, and many a reveller fell wounded.

Some of the officers secured Albert and Frank, while others kept the trio at bay.

Fearful was the destruction of human life.

Officers fell, and lay in twos and threes in different parts of the hall that had but a few minutes before been one dazzling scene of joy and mirth, and now it looked like a slaughter-house, or more representing a battle-field with the wounded writhing in agony, and the dead lying white and pallid, with the features drawn into hideous shapes by the agony of the last dying pangs.

"Don't let him escape," shouted the admiral, alluding to Hal.

"What do you mean, you parchment-faced old sinner?" Hal said, turning abruptly, confronting the infuriated old sailor.

"Yah! would you strike an admiral of the king's navy?"

said the old fellow, putting his arms up in front of his face to guard off the blow he expected.

"Look here, you raspberry-nosed old brute, if you say another word I will choke you."

Hal looked stern, and Admiral Banjemore, not liking the idea of being choked, slunk out of the way; even the pretty Bella, that still clung to Hal's arm, seemed half frightened.

"Don't hurt him," she said, imploringly; "he's a friend of uncle's."

"No, my pretty," Hal said, laughing. "I only threatened him to keep him quiet."

The officers had reached the door by this time with their two captives, and were going away in triumph, when there was a sudden rush made from the road that nearly sent them sprawling.

Some stalwart fellows made an attempt to capture our hero.

"Forward, friends!" shouted the leader, in great excitement. "This Black Hawke—"

"You allude to me?" said Merlin, turning on them with his sword drawn.

"Dead or alive," said the interferer, "we mean to take you."

"Then you will not take me alive; so try your best."

Many more gentlemen joined in the attack, who seemed to think it good sport to hurt a highwayman.

The ladies were of quite a different opinion.

They admired the gallant fellow for his courage.

"Cowards!" said Merlin. "At least twenty to take one."

The men laughed.

"Come on, one at a time," Merlin said again, "and I will fight foot to foot and sword to sword. If I fall by the sword of my first combatant, the capture will be easy."

A dozen swords were drawn to answer him.

Merlin Hawke stood like a statue waiting for his opponents, sword in hand.

The men who had led on the attack stepped forward.

With a clash their weapons crossed.

Lunge for lunge and thrust for thrust.

Merlin stood cool and parried the blows as they were dealt with furious onslaught.

The lookers-on stood in breathless anxiety, every minute expecting to see one fall pierced through the heart.

They did not wait long.

Merlin made a feint at his opponent, and like lightning his sword was drawn back as his adversary guarded for the expected lunge.

Before he had time to parry, Merlin's sword entered just under his shoulder.

A fearful shriek arose, that made all who heard it shudder.

A death cry.

He did not see that fatal thrust, it was so quick.

With a shriek of horror, the man spun round on his heels and fell prone to the earth.

There was an angry cry from his followers, and they dashed after Merlin.

He had gone, for he thought the best policy was flight, and he knew he could not contend against such fearful odds.

Every one rushed about knocking one another over in their flight.

The highwayman was gone.

Like a lot of madmen the gentlemen rushed about in search of the slayer of their companion.

(To be continued)

THE PHANTOM'S WARNING;

A LEGEND OF THE TIME OF RICHARD THE THIRD.

(Continued from page 56.)

About two hours before noon Glo'ster entered the hall, unattended; he looked unusually sad, and, walking slowly forward with his hands behind him, he came to the upper table, and throwing himself into the seat or temporary throne, he folded his arms across his bosom and sat for several minutes occupied in deep thought. The rich banner hung above him, casting its shadow over his face, and making the dense furrows on his brow appear more gloomy; a slight quivering was visible on his upper lip, his eyes too occasionally flashed wildly, and his hands trembled, all evident gns that he had passed a restless night. At length he summoned a page to bring him wine, who soon attended, bearing a gold cup in his hand, which the duke emptied at a draught. Buckingham and the Bishop of Ely were soon after announced, and Glo'ster arose to welcome them. After some short conversation, the bishop retired into the chapel on the eastern side of the Hall, and left the two dukes alone.

"The brat has arrived," said Buckingham, "and sends his services to your grace. By Heaven, my lord, he hath a froward tongue!"

"Which we will clip with speed," answered Glo'ster, "ere we be many hours older. I will meet this baby prince anon: to-night he sleeps with York in the Tower; to-morrow night, and all be well, he sleeps in Abraham's bosom. Saw you Hastings? Will he grace our wedding?"

"No, by our Lady," replied Buckingham; "he said that he must pay his devoir to the prince, and would meet your grace with the council in the Tower this afternoon. Methinks Shore's wife did motion him to stay, for she was by during our conference."

"Now, by Saint Paul, may I never see the light again," said Glo'ster, "if he ever leaves the Tower with his head on. As for that strumpet Shore, she shall do penance when I am king."

"It were well to humble her pride," answered Buckingham; "but, by Heaven, she is a goodly dame—such eyes and lips, and such majestic gait! Marry! she looked more lovely than when seated by Edward's side, adorned like a queen. There was a sadness, too, upon her face, which did conspire, with all her other beauties, to make her look more like our lady's face that hangs in Westminster."

"Come, cousin," said Glo'ster, smiling, "if thou goest on this way, I shall conclude that thou art only waiting for Hastings' death to wed her; thou art of a surety bewitched by her charms, for never did I hear thee praise woman so before. What think'st thou of my Lady Anne; would'st wed her, if she consented?"

"No, by the Holy Mother," said Buckingham, "I would not, nor any one who cursed so deeply as she did curse your grace but yesterday, and yet she's not ill-favoured. But see, she comes! By Heaven! lovely as an angel form: nay, now if I was asked to have her for myself, methinks I would repent me of my oath, and answer 'yes;' and one hangs on her arm too, exceedingly beautiful."

While Buckingham was speaking, the Lady Anne approached accompanied by Bridget Crosby, who was arrayed in white, and might have rivalled by her charms the famed Houris of Mahomet's Paradise. The Lady Anne, who appeared the most stately of the two, had her train borne by two young maidens, while four others of equal beauty followed behind. Their dresses were of rich white silk, embroidered with silver flowers. Anne's excelled the others in the richness of its ornaments, her train being of white satin-velvet with a border of golden stars. The sunbeams fell upon them from the gaudy windows, mingling a thousand hues with the splendour of their drapery.

As Glo'ster and Buckingham approached them a band of musicians struck up a lively air from the gallery in which they were stationed. Just then the hall-doors were thrown open, and upwards of a hundred nobles and knights entered and joined the train, in exact order, filing off in the direction of the chapel, in which the ceremony was about to take place. As soon as the wedding train had departed, the hall was nearly filled with the followers of Glo'ster, and the adherents of other lords who were his friends. Lovel and Catesby were also amongst them, and, having had their instructions, were busied in sounding the praises of the duke among the soldiers, while the menials were preparing the banquet against the return of the party from the chapel.

"How now, my man of war," said Catesby, "art thou in love with that banner which thou gazest on so fixedly?" addressing a man in armour.

"Marry! I have loved it ere now," replied the soldier, "and shown many a brave fellow down the gateway of darkness in its defence; but methinks it will be long enough ere I shall be called upon again to guard its golden lions."

"Why thinkest thou so?" inquired Catesby.

"Nay, by my troth," replied the soldier, "I should be wanting to think otherwise. When children are to become our rulers, what need we of banners unless they are to be hung in the nursery?"

"But is not the Duke of Glo'ster Protector?" said Catesby. "Now, by the mass, I thought thou hadst known his grace better than to have supposed that he would long let a soldier remain idle."

"I have seen his grace active enough, I trow, when in the field of Tewksbury," answered the soldier; "but men reigned then as kings, not beardless brats, like this young imp of Edward's, just loosened from his leading-strings."

"Thou art a d——d traitor," answered another soldier, who bore the arms of Hastings upon his helmet, and had been listening to the follower of Buckingham, for such he was, who conversed with Catesby; "none but a cut-throat knave like thee would speak against the royal prince."

"Hast thou been to shrift this morning," said the follower of Buckingham contemptuously, "that thou dost dare to beard me thus, or has Mistress Shore, thy master's ruler, insured thy life, that thou takest such license?"

"Thou art not my confessor," replied the soldier, "neither shall I answer thee but as a loyal subject, which I am, and thou a poor, mean-hearted traitor, who, instead of upholding the young king, wouldst take 'vantage of his youth, and take part with those whose hands are ready now to strip him of his rights."

"Were not this a day of merry-making," answered the follower of Buckingham, unsheathing his sword, "by the cave of hell I would cut out that mischief-making tongue of thine, and throw thy body into the court-yard."

"Thou art a mean braggart," retorted the soldier, also drawing his sword, "a base varlet. I saw thee in Guildhall throw up thy helmet and shout for King Richard, when that thy master, Buckingham, attempted to poison the ears of the good citizens with forged lies touching the honest birth of our young King Edward. Go to, thou art a villain!"

"Nay, now thou hast reflected on the good duke whom I serve," answered the follower of Buckingham, "I call thee villain in return, and thus confirm it," saying which he aimed at him a blow with his sword, which the other dexterously parried, rushing in upon his opponent at the same time, and bearing him to the floor, where he would have despatched him had not Catesby interfered, and Glo'ster and his party at the same moment re-entered the hall, which was in the greatest tumult.

"What means this?" exclaimed Glo'ster, quitting the arm of the Lady Anne and springing forward with his sword uplifted. "Are ye Turks that ye must be at each other's throats on every occasion, disturbing by your brawls the quiet of our mansion? For shame, put up your swords. My Lord of Buckingham, this is a follower of yours; I pray you learn their quarrel, and inform me of it."

Here Catesby interposed, and began to narrate all that our readers are already acquainted with, trying, however, to throw the blame upon the follower of Hastings. Glo'ster knit his brows, and, bidding them to keep at peace, and join the feast, went and seated himself by the Lady Anne, who already occupied the throne. Drums and trumpets and cymbals also began to sound, as the signal for commencing the banquet. Barons of beef, and hogs and sheep, stood upon the table on huge silver vessels and large dishes of pewter. Game of every description was also there, smoking, and sending up their savoury steam to the lofty roof of the hall. At the high table where Glo'ster presided, the greatest order was preserved, and, as the different dishes appeared, they were cut off, then passed to the next table, where the knights were seated, and from them handed to the common soldiery, or servants, at the lower end. Wine was circulated on every hand without distinction, saving that the costliest vessels were placed at the upper end; but even the soldiers had their beer-horns filled with it on that day, with orders to drink *ad libitum*. A hundred voices were in conversation at a time, and, as the wine circulated the noise increased; mirth and laughter reigned unbounded at the lower tables of the hall. Even Buckingham was uttering soft words to the fair Bridget Crosby who was seated beside him.

And Glo'ster also had succeeded in drawing faint smiles from his fair bride, to whom he was very attentive, for her beauty on that day would, for a moment, have divested the devil of evil thoughts to work woe upon one so lovely.

"Seest thou, Anne," said Glo'ster, "how closely my Lord Buckingham is besieging sweet Bridget? By my dukedom, she is a comely wench, and many a coronet has sat on brows less lovely."

"She is worthy of a place in a prince's heart," answered Anne; "were I a lord I'd sooner wed her than many a haughty dame who holds her head highly in the dignity of titles, for Bridget hath that which rank giveth not, a faithful heart and a clear conscience."

"Have not all women faithful hearts?" inquired Glo'ster, fixing his dark eyes upon Anne as he spake.

"Faithful enough, I trow," replied Anne, colouring highly as she spoke, "when, like Bridget, they are a guerdon worthy of being received, rich in their own first love, and free from all attaints."

"Now, by the Holy-rood, thou speakest in parables to me," said Gloster, "for I have always deemed that woman's heart was like her kirtle, easily altered to the latest fashion."

"Thou mayest have deemed rightly," replied Anne, "but in sooth it is then only an old kirtle; however its new form may gloze it, the eyelets of the former needle remain, and, though it be of costly stuff, 'tis of less value than the shepherd's new gaberdine."

"Thou hittest me hard, fair wife," answered Glo'ster, knitting his brow. "What thinkest thou of the crown, then? it descends by entail. Beshrew me, thou canst not say but it is new to him who never wore it before."

"I grant ye that, my lord," replied Anne, "so are its cares; but yet methinks that he who wears it should also have a charmed life, for 'tis the magnet that draws down the steel, and entails but seldom does embar the blade's approach. I wot not how it first became a curse, but he who wears it is enmined in bale; he is the target which ambition aims at."

"How now?" inquired Glo'ster, turning to his page.

"Your grace's presence is desired at the Tower," said the page.

"We will be there anon," replied Glo'ster. "Come, my lord of Buckingham and Ely, we must leave these fair ladies for a time, for graver matters crave our attention; I beg you to attend me to the council."

Then, addressing his guests generally, he arose and said,

"Let not our absence be a damp upon your mirth, whatever Glo'ster owns is yours. I see many a face among you that has with me looked on the storm of battle, and fought it bravely by my side in many a well-won field; to all I say, make merry now. There have been nights when we have made our shields our pillows, and slept with naked swords grasped in our hands, wearied with long fatigue, quick march, and breathless charge; but then we murmured not, for victory kept watch around us, and glory made our slumbers light with golden dreams. We had no wine cups, then, soldiers, to make merry with as now, but I, your leader, shared the same fatigue, slept on the self-same field, felt the same midnight wind steal o'er my limbs, quenched my thirst at the same meadow-stream, where hundreds knelt to drink. Who is there here can say that Glo'ster wrapt his limbs in feathery down when his brave followers pressed the dewy sod?"

"None! none!" rolled from a hundred voices.

"I cannot forget your brave deeds at the field of Tewksbury," continued Glo'ster, "when we humbled the pride of the house of Lancaster to the earth, and took captive their only hope. Since then the rose of York has raised its head, and still waves unmolested. I call on you to rally round your Protector that he may guard the prize."

"Long live King Richard!" rose like the sound of thunder.

"I thank you, friends, but that is not my wish; but should the crown fall into feeble hands, it will be time for me to guard it then, and keep it safe from those who long in vain have sought it. Never shall the royal Lion that has so long floated in victory over many a bloody field, fall to the earth unclaimed, while Glo'ster's hand can lift it, and swords like yours can hem him round in safety."

(To be continued.)

BLACK HAWKE, THE HIGHWAYMAN.

A WELL-AIMED SHOT.

CHAPTER XVIII.

TWO HIGHWAYMEN IN NEWGATE—THE INTERVIEW THROUGH THE HOLE IN THE WALL—THREE CAPTAINS MEET—A DESPERATE STRUGGLE BETWEEN HAL HUNTER AND WILL MERRY—THE RESCUE FROM THE GALLOWS AND A DREADFUL FIGHT WITH THE SOLDIERY.

So suddenly had the highwaymen disappeared that the astonished revellers doubted whether they had left the Hall; consequently a search ensued, but to no purpose.

They had effectually escaped.

The officers carried off their prisoners in triumph, and in the morning, when the young knights of the road returned to consciousness, they found themselves lying on straw in a cell in Newgate.

Albert raised his head and looked vacantly around him; he was alone in a miserable cell, faint and weak from the loss of blood.

His wound had been roughly dressed.

He had fallen into a deep reverie, from which he was awakened by the gaoler entering.

A big, rough, burly-looking fellow, dressed in the prison costume; he had brought his prisoner's breakfast—a huge piece of dry bread and a jug of water.

Albert cast it disdainfully away as the man set it down in front of him.

"What am I brought here for?" asked Albert.

"Why, we likes to make the acquaintance of such birds as you," replied the gaoler; "you will do a dance in the air outside in a day or two."

Albert waved his hand for the man to retire; he could see he was a brutal fellow, that took delight in tormenting his captives.

Albert buried his face in his hands as though to shut out his miserable thoughts; it was the first time he had been in such a place, and he saw little hopes of getting out again.

Frank was of quite a different opinion.

He had often been there before, and escaped each time by the aid of his faithful comrades; therefore he still cherished

No. 9.

the hope of escape; he knew his companions never deserted one another when any of them were in danger.

He had awakened rather early, and, to pass his time away, he was whistling all the dances he had heard at the Duke of Cleveland's.

Albert, who was in the next cell, heard some one whistling, and had wondered who it was, and how they could be so cheerful under such circumstances.

Frank discontinued his musical entertainment as the gaoler entered, and sang out,

"Hullo, what have you brought me for my breakfast?"

The man gave a grunt, and put the bread and water down.

"Do you think that a gentleman of my station can digest this muck?" said Frank, "I who live on the best of delicacies."

"Other people have to pay for them," the gaoler replied.

"I don't pay for this, and those that do might send a fellow something nice."

"You won't have many more breakfasts before you swing."

"Thank you for your cheerful information," said Frank; "but wait a minute, where is my friend?"

"In the next to this."

"How is he? Have you seen him yet?"

"Yes; and he don't seem to like the idea of having to swing in a day or two."

Frank frowned darkly; the gaoler's words went through him, as though he had had a knife thrust in his heart.

Turning on the gaoler, he said, savagely,

"Go; that will do; leave me."

The man retired grinning; he saw the effect his words had taken.

Frank listened to the sound of the heavy tread of his late visitor until the echo died out of hearing, then he soliloquised,

"There's a spiteful brute; takes a delight in tormenting a fellow. I shall owe him one."

He pondered for a few moments; then his eyes wandered searchingly over the wall, as though he had suddenly thought of something.

"I think this is the den," he said; "only I am blowed if I don't almost forget which side it was. I see."

He jumped up as he finished speaking, and, reaching the wall, he took several bricks out, after some fumbling.

"Albert," he whispered, putting his head to the hole.

Young Montague started and looked round in surprise

"Some one called my name," he said.

"Some one did," repeated Frank.

"Who, and where are you?"

"Here; your comrade, Frank."

The young nobleman gave a cry of joy as he caught sight of his friend's head poked through the hole.

"This unexpected interview has inspired me with new life," said Albert, speaking to his friend with a frankness that showed his pleasure at seeing one of his brethren. "I thought, perhaps, that you had escaped, or had been sent to another place. I had given up all hopes of ever seeing any of my companions again."

"Never give way, old boy," said Frank, speaking cheeringly; "our noble comrades never leave any of their brethren when they are in danger."

"But we are in Newgate, and there is no hope of escape," replied Albert.

Frank laughed outright at the idea of no hope, and said,

"This is the first time you have been here. I——"

"It strikes me very forcibly that it will be the last here or anywhere else."

"Fear not, I have escaped at least six or eight times in various ways," said Frank, "through the faithfulness of our comrades."

"I don't care how soon I get liberated. I cannot stomach the food they provide for their guests here."

"I guess not. It's awfully dry and very disgusting," Frank remarked. "Here comes that spiteful sentry. I shall give him a dig when I get the chance. Good-bye, old boy, keep your pluck up."

"Good-bye," said Albert, as his friend's head disappeared and the goaler entered.

"Who was you talking to?" asked the gaoler, looking round suspiciously.

Receiving no answer he entered Frank's cell; he found that ingenious young gentleman sitting on his hard stool looking quite cool, waiting for him. Our young friend had replaced the bricks as he heard the fellow entering Albert's apartment, and had resumed his former position as the big key was put in the lock and the door swung open with a bang.

"Well, old chap," said Frank, "have you brought any good news?"

A cunning smile lit his swarthy features as he answered,

"Yes, the governor has received a warrant for your execution."

"That's worth knowing."

"You won't know much after to-morrow."

"I like you," said Frank, speaking in an impressive tone of voice. "Look here, how much will you take to let us out?"

"Couldn't do it," replied the gaoler, "it's more than my life's worth."

"I have no doubt of that," said Frank, laughing. "I don't mind paying twice its value."

The man looked savage, and retired in disgust.

While this was going on in Newgate, Captain Hawke and his comrades were not idle.

Will Merry had promised his fair companion that he would see her some future time, and, giving her to the care of her friend, who had come to take her home, he made his way to an inn kept by a worthy landlord, who seemed to know the captains very familiarly.

Will winked to mine host as he entered, and that worthy individual showed him to a very cosy room kept especially for private customers.

As Captain Will entered Merlin rose, looking very much flushed through the excitement of the night's adventure.

That had been the appointed place for them to meet if anything occurred that should separate them.

They never went out on any adventure without appointing a place where they could meet, though they seldom had any occasion to part; but on this night it could not be prevented. Frank and Will would have fought for their leader, but, unfortunately, they each had the charge of a fair partner that prevented them from giving their valuable services to the aid of their companions.

Perhaps it was better as it was.

Had they been free they would have fought to the last, and would probably have been captured, as most of the gentlemen had taken part to aid the officers to secure the highwaymen.

The two chief captains were conversing about the liberation of their friends, and were imbibing in a bottle of old wine when they were both startled by the door being burst open, and Hal Hunter rushed in, looking haggard and white; his sword, held in his hand, was red with blood that still dripped from its point.

As he sank into a seat he pointed to the wine.

Will Merry understood what he indicated, and hastened to his side with the reviving draught.

Hal was overcome by some fearful fatigue; his still bloody weapon had fallen from his grasp, and his arms hung loosely by his side; his features were clammy with the perspiration that rolled down his cheeks; his eyes stared wildly from their sockets, and his tongue protruded from his mouth covered with foam.

Will Merry gently held his head back while he poured the wine down his throat.

Merlin stood and looked on in reverential silence.

Hal's whole frame quivered as the wine was forced between his clenched teeth, his eyes wandered about the apartment, and finally rested on his two comrades.

He brought his hands up to his temples with such suddenness that, had not Will got out of the way, he would have caught the ascending arms in his face, which would probably have floored him.

"Away, away!" shouted Hal, making a gesture to his astonished friends to move from his side, "I will not be secured! No, I will not be hanged! I did not mur——"

His voice sank to a whisper, and again his limbs relaxed.

His brethren were quite astounded at their friend's sudden attack.

"What can be the meaning of this?" asked Merlin.

Will Merry shook his head in the negative, and looked inquiringly at their indisposed friend.

"He must have been pursued," said Merlin, again speaking, "and, to effect his escape, he has slain some one that he did not intend to die."

"Ha, ha, ha!" laughed Hal, like a maniac, "you shall not take me! My Captain Hawke will come to my rescue soon."

"I am your captain," said Merlin, approaching Hal; "you are safe now."

"Liar, away!" shouted Hal, frantically. "You are officers."

"No, no!" said Will Merry, speaking consolingly. "Come, old boy, you are safe. We are your friends."

Hal made no reply, but looked maliciously at the speaker.

In another instant, and before Will had time to defend himself, Hal sprang upon him, and they both fell heavily to the ground.

Merlin rushed to their assistance, but he could not release Will from his assailant.

Over and over the trio rolled, struggling dreadfully, each trying to free themselves from the madman's grasp, that held them so tightly.

Merlin rose to his feet, and with a sudden jerk, freed Will from the maddened clutches of their friend.

Will Merry was severely pulled about.

His face was scratched, and his hair had been pulled out by handfuls.

He was wiping the blood from his face, when he was again attacked by his own comrade, and, with the convulsed fingers buried in his throat, he was borne to the ground, half strangled.

Merlin was paralysed.

He had never seen any of his own friends in such a state before.

He feared the struggle would end fatally either with one or both.

The scene was awful to behold.

On the floor they both rolled over each other, struggling and plunging about fearfully, Will Merry only trying to release himself, without hurting his companion, while Hal was trying every way he could in his mad state to throttle and bite his adversary.

Will released himself, and was gaining his feet.

Ere he could rise, his assailant dashed at him.

Will stepped aside, and Hal's head came with a fearful blow against the edge of the table.

One groan escaped his lips, and he fell prone to the floor.

The sudden concussion stunned him, and he laid quiet.

That ended the struggle.

Merlin Hawke looked regretfully at his companion, and summoned the hostess to remove him to a chamber, and bring him back to consciousness.

"By Jove! that was an unexpected struggle," said Will, recovering from the effects of the awful mauling he had received.

"I cannot imagine the cause of his going off like that," returned Merlin.

"Our friends are undoubtedly in Newgate, and within a few days will be condemned," said Will Merry. "It will take us some time to return to the haunt and get whatever band we shall want, and then come back to London."

"As soon as Hal recovers, we must start," Merlin said.

Hal was some time before he began to show the least symptoms of recovery; but with the careful attention of a pretty nurse, he slowly revived.

There was a strange, wild look in his eyes, and an agitated expression on his countenance, that plainly showed there was something on his mind that worried him.

It was very late in the evening before he had recovered sufficiently to get up.

"Well, old boy," said Will Merry, taking his friend's hand, "are you better?"

"What has happened?" inquired Hal, speaking very feebly. "Are we safe? How did I get here?"

"Don't you remember rushing in here?" said Merlin.

"No," replied Hal. "I remember—remember——"

His lips quivered, and he seemed as though his voice would not give utterance to another word.

He buried his face in his hands to hide his emotion; the tears trickled between his fingers as he turned his face to the wall.

"Come, come, comrade," said Will Merry, laying his hand on his friend's shoulder.

"What's the matter, Will?" asked Merlin. "Have you got a piece of dirt in your eye?"

"Yes," replied Captain Merry, in a husky voice, as he wiped the tears that had forced their way to his eye-lids. "Come, Hal, old boy, don't give way like this; it makes me feel as though I had got a lump sticking in my throat and I can't get it either up or down."

He turned his head away to hide his weakness.

He was very much attached to his companions, and so they were all to each other, only Will Merry was very tender-hearted, and he could not controul his feelings, though he did not like to let them be observed; he turned his head aside as I have before mentioned.

"What is it that's been amiss?" asked Merlin of Hal.

Will Merry turned aside as Merlin approached their companion.

"Bother it," he said, rubbing his eyes. "I can't get the piece of dirt out."

Merlin laughed as he remarked,

"Dirty water, my old boy, keeps overflowing."

Will Merry looked all the disgust he felt, and that's more than I can explain.

Hal had been having a desperate struggle to keep down his emotion that ever and anon would overpower him.

"Come, comrade, drink this draught of sparkling wine," said Merlin.

Will stood behind him, waiting for the remainder of the song.

"Go on," he said, "give us the next part."

"Of what?" asked Merlin Hawke.

"The sparkling wine, sir."

"You shall have it."

He got it.

Not the air, but the wine-dregs in his eyes.

Hal could not repress a smile at seeing the wry-face Will made.

"Brayvo!" shouted Captain Will. "Cheer up, comrade, we have exciting business to do to-morrow."

"Eh?" said Hal, in a low, quivering voice. "I would I could cheer up; but last night's adventure has blighted my happiness."

"Say not so," said Merlin. "We brave knights of the road should not be downcast through love."

"No! Hal Hunter is no love-sick spoony, nor neither does he forget his position."

"What has happened?" inquired Captain Merry.

"Listen," said Hal, "and I will tell you."

The trio sat round the fire, and Merlin poured the wine out; he and Will listened attentively to their friend's story.

"When you escaped last night," Hal began, "I was with the judge's niece, Bella. Several times in the course of the evening I was recognised by old Admiral Banjemore; but by threatening him with a big pistol he kept his tongue quiet for a short time. I saw Will escape with his fair companion directly after you had slain that interfering noble."

A look of regret came over Merlin's face as his friend spoke of the deed he had committed in self defence, and he said,

"I should not have done it only I had no other way of escaping; then I had to run for it."

"I saw your retreat," continued Hal, "and thinking that my best plan would be to take home my partner, I accordingly hastened away to prevent any further interruption. I had not proceeded far down the road before I was startled by a terrific shout that rung through the air, and called out in one long breath (the fellow must have had good lungs), 'Stop! highwayman, thief, and murderer! Stand! or I will fire and bring you to the ground.' I was very much astonished at the suddenness of the outbreak, and the lady trembled and clung to my arm. She knew the voice; it was a friend of the judge's, a dandy, who had offered a very handsome sum of money to the judge for her hand, which was greedily accepted by the ugly old brute."

"Which, the money or the lady's hand?" inquired Will, interrupting Hal.

Hal laughed, and said,

"The money."

"Oh," said Will, "there is nothing like being sure."

"Nothing," remarked Merlin, stroking his friend across the nose. "Perhaps you will let a fellow continue his story?"

"With pleasure."

"Thank you," said Hal, recommencing. "In a minute he had reached us even before the strain of his melodious voice had time to die away. 'Release the lady,' he began. I told him to go to the devil, upon which he drew his rapier; I did likewise; but before we had time to cross swords the old admiral (the old wretch seems to hunt me up like the devil), and Bella's respectable guardian, old Judge Blenheim——but to bring my story to a close, they wanted me to give the lady to the parasite and be quietly arrested. I, as a matter of course, refused to comply with either of their wishes, and in an instant the young nobleman rushed upon me, but I shook him off; again he rushed at me, and, with the aid of the other two, they tore the lady from me, though she clung to me affectionately. My passion was aroused by that dastardly act, and before I knew where I was thrusting, my sword flew through the body of the young stranger. Oh, horror! a shriek followed from Bella; she fell to the earth."

He hid his face as he finished speaking, and groaned loudly.

"What followed!" asked Captain Merry, eagerly.

"Officers," replied Hal.

Merlin laughed loudly at the quick reply, and Hal began again.

"I was maddened by the sight; my accursed weapon must have gone through her tender flesh as well. Before I had time to raise her inanimate form a signal brought at least a score of officers to the spot. I saw my danger, and cutting my way through them I started off at a maddened pace. I was hotly pursued; they did not gain on me, though they kept me well in sight. To elude them, I turned down some narrow courts and a street. A terrified shout saluted me from behind, then I remember no more until I awoke to find myself in the care of a very pretty nurse."

"Then we know the rest of your adventure," said Merlin.

"I shan't forget it for some time," said Will Merry.

Hal was told the remainder of his adventure, and as Will concluded they gave a hearty good laugh.

The old wine made them sleepy, and they retired to rest; they were not long before they were locked in the arms of slumber, where they passively lay until morning.

Their horses were brought to them by an ostler who had had the charge of them since they had been in London.

The animals were very fresh, and went on their long journey with a swiftness that soon brought them to the haunt of the Black Hawke's.

*　　*　　*　　*　　*　　*　　*

We will now take another look at the two captives, or rather prisoners, of Newgate.

Two days had not improved our young heroes; they had neither eaten more than they could possibly help during their stay.

Frank sat on his hard couch buried in deep reverie; his face had lost its bright, cheerful look that it had but a few days previous, and his eyes were sunken, and had a strange look about them.

"Two days and nights have we been here, and yet have not heard or seen any of our companions," he soliloquised, doubtfully, his face undergoing a peculiar change as he spoke. "Something must have happened that has prevented them from coming. To-morrow all hopes will be fled unless they come just at the last moment."

He looked searchingly around, and, getting up, he looked through a grating at the back of his cell.

"A cheerful-looking place," he said. "His majesty's court yard for the reception of such guests as I and Albert to take our last promenade before we ascend the ladder that will take us to heaven; but the worst of it is they hasten us by the aid of a rope—very kind of them. Never mind, I will consult my comrade on the cheerful subject."

As he finished his self-conversation he approached the wall and removed the bricks as before.

"Albert," he said, in a whisper.

Albert, who was lost in deep thought, suddenly jumped up, and hastened to where his friend was.

"I thought we should never see each other any more," said Lord Montague, in a tremulous voice.

"Never despair, old boy," said Frank.

"I should not despair only I do not like the idea of that villanous hound enjoying that which belongs to me."

He will not enjoy it much longer."

"There is no hope of our escape, therefore he will triumphantly keep possession."

"There is still hope I know; our companions are too faithful to leave us to the mercy of the law; even if they do not come to-night I shall not give up the hopes of rescue until the rope is round my neck."

Albert shivered at the last sentence, and his hand involuntarily wandered to his throat.

Frank laughed as he saw the innocent way in which it was done.

"Here's our friend coming again," said Frank. "Good-bye."

"Good-bye," said Albert, as his friend's head vanished. "We shall see each other in the morning."

Frank answered as he replaced the last brick.

"The time's drawing nigh," said the gaoler, trying to taunt the captain by his words.

Frank only laughed at the man as though he heeded little what was said to him, though at the same time every word went to his heart's core like a keen dagger.

The gaoler, finding that his taunting words did not take much effect on Frank, went to the next cell, where he met with more success.

"I have got a long score to settle with you," muttered Frank, as the fellow closed the gate. "I shall not forget to pay it when I get free again."

"Why have you come here to taunt me?" asked Albert, of the malicious brute.

The man laughed with savage glee as he saw the effect, and he continued,

"To-morrow morning will be your last day in this land of glory. You may as well make a clean breast of it, and tell us where the rest of the band are to be found."

"Hound!" shouted his young lordship. "By heaven, if you stand there I will fell you to the ground."

The man laughed defiantly.

He would not have laughed so freely had he known the state of his prisoner.

Owing to the smallness of Albert's hands, he had worked the manacles off his wrists, and now he sat with the handcuffs lying across his wrists, but with one hand he held them firmly at the end.

"Have you said yer prayers?" said the fellow, grinning.

His grinning soon changed to a long, dismal, howling visage.

Albert had got his hands free, and he could not stand being taunted by one so inferior, though at the present he was placed over him.

His lordship could not stand the last words the fellow sneeringly put to him, and like a young tiger suddenly he sprang upon his tormentor.

The gaoler was quite astounded for a few minutes. He did not expect to be thus suddenly attacked.

He soon recovered, and a desperate struggle ensued.

Albert would have fared badly—his assailant was a huge muscular giant compared with the slender form of his prisoner.

He had clutched hold of Albert, and held him above his head with his two hands.

In another minute he would have dashed the young nobleman on the stones; but his murderous act was prevented just in time.

Frank had heard the scuffle, and guessed its cause, as he had got his manacles off by the aid of his friend picking them with a rusty nail he found, and in an instant he scrambled through the hole and rushed to his friend's assistance.

Frank slowly lowered the gaoler's arms until Albert's feet reached the ground, then he struck the sinewy brute to the earth with the iron manacles; young Montague seconded the blow with like instruments as he fell.

"That's settled him," remarked Frank, when they had stunned the man by a succession of blows,

"Can we escape now?" asked Albert, looking wistful at the open door.

"No; to attempt that would be sudden death."

"We can but die once, so we may as well in the attempt of escape, as be choked in the morning before a crowd of hooting spectators."

"It would be madness; we should not get twenty yards before we should be made bullet cases of."

"There is no hope for us now," said Albert, despairingly.

"There is hope while there is life," replied Frank, "and I feel confident that our friends will come to our aid even at the last minute."

Albert shook his head despondently.

"We will remove this carcase outside," said Frank.

So they did, and Frank stayed with his friend until the morning.

They were awakened early by a religious personage entering, robed in black.

"Reveal all to me, and you shall be forgiven," he said, after some long talking.

"Go to the devil," replied Frank.

"Think, my dear brethren—"

"Don't lie; our brethren are all honourable gentlemen," said Frank, interrupting him.

"It will not be long before you will be quickly sent to eternity," continued the reverend gentleman; "consider the many sins you have committed, and when you quit this earth you will have to answer before your Maker."

"Then," said Frank, "that will be sufficient. I shall not answer to you, for I know you have not the power of forgiving people their sins."

"But I can pray for you."

"Thank you, I can do that myself."

"Think what a wicked sinner thou art—"

"Look you, go, or by the Lord Harry, I shall turn you out," said Frank, getting exasperated.

The reverend gentleman, gathering up his robe, darted out.

Frank followed, and gave him a parting kick that made the pious gentleman hop away with his eyes turned into the back of his head.

"That's the way to get rid of all such humbugs as he," said Frank.

Albert thought it a very good way, although he did not answer.

Their breakfast was brought in extra early on this occasion, and they had scarcely had time to partake of it when they heard the doleful bell tolling forth their death knell that took their appetite away, and gave them a peculiar sort of stomach ache.

The chaplain again enters, with the hangman, and several other servants that came to attend upon our friends.

Frank takes everything cool, and answers everything he is asked in a manner so that they could not glean any information that they wanted to know.

At the same time Albert is sullen, and will not answer a word that is put to him.

They are led out after the usual ceremony, and ascend the gallows.

Horror! the scene outside Newgate is heartrending!

The young highwaymen's cheeks turn pale, and a thrill runs through their frames.

Thousands of the lowest tribe have assembled to witness the execution.

The hallooing and hooting is fearful. Each person is anxious to squeeze his way to the front, eager to catch a word that may be said, and see the last death struggle.

A fearful yell from the crowd greets the prisoners as they ascend the gallows.

Many a blasphemous oath and curse escaped the lips of some ill-looking brute as he received a descending stick or stone on his head.

Frank looks down upon the crowd, and a flush spreads his handsome face.

The young knights are roughly handled; their arms are pinioned behind them, their legs are secured, then they are placed beneath the noose that will squeeze their life from their bodies, unless there is some providential rescue made in time.

Prayers are read to them.

All hope of rescue has fled, though their eyes search through the crowd of idlers.

The hangman tears the lace cravats from their throats, their coats are torn open, and their throats are left bare for the rope to encircle.

The caps are put over their heads.

Another moment and it would have been too late.

The executioner is about to put the noose over their heads.

A yell of fear, yet defiance, rings through the air.

The young prisoners start.

It is not a shout from the surrounding spectators.

It is a yell that the young highwaymen well recognise.

Another and another follow the first, each time getting nearer.

The people scream, and are scattered on all sides, as a body of black horsemen dash in their midst.

A body of soldiers, that have been under the gallows to guard the prisoners from escaping, attack the intruders.

"Forward, men!" shouts a well-known voice.

It is Merlin Hawke, with his band of brave men, come to the rescue of their friends.

"Thank God, we are saved!" are the words that escape Albert's lips under the tight-fitting cap.

"Cut every one down that gets in your way, men!" shouted Will Merry, setting the example by giving one of the officers in command of the soldiery a cut with his sword.

"Charge!" thundered an officer to his men.

A deafening report followed his command.

Then came shrieks of agony and pain.

Not from their intended victims, but the crowd who make good their flight.

The highwaymen had dashed past the soldiers as the word for fire was given, and, with the swiftness that they whirled round the soldiers, missed their aim, and the highwaymen escaped the intended volley.

But the crowd suffered for it.

The scene is one of fearful confusion.

The soldiers are fighting desperately to guard the prisoners from the attack, and the highwaymen fight only for their comrades.

Men are falling on both sides frightfully cut and gashed.

The three captains lead the highwaymen on to another attack; the soldiers fall like dummies, and the highwaymen gain an entrance to Newgate.

A shout of triumph follows their success.

The soldiers and men that are employed in various ways in prison rush after the daring fellows, but they are beaten back.

The three captains, with some of the men, gain the gallows, while the remainder of the band keep all meddling people down.

The two captains are now released from their critical position.

A shout of "hurrah" rends the air as their faces are uncovered.

The hangman and chaplain are seized, the nooses that were intended for the young captains are put round their sinful old necks, the traps are removed from beneath their feet, and they do a jig in the air.

The rest of the men who were to superintend in the execution are pierced through the head, and then thrown amongst the astonished crowd.

Another minute sees the five captains outside the prison

mounted on beautiful chargers that would give chase to any then kept by government.

A word of command from their president, and the band mustered together.

The soldiers tried to oppose the highwaymen with fixed bayonets.

They soon fell beneath the terrified cut from the highwaymen's long swords.

The crowd were so enthusiastic at the daring way in which the noble men saved their comrades that they could not repress a cheer, and a clapping of rough hands plainly showed our heroes that the spectators were on their side to encourage them, as in some future time their help might be useful. Every one of the highwaymen that had money with them threw it among the crowd.

"Hurrah for the Black Hawke's highwaymen! hurrah! hurrah! hurrah!"

Such was the confused shouting that followed that generous act.

The highwaymen formed a ring round their captains.

Will Merry rode forward, his beautiful plumed hat in hand; he addressed his comrades and the people as follows,

"Now, comrades and public in general, give one last good cheer for our noble leader, Captain Merlin Hawke."

A deafening roar of many voices rang through them in approval to what Captain Will had said.

Captain Merlin Hawke raised his head, and made an elegant bow, then rode away with his companions, leaving the inspired throng to scramble for the spoil.

(*To be continued.*)

THE PHANTOM'S WARNING;
A LEGEND OF THE TIME OF RICHARD THE THIRD.
(*Continued from page* 64.)

As he uttered the last sentence, he seized the royal banner of England in his hand, and waved it aloft amid the shouts of "Long live King Richard!" "Long live brave Glo'ster!" "No baby King!"

The colour quitted the Lady Anne's cheek as she lifted up her eyes to gaze on the duke, who stood with flushed brow on the throne, holding the flag at arm's length, in a warlike attitude, and pointing with his drawn sword to the rich emblazoning enwrought thereon. The guests in the hall also stood up, amid loud huzzas, and the waving of drinking vessels, and deafening shouts, mingled with the sound of music, and the cries of "Long live Richard the Third!"

When the din had a little subsided, Glo'ster and his attendants took their departure, for their steeds had long been waiting in the court-yard. The Lady Anne, with Bridget. Crosby and other ladies, also arose, and left the hall amid the drunken cheers of the guests, and entered the great dining parlour. But even there the noise of the revellers penetrated as they broke out at intervals in rude songs, or drank to the long reign of Richard. For many of Buckingham's followers were there, and had received instructions to prepare the minds of all present for the information that Glo'ster would soon be king.

It does not come within the limits of our tale to follow Glo'ster to the Tower, and describe his interview with Hastings, whom he caused to be beheaded a few hours after his departure from the banquet, neither have we space to follow all his actions until he obtained the crown; we shall confine ourselves more particularly to those which took place at Crosby Hall.

Another morning had arisen, and all sounds of revelry were hushed in the hall; some of the guests had fallen asleep upon the floor, and there remained during the night; others had retired to their homes, and the Lady Anne, attended by Bridget Crosby, who had now become her confidant, were walking in the pleasaunce, or pleasure-garden that extended behind the north end of the building.

It was a beautiful spot, laid out after the quaint manner of the period, and contained many of those old flowers whose names we have yet retained, and many of them are now only to be found in their wild state. Hedges of box were cut into grotesque forms, peacocks and dragons, and fish, and fanciful shapes which had no living forms. By the side of moss-roses and sweet williams, grew wind flowers, and canterbury bells, and adder's tongue, and cuckoo flowers, heart's-ease, and true love, and many others, which were supposed to flower only on particular days dedicated to different saints. Anne appeared dejected, and walked along the serpent-like gravel paths in silence, sometimes glancing on Bridget's face, then on the ground.

"I have a great love for flowers," said Bridget. "Father Philip maintains that many of them are holy, and blow in honour of the saints."

"He is right I trow," answered the Lady Anne, "for I have often taken note of the Christmas rose, which beareth flowers at that time, and hath wrought many miracles, which the good fathers at Glastonbury avouch. The snow-drop also appeareth about the time of purification, an emblem of purity."

"And the yellow crocus," said Bridget, "puts forth on good St. Valentine's day, and the daisy on St. Margaret's, for it is Margaret's herb, and I have some rhymes written by one Geoffrey Chaucer, where he says,

"'And in special one called so of the day,
The day's-eye, a flower white and red.]
And in French called *La belle Marguerite*,
O commendable flower and most in mind.'

"Which we do even now call Margaret's flower."

"And the early daffodil," said Anne, "blows on St. David's day, and the golden pilewort on St. Perpetua's, and the crown imperial never fails to appear on the celebration of St. Edward."

"Marry, but Our Lady's smock is a flower that always obeys the Holy Virgin's behest, and cometh to commemorate her annunciation; a true type of her innocence are its silvery bells," said Bridget.

"So have I deemed in sooth," replied Anne, "that the bright marigold is like the glory that circles her holy brow, and Father Ambrose avouches that it was named Mary's-gold, after the halo that emanates therefrom, which we see enwrought on the chapel window; the blue-bell also cometh on St. George's day, for it was a colour he loved when on earth, and a flower he held sacred."

"And I have made comment of many," said Bridget, "that others have made no mention of, such as the yellow flag, flowering on St. Nicodemede, and the red poppy on St. Barnabas' day, and the scarlet lychin on St. John the Baptist's; but most white flowers appear in honour of the Blessed Virgin, and the white lily never fails to grace the day of her visitation, but the midsummer rose always begins to fade at the feast of Mary Magdalen."

"There are many mysteries hidden in flowers I trow," replied the Lady Anne, "signs and resemblances that we wot not of, and deep meanings which were known to the holy fathers of old, but are now forgotten; I would that we were conversant with all their types and sacred emblems."

They had by this time reached an old summer-house, dark with the twines of ivy, and redolent with the perfume of woodbine, and here they seated themselves, listening to the birds that chanted their merry songs from the surrounding trees—for the wealth of acres stretched out behind Crosby Hall, rich in gardens and pastures, and fruitful orchards.

"I feel very spiritless this morning, sweet Bridget," said Anne, sighing deeply; "I had but little sleep all night long, and what I had was broken by frightful dreams, enough to make a brave heart blench; my husband, too, awoke me, thrice calling on Clarence and on Hastings in his sleep, and trembling like a guilty wretch whose reckoning hour is come."

"I do not love his grace," said Bridget, "so well as I was wont; methinks there was but little need to take off Hastings' head, as they did yesternight."

"And is the good lord dead?" said Lady Anne. "Ah, well-a-day, and I did fear 'twas so. Bridget, it will be my turn next to die, for in his sleep last night I heard him mutter my name, as if he thought that I was pleading for my life; I heard him say distinctly, 'Anne my wife must die,' and then he clutched me fiercely by the arm, until I shrieked for pain, and he awoke and said, 'hush! hush! 'twas but a dream.'"

"Holy Mary shield us!" ejaculated Bridget; "in sooth I do believe, that in our dreams we are forewarned of things that come to pass, and that good saints do visit us in visions, and that the spirits of those we loved, or have injured, hover around our pillows, blessing us in sleep or filling our minds with thoughts of bale and terrible images."

"Oh, Bridget!" exclaimed Anne, "my conscience oft reproaches me, and my heart quails within me when I think of those who are no more; and all that I have loved and doated on are gone; indeed, I would not wish to live, and yet I fear to die. I dreamed last night that the young princes lay lifeless on a wild sea shore, and oh! methought their cold, dead fingers were pointed to me; and as I gazed, a huge wave came and washed me in the sea, and on the yeasty waves we all three rode—the living and the dead! and that the foam in its fierce fury loosened their pale arms, and then they clasped me, cold as chilling ice, and then a voice came from the deep—it sounded like my Edward's—and called me to come away; and then methought the waves assumed Glo'ster's face, and that on every ridge his arm arose grasping a bloody sword, the very same with which he slew my lord at Tewksbury. Then the scene changed, and I was here in Crosby Hall in bed alone, and men in armour came with daggers in their hands, and held a lamp above my head, and as one uplifted his arm to strike me, I shrieked with fear and woke, and then I slept again, and the same men appeared with lights and daggers. Oh, Bridget, I do fear that ere many more days are darkened, I shall have run my race; but I am half prepared, such bodings are true warnings."

"Ah me! I like not your dream, lady," said Bridget, "and in these large chambers, and winding galleries, any one might come and take away our lives ere one could cry, 'God help me.' I would my father were alive and in this home again, and you would leave these plotting courtiers, and dwell with us. Make known unto the prioress your fears; methinks she would protect you, for no one dares to invade the sanctity of the Priory."

"Thou deemest wrong, fair Bridget," replied Anne, "the assassin's dagger hath reached the holy altar ere now; and I am Glo'ster's wife, I know not how, no more than the poor bird that trembling gazes on the dreaded serpent until immersed within its jaws, when it should have flown away. I cannot flee away; he hath a power over me which I cannot resist, a spell I cannot break, although it leads me on to death."

Anne threw her head upon Bridget's shoulder, as she uttered the last sentence, and wept bitterly. At length a page entered the garden, and announced a message from the Duke of Glo'ster, summoning her to Westminster to be crowned queen. A deep shuddering pervaded Anne when she heard the news, and had not Bridget supported her she would have fallen upon the flower-bed by which she stood. When the page had received an answer that she would attend shortly, and had retired, Anne again gave full vent to the current of her sorrows."

"Oh, Bridget," said she, "I go to be made queen; happy should I be to live with thee, and pour my sorrows on thy bosom, but now I shall have no one to listen to me. None but

the liveried menials of a court, ready to fulfil their king's behest to bring the goblet or the dagger. It will not be for aye, Anne's days are numbered."

"Nay, lady, say not so, his grace may yet mean well," replied Bridget; "and you can again return to Crosby Hall, and I will shew you all the flowers, and old Cornelius, the gardener, will tell us all the names they bear. Stay not away, sweet lady; I do love you as my mother, and will be more than a daughter to you. Importune his grace to let you soon return, even when your coronation is over."

"I will! I will!" answered Anne, "my heart can never be wholly desolate while it has one like thee to cling to."

They again embraced each other, and separated in tears just as Lord Stanley appeared at a turning of the garden walk to urge her departure. Steeds were in readiness in the courtyard; the one which Lady Anne mounted was richly caparisoned, the trappings were of gold and silver, and the saddlecloth was emblazoned with the arms of England. A knight in armour held the bridle, and at the sound of the trumpet the lady and her attendants disappeared, and the ring of their horses' hoofs echoed through the arched hall, mingled with the dying cadence of silver-snaring trumpets.

CHAPTER III.

THERE was a sound of merriment in London: bells were ringing and bonfires blazing, and voices shouted in the streets, "Long live King Richard and his Royal Queen." Many a brawl ensued, and many a sword leaped from its scabbard on the night that followed the coronation of Glo'ster; for parties met in the thoroughfares of the metropolis, as they returned from their late revels, and shout was opposed to shout, some exclaiming, "Long live the house of Lancaster! Down with the white rose of York," which was answered by "Down with the bloody house of Lancaster! Long reign King Richard the Third!" for a strong feeling still existed among some of the citizens in favour of Queen Margaret. Others also exclaimed, "Long live King Edward the Fifth! Down with the Usurper," for Glo'ster had already become obnoxious to many through his acts of cruelty; indeed, there were proofs given afterwards of his unpopularity, when such numbers revolted, and joined the standard of Richmond; for during the two years of his reign, and the one which preceded it, he had been the means of shedding more royal blood than had been spilt in many battles.

But, amid all these mingled sounds of joy and tumult, there was one sad heart, and one thoughtful brow on which the crown sat heavily—a cavern of dark ruminations, which the splendour of a diadem could not radiate; for Queen Anne had retired alone, to sigh over her sorrows in Crosby Hall, while King Richard kept his court, and pursued his daring plans in the palace.

Several days had elapsed since the coronation, and during that time the queen had resided in the south wing of the hall, while the great dining-parlour and throne-room were put in order, and decorated with becoming splendour for a queen. It was a portion of King Richard's policy to spare no wealth, which might add to his greatness in outward show, and yet appear as if done solely for the comfort and love he bore to his wife, which could not fail of being rumoured abroad, and would in the end serve as a cloak for the furtherance of his designs. It was his intention, after the death of Anne, to wed the daughter of Queen Elizabeth, widow of Edward the Fourth, and thereby prevent Richmond from laying any claim to the crown through marriage, thus hoping to crush for ever the power of the house of Lancaster. How far his plans were succcessful history has recorded; and Shakspeare has also thrown the poetry of undying thought over his deeds, which will live when the annals of history are doubted. It only comes within the limits of our narrative to dwell upon such portions of his life as were connected with the fate of his queen, and took place within Crosby Hall.

All the old furniture had been removed from the great dining-parlour, and it had been fitted up in the most costly style; almost every quarter of the globe had contributed to its splendour: for the many wars in which England had engaged during the last three reigns had made a great revolution in the domestic arrangements of the English, causing them to import and copy the manufactures and luxuries of foreign nations ; there being as much competition among the English nobles in outvying each other in showy grandeur as there is in our day in two rival houses of Bloomsbury endeavouring to eclipse each other in dress. The dining-parlour walls were now hung with rich arras of purple velvet, edged with gold, which reached down beyond the wainscoting : there was something heavy in its richness—an appearance of solemn splendour, but this might be owing to the dim light which streamed forth in such a variety of hues from the deep-dyed windows. The chairs—or rather stools, for such they might be termed when compared to what we now use—were also covered with velvet cushions, matching the drapery upon the walls ; the woodwork was black and bright, and wore the appearance of ebony—and was richly carved, or rather heavily, for there was a massiveness in the foliage thereon enwrought. In place of rushes the floor was now covered with carpet, or more properly tapestry, for the trees and flowers were worked upon it after the manner of modern embroidery, but ruder than a girl's first sampler, and much after that fashion. The trees were all made to rule, triangular, with a shaft in the centre for a stem, bearing no bad resemblance to a dunce's cap placed upon a walking stick. The flowers also appeared like cherries fastened upon a splinter of wood, each matching each, as old women array them to catch the eye of passing urchins. The colours were gaudy in the extreme, and at a distant glance gave you no bad idea of the drapery of harlequin. The table was of old English oak, covered also with a cloth of velvet, in union with that upon the walls. At one end of the room stood a recess : it was so formed as to face the entrance door ; its leaves were thrown open, and displayed a rich array of plate, gold and silver, and in curious devices, some of them bearing the impress of the royal arms of England. The iron lamps were also removed, and others of silver swung in their places, bearing the forms of flying dragons. Such was the appearance of the dining-parlour ; part of the furniture had been removed from the palace, for Richard had his secret reason for keeping his queen at Crosby Hall, and had intended proposing what she so eagerly solicited.

But the throne-room above, if it was possible, excelled the lower apartment in grandeur. It was hung with the richest drapery, tapestry of gold and silver, on which was represented, in no mean style of execution, the wars of the Titans ; gods stood out in gold, upheaving massy mountains of silver, and tearing up rocks from their bases, or grasping trees in their hands, while others showered the forked lightning from above, or darted down golden thunder-bolts. At the end of the apartment, facing the chamber door which we have already described, stood a splendid throne, or chair of state, and of sufficient dimensions to contain two persons ; it was raised three steps from the floor, and surmounted by a canopy of crimson velvet ; the cushions and curtains were also of the same costly material. On the top of the canopy were two crowns, resembling those worn by the king and queen of England. A golden boar stood grinning above these, as if looking on the splendour below in triumph. This was the king's crest, when duke of Glo'ster.

The chairs, or settles—for they were shaped much like the high-backed benches we now see in tap-rooms, only lower at the back—were also covered with crimson velvet ; white roses of silver were emblazoned upon them. Over the fire-place, which alone was unencumbered with drapery, hung several valuable pictures, the productions of eminent masters, which were brought to England among other spoils of war. Marble statues, too, ornamented this apartment, such as had once graced the galleries of Italy. In this room were seated Queen Anne and Bridget Crosby, side by side, upon one of the richly-covered seats. It was night, and silver lamps shed their bright beams over the apartment ; the oil was perfumed and sent forth a pleasant odour. Everything around wore an air of comfort and majesty, but the pale face of the queen unharmonized with the scene. There was a deep melancholy upon her brow, and a tear stood upon her silken lashes ; even Bridget sat with folded hands, like one who dared not offer comfort, and was attentively

listening to the queen, who had paused in her conversation to gather strength to proceed, for she appeared greatly excited.

"Was it after the shedding of blood in the field of Tewkesbury," said Bridget, "that the Prince, your husband, was murdered ?"

" Alas !" sighed Queen Anne, "it was ; had he fallen in the fight he would have saved me many tears. But he died nobly—heaven rest his soul !—asserting his rights, even in the teeth of those who took his life, and might now have been England's king, but for the dagger of my present lord."

" May heaven forgive him for the deed !" ejaculated Bridget·

"Amen !" responded Anne ; "and may the Holy Mother intercede for him for murdering my husband's father."

"It was a dark day for England," said Bridget, "when they first gathered the white and red roses, and from the fairest flowers drew the foulest factions."

"Little rest has my country had from that hour," replied the queen ; "it has caused many a son to shed the life of his father, and father of son. Ah ! woe is me since the red rose fell—since the house of Lancaster was shorn of its plumes, for then I lost one who was a dove to me, but to his enemies a sweeping eagle. And I have been deluded by the wily tongue of a poisonous serpent more subtle than that which tempted our first mother."

" Think you, my lady," enquired Bridget, "that his majesty gave sanction to the destruction of the princes in the Tower ?"

"I am too certain of it," replied the queen, "even as much so as if I had heard him give orders for their death ; nay, I do believe that Dighton and Forrest, whom the king has appointed for our guards, were they who smothered the pretty babes. 'Tis well well known that they destroyed Clarence, and for their villanies have been advanced by the king. Oh, Bridget ! whenever I look at Forrest methinks there is murder written on his brow, and it was such a face as his that bent over me in my dream with a dagger in his hand."

"But," continued Bridget, "I heard his majesty say that if any of your attendants were obnoxious he begged you would discharge them ; marry, I would not allow such a brace of unhanged knaves as they appear to come in my presence."

(To be concluded in our next.)

BLACK HAWKE, THE HIGHWAYMAN.

MINNETTE.

CHAPTER XIX.

WILL MERRY KEEPS AN APPOINTMENT—HIS DREAM OF LOVE—AN INTERRUPTION — THE DUEL—THE SECRET PANEL—CAPTAIN WILL ENTOMBED ALIVE — CAPTAIN HAWKE STOPS A COACH ON HAMMERSMITH BRIDGE, AND SAVES A FAIR LADY—THE ROBBERY—MERLIN HAWKE FALLS INTO THE HANDS OF A BAND OF OUTLAWS, AND IS HANGED.

"WHICH way does my friend take?" asked Merlin.

"I have an appointment to keep," remarked Will Merry.

"With a lady?" asked Hal.

"As beautiful as one," replied Will.

"If it is the same one as I saw you with at the masquerade she is beautiful indeed," said Merlin.

"It is the same."

"Then, may you meet with success," replied Merlin Hawke.

"If I meet with any fellow I shall pitch into him," said Will Merry. "And now you know my business, may I ask where our friend Hal is going?"

"You may," replied Hal.

"But would you answer?"

"Yes."

"Then let's hear your adventure on hand?"

"It is a sad one. I am going to the judge's in disguise to see his niece, if she still lives, which I shall ascertain to-night."

"We," said Frank, insinuating himself and Albert, "shall go to the haunt."

"I shall be there in a few days," said Merlin, "until then au revoir."

They each rode different ways, except two who were going to the haunt with the band.

Will Merry rode as far as Kensington, when he halted before a magnificent mansion that lay back from the road.

Dismounting his steed, he knocked at the door.

His summons was answered by a handsome-looking page, and he was ushered into an elegantly-furnished apartment.

"You will say that Captain Delmore requests an interview with her ladyship, Ellen," said Will Merry.

As the page was about to retire, a lady of magnificent grace and beauty glided into the room, her long silk dress trailing the ground that gave her a grand stately air.

Captain Will's handsome face flushed as his gaze rested on her heaving white bosom that was exposed by her low dress

"Captain Delmore," she said, smiling pleasantly at him as she spoke, "I thought you had forgotten your promise."

"That is cruel to speak thus," said Will. "How could I forget one so fair and beautiful?"

"You flatter me," she said. "Come, this is not a fit place for us; we will go to a more secluded place."

Will followed her.

As she led the way up a spacious staircase he rather liked the idea of being in a secluded place with such a fair companion.

"This will be a more fitting place for our love-making," said Lady Ellen, coquettishly, as she pushed open a door and entered an apartment that would have graced a palace.

Will Merry looked round in surprise at its costly furniture. She threw herself carelessly on a couch.

Will took his seat by her side.

He felt in a very critical position to be alone with one so fair.

Her beauty would have tempted an anchorite.

Will was more quick and passionate than that solitary being.

His hot blood mounted his cheeks, as her soft, pliant, round arms were encircled round his neck, and drew him passionately towards her.

He seemed to be in a trance; her tempting beauty made him forget all the honour he held the fair sex in.

Their lips were glued together in passionate kisses, when Lady Ellen sprang to her feet.

Captain Will made a clutch at her, but she vanished before he had time to stay her.

In a few minutes she returned. She had changed her attire. She blushed as she caught the captain's gaze fixed on her.

Will was enraptured by her surpassing beauty.

"I have not been long," she said, as she glided down by his side. "I was hot in my other dress."

Certainly she had changed her dress to advantage, as Will thought.

What she had on when she re-entered the room where Captain Will sat—rather surprised at her abrupt departure—could scarcely be called a dress.

It was a light gossamer robe, fastened round the waist with a silk girdle, open in front, so that when she walked, you could see the whole of her delicious breast.

Will muttered some inaudible reply to what she had said, and passing his arm round her lissom waist, pressed her form to his.

Such contact as this would make delirious a man less impressionable than Will Merry.

As for him, he was in dreamy ecstacy.

Never in his life before had he beheld such rare loveliness of form; so rounded, firm, and seductive a bosom; such softly proportioned and large limbs.

Her robe clung to her limbs, as she threw herself into different attitudes, and showed every wrinkle in her well-moulded limbs.

Lady Ellen's mind seemed to be wandering. Yielding to the fiery influence which was possessing her lover, their kisses grew hotter, and at length, forgetting everything but the present, she lay half-fainting in his arms, and yielded up to his love.

Their dream of passion over, reflection came to his mind.

A look of regret seemed to pass over the highwayman's face as he sat toying with her long tresses, that hung in profusion over her shoulders.

Lady Ellen nestled her head on Captain Will's breast.

He could feel the warm thrill of her pliant form beneath his own, and as their lips met, she looked reproachfully at him.

"I feared you would not come," she said, after a long time of silence.

"Not come?" he said, tenderly. "Could I stay from you? I feared, too, that you might be in danger."

"Why, darling?"

"Through taking the part of that highwayman."

"He is a noble fellow, and has been driven to what he is."

"But you might have been taken for aiding him in his escape."

"Lady Ellen Curtis," he said, "my love for you would make me dare more than that."

"But was it not a strange idea?"

"How else could I act in such a case? He has on more than one occasion saved my life, and for his generous courage I could not see him taken."

"You are so daring and brave, Captain Delmore. What other name shall I call you?"

"Will, dearest—call me Will."

"It was so generous of you to aid him in his escape."

"Not so generous as you are beautiful."

"But had you been taken?" she said.

"In all probability I should have suffered."

He had not told her that he was one of the brotherhood belonging to Captain Merlin Hawke; neither did she think for one instant that he was a highwayman, though he had been accused as being Will Merry belonging to the band of highwaymen known as Black Hawke's.

Which was an undeniable fact.

But he strongly denied it.

And she believed him, loved him, and now he feared to undeceive her by telling her the truth.

Looking at her, as they sat entwined in each other's arms, he felt that he could not lose her.

Yet he feared to reveal to her his proper character for fear that it should make her unhappy.

"Yet she must know it sooner or later," he said to himself, "so here goes. What if I were not Captain Delmore?"

"Not!"

"What if I were Captain Will Merry instead?"

"Will! Dear Delmore, you are really not in earnest?"

"But how if I am Captain Will Merry?"

"It would break my heart," she said; "but I should still love you."

"I am not worthy of such confiding love."

"Why not?"

"No matter now, I may be more worthy of your love some day."

He kissed her with a long, lingering kiss, and again thought how beautiful she was, then sighed sadly.

"What is the matter, Will, dear?" she asked, seeing that he was lost in deep thought.

"Nothing, dearest!" he said. "Do you love me very much?"

"Do I love you, Delmore? How can you ask?"

"Something seems to tell me that you love more than me?"

"That is unkind."

Smiling tenderly in her face, he said,

"Why do you love me?"

"I could not help it," she answered, blushing.

"Yet we are comparative strangers," he said; "a day may come when you will regret this."

"Never, Will, dear! never!"

"You are betrothed to another?"

"I will never be his, I would rather die!"

"He has the right to claim you?"

"He shall not have me, Delmore; I will only be yours, so that you are always true."

"You are rich," he said, "Ellen; you would not give your love to one so poor as I am?"

"Poor?" she said, doubtingly.

"Very poor."

"It cannot be. Your jewels are worth a dukedom."

"To-morrow I may be hunted from place to place like a murderer by the hands of the law !"

"Will, dear !"

"An outlaw !" he said.

She shuddered, and clung to him with a startled cry.

"How, then, my dearest, would you still love me ?"

"Through all," she said, passionately ; "let your fate be what it may, I will be yours until death part us."

"Poor trusting girl," he thought, tenderly, "if she but knew my real character it would crush her dreams of happy joy. I will keep the knowledge from her while I can."

Then he said aloud,

"Be always true and confiding, and we shall know nothing but happiness, and whatever I may seem to others I shall remain true to you."

That was all she wished for.

Her head was lying lovingly on his breast, her face buried on his shoulder, and her white arms twined closely round his neck ; he had got one arm round her supple waist, and with the other he was playing with her hair that hung in massive curls.

Their love dream was brought to a sudden climax.

The door of the room burst open, and in rushed a tall, handsomely-dressed cavalier.

She sprang away as the intruder entered.

Captain Will leapt to his feet, drew his sword, and waited for his enemies.

He thought not of his own danger ; his solicitude was for her sake, and, supporting her half uncovered and fainting form, he awaited the attack.

"Highwayman and murderer !" cried the infuriated young nobleman, as he advanced towards Will, "you shall suffer for this dastardly act of stealing on the privacy of a lady."

Will Merry laughed scoffingly.

His assailant made a sign towards the door, and six retainers rushed in.

"Take the lady from that fellow," said Lord Belmont, Lady Ellen's betrothed husband, "and remove her to her own room."

Lady Ellen clung tightly to her companion for protection ; she hated her intended as much as she now loved her new champion, and that was a great deal, as Will Merry could plainly see, and he said,

"The first one that comes within reach of my sword will fall uncomfortably hurt."

He spoke with such cool determination that none of the men cared about being the first to attack him.

Lord Belmont got awfully excited, and shouted,

"Do your duty, men, or, by Heavens, you shall all suffer for your cowardice."

Two being rather more courageous than the rest advanced. One fell bleeding as he laid his hand on the lady's arm.

The other shrunk back horror-stricken.

"Number one," said Captain Will, pushing the man's prone body aside with his foot.

"Cut him down where he stands !" shouted his lordship. "Are you such cowards that you will see one of your own companions slain in cold blood by such a ruthless hound ?"

His words seemed to have the desired effect upon the retainers.

With a rush they all ran forward.

"If any of you have respect for your lives keep back," Will said.

They heeded not what he said.

Before he had time to resist, but not before another fell wounded, they closed upon him.

Two held his arms secure, while the others took the fainting form of Lady Ellen from him.

Desperately he struggled to release himself,
But in vain.

His heart beat wildly against his breast as he saw the lady taken away.

"If you are not the cowardly cur you look, fight me sword to sword," said the captive, alluding to Lord Belmont.

"Release him, men, and retire," said his lordship, his face getting crimson with passion. "I will answer to him with my weapon."

"A brave remark," said Captain Will. "It is more than I expected from you ; though I am sorry to say you will require the service of these interesting gentlemen to remove you with these two here."

He meant the two retainers that he had so kindly rendered useless.

A cunning smile spread the young nobleman's face, and his lips curled scornfully as he drew his rapier.

Will Merry was slightly taken aback by his opponent. From his courage and strength as that of a lion's he was a good swordsman, and could cope with his rival in every way.

Will Merry enjoyed the fight.

His opponent by degrees backed him step by step, until he had him on the threshold of the door ; then, forcing him against the opposite wall, he made a quick cut,

Captain Will parried it quickly.

The next instant his sword went through his adversary's right side.

Maddened by the pain, he dashed at Will, and made a lunge.

Will Merry stepped back, and guarded the thrust.

Lord Belmont laughed a low, devilish, mocking laugh, as he heard a sharp click.

A panel glided aside behind Captain Will.

The next instant he had disappeared !

As the panel glided back into its place, he felt his feet slip from under him, and he fell backwards.

His brain seemed to whirl, his eyes were dizzy, and a sickening sensation came over him as he felt himself falling down a deep, dark, loathsome chasm.

Down, down he went, until he reached the bottom, where he lay stunned and bleeding.

During this time Merlin Hawke had not been idle.

He was riding down the Hammersmith Road, when Fair Rosamond paused suddenly, pricking her ears forward, and stood as though listening.

"Well, my beauty," said Merlin, caressingly patting his animal's glossy neck, "what is it you hear ? Is there anything coming ?"

The horse threw up its head, as though in acknowledgment of its master's enquiry.

Again the sound came.

This time nearer, and the noble creature stood like a carved statue.

The distant sound of a coach coming rapidly down the road.

Coming swiftly towards the highwayman, awaiting its approach.

He stood on a bridge. About half a mile ahead of where he stood he could see a coach coming towards him with terrific speed.

The horses dashed along as though mad under the lash of the whip that the driver laid on them.

One glance, as they came on, told him the purpose of their flight, and his dark eye flashed as he drew a pistol from the holster.

"The abduction of some lady," he muttered. "A helpless lady, perchance. Rosamond, my beauty, we are wanted to the rescue."

A touch upon the rein, and Fair Rosamond turned to face the coming equipage.

The vehicle had come so close that he could see a lady at the window, her white, lovely face pale with fear at the thought of being taken from her home by some dastardly ruffians.

But as her gaze fell upon the handsome features, and rich, costly dress of the young horseman, a look of hope brought a glow to her cheeks, and she exclaimed,

"Save me! Oh! save me!"

"From whom, sweet lady?"

"These fearful men; they have taken me from my home, while I slept. You will not let them take me?"

"Not while I can use my sword."

He had not time to say more.

"Stand aside!" shouted some one from within the carriage.

"You come and stand outside," said Merlin, "and try your skill in swordsmanship."

"Curses!" he exclaimed, savagely. "Drive on coachman."

"He had better not, without he wants to fall off his box."

Merlin had stopped the carriage by presenting a pistol to the gaze of the postillion.

That had a momentary effect.

With a sudden jerk they came to a halt.

The men sat shivering as though they had suddenly been seized by delirium tremens.

The smell of the powder as Merlin put the barrel of the pistol against their noses was too strong for their nerves, it had overcome them.

"Let us resume our journey, or I will blow your infernal brains out!"

Merlin laughed as he approached the window; he put the cold barrel of his pistol against the profligate's forehead in such a manner that the man's eyes seemed to fix their gaze, and cause him to squint frightfully.

"You see," said Merlin, "that my weapon has a very long tube and holds a considerable lot of lead, and if you make the least movement the contents will immediately mix with your brain—that's if you have got any—and it will make a very nasty mess."

Like a savage tiger brought suddenly to bay by a daring hunter, sat the maiden's abductor, not daring to move because of the gallant highwayman's gleaming weapon that was uncomfortably close to his forehead.

The lady trembled in every limb for fear the pistol should go off.

"Well, sir," said Merlin, at length, "may I ask what you want with this lady?"

"She is my daughter," said a middle-aged man, vindictive and cunning-looking; he had been shivering up in the corner of the carriage, but now had summoned up courage, "she has run away from her home, and now I am going to send her to her aunt's."

"It is all false," said the maiden; "he is not my father; he is a wicked old uncle who lives with papa, and he has sold me to this man (alluding to the one Merlin kept at bay) for a large sum of money."

"Your words tell me what you have said is true," said Merlin; "his assertion seemed so very much like a lie that I should not like to trust you to his parental care. Now, gentlemen, you will be kind enough to alight, and having seen the lady safe from your clutches I must attend to my own interesting occupation."

Neither of the shivering curs seemed inclined to move.

There was a murderous gleam f the elder of the two.

"Shoot him down!" he cried.

"I have another pistol; I always like to serve my friends alike; one each for you."

In obedience to his companion's kind instructions he had drawn a pistol from his belt, and took deliberate aim.

Before he had time to pull the trigger Merlin flung the door open and dealt him a fearful blow that knocked the weapon from his grasp.

It discharged as it fell to the ground, and the bullet stuck in the fellow's leg, and he moaned miserably.

Merlin Hawke handed the lady from the carriage.

Then turning to the baffled abductors, he said,

"You will oblige by giving me your money."

They looked at each other in utter astonishment, the demand came so cool and deliberate.

"Your money," he said again, pulling the trigger of his weapon about impatiently that made them feel very uncomfortable. "Quick, or you shall have the contents of this!"

They gave a start, and handed their purses to him reluctantly.

To avoid having the contents of the formidable weapon they complied with his wishes.

"Your jewellery," he said, putting their purses in his pocket.

The howl that the youngest gave was awful as he drew his rings from his fingers; his friend seconded the chorus by a miserable groan as he parted with his gold snuff-box, and had the pleasure of seeing them with their other jewels dropped into his pocket.

"Go now," said Merlin, "and the next time we meet under any such circumstance, you will not leave me without weighing a few drachms more than your usual weight."

A murderous gleam played about the eyes of the youngest as Merlin turned to go.

"Curse him!" hissed the infuriated libertine. "He shall not escape with my property!"

"Fire!—fire!" shouted his companion.

He did fire.

The bullet struck our hero in the side.

The suddenness of the attack made him reel, but only for a minute.

He was bullet-proof, as they plainly discovered when he took the bullet that had been fired at him and threw at the cowardly cur who had fired it, which struck him on the tip of his nasal organ, and drew the ruby.

"May I ask to whom I have rendered this slight service?" asked our hero.

"My name is Alice Warren," was the reply.

Their conversation was brought to a close by the approach of a horseman, evidently in great excitement.

"Alice!—my daughter Alice!" he said, his voice tremulous with emotion. "Saved!—saved! Whose generous act is this to save you? You, sir?"

Merlin bowed as the old gentleman took his hands in his own grasp, and squeezed them gratefully though not tenderly.

"The villains wanted to run away with my child. Oh! the wretches! I'll blow the brains out of your treacherous uncle, d——n him, I will."

He embraced his daughter tenderly, and the tears stood in his eyes as he spoke to her.

"Who am I to thank for this kind deliverance?"

"My name is Merlin Hawke," replied our hero.

"Then Lord Warren's house is always open to whenever you may chance to come ; but you will return with us to-night, it is too late for you to go anywhere."

"Your invitation gives me much pleasure," said Merlin ; but you will excuse me this evening."

With many hems and grunts the old gentleman parted with him, making him promise he would see them in an evening or two.

Merlin Hawke had not proceeded far after leaving his new acquaintance, when suddenly he was set upon by a gang of ill-looking, murderous wretches.

He was roughly dragged from his horse and beaten about the head with huge sticks.

"Revenge ! revenge !" they shouted, as they bound and gagged him.

He was powerless in thei hands.

To have tried and resisted would only have been exerting his strength to no purpose.

His hands and feet were securely bound, and he was alone in the hands of a band of desperate, ruthless villains, who would not scruple at anything.

Horror ! what were they going to do with him ?

He felt his cravat torn from his throat, then a thick cord was placed round his neck, and he was pulled along the ground.

He could feel the cord cutting into his flesh.

His eyes were starting from their sockets, his nose swelled to such a fearful size that he thought it would burst, his tongue, bloody and parched, protruded from his mouth.

His senses whirled, the rope was jerked several times, and then he remembered no more.

CHAPTER XX.

FRANK MORTON AND ALBERT MONTAGUE ARE RECOGNISED AND PURSUED BY THE OFFICERS—THE HAUNTED HOUSE —THE GHOSTS THAT VISIT IT—HOW THE HIGHWAYMEN FRIGHTENED THE OFFICERS—A RIDE FOR LIBERTY AND THE DISCOVERY OF A FRIEND GIBBETTED.

OUR two friends did not return to the haunt with the band as they had said they would do.

They had been confined in Newgate quite long enough, and now they were out they wanted to see a little life, though they had seen a great deal of excitement at the time they were saved from the gallows.

It was not long after they had left their comrades, and were quietly riding down the road, ready to make the acquaintance of any traveller that might come within ear-shot, when "Hold !" was shouted by at least twenty voices behind them.

"D——n those fellows' impertinence," said Frank, "they can't let a chap alone when he is quiet. That's clever," continued Frank, lowering his head to let a bullet pass over that came from one of the officers, and travelled with great velocity in a straight line for Frank's skull, and would have taken off his favourite top curls, but he heard it coming and prepared accordingly.

"That's nearer," said Albert, helping the foremost officer off his horse with a bullet.

They laughed at the fellows' ugly faces and rode on.

The officers swore like a lot of troopers, and rode after them.

"The haunted house," muttered Frank.

The officers were getting unpleasantly close, and he thought it would be a capital place to hide in.

Turning down a lane on the left that ran out of the road, Frank guided his horse through a thick hedge, and entered the ground that surrounded the Haunted House, closely followed by his comrade.

By the time the officers reached the corner of the lane, the two adventurers were safely concealed in the Haunted House.

The officers concluded that they had gone down the lane, and given them the slip.

They dispersed, and went in different directions to catch the runaways.

Frank's horse, who was put in the kitchen with his friend's animal, neighed as she heard the officers gallop away.

"Did you hear that, Albert ?" asked Frank.

"What ?"

"One of our horses laughed at the idea of those blockheaded fools ever catching us."

The officers soon returned, swearing vile oaths, and looking savagely at one another.

"Blackguards !" said Frank. "D—n their infernal impertinence for using such offensive language to gentlemen like ourselves !"

"Curse them !" said a loud voice under the window. "I'd have sent a bullet through their cursed carcases, if I'd had my will, when we got them the other day !"

"You confounded son of a nigger, if I don't hit you where the flesh doth most predominate, may I be swallowed by an alligator !" said Frank.

The prominent part of the officer's person presented a very favourable mark, as he had stooped to pick up something.

Frank availed himself of the opportunity, and fired.

The officer stumbled forward.

"Ah," he yelled, "murder ! Oh, I am shot !"

Then he indulged in some peculiar antics, jumping about with wonderful agility, and making the air ring with his yells.

"What a devil of a row he is making," said Albert, "any one would think he was hurt."

"I shouldn't wonder if he was," replied Frank, coolly.

"Where is the infernal thief who shot me ?" roared the infuriated officer, limping. "Search for the d——d hound !"

"Have a cigar, old boy," said Frank, and let that noisy fool have another in the other side."

"We had better not," said Albert, as he took a cigar, "they might see where it came from, and that would cause a disturbance."

"That's a wise speech," Frank said. "I wonder what sort of wine the spectral gentlemen keep in this old place ?"

"I am very dry."

"We must find something to drink."

"Where ?"

"Here."

Albert shivered.

"All right," he said, "go and look for it."

"I intend to."

"Glad to hear it, and I'll find some wood and make a fire while you are gone."

"No you won't."

"It's cold, and a fire is a great benefit."

"You can light it after you have been with me."

"Where to ?"

"The wine cellars ; we may find an old bottle or two."

"I have a great objection against going into wine cellars."

"Not when the wine is kept there."

"It isn't that ; only that there might be a few stray spirits taking care of the wine."

"Nonsense ! come on."

"I would rather not ; my legs are tired, and running up and down rickety stairs is not good for a fellow's breath."

"Humbug!"

"Well, if you are frightened to go down alone, I suppose I must come to take care of you."

"It is well to have some one to protect you in case of an accident."

"The officers are awfully quiet," said Albert, "what if they have sneaked in below?"

"We shall have the trouble of turning them out."

Frank waved his sword heroically, and led the way downstairs.

The old stairs creaked miserably as their heavy steps trod them one by one.

"A dismal crib this," Albert remarked.

"Very quaint," replied Frank.

Every word they spoke rang wildly through the deserted mansion, and an unearthly echo seemed to answer them.

"That's a miserable response," remarked Frank; "it sounds just like a lot of little imps repeating a fellow's words."

They reached the wine cellar.

Frank entered first, holding a light in his hand. They began to search for the bottles.

Which they found plenty of—empty.

"I don't think we shall get much wine here," said Albert, who felt much more comfortable upstairs than in a loathsome cellar.

"So it seems," said Frank; "but look away."

"Let's look behind this crate," suggested Albert.

The hamper spoken of stood at the back or the cellar.

"Better look inside," said Frank.

They did.

It was tied tightly down and filled with straw.

Amongst this straw there were some bottles.

Frank extricated one from the straw, and handed it to Albert.

"Here's one full to the cork," he said.

"Any more?" asked Albert, looking with satisfaction at the one he held.

"A dozen or two."

"Then we will have two each for the present, and stow the others away."

They took the required number and left the cellar, shut the door, and went upstairs again.

A fire was kindled, and sitting close by it they began to wiff away at their cigars, and discuss several little adventures that had taken place.

"Are those blackguards gone?" asked Frank.

"You had better go to the window and look," advised Albert.

He did.

But soon returned to his seat as a shout came from under the window.

"Here they are, mates," shouted one of the energetics as he caught sight of the highwayman's inquisitive face at the window, "the very two we want; we will have both."

"I wonder whether that man prays of a night?"

"Why?"

"Because he just told a lie."

"What was it?"

"He said he would have us both."

"An error of miscalculation."

Here the officers commenced a terrified hammering at the door.

"What infernal hard hands they must have," said Frank.

"Keep it up," said Albert. "Pretty amusement, so long as the door don't fall."

"That would be anything but amusing."

So Albert thought, but said nothing.

"Surrender!" shouted the officers.

The highwayman laughed.

"In the king's name, open the door!" shouted the same individual.

"What the devil do they think we care about the king?" said Frank.

"Don't know," said Albert. "I care little for his gracious majesty's power."

Frank went to the window.

"What will you give us to let you come in?" he asked.

"We will shoot you if you don't open the door."

"You shan't come in now," he said, "you are ungrateful, and I don't like the company of ungrateful people. We in general quarrel, and from quarrelling we fight, and at the termination of the fight the ungrateful person is sure to get hurt."

The fearless fellow hung half way out of window.

He was a very good target for the fellows below to practice on.

Just then one of the officers was thinking the same thing, and taking a pistol from his belt he was about to fire.

Frank saw his danger, and bobbing in, he put the end of his thumb to the tip of his nose.

(*To be continued.*)

THE PHANTOM'S WARNING;

A LEGEND OF THE TIME OF RICHARD THE THIRD.

(*Concluded from page 72.*)

"Twould be of no avail," replied Anne, "I should but remove the savage tiger for the prowling wolf, the fierce hyena for the subtle crocodile. No, he has too many instruments at his bidding for a frail woman to resist, and he hates me on account of my father, Warwick, who many a time overthrew his strongest measures."

"I fear there is too much truth in what you have stated," said Bridget. "I have a maiden aunt in Kent, let us fly to her; the honour and long services of my family will be a sure protection to us, and I have a friend in the mayor."

"I thank thee, Bridget," answered the queen, "but I am King Richard's, and to fly would be unworthy of the daughter of Warwick; moreover, the mayor is his friend, and already does

his behest without a murmur. Bethink thee, maiden, there is no escaping his power; besides, my father met his death valiantly, nor should his daughter be a craven."

"It ill becomes me," replied Bridget, "to advise one so high born as yourself, but a man can defend himself better than we, and to die in a battle-field is far nobler than to be stabbed in bed. Methinks that even your brave father would fly from the odds of darkness and assassins."

"Mine may be but idle fears after all," said Anne; "and if they are not, there is none to mourn for me, I trow; neither do I wish to live, for there is a worm gnawing at my heart whose work will soon be done, without the aid of steel or poison."

"It may be so," answered Bridget, "but methinks what he

has done would make any one fear ; in sooth, I would not trust him. Oh, do not, if it be but to save one heart from sorrowing, for mine would break were you to leave me, and oh, how awful to be murdered !" and Bridget buried her face in her hands, while her loud sobs at intervals broke the silence that reigned in the apartment.

The queen replied not for several minutes, but threw her arms around Bridget, while the tears gushed from her eyes and trickled down her lovely cheeks like rain-drops stealing down the stem of a lily. At length she said,

"I will go with thee ; take me to a place of safety ; let me spend the remainder of my days with thee in retirement."

"You would not leave us to-night, fair wife ?" said King Richard, closing a secret door just behind them, by which he had entered and stood unobserved long enough to hear that portion of their conversation which related to himself. "Nay, thou givest one but a cold reception," continued he, knitting his brows, for neither of them had as yet spoken, but clung to each other in fear, for they had not the most remote idea of his being so near at hand until he spoke. At length the queen mustered resolution enough to speak, and said, in a tremulous voice,

"Methinks your majesty might have apprised me of this honour, for we were unprepared for a visit at this hour."

"Beshrew me," answered King Richard, "for want of courtesy ; I know it has become much the vogue of late for the husband to give a long notice to the wife, in case she should have pledged her word to visit a play, or walk with some very dear friend, or be out at a dance, or have company in her own chamber whom it would be uncourteous to intrude upon ; but, by the holy rood, I thought there had been exceptions among kings and queens."

"That exception extends to me," answered Anne, "and Bridget Crosby is the only one I would wish to honour with the name of friend ; but there are those around my person, when you are absent, who intrude upon my privacy at their pleasure, with as little ceremony as if they were my equals."

"True, fair wife," replied Glo'ster, with a sneer, "but methinks it is necessary that some one should look to your safety, were it only to receive your commands at parting, for I was not aware until to-night that it was your intention to take so unceremonious a leave of us. Marry, you should have apprised us of your wishes, that an escort might have been in readiness, for it ill becomes a queen to journey alone."

"I scarcely deemed," said the queen, "that your majesty took so deep an interest in my weal, for many days have elapsed since you deigned to honour me with a visit."

"True," answered the king, "but thou canst not accuse us of paying no attention to thy comfort," casting his eyes around the splendid apartment ; "and thou art well aware, I trow, that affairs stood not in the best position when my subjects made me to take the crown. But thou shalt not complain ; I intend sharing thy company to-night, unless, indeed," added he, contemptuously, "thy fair counsellor Bridget would be a preferable companion."

"I intrude not myself upon her majesty," said Bridget, undaunted by the king's presence ; "but methinks it would ill become me to see her sit day after day alone, or her only companions armed ruffians, villains who would murder their own father for gold—ill guests for a lady's society, I wot."

"Softly, fair maiden," said King Richard, gazing on the lovely and high-spirited Bridget, as much in admiration as anger. "By the Holy Paul, methinks thou holdest my friends in small repute to speak thus lightly of them."

"I hold them in as high repute," replied Bridget Crosby, "as every honest person ought, and, perchance, as much as thou dost, O King, for as they act to others, so would they be tempted to do with thee for a higher guerdon."

"By the mass, I do believe thee, fair damsel," answered Richard, "and, if they be such as thou sayest they are, I will be rid of them."

"If," answered Bridget, looking full upon the king's face until he quailed beneath the purity of her glance and the consciousness of his own guilt ; "if—thou knowest they are ; thou wert not wont to hearken to if's when thou orderedst Hastings to be beheaded."

"Now, out upon thee for a cursed hag !" shouted King Richard, drawing his sword and shaking it in Bridget's face, while his rage scarcely left him utterance. "Art thou here to take note of my actions and construe them as thou pleasest ? Out of my sight, I say, or, by hell, I will draw a curtain over thine eyes !"

"Nay, thou darest not to touch me," exclaimed Bridget. "King as thou art, thy betters were beholden to my father, and, wert thou to draw one drop of my blood, there are ten thousand daggers in this city which would leap to my revenge. But I leave thee ; and thou, fair queen, beware of him. The hall of my fathers has not yet been polluted with the blood of murder. Nay, thou darest not to strike me ; there is blood enough upon thy hands, I trow." And Bridget left the apartment, followed even to the door by Richard, with his sword pointed at, yet not daring to strike her, so much had her proud bearing and the boldness with which she confronted him over-awed his spirit, which shook beneath the terrible truths she had uttered.

For several moments he paced the apartment with rapid strides, his brow flushed with rage, and his dark eyes flashing wildly and frightfully upon the queen, who still maintained her seat, although trembling like the last leaf of autumn, and expecting every moment that the storm of his passion would burst forth. But no ; he had learnt "to smile and murder while he smiled," and soon walked himself into an apparent calmness, which was more dangerous than his anger, and approaching the queen he said,

"Hie thee to bed, sweet wife ; I will be with thee anon."

The queen took up a silver candlestick, and lighting the waxen taper, walked with tearful eyes into the sleeping-room, without even summoning her female attendants. Without unrobing herself, she knelt before a crucifix, and remained in prayer for several minutes ; when these were finished, she continued to kneel, with her hands clasped, and her long bright hair falling in disorder over her face. She was indeed a picture of beauty in sorrow, for as she removed her long tresses with one hand, and continued prostrate, the light fell upon one side of her face, revealing a profile such as hath but seldom been excelled in the fairest work of sculptor, or the sweetest dream of poet. At intervals she sighed deeply, and when she arose there was an unusual calmness upon her face, melancholy indeed, but resigned, like one whose mind is made up to meet the worst without a murmur. At length she divested herself of her rich robes, and with aching heart she laid her lovely head upon the pillow, and as if pain and care were wearied with keeping their long vigils, she soon fell asleep ; but even while she slept, the bright taper revealed a tear that stood upon her silken lashes, like a sorrowing sentinel that kept watch.

We now return to the throne-room, which adjoined the sleeping apartment, where Queen Anne had retired and left the king alone, who only remained so for a short time, for Dighton and Forrest, who were at hand, joined him soon after the queen's departure, and were seated at the splendid table with the king, conferring together in a low tone.

"In the garden, you think, would be the most secret ?" said the king.

"'Twould be done the speediest I trow," replied Dighton, "for we might dig a pit in a little time deep enough to hold her."

"Right," said Forrest, "and the best place would be in the gravel-walk, which would escape suspicion, as we might cover it again, and trample it to its former appearance."

"Hold !" said the king, "this must not be ; cannot you dispatch her, so as to make it appear that she died a natural death, for now I bethink me I have given it out that she is grievous sick, and would fain have her buried with great splendour, publicly ?"

"Not well," answered Dighton, "for though we smothered the young princes in the Tower, and did it as quietly as possible without much force, still there was a difference in their faces to what there would have been had they died naturally ; for your majesty may be sure that they will make a little resistance, in spite of our persuading them that it is all for their benefit."

"Well, you know the best," said Richard, "and I leave it

entirely to yourself. Could you do the deed without marks of violence I would increase your reward ; but if not, then bury her in the garden. And now good night, and let me see you early to-morrow at the palace," saying which, he left the apartment, muffled in a large cloak, and walked alone to the palace, unknown even to his menials.

He had not long retired before Bridget Crosby entered by the private door by which the king obtained ingress.

As she entered without making the slightest noise, neither Dighton nor Forrest perceived her, for they were too busily engaged in devising a plan to dispatch the queen without leaving marks of violence that they might obtain the increased reward. Bridget Crosby stood in the shadow of the rich drapery that covered the wall, and listened to their various schemes for murdering the queen. We will not attempt to give their conversation, for it was such as blanched the brow of the brave Bridget, and drove the blood coldly back into her heart ; for they hesitated not to argue over the methods taken to dispatch Clarence and the young princes, and entered into the details as minutely as an anatomist, only in language too horrid to be repeated. At length they decided upon first having the pit in readiness, in case they should not succeed in taking away her life without marked violence, and they retired for that purpose.

They were no sooner gone than Bridget entered the queen's apartment, and acquainted her with what she had heard, advising her also to prepare for her escape by the private door ; to which she readily consented, and was soon in readiness for her departure, refusing to take with her the least trifle that had been presented by the king, and only confining herself to a few necessaries, which were her own before her marriage with Glo'ster, together with her jewels. But an unforeseen accident prevented their escape, for in closing the secret door Bridget had neglected to secure the spring outside ; in vain she tried to force it open by main strength ; she might as well have attempted to force down the massy walls. The door that led to the staircase in the garden had been secured by the murderers when they went out,—this was done by their taking down a thick bar of iron which fell upon a staple ; there was no means of securing the door inside to prevent their return, neither was their any fastening to the queen's sleeping-room. They consulted together for a few moments, and, finding that all means of escape were for the present cut off, again entered the bed-room, and placed a table against the door, which would at least leave them a little time to parley with the murderers, who were not long in returning from the pleasaunce, and attempted immediately to force open the door.

"What is your business with the queen ?" said Bridget.

"We will acquaint her in person," replied Forrest, "and in return might demand yours, for his majesty said that she was alone."

"Mine is to protect her from the design of his majesty," answered Bridget, "and to bid you retire, or I will arouse the household."

"But you must first reach them," said Dighton, forcing open the door, and overturning the table.

"You would not murder your queen," said Bridget, turning pale as she spoke, and gazing upon the hardened brows of the ruffians. "She has never injured either of you. If it be gold that tempts you to this act, I will give you more than this deed will bring you ; and methinks you have shed blood enough already."

"By Our Lady, the maiden speaketh fairly," replied Forrest. "I am for the gold, and let the bloody-minded king do his own work. I have too much upon my hands already."

"So have not I," replied Dighton. "We are the king's subjects, and bound to his behests, which, if we do not fulfil, our lives are not worth so much as a struggling kitten's in the Thames."

"Now, out upon thee," said Forrest ; "hast thou forgotten what vows thou didst make after our last act, and swore by Holy Paul thou never wouldst do the like again ?"

"True, noble chicken-heart," answered Dighton, "but I have been shrived for that deed, and thus I do repent," saying which, he plunged a dagger into the back of the queen, who was kneeling before the crucifix, and she fell forward with the force of the blow, grasping the feet of the holy image in the agonies of death.

Bridget flew to her assistance, and bent in mute sorrow over the bleeding form of the queen, for so unexpectedly had the blow been dealt, that even Forrest stood for a moment wrapt in speechless astonishment ; then turning, he exclaimed, "Remorseless villain !" and plunged a dagger up to the hilt in his bosom. "Thou wouldst have told the king of my willingness to have spared the lady, wouldst thou ?" continued Forrest, gazing upon his companion, who lay at his feet. "Tell him when ye meet together in hell, damned fiend ! It was thou who first steeled my heart to murder—first drew me from the path of honesty, and poisoned my ears with reports how gold was won in serving kings, making me peril my soul for filthy lucre, and when I refused to plunge deeper into crime, threatened to bring me to justice. Nay, grin at me, wretch, and gnash thy teeth, thou grey-headed murderer ; thou hast grown hoary in crime."

"Oh !—oh ! curse thee !" groaned Dighton, and throwing out his arms, expired, his lips curled up even in death, as if a curse yet lingered upon them and he had died without giving it utterance.

The light from a lage waxen taper fell upon the cold faces of the dead, as they lay outstretched upon the floor. That of the queen's was calm as one that sleepeth, but her beautiful ringlets were unbound, and the gory stream that issued from her wound mingled with her long hair.

Bridget knelt beside her with folded hands and anxious eyes gushing with tears, that fell upon the cold bosom of the queen.

Forrest stood by, with one hand shading his eyes, as if to hide himself from the horrid sight, while his other yet grasped the dagger which was dyed with the blood of his companion.

The silver crucifix glittered in the pale light, and the rich drapery of the bed hung in light and shadow, as it fell upon the folds of the hangings.

Forrest then retired, and the hoofs of his steed rung upon the silence of the night as he hurried from Crosby Hall.

NOTICE.—In our next Number will be commenced a new and highty interesting Story.

BLACK HAWKE, THE HIGHWAYMAN.

SIR MARMADUKE GREVILLE.

CHAPTER XX.—(*continued*).

The officers grew exasperated.

To be made derision of by highwaymen was more than they could stand.

They hammered away at the door with right goodwill, but finding it did not yield to them, one suggested that they should go round the back way and force an entrance.

"What shall we do," said Frank; "the artful devils are coming round the back way."

"Let them come," said Albert, "they cannot do any harm till they get in."

"They will soon effect an entrance. The door is open."

"Hullo!" said Albert, "what is this?"

"What?"

Albert pointed to a cupboard.

"Let us go and see," said Frank.

They did.

"I have just thought of an idea," said Albert.

"Let us have it then," said Frank; "it must be something good or you would not think of it."

"These," said Albert, taking two large sheets out of the cupboard, "will do for us to disguise ourselves in."

"I don't see the force of that," said Frank.

"I don't suppose you do, but if you will listen I will tell you what I propose. This is a haunted house we are in."

"Precisely."

"It is supposed that spectres from the other world visit this mansion, robed in white."

"Yes!"

"Then suppose we put these sheets over us and black our visages, and wait for these unwelcome guests who are forcing their way in against our inclination."

"We shall be nigger ghosts, if we black our craniums!"

"It will be all the more hideous."

"Bravo!" said Frank, giving his comrade a smart smack on the back, by way of approval.

They had hardly put the idea into execution, when there came a rush of heavy feet ascending the stairs.

"Look a-live," said Frank, throwing the white robe over himself, and pulling it tight down each side of his face.

Another minute and the officers were rushing in the room.

"Oh, oh! boo-boo-ooo!" said one of the men, catching sight of the two motionless figures, standing side by side with outstretched arms.

"What the devil's the matter, you shivering cur?" said the leader of the officers.

"Oh, lor! I saw 'em—boo-boo-ooo! They are gone."

"Saw what, d—n you?"

"Ghosts," shouted the frightened officer; "they are gone—vanished like two shadows."

The rest of the force stood in utter amazement, looking at one another, with opened mouths.

It is a wonder one half of them did not fall down the throats of the others, their mouths were open to such a frightful extent.

They were suddenly brought to action by the voice of their leader sounding in their ears like a thunder-bolt; in an instant their mouths closed with a bang!

Frank and Albert were standing behind the door when the officers rushed in, and when the last one entered and got frightened the *ghosts* thought it their best opportunity to escape while the fellow's head was turned aside.

Which they did.

And during the time the officers were making ugly faces at one another they gained the kitchen, where their horses were left, and were soon mounted and galloping down the road.

They looked like a pair of demons escaped from the lower regions. The sheets they had round them were flying behind them like the sails of a ship, and their long massive curls hanging round their black faces presented a most peculiar sight.

"There they go!" shouted one of the officers, who, hearing a noise, went to the window; "ghosts or no ghosts, they can ride!"

"Bring them down if they won't stop!" shouted the infuriated leader, helping one of his men down with the toe of his boot.

"Stop, in the king's name! surrender!" shouted one of the valiant officers.

"What a set of asses," said Frank, "they always use the same words about surrender, in the king's name; it is getting quite stale."

The officers were about half way down the road when our young adventurers turned the corner, and divesting themselves of their disguises and rubbing the black off their faces, they galloped across some fields and so eluded the officers, who, arriving at the top of the road, were in a fix at finding their intended captives had escaped and out of sight, and, by way of excusing themselves, they let loose their vengeance by swearing at one another, and rode away, greatly disappointed.

The two captains rode away, quite heedless of where they were going until they were brought to a halt by hearing a faint groaning, evidently from some one in great distress.

The young highwaymen were always ready to help any person in distress, and, hearing these groans of pain, they looked anxiously about to discover from whence it came.

"Ah!" shouted Albert Montague, in surprise, backing his horse a few steps.

"What is the matter?" enquired Frank, eagerly.

"Look—look there! Some poor man has been roughly treated; he is bound hand and foot."

Frank looked in the direction indicated by his companion.

He closed his eyes to shut out the horrible spectacle.

Hanging from a branch of a tree was a man, young and handsome.

His dress was of a costly material.

It was clearly to be seen that he had been very roughly treated.

Perchance a traveller set upon by a set of vagrants, who had robbed him, and, fearing that he would send the officers in their track, they had bound his limbs together with ropes and hung him to the tree, where he would die a long, torturing death.

"This is some cowardly work," said Frank, as a tear trickled down his cheek. "By heavens, if I knew who did it I would crush their craven lives out; it must have been the work of more than one. But to work, Albert, and release the poor fellow."

Albert held the reins of his comrade's horse, while Frank stood on the saddle, and, by the aid of a stiletto, he cut the cords that held the form of a fellow creature from the earth, and would soon have crushed the life out of its body.

As he severed the cords, he put his arm round the waist of the unconscious form and lowered it to Albert, who gently laid it on the sward.

To unbind the cords which were so securely fastened round the body was the work of a minute.

Frank fell back in horror and amazement, and exclaimed,

"My God, it is our president!"

Albert Montague seemed speechless, so sudden was the shock; he knelt by the side of Merlin, and, taking one of his hands in his own, he turned his face from his companion to hide his emotion. He was overcome by the pleasure of Providence guiding them towards that fatal spot in time to rescue their much-beloved president.

Albert owed his life to their noble leader; it was he, Merlin Hawke, who saved his life the night his lordly parent was so piteously murdered.

It will be remembered, dear readers, at the time of the murder of Lord Montague, mentioned in Number 4, page 30, that the other occupant of the carriage, his lordship's own, made his escape by getting out the other side of the vehicle; he ran across the fields, and so got out of sight.

He had kept up his flight for some distance, when he began to get tired; he knew not where he was or where he could go.

He had not been sitting by the side of the road long, when his attention was attracted by the sound of heavy, quick footsteps approaching him. Ere he had time to escape he was assailed by one of his late ruffians.

"Ha! ha!" laughed the bravo, in savage defiance, clutching hold of Albert by the arm, and brandishing a huge knife before his eyes, "you thought you would get off nicely, you d—n young viper."

The young nobleman struggled desperately for his life. In his struggles he knocked the knife from the murderer's grasp as the burly ruffian was about to plunge it into his heart.

The fellow grew maddened at being thus thwarted in his murderous act. He dealt Albert a fearful blow on the face with his clenched iron fist, and knocked him senseless to the ground; in another instant he had gained his bloody weapon, and, stooping over his victim, was about to plunge it into his heart, when an elegantly-dressed horseman dashed up to the spot just in time to prevent that horrible deed from being committed.

In an instant he took the whole scene in at a glance, and, leaning over in his saddle, he dealt the bloodthirsty ruffian a blow with tremendous force that sent him spinning round, and then he fell prone to the earth with the knife in a grasp of iron that would have been buried in the body of Albert Montague had not Merlin Hawke so providentially come to the rescue.

Dismounting his noble steed, Fair Rosamond, he poured some brandy down the throat of the unconscious young heir of Albion Hall, and, getting some water from a brook close handy, he bathed his temples, and soon brought him back to consciousness.

Albert looked vacantly around him, and, seeing the prone body of his would-be murderer, he shuddered.

Merlin spoke kindly to him, and soon Albert Montague related the whole to his preserver.

Merlin looked contemptuously at the ruffian murderer, and, turning the inanimate body over with his foot, drew his sword.

"No," he said, putting his weapon back, "I will not stain the blade of my sword with his vile blood."

He then took a pistol, and, putting the tube to the bravo's ear, blew his brains out; he then put Albert on his horse in front of him, and rode to the haunt of the Black Hawkes, and gave him to one of the females whom they kept there to wait upon the captains of the band.

A strong attachment grew between Merlin and his foundling, and when Albert got well and perfectly recovered from the effects of the fearful catastrophe that had placed him under Merlin's charge, Merlin Hawke consulted him about returning to his home, but the boy was too sensitive, and said that he knew it was his uncle's work.

Merlin Hawke being satisfied with what he said, Albert remained with them.

Three years then elapsed, and Albert was then seventeen (being only fourteen when rescued from an untimely death). He then became a member of the Brotherhood, and in a short time, for his bravery and many gallant acts, he was made captain.

He then swore on an oath before the whole band that he would avenge the death of his father, and when his villanous uncle thought that he had got all obstacles from his path and was mounted to the top of the precipice and surrounded by the highest of fashion and perhaps about to take a bride, he would then appear and hurl him to the bottom, and have him brought to justice.

This it was that caused that strong affection which overcame him as he knelt by the side of his preserver who had saved him, and been so kind and protected him as a brother would.

Albert kissed the hand of Merlin and then the point of his sword, and holding it towards heaven, he took a fearful oath to avenge this cowardly act.

Frank looked at his companion in astonishment to see the sacred way in which he pledged the vow of vengeance; he felt quite as sorrowful and grieved as his friend, but being of a more reckless and careless nature, he did not show it as much as Albert, and as for avenging the wrong his president had suffered, he would track the culprits through the world but what he would catch them.

They had tried their best to bring Merlin Hawke back to consciousness, and now he slowly opened his eyes. Frank then held his head on his arm and poured some water down his throat, that they had got from a stream.

Slowly he got up by the aid of his friends, and taking a flask from the breast of his coat, he took a long draught.

That seemed to revive him, and taking a hand of each of his friends in his own, thanked them in a low, tremulous voice, for their kind, timely deliverance.

He then related to them the way he was suddenly attacked, and gave the description of the ruffians who had nearly sent him to perdition.

"Where is Fair Rosamond," inquired Frank.

"I know not," said Merlin. "I remember hearing some of the fellows giving very dismal howls. I presume she did her best to put a few *hors de combat*."

"She is one of the most faithful animals in existence," said Albert. "I recollect the way she served that sneaking officer that was about to lay his ugly hands on my shoulders, at the 'Chequers' Inn, one evening, and she, thinking he had no right to take liberties with a gentleman, lifted him out of the yard by the hair of his head."

"By jove," said Frank, "she is an animal worth a fortune."

"I would not take two for her," said Merlin, proudly; "We will see if she is anywhere about here."

"Perhaps she has gone to the Haunt," remarked Frank.

"That is very probable," Merlin said; "it would not be the first time."

"Perhaps those fellows have taken her," said Albert.

"If they have," said Merlin, "they shall have her; many envious devils have tried that game on, but soon came to grief with a bruised shin, or gone away minus of half-a-pound of flesh off one of their shoulders. If any did get on her back they soon came off head first."

"If such is the case," said Albert, "and those vagrants found they could not take her, they may have slain her."

Merlin's face changed in an instant; he had not thought of that.

"Come, my friends," he said, "and if the case is as you surmise, let those who have done it, look to it; by heavens I would slay a whole nation to get at the right one!"

They rode away, Merlin Hawke sharing part of Albert's horse, his face wearing a troubled, though determined look.

They had not ridden far when their attention was drawn towards a beautiful black, slim-looking animal lying on the ground. Merlin almost lept from the saddle, but Albert held him back.

The noble creature turned its head at the sound of the approaching horsemen, and tried to get up but fell heavily on its side again.

Merlin got down and ran towards his faithful animal. Fair Rosamond neighed as though in recognition of her master, and threw her head up, that plainly showed she was pleased that her master had come to her.

Merlin bounded forward, and threw himself by her side; he put both his arms round her glossy neck, and cried, in a voice tremulous with emotion.

"My beauty, Fair Rosamond! Oh, that I knew who did this cruel, cowardly act!"

The horse licked its master's hand affectionately, and caressed him as tenderly as a child. It was quite an affecting scene to see a horse lying severely wounded, and its master, a young, handsome cavalier, with both his arms twined round his animal's neck weeping like a girl; Albert and Frank were obliged to use their cambrics, it had overcome them. Never had they witnessed such affection between anything or any one before in their lives.

A thing, a beast that is used to carry its master about wherever the rider liked to guide it by the rein; then to see such love that it showed at the pleasure of seeing her master by its gentle movements and actions. If it could only have spoken it would have told its love for her master, truer love than any woman ever confessed to a lover.

"Come, captain," said Frank, "let us attend to her wants."

Merlin rose, slowly and reluctantly, the tears streaming down his face.

"This cruel work," he said; "I would rather have suffered death than this should have happened."

"Yes, yes," said Frank, soothingly. "We may soon get her round."

"Why should they have hurt her," said Merlin, "an animal so true, loving, affectionate, and gentle?"

Merlin examined the wounds on his faithful steed with a sorrowful look.

There were two deep gashes just below her neck, and one on her loins.

Merlin Hawke gave Albert a prescription, and sent him to an apothecary, which was about five miles from where they were.

Albert started off like a weasel, and by the time he returned Merlin had washed the wounds. He was a good veterinarian, he had studied the different diseases of horses from his boyhood, and had often found it a very useful knowledge, as he did in the present case.

The noble steed laid as quiet as a lamb while she was having her wounds dressed.

When they had finished and bound her wounds with some linen, which they tore off a certain under wearing apparel, Merlin gave Fair Rosamond a dose of medicine, and in a short time she felt much better and more happy than she did an hour previous to her surgical attendance.

Merlin felt quite proud as he paraded her up and down to get her strong upon her legs.

She soon got fresh, and seeming eager for her master to be upon her back, Merlin Hawke mounted the saddle gently, and the trio rode away.

They had not proceeded more than three or four hundred yards when they saw lying on the ground, writhing and twisting about, four of Merlin's late assailants greatly disfigured by the hoofs of a horse; very probably they were the hoofs of Fair Rosamond.

Which they were.

The men had tried to capture her.

But she did not see it.

And, as Albert had suggested, they tried to stay her.

She, being a very sensitive horse, retaliated, and, as our hero said, laid four *hors de combat* in the conflict.

The blood ran in rapid streams from the capacious wounds she received in the fight, which made her very weak (the loss of blood, not the fight), and not liking the idea of lying with such low, base ruffians, she trotted to the part and hid where her master found her.

"By heavens! they are some of the hounds who beset me," said Merlin. "They won't kick about much longer."

So saying, he drew a pair of pistols from the holsters and fired. Frank and Albert fired one each; their shots took effect, and the men gave several spasmodic kicks and then laid quiet, never to move again without some one moved them.

Merlin bade his comrades farewell, and rode away.

The two captains made their way to an inn, where they did ample justice to a good meal, and then rode away, ready for any adventure that might befall them.

We will follow our hero, who is riding along at a very moderate speed, deeply burried in thought.

He is making his way to Oxfordshire; he is now not many miles from Chipping Norton.

He is making his way to the estate of Sir Andrew Greville.

He dismounts his bandaged steed, and conceals her under a thicket belonging to the estate.

"Stay here, my beauty," he said, patting her glossy neck. "I shall soon be back, Fair Rosamond, and shall want you to be ready."

With a stately step he trod the ground, and mounted the steps as though the place *belonged to him.*

His summons at the door was soon answered by a tall, gaunt, cunning-looking flunkey, with his hair looking as though he had been running with the cook, who had thrown a bag of flour at his head.

But such was not the case; it was done because his master ordered it to be so to distinguish his station in life.

The flunkey looked at our hero contemptuously, and asked him what he wanted.

Our hero, without answering, looked at the flunkey with disgust.

Merlin could not repress a laugh as his gaze fell upon the fellow's legs.

"By the Lord Harry!" as Hal Hunter would say. He would have been surprised had he seen the legs of the gorgeous flunkey; of course, they were a pair of legs; from his knee to his ankle they resembled two broom-handles, tied round with a piece of tape.

Had he lived in the present age, we might have made an excuse for him under the plea that his calves had disappeared through the cattle plague; but no such catastrophe plagued the country in his time. The beasts were all healthy, and every day went out to graze. It is very probable that his calves went out to graze, and forgot to return.

But before we enter any further on the subject of the flunkey's personal appearance we will return to our hero, who has been patiently awaiting for an answer.

"Well, you interesting-looking object?" said Merlin.

"Well," returned the flunkey, curtly, "who does yer wish to see?"

"Some one a little better looking than you."

"Then yer needn't look in the glass."

Merlin exerted his toe at the retreating flunkey; but missing its intended spot, his foot slid between the legs of the before-mentioned individual, and he fell heavily to the ground, as straight as a lath.

The fellow soon gained his feet, and began to make a noise as though he was hurt.

Merlin Hawke, not caring about seeing any of his old friends, slipped a piece of gold into his hand.

That had an electric effect upon him.

The next instant he made a bow that quite surprised Merlin to see him do it.

"Is her ladyship in?" asked Merlin.

"Yes, me lord," replied the flunkey, politely.

"Is she quite well?"

"Yes, me lord."

"And alone?"

"Yes, me lord; her ladyship has been very ill up to the last few days, and now she is better she won't see anybody—not even Sir Andrew.

Merlin seemed pleased to hear that Lady Florence would not see any one.

"Where is Sir Andrew?" he said.

"He is out, me lord; but his brother is in, and so is Henry Ashburne."

Merlin shuddered as he heard that name; then he asked, with a troubled look on his handsome countenance,

"How is Captain Ashburne?"

"Better than he was. We all thought he was going to deliver up the ghost."

"What do you mean?"

"Why, don't yer know, me lord?"

"No, my man, I do not."

"Then I'll tell you. We thought he was a going home—going to kick the bucket."

Merlin looked rather bewildered at the fellow for a few moments, then he imagined to himself he meant that Henry Ashburne had nearly died.

"What has been the matter with him?" inquired Merlin Hawke, innocently.

"Why, somebody gave him a dig in the ribs that nearly sent him to kingdom come."

"I should say it would have been Ashburne gave in if he had died."

The flunkey grinned and opened his mouth like an alligator.

Merlin felt uncomfortable, and got a few steps back out of the way until the man shut his mouth.

"Can I trust you with a secret?" said Merlin.

"Yes, me lord," said the liveried statue, eagerly.

"Then, if you will tell her ladyship that Merlin wishes an interview with her, and you do it quietly, and not let any one know I am here, I will reward you handsomely."

The flunkey waited to hear no more; but took three steps and vanished up the stairs in a minute. Before Merlin had time to see whether he had gone, he returned and conducted him to a handsomely furnished apartment.

Merlin gave the powdered lackey a handful of gold, and he had hardly left when Lady Florence entered, looking pale and trembled.

Merlin Hawke rushed towards her with outstretched arms; but she waved him back with her hand.

"Dear Lady Florence, when—"

She put her hand up to stay him speaking, then she said slowly, and in a cool tone,

"Merlin, why did you dare so much as to come here?"

"My dear Florence, I would dare anything to see you."

"You must leave this place immediately. Were you discovered, it would prove fatal!"

"Yes, dearest, I will leave it if you will accompany me," he said; "you are not happy here. Come, leave this cursed place!"

"No," she said, in a determined voice, "would you disgrace me by taking me from my husband's house again?"

"Lady Florence," he said, quietly, "I have come to take you from that vile man whom you were forced to marry because you thought I were dead. He, who has robbed me of you whom I so loved, and put all my trust in, thinking that you would be true to me; and when I returned to claim my property which he now enjoys, and wed you, imagine my feelings when I found you were the wife of the man—my greatest enemy and peace destroyer! I have seen you, dear Florence, shrink when you heard his footsteps, and shudder at the sight of him."

Lady Florence buried her face in her hands as he continued,

"I will not leave the house without you."

"If you have not quitted my presence within two minutes, I will alarm the house!"

"Will you come?" he said.

"No!" she answered. "Go!"

"Then, by the saints," he said, "you shall see that I have been true to you."

As he spoke he drew his sword, and tearing the front of his coat open, he took hold of the blade of his weapon in the middle, and put the point to his breast.

Another instant, and the cold steel would have pierced his heart.

Lady Florence gave a loud shriek and ran towards him in time to stay his hand that was on the jewelled hilt of his sword from thrusting the blade through his body.

His arm lowered as she, fainting, fell upon his breast.

"Now is my time," he muttered, as he kissed her forehead, and raising her lifeless form on one arm, he dashed down the stairs and left the house in a trice.

Her shriek had been heard, and the whole house was alarmed.

Merlin gave a defiant yell as a whole troop of retainers, headed by Marmaduke Greville and Henry Ashburne, dashed after him.

CHAPTER XXI.

HAL HUNTER'S JOY AT AN INTERVIEW WITH THE PRETTY BELLA—WHAT HAL GAVE A SPY FOR LISTENING—WHAT THE SPY GOT HAL FOR GIVING HIM A DIG—BELLA LIBERATES HER LOVER—THE ELOPEMENT, AND MEETING AT THE "CHEQUERS INN."

HAL HUNTER rode along for some distance in deep thought. Many a traveller passed him on the road ; had he been on any other errand to the one he now had on hand, the travellers would not have got off quite so free.

He had ridden some fifteen miles when his horse stopped at a wayside inn. Hal was so deeply involved in meditation, he did not notice his horse stopping until an ostler came out and took hold of his steed's bridal, then he said,

"Of course he wants a feed ; so do I."

"Yes, sir ; come a long way ?" said the ostler.

"Give him a good feed, brush him down, and be ready in half an hour."

"All right, sir."

Hal entered the inn, and ordering a sumptuous repast, with plenty of wine, he satisfied his enormous appetite.

When the worthy host entered he looked at Hal in blank astonishment ; he was doubtful whether he was the same person.

Hal Hunter had changed his coat ; that is to say, he had turned it inside out, and instead of being a bright scarlet trimmed with gold lace, it was a bright blue trimmed with silver lace ; he had also taken the black plume from his hat and altered it to match his coat.

The landlord was quite surprised, so quickly had Captain Hunter changed his dress.

Hal paid his bill, and was once more on the road.

A good ride soon brought him to the respectable residence of Judge Blenheim.

He was considering by what means he could gain admittance, when he looked up at the window and there beheld the object of his thoughts.

A sign from pretty Bella, and he dismounted and ran up the steps as she opened the door to him.

They were soon locked in each other's arms, and kisses were lavished on each other plentifully.

"My dearest Bella," he said, "I cannot express the happiness I feel to see you once again."

She answered him by a loving look, and an affectionate squeeze with her soft round arm.

"I dreaded to come," he said. "I feared that my weapon had gone through you as well as that interfering fellow."

"No," she said, earnestly. "I thought they would hurt you when they all rushed upon you like a lot of dogs."

"No, my love. They did not hurt me ; but tell me, dearest, is his lordship severely wounded ? It is his own fault, not mine, if he is."

"No, Hal dear, he is much better than he was, though he is very weak now."

"I am glad to hear it. He won't be able to trouble you for some time."

She laughed a light silvery laugh that sent a thrill to her lover's heart.

"Is your uncle in ?" Hal enquired.

"No ; he has gone to town."

"I am happy to hear that," he said, "that is another pleasure I did not anticipate."

His horse was given to one of the stable-boys, and Hal made himself jolly with his fair, trusting companion.

The time seemed to pass quicker than it ever did before ; every hour seemed but a minute.

It was a very dangerous time for a reckless fellow like Hal Hunter, quick and passionate as was his nature ; but he let not an evil thought enter his mind, though had he wished to have acted dishonourably he would have found her a very easy victim.

He loved her the better for her true, innocent, trusting confidence, and sooner than he would have taken advantage of her he would have chopped off his right hand.

Her head was lying on his chest, and her pretty face upturned to his, when she started.

"What is it, my dear ?" he said.

"I fancied I heard a noise outside," she said, in a whisper.

Hal put his hand on the hilt of his rapier and listened.

He rose and crept to the door, and opened it with a jerk.

As he did so there was a scuffling of feet, and the page retreated with wonderful speed, but not in time to prevent the point of Hal's sword entering the seat of his breeches.

The boy was at the top of a flight of stairs that led to the kitchen when he felt the keen point of the highwayman's rapier enter a very uncomfortable part of his person.

With a yell and a leap he landed safely at the bottom.

Hal Hunter felt much more satisfied at finding the listener than he would have been had he not seen him.

"He won't be in a hurry to listen again," said Hal, taking his seat by the side of his companion.

"It was very wicked of him to listen," she said.

Hal felt quite enthusiastic at the pretty way she had of articulating her words, and could not help kissing her.

It was getting very late, and Bella expected her uncle to return every minute, and she began to get anxious for the safety of her lover that he should go.

Hal was quite as anxious as her, still, neither of them liked ; twenty times he kissed her and said good bye, and each time he would have something more to say, and every time he rose to go he lingered behind and they seemed reluctant to part.

Thus they kept on for about two hours, until at last their courtship was brought to a sudden crisis.

Judge Blenheim burst into the room with such suddenness that it made the young lovers start and look at the abrupt intruder in surprise.

"You here again ?" said the judge, savagely, showing his fang-like teeth.

"Ah, how do ?" said Hal, in a reserved tone. "I hope you are not fatigued after your long journey ?"

"What do you mean, you insolent hound ?"

"My dear sir, I hope I have not offended you ?"

"Offended be d——d, sir ! How dare you come to my house when I am out ?"

"Well, my dear sir, I hope you will not judge me wrongly, but, upon my word, I came from London to enquire after your health."

"How dare you take such a liberty to come to my house ?"

"Merely for old acquaintance sake ; I never forget old friends. But pray, my dear judge, let me persuade you not to get excited."

"Excited—excited, sir ? Is this not quite enough to make any one get excited—to return from a long journey and find a thief—a highwayman, in your house, with the audacity of the devil, trying to wheedle the affection of my niece, a lady left in my charge ? Away with you ! go from my house."

"Upon my word, my dear judge, you have put yourself in' an unnecessary passion upon no grounds."

"What, you villain, you would deny the truth ! D—n you for a liar !"

"Come, be seated, and get cool ; you will then find that you are under a delusion."

This was more than he could stand ; he rushed out of the room like a maniac, and within two minutes he returned with three men-servants.

"Remove him to the lock-up room, men."

"I am ready to comply with whatever you may wish, my dear judge. It is a pity you should have disturbed those gentlemen."

"Do—what—I—bade—you," said Judge Blenheim, putting a deep emphasis on each word.

The men took their places—one each side, and one behind their prisoner.

Hal put two aside with his arm and held out his hands.

The pretty Bella ran gaily up to him, and clasped his hands affectionately.

"Good-bye for the present, my dear," said Hal, and, to the mortification of the envious old judge, he saw his pretty niece kiss the reckless, handsome young highwayman.

Bella made a peculiar pretty grimace at her wicked old guardian as he marched after his prisoner to see him secured.

He then went for a body of officers to take a highwayman he had *captured*.

The body of officers came ; about a dozen to take one man ; but, greatly to their disappointment and surprise, when they went to take their prisoner as they thought, the door of the lock-up was open, and he was missing.

A search was then made through the house, but to no purpose ; he had escaped clearly. The judge began to feel frightened. Could it be possible that his niece, for whom he cherished such strong *friendly* love, could have eloped with the daring fellow ?

It must be so ; they had both so strangely and quietly disappeared.

The judge raved, and fearfully he stamped across the room, wreaking vengeance on his own head by pulling his hair out by the roots as the thoughts flashed to his mind of the way he had been cleverly tricked by a highwayman, whom he had, with his own hand, locked in a room that would almost have stood a bombardment.

He dispersed the officers in different directions, and sent them in search of the runaways.

Not a minute after the judge had locked Hal Hunter in the prison—a rather more comfortable one than the generality of them—Bella glided quietly out of the room where she was sitting with her uncle, and, getting the key of the prison door, she had soon unlocked it and liberated her lover from his place of confinement.

Hal persuaded her to elope with him.

At first she strongly objected to his propositions, but, with a little coaxing, she consented, and they rode away unperceived.

They soon reached the " Chequers Inn," where they were made very comfortable.

"You are quite a stranger, Master Hunter," said Minnette, who waited upon them.

"Yes, Minnette, I have been very busy ; but I hope you have seen some of my friends ?"

"None," replied the young hostess ; "as for Master Merlin I have not seen him for a very long time."

Their conversation was brought to an abrupt close by the sounds of a rush of heavy feet, and a clamour of many voices.

Bella turned deadly pale, and shuddered coldly. Her lover felt anything but comfortable under such circumstances, though he did not let her see that he feared anything.

It was Merlin Hawke who had entered so hotly pursued. The retainers had overtaken him before he reached the inn. Fair Rosamond thought they were coming rather too close, so she sent out her hind legs, and sent the foremost of the hirelings sprawling.

When Merlin dismounted with the inanimate form of Lady Florence in his arms, he said a few words to Fair Rosamond, who understood their meaning, and dashed off at a terrific speed.

The retainers fell back to let the faithful animal pass ; none appeared to like the idea of stopping her.

Merlin Hawke took the opportunity of entering when his horse had scattered the hirelings.

Immediately he entered, Minnette came to his assistance and relieved him of his lifeless burden ; the doors were closed upon his pursuers, and terrific hammering ensued.

Hal Hunter, recognising the voice of his president, hurried to welcome him.

A cordial greeting took place, and they each related to the other their adventure ; they gave a hearty laugh at the idea of them both coming to the same place with the same design.

That was to keep the ladies there until they could convey them to the Haunt.

"Open the door," shouted Henry Ashburne, "or by Heavens ! you will have this cursed den of thieves pulled down over your heads !"

"In the king's name send forth that robber and murderer," shouted Marmaduke Greville.

Receiving no answer they grew exasperated, and again battered away at the door with good will.

"Go it, my hearties," said Hal, who had put his head out of a little Gothic window.

Captain Henry Ashburne drew his sword in hopes that it was his late antagonist.

"Put that plaything away," said Hal, waving his hand.

"Who are you ?" demanded Captain Ashburne.

"What the devil's that to do with you ?"

"Open the door," cried the infuriated young soldier, " or I will shoot you as an accomplice !"

"Don't talk foolish, my boy," Hal said ; "go away and don't make a noise."

The young soldier grew furious ; his wrath was uncontrolable, and, as Hal had disappeared from the window, he called out in a voice of thunder,

"Merlin Hawke, highwayman and robber, come forth and answer at the point of a soldier's sword for your dastardly work."

Merlin's lips curled scornfully, and he laughed a mocking laugh at the words.

"They are making a devilish row out there," said Merlin.

"They seem to have taken a particular wish to make your acquaintance."

"Yes, d——n them ! I have none for theirs."

"Young Ashburne has good lungs."

"He appears to be more anxious than any of the others to come in ; shall I open the doors and let him in ?"

"That is as you wish," replied Hal.

Before they had time to say more, Henry Ashburne shouted out at the top of his voice the following words,

"Merlin Hawke, highwayman and robber, liar and cur, assassin and poltroon, if you are not the wholly cowardly white-livered runaway, and have one spark of manhood left in your craven breast, come forth and answer, sword to sword, for your many dastardly actions, unless you fear the point of a soldier's sword."

"Merlin Hawke does not fear the point of a soldier's sword, or either the owner !" said our hero, as he flung the door back and stepped out proudly ; his challenger's words seemed to electrify him and cause the hot blood to mount his handsome features and the veins on his temples to swell out like cords. "Guard for your life, bounceable strut, this is a duel to the death, Henry Ashburne !"

"To the death !" repeated Henry Ashburne.

It would not have been many minutes before it would have proved a duel to the death had not Marmaduke Greville put a stop to it by having Henry Ashburne taken away by the retainers.

Merlin Hawke was stung to the heart by the insulting words of his opponent, and, maddened by desperation, his sword parried and thrust with such velocity that it looked like forked lightning darting about.

Had not Captain Ashburne been saved at that instant he would have fallen to the ground a lifeless form.

None seemed anxious to bar the way of Merlin Hawke as he re-entered the inn.

A yell of defiance rang through the air, and the officers that were sent in search of the escaped prisoner dashed into the inn.

"Oh, lor !" said Hal, " the game's up."

"No it ain't," said Merlin.

The leader of the officers then approached them and said,

"You are my prisoners !"

"Are we ?" ejaculated Hal.

"Yes," the officer replied.

"Then, my good fellow," said Merlin, "you are mistaken."

"No I ain't, captain ; you have had it all your own way long enough, and at last the game is up."

"That is what I said," Hal remarked.

Merlin gave his companion a peculiar wink, the meaning of which he perfectly understood.

"You must have the bracelets on," said the leading officer, producing a pair of handcuffs for each of them.

"Put them away," said Merlin, determinedly.

"It's no good of you resisting," said the officer, "there is twenty of us at least."

"And is that not enough to take two without putting manacles on our wrists?" said Hal, in a tone of disgust.

"Well, you see, captain, it is only to keep you quiet."

"Any way we are not going to have them on."

"If you will come along quietly, you can walk without them ; and if you try to escape you will soon be brought down."

"All right, my man," said Hal, who had still got the pretty Bella clinging to him, timidly.

Lady Florence had not yet returned to consciousness ; she was under the care of Minnette.

Hal whispered a few words to Bella Claremont, that seemed to make her a little more happier than she was before.

The two highwaymen seemed very indifferent and careless as they were marched away between the *valorous* officers.

They had not proceeded far down the road when a clatter of many horses' feet were heard galloping towards them.

The officers turned pale as they saw a body of handsome stalwart men, armed to the teeth, and mounted on powerful steeds of spotless black.

"Black Hawkes ! My God, we are lost !"

And such were the remarks that escaped the quivering lips of the officers.

Merlin gave a defiant, demoniac laugh that curdled the blood in the veins of all who heard it.

The men gave a shout as they recognised their captains in the midst of the officers.

Fair Rosamond galloped in front of the men, to lead them to the scene of confusion and rescue. It was she who had been the messenger to the Haunt, and brought the band with her.

She bounded forward as she recognised her master, and in a minute she had made a passage through the officers, and was once more by the side of her affectionate owner.

Another instant and the highwaymen have penned the officers in.

To tie the officers on the backs of their horses with their heads to the animal tails was the work of a few minutes !

That being completed, they sent them off at a sharp speed, to roam about where they liked.

Merlin Hawke and Hal returned to the inn while the highwaymen secured and made prisoners Marmaduke Greville and Captain Ashburne.

A shout from the men welcomed their captains as they came from the inn. Merlin Hawke with Lady Florence, who by this time had recovered and did not regret the abduction, and Hal looking quite proud of his lady-love, who was leaning on his arm and looked exceedingly pretty through the excitement that had given her a slight flush.

The retainers, who were making good their flight, were suddenly brought to a stop by heavy hands lying on their shoulders.

The highwaymen, by order of their president, gave chase and brought back the runaways.

They were then put in couples and tied back to back with their hands securely bound to their sides.

They were not long on their feet after they were tied together.

Some tried to walk sideways, but one of them getting out of step, they soon came to grief ; others would take it in turns to give each other a ride, that is, the one that was walking would carry the other on his back until he kicked his foot against a tuft of grass, or by a sudden jerk fell to the ground, and at last, by various ways, they all were rolling over each other on the ground.

"You see, Henry Ashburne, what I can do," said Merlin Hawke, mockingly, "I might have had you killed long since had I chosen, but I want you for another *purpose*, as I do your friend, Marmaduke Greville. You will accompany us, gentlemen. You shall be taken *care* of. It will not be long before Sir Andrew will join you. Bind and blindfold them and follow to the Haunt."

The last part of his speech he addressed to his men.

Within five minutes the band of noble men that defied even the law, were on the road to the Haunt of the Black Hawkes.

(*To be continued.*)

A LEGEND OF OLD LONDON.

CHAPTER I.

THE hour was late : the lights in the dwellings on London Bridge were one by one disappearing, and scarcely a sound broke the stillness which prevailed over the city. The night was cloudy, but the evening star shone out when not obscured by the dark masses of clouds which crossed it at intervals. In the east appeared the broad red disc of the moon, lighting up the turrets of the white tower, and throwing on the river a lurid glare, which became brighter and brighter as she ascended, until the noble stream reflected every surrounding object like a vast mirror. The tide was running up, and the water sparkled brightly in the moon-beams as it dashed upon the starlings of the old bridge. The vessels moored alongside the quays rocked to and fro with the current, and the night-wind in faint and fitful gusts sighed mournfully among the rigging.

On the deck of one of the large craft, lying off Galley Quay, two men were engaged in earnest conversation as they paced to and fro. One of them was a short sturdy figure, dressed like a mariner of that period ; the costume of the other, a tall elegant youth, was rich if not splendid ; yet there was a familiarity in the tone of the sailor which ill accorded with the contrast in their appearance.

"I have weighed the chances, Master Alleyne," said the young man, "and am still resolved to risk all for her dear sake."

"You will thrust your head into the lion's mouth, then," remarked the mariner ; "you will cause your uncle to renounce you, and bring upon you the ban of the church—and for what, I pray ? for a pretty face—a pair of black eyes, which may be found as beautiful in the head of a Christian lass."

"Prithee cease, Alleyne !" cried the youth impatiently, "thou dost but torment me. I tell thee I will risk all for that face ; therefore no more of thy sage preaching, but help me with my plan."

"Master Arthur," said the sailor, making a dead stand and fixing his eyes earnestly on the youth, "you may laugh at the preaching of an old sailor, but he gives you wholesome advice. Twenty years ago your uncle gave me a start in the world—released me from prison, helped me with money, and gave me letters to many rich merchants across the seas. To him I owe all I possess ; shall I then counsel one whom he dearly loves to play the truant and leave him in his old age ? No, Master Arthur, go seek some one who loves not you and yours—I cannot, I *will* not assist you."

"You are a churl, Alleyne," replied the youth. "I wot not that I should ask of you in vain ; but the master of the Falcon has become rich and proud, and hath no favours for citizens' sons."

"The master of the Falcon (heaven bless the good old man who made me its master !)" rejoined the sailor vehemently, "warns you of your danger. The breakers are ahead, Master Arthur, take heed and slacken sail, or you are lost. Ah ! little thought I, when you came to your uncle's, a curly-headed boy, scarce three years old—an orphan, the picture of your sainted mother, and mild and gentle as that sweet lady—that you would become so wild and wilful ; but go your way, sir, I will not assist you, and may the deep sea sink those who do."

The skipper resumed his walk, and the young man remained mute for some moments, looking vacantly on the rushing tide ; at length, with an apparent effort, he attempted to renew the conversation.

"Master Alleyne," said he, "you spoke of my uncle's love : methinks he is of late estranged from me."

"He thinks it time, perhaps, to curb you," replied the master, with the licence of long acquaintance. "He has heard of your mad pranks : he would make a man of you, master Arthur, and wean you from the wild youths you consort with."

"Excellent morality! most philosophical conclusion!" said the youth, with a laugh. "Who would have looked for such wise sentences from the master of the Falcon? 'Fore George, thou should'st have been a priest, Alleyne!"

"It is the spring time of youth and hot blood with you now," observed the mariner; "but storms and tempests will come, and tears and repentance—"

"Storms and tempests I can brave, tears are for women and children, and repentance for dotards," said the youth, haughtily.

"You are acting unwisely and cruelly," said the master of the Falcon; "your uncle loves you dearly, and your leaving him will break his heart."

"I am sorry to leave the old gentleman," said the youth, with a forced laugh, for it was on that subject alone that he was vulnerable. "I am sorry too, to leave merry England; but what can I do, friend Alleyne?"

"Do?" replied the sailor, who thought he could discover something like irresolution in the querist. "Do? why make up your mind to think no more of the girl, but turn your eyes upon some citizen's fair daughter: London lacks not sweet faces and comely figures."

"True, Alleyne; but the world has not another whom I love."

"Ah! I was once like you," sighed the master; "no one was nimbler in pavise or galliard. I have danced with the fairest in this good city; but grey hairs and wrinkles came at last, and warned me that such follies must have an ending; yet, the saints be praised, I looked not on the dark-eyed daughters of that accursed race, whom God in his wrath has scattered through the wide world. Heaven help you, sir! whither would you fly?"

"To Holland," replied the young man.

"You will find no refuge there," remarked the sailor.

"I will make the trial, Alleyne."

"Do so then," said the master angrily, "but seek some other vessel for your purpose: the Falcon shall not carry you." With these words he dived below, and left the gallant to ponder on what he had heard.

"The Devil take the old churl!" muttered the youth; then giving a low whistle, a boat, which was lying off the quay, came alongside the vessel. He jumped into it without uttering a word, and the next moment it was gliding silently up the river.

CHAPTER II.

STARTLING NEWS.

THE "courteous reader" is referred to the minute old antiquary Stow for a description of Cheapside; or, as it was then called, the West Chepe, "before the great and dreadfull fire," which laid ancient London in ruins. What that great thoroughfare was in those days may be easily imagined by any one who has observed the appearance of the High Streets of our country towns, into which modern improvements have not yet crept. Let the reader, therefore, endeavour to forget its present appearance, and picture to himself a broad thoroughfare, with a closely packed row of houses of unequal heights and sizes on each side. Let him fancy the quaintly carved and grotesque-looking figures which supported the upper stories of the various dwellings, the weathercocks which crowned many of the gables, the large many-paned windows, the huge oak rafters which intersected the walls, and, above all, the numerous sign boards, which swung over the heads of the passengers, upon which griffins, dragons, lions of all colours, and various other heraldic monstrosities, sprawled in truly Gothic variety. Here and there a tall elm might be seen rising majestically above the houses, its rich foliage darkened by the tenements of the "Burgher Rook," as Horace Guilford so aptly terms that social bird, while the jackdaws had taken undisturbed possession of the church towers. In those days a man might talk to his neighbour at mid-day, in Cheapside, without bawling at the top of his voice; but the head-splitting din now constantly heard in that neighbourhood has driven the rook and the jackdaw for ever from the spot.

Early one fine morning, just as the good folks of the West-Chepe were bestirring themselves for the day, the master of the Falcon was seen to give a hearty tug at the great bell of Master Richard Herlion's house, near the church of St. Mary-le-Bow. The outer gate quickly opened at the summons, and the honest face of the sailor being recognised by the porter, his arrival was immediately announced to Master Herlion.

Richard Herlion was a merchant of great wealth and unblemished reputation, and had held the office of alderman several years, to the very great satisfaction of the inhabitants of the ward of Chepe. He had long been a widower, and his children had died in their infancy, one of them having been lost in a tumult which had taken place in the city many years back; but he had a nephew upon whom he doated, whom he had humoured and indulged to an absurd degree, to his own disquiet and the youth's total ruin. This nephew was no other than the young gallant who has been introduced to the reader in the previous chapter. To complete the catalogue of his wild tricks, he had lately fallen desperately in love with a beautiful Jewess, the daughter of an old Israelite, residing in the city. How this acquaintance first commenced, nobody knew; and to the surprise of every one, his uncle was as yet ignorant of the fact, although with his neighbours it often formed the subject of conversation. Arthur had been seen by more than one of his uncle's friends walking with a tall elegant female in the outskirts of the city, and scandal soon set afloat the story that the alderman's nephew was enamoured of a Jewess. Nay, some had gone so far as to say that they had seen the damsel and her lover disembark at the Temple Stairs and proceed to the young man's lodgings in the Strand; yet Master Herlion was, as yet, entirely ignorant of his nephew's strange attachment. The master of the Falcon found his old friend and benefactor sitting at his morning's meal, which in those days was a substantial one. No slops; no toast or muffins drenched in butter, and rendered more abominable by hot draughts of tea or coffee, then spoiled the digestion of Englishmen and helped them to the blue devils. A round of beef, a huge ham and a cold pasty, displayed their charms on the alderman's breakfast table, and a large silver flagon stood foaming to the brim with ale.

"Ah! Alleyne," said the old citizen, extending his hand to the sailor, "you are early, but you are welcome."

"I have much to tell ye, sir."

"Well, sit ye down, and when we have taken our meal, I will hear what thou hast to say."

Alleyne needed no second bidding, but instantly commenced a vigorous attack upon the good things before him. The alderman supposed that his visitor had news of a totally different description to that which he was shortly to hear, and therefore betrayed no eagerness to receive his news; but when the master of the Falcon acquainted him with his nephew's conduct, grief and indignation by turns made the old man rave like a maniac. Grief, however, predominated when he learned that Arthur meditated an escape from England with the object of his affections, and Alleyne left him half inclined to doubt the humanity of his interference.

CHAPTER III.

EVIL TIDINGS.

IN one of the narrow, dirty streets leading out of the principal thoroughfare near Aldgate, lived Abraham the Jew. He had long been a widower; but one child, a daughter, the most beautiful of her sex, consoled the old man for all the afflictions which had befallen him during his residence in England.

(To be continued.)

BLACK HAWKE, THE HIGHWAYMAN.

THE PAPERS CHANGE HANDS.

CHAPTER XXII.

CAPTAIN WILL MERRY RECOVERS FROM HIS FALL, AND
FINDS HIMSELF IN A VAULT—ESCAPE FROM A LINGER-
ING DEATH—THE SLEEPING CHAMBERS—THE AVENGING
MARK OF THE BLACK HAWKES—LADY ELLEN ELOPES—
PURSUIT, AND A FIGHT FOR A LADY.

CAPTAIN WILL MERRY knew not how long he had been
lying in that dark, loathsome cellar when he returned to consciousness; his limbs ached, and his head seemed dizzy and
light.

"Where the devil am I?" he soliloquised, and, putting his
hands to his head, he mused for a few moments.

He suddenly started, and, staring wildly around him, he
exclaimed,

"Curses on him! I remember all."

Again his gaze wandered round his gloomy prison.

"There seems no way of exit. I cannot stay here to die
a miserable, lingering death, and none of my companions to
ever discover my body that would lie and rot here. No!"
he shrieked, "I will not stay here."

He then jumped up and groped round the wall.

He shuddered as his hands went over the wet, mildewy,
and slimy wall.

Again he shuddered, and, drawing his hand across his forehead, he muttered,

No. 12.

"Am I to die entombed alive in this beastly place?"

Just then he caught his foot in something, and he fell
heavily to the earth.

Slowly he raised himself on his knees to put his hand on
the wall, as he thought, instead of which his arm went
through a gap, and he fell forward.

Again he raised himself, inspired with fresh life at the hopes
that the hole through which he fell would lead to an escape;
but in his ascent his head came in collision with the jagged
wall that caused his skull to swell a considerable size larger
than was comfortable.

His hand wandered reflectively to the injured part, and he
muttered a curse.

The place was pitch dark.

He put his head through the hole, but he could not see an
inch before him.

"Thank Heaven for that," he said, as a gush of fresh air
blew past him. "That refreshing breeze has given me strength,
and it may be that I could discover the opening through
which it came if I can get through this d——d hole without
breaking my neck."

He managed to get through without breaking his neck, and,
groping about, another gush of wind blew past him.

He stooped down to discover where it came from.

A cry of joy escaped his lips as his hand came in contact
with an iron grating, through which the breeze found ingress.

He looked through, but that was also dark as the others, though the air came through fresh and fragrant. It was evident that, could he get the iron grating up, he would once more stand in the fresh air free.

He worked away with a good will, but it seemed to resist his every effort.

But Will Merry would not give in while he had strength, and, giving a sudden wrench, it loosened.

Another and another jerk he gave; each time it relaxed more and more.

One more desperate effort, and a jerk that would have pulled the side of a house down, the grating came up in his hands, and he staggered back with the sudden jolt.

He soon lowered himself down, and found himself in a long, narrow passage that had been cut through the ground to make a secret way to the vaults he had just left.

Reaching the end of the passage, which was very long, he found himself at the bottom of a very deep pit some fifty or sixty feet from the top.

To ascend this was his next task.

But how was it to be done? The sides were quite straight and there were no steps or ladder to get up by.

Then how was he to get up?

He thought that was as bad as the other place, save that he had the fresh air, instead of being stifled in a damp, loathsome cellar.

He gave a cry of joy as he saw a rope that hung from the wall.

He had not perceived it before, and it was not long before he was trying its strength after he had seen it.

"Then this is what is used to descend by," he said. "By Jove! not a bad contrivance; I will try my hand at monkey climbing."

So he did.

Once more he stood on firm ground.

He was in a shrubbery at the back of the house, by its appearance not often inhabited.

He surveyed the position of the house, and, looking enquiringly at a window, he said,

"I wonder if that is her room? I will see."

How was he to get at it?

That he quickly discovered.

Clambering up a high poplar tree, he leapt from a branch that hung towards the window and caught hold of an iron bar that went across the casement.

He tried the window.

It was not locked.

His heart throbbed with joy at the thought that Lady Ellen slept there.

He entered as quietly as a thief, and approaching the bed, he removed the covering off the head with trembling hands.

His brow grew dark and he fell back as he saw the face by the aid of an oil lamp that burned close by.

"Curse you!" he muttered, "if you were awake I would make you answer for your cowardly, treacherous act; as it is, you shall have something to remember me by."

He approached the bed again, and taking a bottle from his pocket, he poured some of the liquid it contained in the palm of his hand, and dipping the point of a stiletto in it, he drew it across the sleeper's forehead.

"There, my Lord Belmont," said Will Merry, as he saw a bright blood-red mark appear on the forehead of the unconscious nobleman; "I shall know you by that mark, and the first time we meet I will make you repent your treachery."

He then left the chamber and entered another as noiseless as a cat.

That was an empty one.

He swore, and left it in disgust.

He stopped and listened.

The place was wrapped in sombre quietness, and a glimmering moon-light, that threw its soft blue rays through the sky-lights, gave the place a very gloomy appearance.

Being certain that no one was stirring, he quietly opened the door of another bed-chamber.

His handsome face flushed with pleasure as he approached the bedside.

He stooped over and kissed the forehead of the sleeper.

She moved.

Will Merry stepped back, and for a few moments he seemed mentally lost in a reverie.

"Yes," he muttered, "she must come with me to-night."

He then gently touched the sleeper again.

Lady Ellen, for it was she, started up in bed.

Will Merry spoke her name in a low voice.

She looked at him inquiringly.

"Have you forgotten me, dearest Ellen?" he said.

She rubbed her eyes with her knuckles, and again looking at him, she exclaimed in surprise,

"Oh, Will, dear, is it you? I feared that you had come to harm."

"Thank heaven!" he said, "I have escaped his treachery."

Captain Will was in a very dangerous position.

He had got his arm round the white round shoulders of Lady Ellen, and his head resting on her beautiful breast.

Her head was resting on her lover's face, and her soft arms were twined around his neck.

Their kisses grew quick and passionate, their hearts throbbed quickly and irregular, their conversation grew low, and their breath came thick and hot.

This was more than Will Merry could stand.

To have the soft, warm and uncovered form of a lady so beautifully made as she was.

His hot lustful nature was growing inspired by her beauty. In another minute he would have given way to his feelings that were so fast overcoming him.

But slowly releasing himself from her passionate embrace, he kissed her and said,

"You will dress, dearest, while I am gone to prepare a conveyance?"

"I cannot. I must not leave," she said.

"Would you stay here to be wed against your will to that coxcomb of a lord?"

"No, no, Will, dear; but I dare not leave."

"Why not?"

"Because my uncle would have the country searched through to find me, and send you to prison."

"They would not find you were they to search the world through."

"Where would you take me?" she inquired, in wonderment at his words.

"To a place where you would be more happy than you are here."

"I should be happy anywhere with you, Will, dear."

"Then, come."

She did not answer him—his words had taken the desired effect, and with a little persuasion she soon consented to his propositions.

Will Merry soon reached the stables, and harnessing his own horse with another, he put them in a carriage.

When he returned, Lady Ellen was ready and waiting.

Slowly and cautiously they descended the stairs, and going through many doors they reached the awaiting vehicle.

Lady Ellen was soon seated inside, and in a minute Will Merry had mounted the box, and was driving on like an accomplished coachman.

Captain Merry had not seen a cunning, grinning man watch him as he returned after preparing the carriage for his lady love.

As Captain Will started off, the owner of the face that had been watching him disappeared, and within five minutes the whole of the inmates of the house were aroused and acquainted with the fact that Lady Ellen had eloped.

The men servants were soon armed with various kinds of weapons, and like a pack of wolves they rushed in pursuit of the runaways.

Will Merry had come suddenly and unexpectedly to grief; while turning a corner of a road rather too sharply the carriage overbalanced itself and rolled into a ditch.

He had just got the lady out, and was about to release his horse from the traces and start off, when the men rushed to the spot.

Another minute he was their prisoner.

Will plainly saw it would be no use for him to resist against such odds, and, like a wise man, he gave in quietly.

"Well, my good men," he said, "what do you want?"

"The lady," said one of the men.

"Take her; and be careful how you use her," said Will Merry. "I shall return and see his lordship to-morrow."

"You ain't gone yet," said one man.

"No, nor he ain't a going either."

"Indeed," said Will, "who will stop me?"

"We will," shouted at least half-a-dozen.

"The first that attempts to bar my way falls," said Captain Will Merry.

Three threw themselves in his path.

Two fell considerably injured.

The other slunk away.

Will then whispered a few words to Lady Ellen

He bid her adieu, and left her.

Two more stood in his way.

They soon went out of it.

He caught hold of each by the throat, and flung them aside.

None of the others seemed to like the idea of stopping, and Will Merry strode through them to where his horse lay.

It was the work of a minute for him to prepare his steed for a long ride.

While he rode away prepared for any adventure that might befall him, the men led Lady Ellen back to her home.

Captain Will felt himself again; he was on the road, the moon was shining like a silver sea, and clusters of radiant stars were out.

Will felt particularly inclined to plunder somebody.

Somebody came—not the sort of person Merry wanted—but he believed in making beginnings as soon as possible.

The traveller was a young, slender fellow, dressed in black, and with a white necktie. He was evidently a curate, or some member of the clergy.

Captain Will nodded to him, asked him what he had in his pocket, and tapped the butt of a pistol by way of hint.

Much to his surprise, the young man stopped deliberately, and said,

"I have nothing to give you, but, if you would serve a fellow creature, shoot me through the heart."

Will stared. The young man stood calm, and with a bitter smile.

That bitterness—the sadness of its being set so deeply on so young a face—touched Will Merry, and he said, kindly,

"If I can serve you in any other way I will with pleasure, but shooting people through the heart is a little out of my line. Are you poor?"

"A wreck in heart."

"And pocket, too, I suppose?"

The stranger bowed his head.

"Then, take this," said Will.

He drew a heavy purse from his pocket.

The young man went back.

"A robber's gold!" he said. "No."

"A robber's gold! Nothing of the kind; it was presented to me last night by one of the first gentlemen and most infernal scamps in London. Take it, my dear sir; it's only fair, for it's ten to one that when you get rich I shall stop you the first time we meet."

The stranger eyed it greedily.

"It would give me life," he said; "all for which I live—revenge!"

"That's the thing. Revenge on whom?"

"On him who ruined me!—the thief that stole my bride and dishonoured her!"

He paused before he said any more; then he continued, in a thick, whispering voice, and his eyes staring wildly,

"And murdered her!"

"The traitor and villain," said Captain Will, "he deserves to have his neck stretched."

"Ah, ah, ah!" laughed the young man, with a strange savageness, "I can now track him through the world, and I will slay him when first we meet."

"That's the thing," said Captain Will. "Kill him—follow him, and have revenge!"

"Aye! I will kill him," said the stranger.

Their conversation was brought to a close by the sound of an approaching vehicle.

They both drew under the hedge in the shade, and awaited the coming carriage.

Captain Will Merry prepared his pistols for use.

"A moment—and I will speak further," said Will Merry. "I must attend to business; there may be something worth having."

A chariot, drawn by four swift horses, rolled towards them, but came to a sudden stand as Will Merry reined across the road to bar the way.

"Who stops the path?" thundered an angry voice from the carriage.

Captain Will was riding to the window of the carriage when the stranger leapt forward like a maniac.

Will had no time to say a word or interfere with the quick and bloody tragedy that followed!

He heard a woman shriek; saw the stranger open the door and leap into the carriage.

There was the sound of an awful struggle; low, quivering sobs of dying agony, and then the stranger came forth; he had a dagger in his hand, red to the hilt.

"What have you done?" Captain Will asked.

The stranger laughed maniacally, and holding up the gory dagger, he said,

"Look at this bloody weapon. Look in there and see him who has been the destroyer of my life and happiness. I have revenged the death of my wife, and saved another from ruin. Look in there."

And Will Merry peeped into the vehicle. He had seen sights of horror in his lifetime, but never such a sight as now he saw. The carriage was deluged in blood. A human form lay huddled at the bottom, dabbled in red streams that still were flowing from a myriad of gashes; and on the seat, with the terror of death in her face, sat a young and beautiful girl, pallid and shuddering.

"On," shouted the stranger to the coachman, as Will Merry recoiled in terror from the window, "let the wanton lie on her dead paramour's treacherous breast, and call him back to life if she can!"

The terror-stricken driver lashed his horses, and dashed on. The carriage, with its ghastly burden, rolled along the road rapidly.

Sheathing his bloody dagger, the stranger strode away.

"Awful, but just retribution," said Will Merry, "and the most unpleasant adventure I have had for a long time."

His next was more pleasant, and altogether of a satisfactory nature. Two gentlemen were coming down the road towards him. Each had a lady with him, and they seemed a merry party. Will Merry liked to hear people merry; it was a sign that their pockets were in a healthy state.

"In such a case as this," he moralised, "I do a good action. These gentlemen are evidently bent on some sinful enjoyment with their fair and frail companions. It is very wicked of them."

So he drew his pistols, faced the astonished party, and called out,

"Stand!"

"Hullo!" yelled the gentlemen, "what the devil's the matter now?"

"Nothing," he said, politely, "except that I wish to make acquaintance with such a merry party, and ask for something to keep in remembrance."

"A robber!" said one of the gentlemen, taking his arm

from a lady's waist, "a plundering scoundrel, with a pistol in his hand."

"And several more in his pocket," said Captain Will. "What a handsome ring you wear, and that watch-chain, too ; it is superb !"

He finished his brief speech of admiration by putting his pistol quite close to the gentleman's nose. The gentleman was by no means a coward ; and his sense of chivalry was quickened by the fact that there were ladies to protect. Still it was perilous to resist, for some of the highwaymen were simply merciless murderers, who would scatter the brains of any who did not immediately comply with their demands. Captain Will Merry and his comrades were comparatively gentlemen.

"If I had space," the gentleman said, "and were it not that the ladies would be alarmed, I would answer your demand with my sword."

Will Merry liked that. He drew his pistol back immediately.

"Come," he said. "Will Merry never yet refused a challenge, and nothing pleases him better than a passage of arms with a gallant man."

The lady clung trembling to her companion.

"Do not fear," said Captain Will. "Our fight shall simply be a trial of skill. I am no assassin robber, as my name might tell you."

He removed his mask. His handsome face looked noble. The ladies were re-assured, but the companion of the gentleman with whom Will Merry was going to fight, looked anything but courageous.

The fact was the sight of weapons always made him feel uncomfortable.

The highwayman noticed that ; he hated cowards.

"Your friend," he said, as the gentleman stepped forward, "does not look quite at ease. Perhaps he would like to have first go in."

The other's lip curled.

"He has a very weak constitution, and the sight of any weapons will bring on strong symptoms, as you see."

Will Merry did see.

The man was trembling so violently that the ladies were obliged to support him.

The other cast his hat on the ground, and drew his sword.

Will Merry alighted, removed his hat, and unsheathed his blade.

"My purse," he said, "it is well stocked, as you see—my rings, and jewels, against yours."

"Very well ; what shall decide ?"

"The first three points."

"Guard then !"

Their swords crossed. The ladies stood motionless, gazing with admiration on the handsome highwayman, and on their own brave gentleman. The other one tried to look heroic, but failed.

There was a faint, low, clinging clash, then a sudden glitter, and a louder ring of steel. The ladies gave a shriek. They thought Captain Merry's weapon had gone through his opponent's breast.

But Will Merry was too good a fencer to so misjudge his distance. He had made his point, but without touching his man.

"One to me," said the gentleman.

"Two to me," said Will Merry, hitting his combatant in the same place that he had got a hit.

The weapons met once more.

The gentleman got a point with remarkable rapidity.

Will Merry parried just too late, and got a second dig exactly where he had got the other.

"That makes us even," said the gentleman, laughing.

Will Merry bowed, and said,

"The next point will be for me."

"For me," said his opponent, "if you don't watch it. Guard !"

Again their weapons crossed, and Captain Will did watch it.

"This one is for me," said the gentleman.

So it was, but the lunge was counter. The point of each one's sword was at the other's breast.

"Beautiful play !" said Captain Will. "This duel gives me pleasure."

"The last lunge was a draw," said the gentleman.

Will Merry bowed in acknowledgment.

Again the weapons crossed, this time to see which would prove victor.

"I have won," said Will Merry, as he hit his opponent on the arm.

"I have heard of you somewhere," said the gentleman.

"I have been there often," said Captain Will, laughingly.

"I meant to say," the gentleman continued, "I have heard of you very often, but never believed till now that a highwayman could be a gentleman."

"He can be," said Will Merry, as the other handed him his purse and jewels, "when he is treated as one."

"These things," said the stranger, "I have lost fairly ; but the ladies——"

"Well, the ladies ?"

"I must defend them, even if a second trial of skill has a more serious ending."

"I so much honour their brave champion," said Will Merry, "that I will not run the risk of killing him ; but your companion is so brave in aspect that I would fain try his mettle."

The gentleman did not care about having his mettle tried.

"Come, sir, will you fight for your property ?" said Will Merry, to the trembling cur.

"Not with a high—a—highwayman," said the coward, his teeth chattering together. "I don't fight."

"Let us try a shot at forty feet. I will shoot the plume from your hat without hurting you. You try and do the same."

"But the bullet might hit you !"

"I will chance that."

"But—but—I—I—do—not——"

Seeing how the craven shivered, Will Merry grew angry ; his late opponent looked all the disgust he felt, and the coward's lady was distressed by her lover's want of manhood.

"Then stand and deliver !" said Captain Will ; "every coin, every trinket. By Jupiter ! if I had your constitutional malady, I would hang myself !"

The coward gave up all his valuables, and sneaked like a beaten cur to his lady's side, who looked ashamed of her lover's cowardice.

Will Merry's late opponent uttered an exclamation of disgust at his friend's want of courage.

Will Merry mounted his horse, said farewell to the party, and rode away.

His adventures were not over yet ; his last one having been altogether so satisfactory, he was in no hurry for another, but, as is usually the case when a man does not care which way it is, he was not long before he got into a row.

He was letting his steed go very leisurely down the road, having removed the mask from his face, and taken to thinking, when he found himself suddenly confronted by a horseman dressed in black, and with his face covered.

In an instant Captain Merry's face looked terrible and grim.

"Stand !" said the strange horseman. "Stand and deliver !"

Our highwayman laughed.

"One of our old enemies," he said. "This is as it should be. I am Captain Will Merry."

The black horseman uttered an oath, and fired right at the captain's head.

But quick to see, and quite as quick to act, Captain Will

lowered his brow, and the bullet went over, leaving him uninjured.

The next minute his sword was at the throat of his assailant.

"Dog!" he cried, "the brethren of the Black Hawkes shall have one foe the less."

So they did.

The other backed his horse, drew his sword, and stood at bay.

Will Merry could not wait; he hated the whole band to which his foe belonged.

His weapon descended, and would have cleft his opponent's head in two had not the man guarded well.

They fought. There, beneath the calm and silvery moon, their weapons rung and clashed, while heavy thrusts were given, and desperate fighting done.

The contest was brief.

Will Merry was always masterly, rapid, and skilful to the utmost; excited as now he was, his rapidity and skill was marvellous.

Our hero fought to slay, and in less than five minutes his foe reeled from the saddle, dead.

"One the less out of the way," said Will Merry, as he made a cross on the fallen man's forehead. "His comrades will know who to thank when they see him. That mark never leaves them, living or dead."

And leaving his late combatant where he fell, the daring highwayman rode away.

He had not ridden far, when he stopped at an inn.

"Well, my pretty lass," said Will Merry, as a girl of very attractive appearance entered the room where he had comfortably seated himself.

The girl blushed as the handsome highwayman drew her round pliant form to him and kissed her.

Will Merry was a notorious sinner where ladies were concerned.

Captain Will had not noticed a man that stood at the bar as he entered; the man watched him with a cunning, vicious leer from under his slouched hat.

"I want to speak with you," said the man, addressing the landlord.

"What is it, Bill?" enquired mine host.

"Well, if you can spare a minit, I'll tell yer."

"Come in here."

The man followed the landlord into the parlour.

"Did yer see that gentleman," said Bill, "that came in about five minutes ago?"

"Yes; a traveller I should say."

"Would yer? Well, I can tell you who he was."

"Well, let us hear."

The man looked cautiously around the room, and speaking in a whisper, he said,

"It is Will Merry, captain of the Black Hawkes."

The landlord looked at the speaker in blank astonishment, his mouth wide open, and his eyes straining out of their sockets.

"A captain of the Black Hawkes?" he exclaimed.

"Yes; and there is a thousand pounds reward for his capture. What do you say, we've got a good chance?"

He slapped the landlord on the back, and gave a peculiar cunning wink.

"Then I will send to Bow Street."

"Nothing of the sort; they will take all the honour of his capture, and half the money. Leave it to me. All the reward shall be ours."

"But we shall lose him. He has often got away from half-a-dozen Bow Street runners, so I know we shan't be able to take him by ourselves."

"Who said we could? I have got some mates not far off. You keep a sharp look out, and if he attempts to escape, give a signal, I will fetch my mates."

Meanwhile, Will Merry was with Polly; he had laid aside his weapons, and was sitting with the pretty little girl on his knee, forgetting all about everything in the world except Polly.

Reflection might have brought remorse, so Will did not reflect; he was quite content with the pleasure of the time, and all the joy the yielding love of the inn-keeper's daughter afforded him.

Suddenly there was an uproar at the room door; Polly sprang from the highwayman's arms, and, hastily arranging her disordered hair, ran to the window.

A party of armed men were outside; she heard the name of Captain Merry mentioned.

"Fly," she said, "to my room; you can escape from there; but to stay here would be death."

She opened a sliding panel in the wall as she spoke.

Rendered forgetful for the moment by her excitement, he was about to go, when her father's voice was heard at the room-door.

At the moment, and before he had time to recover his hat and sword, the door was burst open, and his foes appeared.

"Seize him!" said the man, who had fetched his companions. "He cannot resist, for he has no sword."

Captain Will looked round for a weapon.

His foes were advancing, when, like an angel of light, Polly sped to the highwayman's side with the fleetness of a fawn.

She had brought him his sword.

"Thanks, sweet Polly," he said, pressing her to his heart.

"Now I am ready for you, gentlemen."

CHAPTER XXIII.

CAPTAIN MERRY IN TROUBLE—ONE-EYED BILLY'S JOURNEY—A MEETING, THOUGH NOT A PLEASANT ONE—THE HORSEMAN.

THE landlord stepped a single pace inside the chamber when a wave of Will Merry's sword caused him to halt with more haste than dignity.

The gallant and dashing robber took advantage of the brief pause to harangue his enemies.

"Gentlemen," said he, "to what unforeseen circumstance am I indebted for the honour of this visit?"

"Seize him!" shouted the host.

"Down with him! Secure him!" shouted the fellow who had given information. "Five guineas each if you take him alive!"

"Back, if you value your worthless lives!" exclaimed Captain Will.

One more daring than the rest pushed forward.

He was armed with a huge bludgeon, and raising his weapon in the air made a blow at Will's head.

The highwayman drew back, and the blow descended harmlessly.

Swift retaliation followed the daring assault.

Captain Merry's sword gleamed through the air, and with a scream the bold assailant fell back amongst his companions.

A perpendicular gash disfigured his forehead, his nose was cleft in two, and his lips divided by the keen weapon.

Blinded by the blood that flowed in torrents from the wounds, and mad with rage to think that his ugly visage was thus rendered still more hideous, the fellow staggered to his feet and hurled his bludgeon at the head of the gallant highwayman.

The weighty missile hissed through the air with a vengeful noise.

Had it struck its mark Will Merry's fighting and love-making would have been stopped for a time if not for ever.

But the cautious captain of the Black Hawkes avoided it by politely bowing to his adversaries in general, and the piece of timber pursued its flight till it came in contact with the window, which it shivered to atoms.

"You shall pay for this!" roared the angry Captain Merry.

He made a step forward, and his bright weapon gleamed like a meteor.

With a groan the man fell back on the floor.

"Dead!" exclaimed Will. "Who is the next patient requiring bleeding?"

There was a pause.

None were bold enough to venture within reach of that glittering weapon.

Life has its charms for all men, be they of the highest or lowest grade.

The men who sought to capture Will Merry were most decidedly of the latter class; footpads who combined poaching and hen-roost robbing with their recognised profession—men who would have been hireling assassins had they not lacked the courage necessary for the performance of deeds of bloodshed.

"Down with him! Seize the rascally robber!" roared these ruffians, each of whom had as many crimes to answer for and more cruelty than the gallant highwayman they designed to take captive.

No one, however, seemed inclined to set the example.

The landlord had disappeared from the scene along with the man who had first planned the attack.

Captain Will kept his face towards his foes, though he declined to make an assault, preferring to keep his sword ready for use rather than destroy its temper and edge by contact with the bludgeons and pokers of his assailants.

A sudden shriek from Polly caused him to turn sharply round.

At the same moment a pistol bullet whizzed past his ear.

From the secret door which Polly had thrown open the landlord had watched for what he considered a favourable opportunity to lay the highwayman low by a well-aimed shot.

Polly's sudden exclamation, and the captain's subsequent sudden movement, caused the bullet to miss its billet.

Will Merry strode towards the ruffian, sword in hand.

"Die, cur!" he exclaimed.

But ere he could strike, Polly thrust herself between her father and her lover.

"Spare him," she exclaimed, "spare him, for he is my father!"

"Mercy!" faltered the wretched man.

"What mercy would you have shown me?" demanded Will.

The man made no response.

"For *my* sake!" pleaded Polly.

"For your sake be it then," replied Captain Will. "Wretch, your life is spared!"

The trembling man rose from his knees, and would have slunk away.

"Stay!" exclaimed the captain of the Black Hawkes. "Ere you go, place your remaining pistol in your daughter's hands."

The man was about to do so; but suddenly his look of crest-fallen gloominess changed into an aspect of exultation.

"Ha, ha, ha!" he laughed. "Bravo!"

At the same time Will Merry fell to the floor stunned by a blow from a bar of iron wielded by one of the gang.

With a loud shriek Polly sprang forward, and threw herself upon his body.

"Father!" she cried, "he spared your life when it was in his power."

"Out with you, vile slut; his life is worth a thousand pounds to us."

"What is your own life worth, father?"

"Silence!"

"I cannot. I will not see him slain!"

"Pooh! silly girl; we are not going to kill him. We get more by keeping him alive."

As he spoke he rudely pushed his daughter to the door.

"To your work girl, to your work!" he exclaimed. "If you are disobedient, you shall suffer for it."

During this time the other ruffians had bound Captain Will hand and foot.

"Where shall we put him?" they asked.

"In the old back room, upstairs."

"Do you think that is strong enough to contain him?" asked the man, whose information and knowledge of Will Merry's person had brought the gallant rider to his present plight.

"Strong enough? Aye, I should fancy so."

"He's a desperate dare devil fellow."

"Well, he must be a clever fellow to get away now I've tied him up," said the ruffian who had busied himself with the cords.

"Lift him up and take him away," continued the host.

The men raised the still inanimate form of the brave fellow to their shoulders, and staggering beneath the burden, made their way up the winding narrow staircase.

The landlord threw open a door and motioned them to enter.

The room had not been used for some considerable period.

It had formerly been the rendezvous of a gang of smugglers, with whom the landlord had done business, and both the walls and the door were thick and strong for purposes of defence in case of attack.

The furniture consisted of a heavy oak table and two chairs, minus the greater portion of their seats.

Into this dirty, unswept apartment, the ruffians thrust Captain Will Merry, throwing him on the floor with no more care or feeling than if he had been a log of wood.

After glancing round the room to see that all was secure, the landlord locked the door, while his friend departed with the intention of giving information to the constabulary.

The name of this ruffian was William Scott, or, as he was more generally called, One-eyed Billy.

The origin of this singular cognomen was well known to every one in the neighbourhood of the inn.

Billy was an informer as well as a trainer of young thieves and poachers.

It was his custom to entice lads into some trifling act of felony, and then, by working on their fears, induce them to become his pupils until such time as they were fit for some grand plundering expedition.

From these expeditions Billy always took care to absent himself, though he was always at hand to receive the booty.

In those times the laws were more severe, or rather more cruel than they are at the present time.

To steal property of the value of *five shillings* and upwards from a dwelling-house was a crime which death alone could expiate!

Consequently the hangman's time was well occupied, and the mob, by frequent gazings upon the brutalities of a public execution, grew hardened, so that the spectacle had none of the desired effect.

One-eyed Billy was in the habit of receiving stolen plunder from his pupils and then betraying them to the police, taking great care to keep snugly concealed till the thieves were executed, so that there could be no evidence against himself, the receiver.

Once this excellent plan failed.

A pupil of Billy's was acquitted for lack of evidence, and, in retaliation for the injury done to his character, the enraged youth, with a red hot poker, burned out his instructor's eye, and would have gone on to further violence had not the timely arrival of some mutual friends prevented the impending catastrophe.

Billy vowed vengeance, but was unable to lay hands on the headstrong young man, who safely escaped to a distant part of the country.

Billy's trade declined after this unfortunate occurrence; however, as he himself remarked on one occasion,

"There wos a werry tidy livin' to be got on that 'ere graft."

He was more than half way on his journey, whistling softly to himself to keep his courage up.

The road was dark, being over-hung with trees; houses were few and far between.

Billy thought that it would be a very particularly unpleasant spot to meet with any evil-disposed person or persons, and he knew well enough that there were persons in the neighbourhood who bore him no good will.

He looked cautiously on both sides of the road, which was skirted by two deep filthy ditches, full of muddy water and decayed vegetable matter.

Suddenly two men strolled into the road before him.

One-eyed Billy halted suddenly, and after a moment's pause, faced to the right about.

There was a low whistle—a signal—and two more men made their appearance.

(*To be continued.*)

A LEGEND OF OLD LONDON.

(*Continued from page 88.*)

They are a curious people the Jews! What a persecution has their race suffered since the accomplishment of that prophecy which foretold their dispersion! Plundered by all nations, and scattered through many countries for centuries past, they are still a distinct race, with which Christians of all denominations are averse to commune. There are many reasons why the Jews cannot acquire a footing in society. The fierce bigotry of former ages rendered them the most wretched of human creatures, and the Jew at the present day cannot forget that he lives among the descendants of those who persecuted his race; hatred of the Christians is a legacy bequeathed to him through many generations. Necessity has made numbers of them worldly and vicious—I speak not of the wretched creatures who may be heard on a cold morning before we rise from our beds with their eternal cry of "closh." These miserable beings are objects of pity, cunning and roguish as they proverbially are, for their privation must be great indeed. I have seen feeble old women, "of the Jewish persuasion" as our newspaper reporters phrase it, sitting at mid-day on the step of a door, devouring a hunch of dry bread—their only dinner, after a fruitless walk of many miles! There is no "shamming Abraham" in this—these poor creatures cannot do it to excite compassion, for they would obtain none. They devour their crust in silence, without a murmur, and prefer a wretchedly precarious subsistence to servitude among Christians. As regards the wealthier Jews, the hereditary dislike of those whose creed they despise cannot be extinguished so soon as some of our soi-disant philanthropists suppose; but, as my fair readers will think I am becoming political, and vote me a bore if I say more on this subject, I will leave the tribe of Israel, and forbear further remark, lest I should be tempted to express a doubt of their "usefulness" to a state, in opposition to the notions of a member of our legislature, who perhaps may have cogent reasons for forming such an opinion. But to my story.

The dwelling of Abraham the Jew was situated in a dirty and miserable quarter of the town; yet it was roomy and commodious. He was rich, too, and therefore had many friends, and of course a few enemies besides those who hated him because he was a Jew. His daughter, it has been said, was fair; and as she did not much resemble her father in feature, there was no lack of scandalous stories in the neighbourhood. These, however, gave Abraham but little uneasiness; he valued not the opinion of the *Christian*. But there was one tale which reached his ear, and caused him some disquiet: report said that his daughter had a lover, and that that lover was a Christian.

The news of his daughter's attachment was gall and wormwood to old Abraham: he loathed the whole race of Christians: he had made up his mind to pay them tax and tollage without a murmur; but that his only chi'd should fix her affections on one whose religion taught him to regard the Jews as creatures scarcely human, was insupportable; he dared not believe it; yet he waited impatiently for a confirmation of the scandal. He did not wait long.

One day, as he returned from the synagogue, Israel, the usurer, took him by the arm.

"Friend Abraham," said he, in an under tone, "there are evil reports of your fair daughter."

The old man winced like a galled horse at this remark, but he smothered his indignation, and replied carelessly, "Idle tongues will be wagging, neighbour."

"Aye, truly," continued Israel, "idle tongues will be wagging, and eyes that be not dim will see."

"How now!" cried Abraham, angrily, "speak ye of your own knowledge?"

"I do," replied the usurer.

Abraham suddenly stopped, faced about, drew up his figure to its full height, and stroked his long white beard.

"Neighbour," said he, "you speak daggers, yet I would fain know more of this matter; prithee let me hear all."

"Your daughter was seen three days ago walking in Finsbury Fields with Arthur Lechmere, nephew of old Herlion, of the West Chepe; he who put Aaron's son in the stocks last Pentecost-tide."

Abraham muttered something about Beelzebub.

"Ay," said the usurer, "Beelzebub and the Christians are boon companions—the devil knows his own;—they talk of another tax on the Jews: their king hath more mad wars to make, and we must find the means, neighbour."

"'Tis ever so with the weakest," remarked Abraham; "we are but strangers here, and our very lives are scarce our own—but you spoke of my daughter?"

"I saw her hanging on the arm of Herlion's nephew," replied Israel, "and I wished for the strength of my youth that I might have smitten the Christian to the earth for his presumption."

"Marked ye her conduct, and heard ye ought of their discourse?" inquired Abraham, still endeavouring to suppress his emotion.

"I saw enough to offend both eye and ear," replied the usurer; "and I marvelled that the fair daughter of Abraham, the son of Simeon, should lay claim to the painted face and the party-coloured hood."

Old Israel was a mean, envious, grasping wretch, who loved to see every one unhappy. He enjoyed Abraham's mortifications; but he had gone a little too far, and the distressed father's blood, which had been seething and simmering during the dialogue, now boiled over with indignation.

"Curse you!" cried Abraham, in a voice hoarse with wrath, and giving the usurer a shove, which sent him staggering into the kennel, he abruptly turned a corner, and hurried home to upbraid his child.

He entered his dwelling with a throbbing heart, and a frame trembling with emotion.

> "The cubless tigress in her jungle raging,
>   Is dreadful to the shepherd and the flock;
> The ocean, when its yeasty war is waging,
>   Is awful to the vessel near the rock:
> But violent things will sooner bear assuaging—
>   Their fury being spent by its own shock—
> Than the stern, single, deep, and wordless ire
> Of a strong human heart, and in a sire."

But the object of his wrath was absent, and he sat himself down to wait her return, and brood in silence on the disgrace he had suffered.

CHAPTER IV.
THE TAVERN.

NIGHT had closed in, and a party of young gallants were carousing in "The Holly Branch" on the south side of St. Paul's churchyard. Among them was Arthur Lechmere, who had sought their company in the hope of diverting sundry unpleasant reflections with which he had been troubled since his interview with the master of the Falcon. He, however, found this no easy matter; his disquiet was soon perceived by his wild companions, who, of course, did not fail to banter him without mercy.

"Why, Arthur, my king o' the round table," cried one, "thou look'st as demure as a maid at her shrift! What ails thee, man?"

"Nay, rather like one who dreads a warrant of Capias," roared a law student; "confusion to all the tip-staff tribe!" and he drained his drinking cup to the bottom.

"He is betrothed to a shrew," cried another, "and becomes melancholic by anticipation."

"Silence!" hallooed a fourth. "Silence, ye bawlers, or we shall have a visit from the city watch, anon."

At this moment a gaily-dressed young man came into the room humming a tune with which his unsteady shuffle kept time.

"Hal Pearce," murmured Arthur, "and drunk as usual."

"Ha! Arthur," cried the new comer, "art thou there? Good even to thee, my king of roaring boys. Wilt thou beat the watch to-night, or break old Turnpenny's lattice? I-I-I (hiccup) I'm bent on mischief—Body o' St. Bride, but we'll scour the Chepe to-night. Will Lovelace, too!"

"Ay," replied the young man whom he had just recognised, "even as thou see'st, Harry; this is the council of asses, and he who brays loudest to-night shall be president for the year."

"Tho ass brays before rain, my boy," said Pearce; "if there be much braying we shall have St. Swithin upon us betimes, and, by my beard, your water is good only for brute beasts. 'Tis a villanous liquor, unfit for the stomach of man."

"A wise saw, a notable saw!" cried the company, and Pearce took his seat among them, amidst a roar of laughter and a very babel of voices.

"Heigho!" sighed Pearce, affecting the pathetic. "I beheld a sad sight as I passed Ludgate. The sergeant-at-arms and his men were dragging a fair young creature to Newgate."

"Ho! ho!" cried the company.

"You may laugh, my masters," continued the drunkard, "but it was a sad sight. She was a sweet creature, and looked far too lovely for a witch. They said she was a Jewess, and had charmed one of our citizen's sons."

An icy chillness shot to the heart of Arthur on hearing these words; he set down the cup which he had just raised to his lips, and with open mouth and outstretched neck awaited the remainder of Pearce's story.

"I could ha' broken the rascal's head when he rudely tore off her wimple, and abused her for a Jew's whelp," continued Pearce.

He had said enough. Arthur rose hastily from his seat, and, muttering an excuse for his abrupt departure, rushed frantically out of the tavern. The buz of astonishment at his departure was unheard by the distracted young man, who bent his hurried steps towards the gloomy prison of Newgate. Doubt and fear urged him forward, and in a few minutes he was knocking loudly at the huge iron-studded gate.

A savage-looking face appeared at the wicket.

"What would ye have?" queried a gruff voice, which contrasted strongly with the faint and hurried tone of that which replied to it.

"Good friend," answered Arthur, "prithee tell me if a maiden—a—Jew—ess—has been brought to your prison since even-song."

The grisly porter, upon whose face the light of a lamp within the gate glared strongly, smiled in derision.

"Blaspheming dog," said he bitterly, "thy sister is here. Miriam, the daughter of Abraham the Jew."

Arthur groaned in anguish.

"May He who died to save us," he replied, "soften thy heart and incline thee to pity—that sweet girl is innocent. 'Tis I alone am guilty. For Jesus' sake be merciful; take this ring, convey it to her, and bid her be of comfort—tell her that all will be well—anon. Here, hold thy hand, there is the ring, and a noble for thyself; be trusty, and I will reward thee."

The porter's huge palm received the ring and the piece of gold, and the next moment the wicket was closed violently, and a loud ha! ha! ha! was heard within.

Arthur gnashed his teeth in despair, the Cerberus of Newgate was not to be bribed; he rushed from the spot, and hurrying along the now deserted streets reached his lodgings, tormented by a thousand alarms for the safety of her from whom he had resolved to abandon friends, kindred, and country.

CHAPTER V.

CONSOLATION IN AFFLICTION.

CUSTOM has awarded many privileges to the story teller: he may bring forward, or keep in shadow certain points in his narrations as he may think fit; his heroes are, perhaps, represented as eating or drinking only once during a space of many months, yet he does not suppose his readers or hearers to be so obtuse as to imagine that they are of the camelion breed, living upon air. They walk off and on the stage like your players, and you are, of course, to suppose that they have performed many things while not before the audience. Having thus twaddled an exordium, we shall proceed to inform the reader that when the master of the "Falcon" quitted

his friend and patron, after making the gratifying communication described in the second chapter, the alderman, having recovered from his first burst of sorrow and indignation, sat down to deliberate on the most expedient means of winning his nephew from the mad attachment he had formed. Various plans suggested themselves to the old merchant; but ere he had resolved on one of them, the priest of St. Mary le Bow was announced.

Father Thomas was a man of dignified mien and commanding stature, with "one of those heads that Guido loved to paint," calm, pale, and thoughtful; "a countenance," as my Lord Bacon has it, "becoming the churchman." Father Thomas was a bitter enemy of the Jews; he hated them because they were unbelievers. Master Herlion's hatred was from the same cause; moreover, he considered the Jews as foreigners, who did a great deal of harm to the trade of the city; so that, as a Christian and an alderman, he was a very conscientious hater.

The priest shook his head at every pause in Master Herlion's relation of his nephew's behaviour, and when it was ended scratched his ear, an action which always shows that a man is much perplexed. At length he spoke.

"The cause of these mad passages is plain," said he, as his pale face flushed deeply. "'Tis the work of Satan—'tis witchcraft; but the church may yet have power to save him."

The alderman looked aghast. This was consolation he had not expected; the thought of witchcraft had never entered his head; it was adding to the misery which had overwhelmed him: his nephew was then on the confines of the devil's territory.

"'Tis well that I am informed of it thus early," continued the priest, without seeming to notice the consternation of his auditor, "and yet 'tis a sad mischance. The evil one has been active in our times. Ye wot how the devil, in the garb of a capuchin, entered the church of Banbury last Martinmas, and how he overthrew the sacristan and——"

"Oh! oh! oh! oh!" groaned the merchant, "that I should live to see my sainted sister's son leagued with Beelzebub!"

"Who is the woman who has done you this wrong?" inquired the priest.

"I wot not," replied the old man, wringing his hands; "but my intelligence is good. Oh, father, help me in this sad extremity."

"I will," murmured the priest, and he arose to depart; "you shall see me after vespers."

He retired, and the old merchant was left to his own reflections.

CHAPTER VI.

THE QUESTION-CHAMBER.

ON the following morning, strange tales were afloat in the city. Scandal had a rare feast—old and young, male and female, poor and wealthy, all tongues were moving on one theme, young Arthur's bewitchment, and his strange disappearance from his lodgings and his usual haunts. Search had been made for him in vain, in all quarters of the city, and it was generally supposed that the evil

(*To be continued.*)

BLACK HAWKE, THE HIGHWAYMAN.

THE INTERVIEW.

CHAPTER XXIII.—(continued.)

Retreat was cut off!

Billy looked at the ditch, but it was too wide to leap across, and too deep to wade through.

His knees trembled and his teeth chattered together as though he had suddenly been attacked with the ague.

Well he might shiver!

The men who approached had all suffered imprisonment through the agency of the wretched fence.

"Now, then, Billy," said one of them, "what devil's game are you up to now?"

"Oh, only going for a—a—walk."

"Ha, ha, ha!" laughed they.

"It's true, upon my word; you know I wouldn't tell a lie."

"Why, you old viper, we all know that you never told the truth in your life, except by mistake," said one of them. "Tell me this instant why you are walking along the road towards town at this time of the night?"

"And if you tell a lie, I'll choke you right off at once," chimed in another, grasping the wretched man by the neck-cloth:

"Let me go!—let me go!" roared Billy.

"Not if I know it. Now, then, where are you going?"

"Going to—to—town."

"What for?"

"To—see—a—a—gentleman."

"Indeed! It must be a queer gentleman if he wishes to see you. What is his name?"

No. 13.

Billy hesitated.

The hesitation, of course, convicted him of falsehood.

"A—a Mr. Smith," he said, at length; "you don't know him, I am sure."

"No, nor you either," said the man who had him by the throat, tightening his grasp as he spoke.

"He—help!" shrieked One-eyed Billy.

"Less noise," growled the man, "or I'll stop your shrieking at once and for ever."

Billy suddenly became mute.

"See what he's got in his pockets, lads," continued the individual, whose grasp caused so much inconvenience to Billy's windpipe.

"Not a bad idea, ha, ha!" laughed another of the gang.

"The d——d old rogue taught us to pick pockets, we'll try our hands on him," said a third.

"He taught us something else, too," briefly remarked the fourth.

"What's that?" asked the others.

"What to do with a fellow when we've cleaned him out."

Billy heard this, and would have fallen to the ground with sheer terror, had not the strong hands of his former pupils sustained him in no very gentle manner.

The expert fingers of two of the party were quickly exploring his pockets.

The booty, though not very valuable, was varied in character.

There was an old leather purse, containing a sovereign and some silver; a jewelled brooch, a bunch of trinkets, some skeleton keys, a pistol (unloaded), a short pipe and tobacco, an improved trap for small game, and a packet of papers.

All these articles were quickly transferred to the pockets of his quondam associates.

One of the party turned the light of a dark lantern on the packet of papers, and sought to decipher their contents.

Being but an indifferent scholar, however, the task was not much to his taste, and, turning once more to the prisoner, the man asked,

"Now, then, old rascal, are you going to tell us what you are after or not?"

Billy made no reply.

He resolved, if possible, to wear out the patience of his captors.

"The old cove is sulky; what shall we do with him?" said one.

"Duck him!" was the response.

"Good!" exclaimed the others.

"But I say, comrades, we mustn't lose him nor yet drown him. Have you got a good piece of cord?"

A rope of moderate thickness, and about fifteen feet in length, was at once produced.

One end of it was made fast to One-eyed Billy's waist, while one of the party held the other end fast.

Two of the party then lifted the poor trembling wretch, one holding his head while the other grasped his legs.

"One!" said he who held the rope.

The others began to swing Billy to and fro.

"Two!"

"Help! help!' exclaimed Billy.

"Three!"

"Murder! mur——!"

One-eyed Billy's exclamation was cut short by the stagnant water closing over his head and filling his mouth.

The men who had thrown him in roared with laughter as they beheld the fence emerge from the pool, mud and moisture dropping from his garments, while festoons of weed decked his head, neck, and arms.

They at once seized him, however, and prepared to repeat the ducking.

"Stop!" exclaimed Billy; "I'll tell you."

"Well, out with it then."

"I was going for the constables."

"I'm blest if I didn't fancy so. Who is to be lagged now?"

"Captain Will Merry."

"Who is he, and what has he done?"

"He is a highwayman."

"Did he ever rob you?"

"No."

"Then what the devil do you interfere with him for?"

"There's a reward offered."

"You greedy old devil, you ought to be choked for this!"

"Help! help!" bawled One-eyed Billy.

His sharp ears had detected the sound of horses' hoofs at a distance.

In another moment the rider appeared, and was speedily in the midst of the group.

"How now? What is the meaning of all this?" the horseman exclaimed, drawing rein suddenly.

For a moment the footpads made no reply.

The new-comer dismounted from his steed and strode into the midst of the group.

"Ha! our old friend, 'One-eyed Billy!'" exclaimed the stranger, as with difficulty he recognised the features of the informer through their coating of slimy mud and filth. "By-the-bye," he continued, "why did you not put the rope round his neck, my good friends?"

"We wanted to find out what he was doing along the road at such a time of night," said one of the men.

"And have you discovered his business?"

"Yes. He's got Captain Merry, the highwayman, stowed away somewhere, and was going to fetch the officers."

The stranger's brow grew dark as night as he heard those words.

Plucking a keen dagger from its sheath, he strode forward and seized One-eyed Billy by the throat.

"Tell me, instantly, where is Captain Merry confined?"

Billy was silent.

Though death was before his eyes, he did not altogether relish the idea of giving up the large reward offered for the highwayman.

"Tell me, or by Heaven I will hack you into fragments with my dagger!"

Billy still hesitated.

The point of the keen weapon pierced his skin, causing blood to flow.

The stranger was evidently in earnest.

"Mercy! mercy!" roared he with the single optic.

"Where is Will Merry?"

"At the 'Cross Keys.'"

"How many men are in the house?"

"Five, besides the landlord."

The stranger gazed inquisitively at One-eyed Billy, but at length came to the conclusion that he spoke the truth.

Lifting the informer on to his saddle without saying a word, he gave his steed a word of command.

The noble animal vaulted across the ditch; its owner followed, leaping lightly from side to side.

In a few minutes more, One-eyed Billy was securely bound to a tree in an adjacent plantation.

"Any outcry on your part will attract a pistol bullet towards your carcase," said the horseman.

Turning to the footpads he said,

"Will you assist me to deliver Will Merry from captivity?"

"We will!" they all shouted.

CHAPTER XXIV.

A RIDE AND A REVERIE—VANDELEUR PARK—THE MEETING IN THE GROTTO—LADY JANE'S RESOLVE—HER VISIT TO ALBION HALL, AND INTERVIEW WITH SIR THOMAS BROOKE.

FRANK MORTON and Albert Montague, after rescuing Merlin Hawke from death, proceeded, as has been already said, to an inn where they refreshed themselves, and then rode away in search of adventures.

Frank was lively and jocular, but Albert Montague seemed lost in thought.

In half an hour he scarcely spoke half-a-dozen words.

"What is the matter with you, old fellow?" said Frank, after trying in vain to enliven his moody companion.

"I was thinking."

"I won't insult you by bidding a penny for your thoughts, but still—I should like to know if they concern me."

"Not in the least."

"Any of our friends?"

"No."

"You are thinking of a lady, then?"

"Wrong again."

"Of an enemy?"

"Right at last."

"Then, if your thoughts concerning him are of so gloomy a nature, I presume his time has almost arrived?"

"Again you guess correctly."

"Then, my dear friend, if you wish to kill him, pray don't let me detain you. Stay, you will require a second; may I offer my services?"

"I fear he would not fight, Frank, even if I challenged him."

"Then, what the deuce can you do with such a blackgaurd?

If I were you I'd thrash him to death with my riding-whip if he refused to fight."

"I shall deliver him up to the hangman if I can only lay my hand on a paper for which I have more than once searched unsuccessfully."

"Don't talk about that gentleman," said Frank Morton. "After our late introduction to him I really feel quite uncomfortable at the mention of his name."

Albert Montague smiled grimly, and rode on in silence.

After a short time the two highwaymen reached a small lane, which branched off from the main road.

"Here I leave you," exclaimed Albert.

"What, so soon?"

"Business must be attended to."

"Right. Well, if you get into any scrape, and I hear of it, I will be with you in quick time."

"Thanks," muttered Albert.

The two friends shook hands and parted.

Albert Montague, after riding for a short distance down the lane before mentioned, leaped his horse over the hedge, and cantered across a succession of rich pastures.

Presently he emerged on to a large open common, which looked black, dismal, and lonely in the gloom of night.

A gibbet stood on one portion of it, and from the outstretched arm of the ghastly tree of death a chain depended.

Beneath were the scattered bones which had dropped from it.

Without heeding the dismal heath, the fearful gibbet, or the raven that croaked its harsh song from the summit thereof, Albert Montague kept straight on his course.

About an hour after parting from Frank Morton he drew rein by the railing of a park, and looked cautiously around.

Not a soul was in sight, and he walked his panting steed gently onwards, occasionally pausing to look round.

It was past midnight, and the moon, rising slowly, began to dispel the gloom.

Once more Albert Montague stopped.

His position was beneath a clump of trees, whose branches hung over the railings.

Not far from him was a road which crossed the heath from the park gates.

Albert Montague watched the road attentively, for he could trace its course for a long way across the heath.

The road, however, was silent and deserted.

After waiting some little time, Albert dismounted from his horse, which he tied to a tree.

He then clambered over the railings and stood boldly in Vanedleur Park, the country seat of the Duke of Cleveland.

With swift, yet noiseless footstep, he passed through the groves of oak and chestnut trees, till the mansion stood before him at no great distance.

All was silent; not a soul seemed to be stirring in the huge building.

Albert drew a scrap of paper from his pocket, and after glancing at it by the rays of the moon, once more scanned the dark windows.

"This should be her chamber," he muttered, "according to the plan she gave me."

He was speaking of Lady Cleveland, the affianced bride of Sir Thomas Brooke.

"I will give the signal," he continued.

He placed his hands to his mouth and imitated the cry of the owl so naturally that any one, not expecting such a signal, would have fancied the sound came from the bird of night's discordant throat.

A moment's pause, and then the soft light of a taper gleamed forth from one of the upper windows.

Albert repeated the signal, and again stood motionless.

The casement was opened noiselessly—the sweet face of Lady Jane Cleveland appeared.

"Dear Lady—"

A gesture stopped the speech of the daring youth.

In a few seconds more the lady's white hand was seen, and a tiny note came fluttering to the ground.

Albert Montague caught it, and kissed it ere he cast his eyes upon the writing.

It contained but few words, though it caused the young man's heart to bound with delight.

Lady Jane had consented to grant her lover an interview.

The note ran as follows :—

"Retire at once from beneath the window ; proceed to the grotto at the end of the terrace. I will be with you in a few minutes."

Albert hastily obeyed this injunction, and ensconced himself in the gloomiest nook of the grotto in question.

It was a dark place even in the brightest sunshine, for a huge cedar tree stood on one side of the entrance and drooped its boughs down over the mouth of the little artificial cavern.

The young highwayman seated himself, and with straining eyeballs watched for the appearance of Lady Jane.

Suddenly a hand was laid upon his shoulder.

"Who is there?" demanded the youth, in low but stern tones, while at the same time he drew a pistol from his pocket.

A low, musical laugh sounded in his ear.

"It is you, dear Lady Jane," said he, stretching out his arms.

Another moment and the audacious young captain of the Black Hawkes had pressed his lips to the rosy mouth of the titled lady.

"But how did you come here?" he asked. "I was watching the mouth of this gloomy cavern."

"See," said she, at the same time drawing a small lantern from beneath her cloak.

By its light Albert Montague perceived that a pedestal, on which stood a statue of Milton, had moved itself on a pivot, and that a staircase leading to some underground regions was visible.

"I am the only person besides yourself who know of the existence of such a passage. My father does not suspect anything of the kind remains, for a few years ago he had many secret passages and hiding places blocked up."

"How, then, did you discover it?"

"A very old servant who died not long ago imparted the secret to me."

Albert Montague continued to gaze down the dark chasm, and remained silent.

"And is this all you have to say to me?" said Lady Jane, gazing up into his face.

The young man started up as though stung by a serpent.

"Pardon me, dearest Lady Jane, if I am silent and reserved. This night is the anniversary of the death of my father. You can scarcely wonder that I am moody, when I see the villain who caused his death holding possession of that property which should have been mine."

"Then it is true, as you stated on the night of the masquerade, that Sir Thomas Brooke is a murderer in intention, if not in fact?"

"It is true, dearest."

"I never doubted it ; he has a murderer's look in his countenance."

"There are papers in his possession, I doubt not, that would fix the deed on his guilty head, if I but knew where to find them. But the day will come! He will betray himself, and then vengeance shall be no longer delayed! Blood for blood shall be the righteous sentence, and the villain shall perish in infamy!"

It would, perhaps, have fared ill with Sir Thomas Brooke had the impetuous youth met him at that moment.

Lady Jane listened to her lover's words with horror. Her father still wished her to wed the master of Albion Hall, and would hear no refusal.

"Dearest Lady Jane," said Albert, when his wrath had in

some measure subsided, "I am indeed the rightful lord of Albion Hall. Will you be mine if I can prove my title?"

The fair girl blushed deeply, and remained silent.

"I love you, dearest; I love you most fondly, with all my heart. Your coming here to-night convinces me that you have some slight regard for me; be mine, then, and renounce for ever all thoughts of wedding with that murderer."

"Dearest, I am yours only," whispered the lady, and the next moment the lips of the happy couple met in a kiss.

The sensation was delightful, but the happiness of the young lovers was doomed to be rudely dispelled.

Several footsteps were heard crunching along the gravel walks outside the grotto; the light of torches threw a lurid glare over the beautiful grounds, and harsh voices were heard.

"I saw him go into the grotto," said one individual, "and I dare say the thief is there now."

"The villain!" exclaimed the Duke of Cleveland. "He shall suffer for this. It is a most infamous attempt to carry off my daughter. Luckily she is fast asleep in her own room."

"Fly, dearest! fly, instantly! Your presence here is not suspected," whispered Albert; and ere Lady Jane could say a word, he had pushed her down into the secret passage and re-closed the trap-door.

He then drew himself up proudly to meet his foes.

They were not long in making their appearance.

Half-a-dozen half-naked, half-armed grooms and footmen, headed by the duke, came rushing tumultuously into the grotto.

"Here he is! Seize him!" shouted half-a-dozen voices at once; and as many arms were stretched forth towards him.

"Hold!" exclaimed Albert, levelling a pair of pistols at the group.

They heeded not, but pressed upon him eagerly. He fired!

There was a loud shriek, and a man fell to the earth severely wounded.

In another instant Albert's bright sword had leaped from its scabbard, and, rushing desperately towards the doorway of the grotto, his foes gave way.

Two remained to attend on the wounded man, the others followed Albert, who kept them well behind him, for he was swift of foot.

He soon reached the spot where his brave steed stood, and, vaulting to the saddle, rode off, unheeding the shouts of the grooms or curses of the furious duke.

Lady Jane retired to her chamber to think over a plan which her lover's words had suggested to her.

She resolved to put that plan in execution the following day.

Accordingly, late in the afternoon of the day succeeding Albert Montague's visit, she ordered her carriage, and directed the coachman to drive to Albion Hall.

Though much astonished that their lady should go *alone*, the servants did not venture to make any remark.

Albion Hall was at least sixteen miles from Vandeleur Park, and it was dark when the carriage reached the gates.

Sir Thomas Brooke's domestics were rather surprised at such a strange visit; nevertheless, they ushered the lady with due ceremony to the library, explaining that Sir Thomas had not yet returned from hunting, but that he was expected each minute.

Left by herself, Lady Jane glanced round the room. She had left her hat and cloak in the carriage, and was attired only in a rich robe of purple velvet.

Presently her eye rested on a box which stood beneath a side table.

She dragged it forth, and, placing a candle on the chimney-piece close at hand, tried the lock.

Finding it refused to yield, she drew a strong-bladed knife from a fold of her dress and inserted it beneath the edge of the box and the lid.

The lock was not made to withstand such rough usage, and soon gave way.

The lid flew open, and Lady Jane beheld several packets of papers of various sizes.

"Now," she murmured, "if I can only find the proof of his complicity with the murderers of the late Lord Montague I shall be supremely happy."

She opened several of the packets and glanced at their contents.

There were the title deeds of the estate; these she placed in the pocket of her dress, and there were many deeds, bonds and mortgages, which she restored to the box.

"My search, after all, has been without success," sighed she, when, as she was lifting a packet from the floor, two folded papers fell from it.

Lady Jane eagerly opened them, and glanced at their contents.

The first was a letter badly written, and vilely spelt:—

"Zur,—I'll cut Lord Montigou's dhrote or heny biddy else for a thousind pouns.
                              "Yrs. BILL THE CRUSHER."

The other was a receipt for a thousand pounds for *work done*, and was signed by the the same individual.

Scarcely had Lady Jane deciphered the contents of these two documents, when they were suddenly snatched from her hand.

Turning, and springing to her feet, the lady beheld Sir Thomas Brooke, whose features were literally white with anger and fear combined.

Quick to think and quick to act, Lady Jane Cleveland instantly decided upon the course to adopt.

Before Sir Thomas Brooke could utter a word, she had levelled the straight, deadly-looking barrel of a pistol at his breast, and in low tones said,

"Not a word! Restore those papers to my hand without uttering a sound or I pull the trigger!"

She stood erect, haughty and defiant.

The guilty man quailed before her; his eye fell, though he still retained the papers in his hand.

Lady Jane made a gesture of impatience.

"Quick!" said she. "Give me those papers, or your blood be on your own head."

CHAPTER XXV.

THE SOLITARY HORSEMAN — RESCUE OF WILL MERRY— DEATH OF THE LANDLORD—ARRIVAL AT THE HAUNT— WHERE IS MARMADUKE GREVILLE?

THE Band of Black Hawke, under the command of Merlin and Hal Hunter, made their way swiftly along the road towards the haunt.

They had little fear of pursuit, for were not their foes scattered—dispersed over the country, while their leaders, Marmaduke Greville and Captain Ashburne, were prisoners?

Nevertheless, Merlin was by far too good a commander to allow his band to straggle.

He kept them together in something like military order.

Lady Florence and Bella Claremont had been provided with steeds, and rode with the leaders.

The two prisoners were on led horses, surrounded by a party of the Black Hawkes.

Lady Florence seemed downcast.

A sense of honour told her she had taken a wrong step in yielding to Merlin's persuasive tongue; but strong love was at the same time combating with that conviction, overthrowing her scruples one by one.

Bella Claremont, on the other hand, seemed completely happy.

She was with her lover, and that fact alone was sufficient to banish dull care from her bosom.

When they had accomplished one-third of their journey they turned aside from the main road, intending to reach the Haunt by a less frequented route.

They had proceeded along the narrow, dark lane for some little distance when Merlin suddenly gave the signal to halt.

"Prisoners, be silent, if you value your lives!" said he.

Every sound was hushed.

It then became evident that a horseman was proceeding leisurely along the road before them.

"Hal, ride forward, and see who it is," said Merlin.

Bella winced a little when she heard the order given.

"Don't be afraid, love, whispered the young man, as he bent towards her and kissed her fair brow. I know how to take care of myself."

Another moment, and he had vanished.

Shortly his voice was heard hailing the solitary rider in the accustomed form,

"Stand and deliver!"

A peal of laughter followed, which puzzled the band.

Another moment and a shrill whistle signified to Merlin and his men that it was a friend.

They rode forward and found Hal Hunter conversing with Frank Morton.

"Why, how came you here, and where is Albert?" asked Merlin.

"I left Albert about two hours ago, and shortly afterwards met these gentlemen" (pointing to four fellows on foot) "who were in the act of drowning a one-eyed individual in order to make him confess his business. That business I discovered was to deliver Will Merry into the hands of the Philistines; so, after settling one-eye, we at once started to rescue sweet Will."

After a brief consultation, the whole party proceeded towards the "Cross Keys" where Will Merry was confined, with the avowed intention of rescuing that gentleman from the hands of his persecutors.

They arrived within a hundred yards of the inn, and then separated into two bodies, one of which remained stationary, guarding the prisoners and ladies, while the others, setting spurs to their steeds, galloped forward and surrounded the house.

The alarmed landlord thrust his head out of the window, and, in faltering accents, demanded the business of the newcomers.

"We want our friend and comrade, Captain Will Merry," exclaimed Merlin, bursting open the door and striding into the bar.

"He—e—is—isn't here."

"Liar!" exclaimed the indignant highwayman.

"It's true, your honour, I assure you."

"Here, lads," said Merlin, "exercise your whips on this fellow's back till he confesses where our comrade is."

In another moment the landlord began to shriek beneath the cutting lashes of the highwaymens' whips.

"No, no, spare him!" exclaimed pretty Polly, rushing in; "he is my father. Come with me, and I will show you where your friend is."

Merlin gave the signal, and the punishment ceased.

He then followed Polly till they reached the door of the strong room in which Will Merry had been placed.

"My father has the key," said the girl; "I know not where he keeps it."

Merlin Hawke called two of his followers, and before their united strength the door soon gave way.

Will Merry welcomed his deliverers with unfeigned joy.

He had expected nothing less than to be taken as a prisoner to Newgate.

"Upon my word, gentlemen," he said, "you have relieved my mind of a great anxiety. When I heard your horses out-

side I supposed it was at least a troop of cavalry come to convey me to the delightful regions of Old Bailey."

"We will take you to much more comfortable quarters, my friend," said Merlin. "Lads," he continued, addressing his men, "help yourself to the best wine in the house."

Such a command was readily obeyed, as may be guessed.

The landlord looked on for some few minutes, but at length his rage became too great for control.

He rushed upon one of the band who was in the act of drawing a cork, and, snatching the bottle from the highwayman's hand, struck him a heavy blow upon the head.

The man fell, but a comrade's sword instantly avenged the deed.

The keen weapon glittered a moment in the light of the lamp, and then was red with blood.

With a curse and a groan the wretched landlord fell dead!

Polly, who had witnessed the sudden and fearful tragedy, gave a heart-rending scream, and fell senseless beside the bleeding corpse of her father!

Then deep silence reigned through the house.

Merlin was the first to speak.

"To your horses, and let us get away," he said.

One by one the men left the bloodstained building, supporting their comrade, whose head was severely wounded by the broken bottle.

"How about this poor girl?" said Will, pointing to Polly; "can we leave her here alone with the dead?"

"What would you do with her?"

"Take her with us."

"What, to the Haunt?"

"Yes. She could leave in the morning if she did not like the place."

"I doubt the prudence of trusting the secret of our rendezvous to strangers."

"This girl befriended me, and tried to save me from the gang of ruffians headed by her father."

"Then bring her with you. We have more ladies without, so that she will not lack society."

Captain Will Merry tenderly lifted the unconscious girl in his arms, and bore her from the room.

His horse had been brought from the inn stables by one of the band, and, mounting, he held Polly before him on the saddle.

She made no resistance, but lay in his arms like a corpse.

The cavalcade was soon in motion once more, and, after a sharp ride, they reached their Haunt unmolested.

Lady Florence Greville and Bella Claremont were shown to a well-furnished apartment, and Polly, who still continued unconscious, was committed to the care of the old woman who acted as housekeeper to the Black Hawkes.

The band unsaddled and stabled their steeds, and Merlin was about to visit Lady Florence, when one of the band approached.

"What are we to do with the prisoners, captain?" asked the man.

Merlin Hawke paused for a moment ere he replied,

"Place them in separate chambers for the present. Give them food and drink if they require it, and assemble the whole band in the Hall in two hours' time."

The man bowed and departed.

When he rejoined his companions he uttered a loud curse.

Marmaduke Greville had disappeared!

Loud shouts soon spread the alarm, and in less than five minutes the whole band were ready to pursue the escaped prisoner.

"How did he escape? Who saw him last?" asked Merlin as soon as he heard the news.

"I left him in charge of Bandy Jim," said the man, who

had asked the captain for instuctions regarding the disposal of the prisoner.

"Where is Bandy Jim?'

There was no response.

A party of men rushed off in search of the missing man, and soon a volley of curses proclaimed they had found him.

Bandy Jim was discovered lying on his back outside the gate insensible from the effects of a blow on the forehead.

The horse he had ridden was quietly browsing a few yards away.

They conveyed the injured man into the house, and administered various remedies to restore his scattered senses.

At length, with a deep sigh, the man opened his eyes and sat up.

"Where is——the prisoner?" he exclaimed. "Where am I?"

Then, in a moment recollection returned, and addressing Merlin, he said,

"It was not my fault, captain."

"Tell us how you lost your prisoner?" replied the chief of the Black Hawkes.

"I was sitting on my horse by his side, when, suddenly, I received a blow and—I—don't recollect anything more."

"Let us go in pursuit!" exclaimed a dozen voices.

"Stay," cried the commanding voice of their captain, just as they were about to rush away. "Remain where you are, and guard well the remaining prisoner. My task shall it be to overtake the fugitive."

He beckoned one man to accompany him, and in a few seconds was in the saddle.

Lights were brought, and by their glare the tracks of the horse ridden by Marmaduke Greville were easily discovered.

With a word to Fair Rosamond the gallant steed bounded away, Merlin's fingers toying with the hilt of his sword in a style which boded evil to the fugitive, should he be overtaken.

Not a word passed between the two men; the only audible sounds were the clatter of the horses' hoofs and the panting breath of the animals.

Half an hour elapsed when Merlin's attendant broke silence.

"I can hear a horse on ahead, captain."

"Indeed; I heard it five minutes ago."

Fair Rosamond seemed to be aware that her master's business was of the utmost importance, and, notwithstanding her late severe wounds, strained every nerve in the headlong race.

The grey light of dawn was rapidly tinging the eastern sky.

They were rapidly nearing the runaway, and, on turning an angle made by the road, he was seen about a hundred yards in advance whipping and spurring as though life depended on his efforts.

So it did for aught he knew.

"Halt, villain!" thundered Merlin.

There was no reply.

"Halt, or I fire!"

Still Marmaduke Greville urged his steed along at headlong pace.

Merlin raised himself in his stirrups, and, levelling his pistol, fired.

But so rapid was the pace at which Fair Rosamond was going that the bullet flew wide of the mark.

Merlin drew his sword, and was soon by Marmaduke Greville's side.

"Villain! cur! coward!" ejaculated the captain of the Black Hawkes. "Turn and encounter me, if you dare."

Marmaduke Greville held up his hands imploringly.

"I am unarmed—I am defenceless. Do not kill me."

"My sword has never taken life save in fair combat," replied Merlin, returning his weapon to its scabbard. "But," continued he, drawing a second pistol, "if you make another movement to escape, my bullet shall enlighten your thick skull as to the state of my temper."

So furious was the pace at which Merlin had ridden, that the attendant was left many yards behind.

In a few minutes he overtook them, however, and stood sword in hand ready to assist his captain if assistance was required.

"Sheath your sword," said Merlin, "and bind this trembling villain afresh."

The man obeyed willingly, and tightly secured Marmaduke Greville's hands behind his back.

Merlin smiled grimly while the man was performing this task, and, when he had finished, said,

"Now place him with his face to the horse's tail, and lead him gently homewards."

"Shall I blindfold him again, captain?'

"Certainly."

The man bound his handkerchief tightly over the prisoner's eyes, and, placing him on the horse in a most undignified position, the homeward journey was commenced.

Merlin's steed began to exhibit the most unmistakable signs of exhaustion.

The poor animal's head drooped, her steps faltered, and her body rolled from side to side.

Merlin dismounted.

"On with the prisoner," said he, "and see that he does not escape. I will follow."

"Do you think you are safe by yourself, captain?" said the man. "There are officers about, recollect."

"I can protect myself," said Merlin, haughtily.

The man bowed, and rode on.

With his prisoner he reached the haunt of the Black Hawkes in safety, and, to prevent a second escape, Marmaduke Greville was placed in a stone cell.

The band then assembled in the hall to await the coming of Merlin, and the sentence on the two prisoners.

But Captain Merlin came not.

True to the feeling which a bold cavalier always has in his heart he led his faithful steed easily along the road.

He was within a couple of miles of his destination when the bright light of a fire fell upon his astonished eye.

The fire was by the roadside, and he knew well enough must have been kindled since he started in pursuit of Marmaduke Greville.

By the side of the fire were three hags, whose hideous appearance would be enough to fill the heart of an ordinary man with superstitious terror.

But Merlin Hawke was not an ordinary man, and it must indeed have been a fearful sight that could have appalled him, or caused his brave heart to beat faster than usual.

He quieted Fair Rosamond, who at first strongly objected to approach the horrid group of deformity and rags.

Then, loosening his sword in its scabbard and cocking a pistol, he continued on his way, with eyes firmly fixed on the grotesque yet hideous scene.

As he approached, the hags stretched out their lean arms and claw-like fingers towards Merlin.

"He comes!" they exclaimed, in harsh, discordant tones, not unlike the shrieking of the owl.

"Peace, vile wretches!" said Merlin.

"Peace! What have we to do with peace? Our delight is in bloodshed, in fighting, in dark deeds of murder. Peace—ha, ha, ha!"

"Stand out of my path."

"Pass on; but not in peace. Troubles await you; evil days are coming when your enemies will triumph, in spite of your bravery and your long sword."

"At least I can meet my fate like a man when my time comes,"

The three hags whispered together for a few seconds, then one of them spoke again.

"Throw us a piece of gold, bonny sir; a piece of bright, red gold, and I will tell you news."

Merlin carelessly threw her a guinea.

"More gold, more bright gold; the news is worth more."

"Here is another guinea," he exclaimed, throwing a second coin.

"More, more! one piece each," continued the hag, stretching out her long hands.

"Here is a third guinea, and not another shall you have, whether I hear your news or not."

"Oh, the bonny bright gold!" muttered the hag. "What a fine thing it must be to be a dashing knight of the road, and to take the gold from every traveller!"

And forthwith the three performed a kind of dance, of the most weird and fantastic kind, shrieking a kind of song all the while.

"Come," said Merlin, "the news?"

"The news! Ha, it is rare news! Listen, you have enemies."

"I know that already."

"You have one who is more crafty than all the others put together. He is now on his way to arrest you, and soldiers with him."

"His name?"

"Simeon Lazarus!"

"Where does he expect to find me?"

"At your haunt. But more gold, more gold, or no more news."

Merlin threw a purse towards them, which was eagerly clutched.

"I know not how you procure your information," said he, "but it is of value to me. Tell me, does Lazarus know how to enter the haunt?"

"He does, by the secret path."

"The secret passage?"

"Aye, there is a traitor in your brave band!"

"And he shall die!" exclaimed Merlin, as he continued his journey.

After progressing a few yards, he turned to ask another question.

The fire was extinguished, and the three weird sisters had vanished.

(*To be continued.*)

A LEGEND OF OLD LONDON.

(*Continued from page 96.*)

spirit who had led him astray from the good faith, had finished the drama, by spiriting him away to other regions. The reputed instrument of Beelzebub, Miriam, the fair daughter of Abraham the Jew, was, however, in safety. The delightful dream of the poor maiden had been exchanged for sad reality; the home of her fond parent for a damp cell in the grim prison of Newgate, whither we must now lead the reader.

The Question-Chamber, or Hall of Torture, was a spacious apartment in the very interior of the prison, lit by a large window at one end; but the dust of many years, and the accumulated tapestry of several generations of spiders, almost excluded the light of heaven. The last scenes in the lives of saints and martyrs, emblazoned on the panes which filled the upper compartments, glimmered faintly in the morning's sun, and cast additional gloom over the vast apartment. On one side was ranged a row of stalls of carved oak, and within sat several men in furred robes and gold chains, the light which streamed through the hall crossing their countenances, but leaving the rest of their persons in shadow. The bald head of an ecclesiastic was seen among the judges. In the centre of the hall stood a large chafing dish, supported on a tripod, its charcoal fire glowing with a crimson heat; near it grinned that hideous instrument of a barbarous age, the rack; on the floor were scattered various iron implements of torture. Suddenly a door opened, and two men, the executioner and his assistant, entered, carrying between them a female form, whose garments were dank with the moisture of the cell from which they had borne her.

As they entered, the female disengaged herself from her grim supporters, and with an apparently violent effort walked slowly but firmly into the middle of the hall. The executioner, with bared arms and untrussed jerkin advanced and trimmed the fire. Then a voice spoke from the stalls:

"Woman, you are charged with the detestable and soul-damning sin of witchcraft, what would ye say?"

The prisoner raised her head, passed her hand across her forehead, and while tears stood in her large, dark, lustrous eyes, falteringly replied:

"Alas! what *can* I say, when all here are against me?"

"Do you repent?" queried the stern voice which had spoken before.

"Repent! Is it a sin to love him then?" murmured the poor maiden, in a voice which was only audible to herself.

"Do you mutter threats against the court?" cried another voice from the stalls.

"Hold!" said the ecclesiastic, who was no other than the Priest of St. Mary-le-Bow—"I question her. Daughter, the church is merciful, will you repent and save yourself?"

"I have nought to repent me of," replied the prisoner.

"Where is Arthur Lechmere?" said the priest sternly. Instantly the prisoner's frame was convulsed violently; she raised her head for a moment, glanced round the hall, and then turning towards the judges, seemed about to reply, when her strength forsook her and she sank on the floor. The men advanced and raised her up, but she was insensible. A long pause succeeded, then the judges whispered to each other, and the priest descended and handed to the executioner a small phial of distilled waters, which restored their victim to consciousness.

"Where is Arthur Lechmere?" muttered the priest, whose stern nature seemed somewhat subdued, as he gazed on so much beauty. Had the prisoner been accused of any other crime, he could have believed her innocent; but he remembered the numerous legends, from St. Anthony downwards, which told of the temptations of holy men by fiends, who assumed fair forms, like that before him.

Miriam raised her head, and looked for a moment on her questioner. "Ah," sighed she, "can a minister of that God whom we all worship join in persecuting a poor weak maiden?"

"Where is your leman?" said the priest, with a frown, "Where is the youth you have betrayed to ruin?

"Betrayed! ruin!" echoed the poor girl, "what mean ye? Oh, that he were here!"

A stern voice interrupted her; it was Master Herlion's. "Witch!" cried he, "where is my nephew? Answer, or we will pull thee limb from limb:" then addressing the priest, "Father, we idle time—the rack hath made the dumb speak ere now."

The priest retreated to the stalls, and the executioner again advanced. At a signal the prisoner was again seized, and spite of her struggles, divested of her upper garment. The embroidered band too, which crossed her forehead, became unloosened, but ere her dark hair descended, her judges caught a glimpse of her neck and shoulders, which it shrouded like a veil. The priest averted his head at the sight.

"She is beautiful as the Virgin," thought Father Thomas. "Oh! that the fiend should dwell in such a sweet form."

Meanwhile the poor girl trembled and panted, like a bird in the net of the fowler. Her colour alternately mounted to her pale cheeks, and then forsook them, and with maiden modesty she essayed to hide what the rude hands of the executioner and his man had so recklessly exposed. Another signal was given, and Miriam the next moment was laid on the rack, to which she was bound tightly with small cords, which the executioner carried at his girdle.

There was another pause, and the fall of a leaf might have been heard in the vast hall.

"Ah, Arthur!" sighed the wretched girl, as her heart fluttered in frightful anticipation of what was to follow, "hast thou left me for aye? then God have mercy on an innocent girl!"

Those who have visited the venerable Abbey Church of St. Alban's, will remember the curious echo in the roof of the aisle, which repeats a stamp of the foot or clap of the hands at a particular spot many times in quick succession. A similar echo was heard above the spot where the rack stood in the hall of Newgate, and the words which the poor girl had murmured were repeated audibly by the rafted roof above. It seemed to the executioner that a voice spoke in reply to the ejaculation of the prisoner, and he started as if a spectre had greeted him. His fear, and the cause of it, was not unobserved by the judges; even the priest looked aghast.

"Ha!" cried he, "*she mutters her familiar—who answers!* Proceed, proceed!" No second bidding was necessary.

The machinery of the rack creaked and groaned, the cords tightened, the wheel revolved, and something snapped like an overstrained bowstring. A convulsive sigh burst from the poor maiden, who swooned under the hideous torture, and lay mute and motionless on the cruel engine.

Again the priest's phial was put in requisition, but his attempt to restore the victim was vain; death seemed to have robbed them of their prey; the body of Miriam was removed from the rack, and borne back to her cell, the judges descended from the stalls and conferred together in suppressed whispers, and old Herlion, covering his face with his furred gown, hurried from the hall, overwhelmed with grief, shame, and remorse.

CHAPTER VII.

THE STAKE.

A week passed away, and no tidings were heard of Arthur Lechmere. He appeared neither at mass nor at merry-making: the choice spirits who mustered at the "Holly-branch" marvelled that he came not; and Master Herlion had taken to his chamber, absolutely refusing to see anybody except his gossip and spiritual pastor, the Priest of St. Mary-le-Bow. All this while the innocent Miriam lay in her damp cell within the prison of Newgate. Hope had deserted her; she prayed for death, but death came not to her relief. Arthur was lost to her—she felt assured of that, and she waited for the sentence which she knew would consign her to the flames. Old Abraham, as may be supposed, was frantic with grief; he had applied in vain at the prison for an interview with his beloved child, but he met only with insult and derision. The gaoler spat in his face; and those who saw the wretched old man daily walking distractedly before the dismal building which contained that which he valued far before his wealth, pitied him not, because he was a Jew and an unbeliever. No tear dimmed the haggard and bloodshot eyes of the old Israelite, yet his rent gaberdine and uncombed beard, and grief-stricken aspect bespoke that mental agony which finds no relief in weeping.

It was autumn, and dank winter had given notice of his approach betimes—the evenings were misty and chilly, and the citizens, gathered round their cheerful fires, mingled with the tales which were wont to amuse them the story of Arthur's bewitchment, the imprisonment of the witch woman, and her approaching fate, not forgetting the disappearance of the young man, which latter, of course, was attributed to supernatural agency.

It was autumn—the mists and fogs which rose from the low, damp neighbourhood of London now began to envelope the city in their heavy mantle: several gloomy days succeeded; then it blew a hurricane and the rain descended in torrents, till the grim figures at the ends of the water-spouts on the steeple of St. Mary-le-Bow seemed to vomit forth another deluge—fit type of the tears that flowed in the house of one who dwelt near it. Dense fogs followed; and early one morning the city was shrouded in almost Egyptian darkness. Anon the sun appeared, and ascended the east like a huge globe of fire, but the fog was still dense and impenetrable. The citizens were yet in their beds, and those only whose business called them abroad at that early hour were stirring; even the noisy, saucy chirping and cawing of the sparrows and jackdaws was not yet heard. *It was not so in Smithfield.* There, near to the place where stood that huge permanent gibbet, to which old records so often allude, where wretched criminals expiated their crimes, and in after ages martyrs perished for their faith, was fixed a large post or stake, and near it was piled a heap of fagots, the preparations for burning a human creature alive. The victim was Miriam, the daughter of Abraham the Jew.

As the sun ascended, the fog gradually thinned, and windows and gables became visible. The city began to give signs of re-animation; various sounds within the walls denoted that the Londoners had risen from their slumbers. Two ruffianly men, who had remained like statues near the pile of fagots, shook themselves,

"And swung around their waists their tingling hands;"

for at that early hour the cold was intense. They were savage-looking wretches, fit actors for the inhuman scene in which they were about to be engaged. As the two worthies conversed together they looked earnestly towards the city gates, which were now thrown open; but the victim came not; the doors of Newgate prison remained closed. Several of those shivering, houseless wretches, which

are always to be seen in great cities, and who had probably passed the night under the stalls and pent-houses of St. Nicholas' shambles, came forth, and drew near the pile of fagots. Sturdy rogues were some of them, who had probably in their time excited other feelings than those of charity in their applications for relief to the good citizens in the fields and lanes in the neighbourhood of London. Others also came to the spot; in fact the crowd was gradually increasing, and the gentry composing it were the reverse of reputable, either in manner or appearance. Meanwhile the east was brightening—misty vapours rolled off, and hung on the hills which surround London; weather-cocks creaked, and flashed back the sun-beams, and the pigeons commenced their morning's flight, while wreaths of white smoke began to rise from the house-tops.

At length the mournful tolling of a bell sounded within the prison, a bustle was heard at the gates, which were thrown open, and a party of bill-men ranged themselves in order for the procession, which was immediately in motion. The sheriffs came forth and mounted their horses, and the word was given to set forward.

The Jewess appeared. The bill-men fell into line, and the sad procession advanced towards the stake. The chaplain of the prison was at its head. The bell tolled dismally, and the priest moved slowly along, repeating the verses of a psalm from an illuminated volume, the gilt ornaments of which had become sadly obscured by his reverence's heavy thumb. All eyes were immediately turned towards Miriam; she was divested of her upper garments; her long dark hair swept over her shoulders, and her feet and legs were entirely bare. Many were there, who, in gazing on those beautifully turned and snowy ancles, forgot that in a few minutes the greedy flames would devour them. She held a lighted taper in her right hand, and walked with a faltering step, but without assistance. Her eye was tearless, but cold drops stood on her pale brow, and glistened in the sickly light of the taper she held: behind her walked the executioner and his assistants, each with a coil of rope in his hand. All the while the sonorous voice of the burly priest was heard, while ever and anon the solemn booming of the death-bell chimed in, as if to render the entrance to eternity more awful.

The procession reached the stake, and halted, and the executioner, taking the taper from the hands of the Jewess, bade her prepare for death. The buzz among the crowd at once subsided, and each one, craning his neck, tried to obtain a view of the innocent victim of a gross superstition. A mendicant friar, clad in a coarse and ragged frock, girt with a rope, and with his cowl drawn over his face, seemed to watch the proceedings with intense interest; but he spoke to no one.

On a sudden, three horsemen advanced at a trot down the road, which led from St. John's Priory at Clerkenwell. They were well-mounted, but plainly dressed, and were apparently of the better class of yeomen. They held on their way towards the city, but espying the crowd which had assembled round the place of execution, they altered their course as if desirous of witnessing the sad spectacle.

"Where is the malefactor?" inquired the foremost horseman, as he reined up his steed.

"It is the witch woman yonder," was the reply.

"Mother of God! so young and so beautiful—it cannot be!"

(*To be continued.*)

BLACK HAWKE, THE HIGHWAYMAN.

LADY FLORENCE.

CHAPTER XXVI.

THE PAPERS CHANGE HANDS AGAIN—SIR THOMAS BROOKE'S
SCHEME—THE TRAP SUCCEEDS—THE DUKE OF CLEVE-
LAND AT ALBION HALL.

WHEN Sir Thomas Brooke perceived that Lady Jane Cleveland fully intended to carry out her threats, his guilty heart
began to quake with fear.

With a trembling voice he said,

"Put away that pistol, and we will talk together Lady
Jane."

"That pistol remains levelled at your breast till those
papers are in my hands," replied Lady Jane.

No. 14.

"But listen——"

"I will listen to nothing, till I have possession of those
papers."

Sir Thomas hesitated.

He was in an awkward predicament, from which nothing
but the most subtle and refined cunning could extricate him.

Lady Jane stamped her foot in an impatient manner.

"Be quick," said she, toying with the deadly weapon in a
manner which made Sir Thomas tremble with fear lest her
finger should press the trigger a little *too* hard.

"You shall have them, on one condition," he faltered.

"I make no conditions. I demand those papers, and am
resolved to have them."

"I only want half an hour, to enable me to quit this house and the country, before the—the—contents of those papers are known."

Lady Jane hesitated for a moment.

"Granted," said she. "Now hand me the papers."

"You will remain here till the half-hour has elapsed?"

"I will."

Sir Thomas Brooke placed the documents in Lady Jane Cleveland's hand, saying—

"One of my servants shall inform you when I have left the building. In the meantime, may I send you any refreshment?"

"No, I thank you, Sir Thomas."

It was well for Lady Jane that she refused the offer.

Had she accepted the proffered hospitality the wine would have been drugged and the food poisoned.

The vile man who caused murder to be done to gain a fortune would not hesitate at another to secure that property, which it had been the object of his life to secure.

With a scowl on his heavy features he left the apartment.

Lady Jane continued to cover his body with the barrel of her pistol, until the door closed behind the retreating genteel ruffian.

Passing into his bed-room, Sir Thomas pulled violently at the bell.

It was answered by his special servant, who was none other than the Crusher Bill, who had committed the foul deed of murder.

In the establishment of Albion Hall, he was known by the name of Black, a cognomen which his looks did not belie.

Black entered the room, and stood before his master in as respectful an attitude as his inborn awkwardness would permit him to assume.

"Do you know there is a lady in the house, Black?" asked Sir Thomas.

Black, alias Crusher Bill, grinned as he replied,

"Yes, Sir Thomas."

"You infernal fool, what are you laughing about? That woman knows our secret, and can hang us both, if she likes."

Black's face grew white with fear, his knees trembled.

"Oh Lord!" he ejaculated, "what shall we do? We shall be hanged!"

"We shall if you make a fool of yourself, certainly. But listen to me."

The man placed himself by the side of his master, and bent down his head.

"She has the papers, and she has a pistol as well," said Sir Thomas; "but she must not carry those documents outside of this house. Can you suggest any plan?"

"I! n-no. What do you mean?"

"You're a fool. I wish to get hold of that letter and the receipt, without getting a pistol bullet in my head."

"Send her some wine with p-poison in it."

"She would refuse it; she has refused."

Black approached still nearer to his master and said, with a fearful smile,

"There's the trap door!"

Sir Thomas started, and a look of anxiety crossed his face.

He knew well enough that his own safety depended upon his silencing Lady Jane; and yet to kill the daughter of a powerful peer was a deed which he might well shudder to contemplate.

Unluckily there was no other resource visible to his mind's eye at that moment.

"It must be so, I suppose. Get all ready; not a word, mind you, to any of the others, and in half an hour's time knock at the drawing-room door to inform her ladyship that I am gone."

Crusher Bill departed to prepare everything for the foul deed.

Sir Thomas Brooke sat in his room shivering with cold and fear, drinking repeated draughts of brandy to enliven his spirits and drive away the demons that seemed to have possession of his soul.

Lady Jane Cleveland sat with her pistol ready and her eye fixed upon the door, half expecting some other attempt would be made to deprive her of her hardly-won treasures.

The time passed slowly.

The half hour, she thought, must surely have expired.

She heard a carriage drive away from the hall at a furious pace.

No doubt it contained Sir Thomas Brooke, and in a few minutes she would be at liberty to depart.

There was a knock at the door and a servant entered—one of the most ill-favoured varlets Lady Jane had ever set eyes upon.

"My lady, Sir Thomas desired me to inform you that he has left the house, and that your ladyship is free to depart as soon as you please."

"That will be instantly," said Lady Jane; "lead the way."

The treacherous rascal took up the light, and, with a profusion of uncouth bows, led the way to the grand staircase.

He tripped nimbly down, keeping close to the wall.

Lady Jane followed with more dignified step.

When she had nearly reached the bottom the stairs gave way beneath her feet.

She made an effort to spring forward, but, unable to accomplish the feat, sunk through the opening and fell into the dark regions beneath.

Three of the steps constituted a trap-door, through which Lady Jane had fallen.

The crafty Crusher Bill had evaded the dangerous steps by making a flying leap, which took him safely to the bottom.

The fall and the fright combined had deprived Lady Jane of her senses, and she lay on the floor of the cellar or vault into which she had been thrown completely at the mercy of the villains.

But they were too much alarmed at the success of their own trick to be able to take immediate advantage of it.

On seeing Lady Jane fall through the trap, Crusher Bill's first idea was to seize every weighty article he could lay his hands upon and hurl it through the opening upon the unfortunate young lady.

Luckily no very heavy articles were at hand; besides, Bill the Crusher had a wholesome dread of his master.

He knew not whether that master willed the death of the young lady, or merely the recovery of the all-important papers.

With hasty steps he rushed up the staircase without staying to replace the moveable trap, and entered the room in which Sir Thomas was sitting.

The master of Albion Hall had swallowed nearly a pint of brandy since quitting the presence of Lady Jane Cleveland.

He was intoxicated, though not sufficiently to be helpless.

He could stand and speak, though unable to do either in a proper manner.

"Well?" said he, as his body-servant entered.

"She's down."

"Have a glass of brandy? Help yourself."

Crusher Bill needed no second invitation.

He poured out a large glassful, which he poured down his capacious throat at a draught.

The dose was repeated with greater deliberation.

"So she's in the vault?"

"Yes."

At that moment a thundering knock at the front door of the mansion made the two worthy villains leap to their feet.

"Who's that?" asked Sir Thomas.

"I—I d-don't know," stammered Bill the Crusher.

"Go down and see, then, fool."

Bill obeyed the order with no very great alacrity, pausing on his way down to replace the trap-door.

As he did so he cast a glance down into the black-looking hole.

He fancied he could discern a heap of something lying on the ground, but there was no time to examine closely.

On opening the door the impatient visitor was discovered to be none other than the Duke of Cleveland himself.

"Is Sir Thomas Brooke at home?" demanded the peer.

"Ye-yes—that is, no, my lord."

"You are an infamous liar!" exclaimed the duke. "Show me the way instantly to his apartment."

"But——"

"But I will have no excuse, fellow; I came here with the intention of seeing him, and see him I will ere I quit the house. Lead on."

With trembling steps, and head in a most confused state, the Crusher conducted the duke to the library.

"Now, let me see your master instantly," exclaimed the peer.

Sir Thomas Brooke knew who was his visitor long before the blank-visaged Black appeared upon the threshold of his sanctum.

"What does he want?" asked the master of the house.

"He wants to see you, Sir Thomas."

"I know that, fool. Do you think I am deaf? What does he want to see me about?"

"I don't know."

"Black, you are the greatest fool in this world," exclaimed Sir Thomas Brooke, as he rose in order to meet his noble visitor.

He entered the room in which the Duke of Cleveland was pacing up and down in an impetuous manner.

"Ha!" exclaimed the peer, as his host entered. "Your rascal of a servant tried to persuade me that you were not at home."

"He made a mistake; though, I am bound to confess, I did not expect a visit from your grace this evening."

"You can guess the reason of my visit, Sir Thomas?"

"No, indeed."

The duke turned sharply.

"I came for my daughter."

Sir Thomas Brooke trembled, and changed colour.

"I—don't——"

"Don't prevaricate, Sir Thomas. I have good proof that she came to this house this evening. It was a most thoughtless action on her part, and one in which I should have imagined you would have had better taste than to encourage her."

"She left half an hour ago," exclaimed Sir Thomas.

"Indeed?" said the duke, looking very much as if he doubted the statement. "Then I have only to apologise for my intrusion, and take my departure."

With a stately bow, he turned and quitted the room.

CHAPTER XXVII.

THE SEARCH IN THE VAULT—LADY JANE'S HIDING PLACE—THE GAOLERS BECOME PRISONERS—LADY JANE ESCAPES AND FALLS INTO BAD COMPANY.

THE visit of the Duke of Cleveland almost sobered the drunken lord of Albion Hall, and threw him into fits of alarm for the consequences of his evil deed.

So great was his terror, that he actually shed tears, and throwing himself upon the floor howled curses on his ill-fortune, which was always compelling him to do deeds of darkness.

In a few moments Crusher Bill re-appeared, and announced that the duke had left the mansion.

"We shall be hanged, sir, as sure as there is a place called hell."

"Do you believe there is such a place?"

Bill the Crusher made no answer; his theology was of the most vague description.

Sir Thomas continued,

"When I was young they told me tales of horror—of a vast lake full of burning brimstone, inhabited by evil spirits of the most fearful kind. But I know better. I know where hell is, and what its torments are like; the evil spirits are here—in my heart! an undying fire consumes my body and withers up my brain! This is hell! I am hell!"

Terrified beyond measure by his master's ravings, Crusher Bill was about to quit the room.

"Stay," cried Sir Thomas; "give me more brandy."

The servant, hardly knowing what he did, filled up a large glass from the first bottle that came to hand.

His master swallowed it without perceiving the mistake till the whole of the draught was down his throat.

It was, however, nothing but water, and the cooling draught had a beneficial effect.

After passing his hand across his brow once or twice, he said in a more calm voice,

"Have you been down to the vault since—she—went down?"

The serving-man shook his head.

"Then go at once, and bring me those papers which have brought all this trouble and vexation."

"I go?"

"Yes, you."

"Alone?"

"Why not, pray?"

"I dare not—the spirits—"

"You fool, what is there to be afraid of?"

This remark nettled Bill the Crusher, and he answered with more warmth than respect,

"You dare not go alone, Sir Thomas."

"D——n!" roared the enraged baronet. "Am I to be insulted thus by my servants? You shall quit the house, and starve, you villain!"

"You know better than to get rid of me in such a hurry, sir; I could tell too much."

Sir Thomas Brooke growled a succession of oaths.

"Come along, then," said he, after a pause; "we will go together."

So saying, he unlocked the door of what appeared to be a book-case.

The shelves, however, swung outwards on hinges, and revealed a narrow dark staircase.

Master and man both paused, each being willing and anxious to allow the other the honour of descending first.

The crafty servant, however, managed to give his master a slight push—accidentally, of course—and to save himself from falling, Sir Thomas was obliged to make the first movement downwards.

The staircase was steep and deep.

When they reached the bottom a little arched doorway barred their progress.

Sir Thomas tried it with his hand, but found it locked,

"Where is the key?" he asked.

"I left it in your room," replied Crusher Bill. "I will fetch it.

He darted nimbly up the staircase, carrying the candle with him

Sir Thomas was left in the dark.

Let us now see how it fared with Lady Jane Cleveland.

The fall deprived her for a short time of consciousness. When she recovered she found herself in a gloomy vault, black as darkest midnight save where a slight and feeble light shone through the open trap-door.

She rose to her feet, and searched for the pistol which had fallen from the bosom of her dress.

That search was unsuccessful.

The papers, however, were still in her possession, a proof that she had not been molested during her temporary insensibility.

She looked up at the trap through which she had fallen, but could discover no means of ascent.

There was a door she discovered after groping carefully round the slimy walls, but it was securely fastened.

She sought in vain for any other outlet, and at length determined to return to the only spot where there was any light, and search once more for her lost pistol.

While so engaged her mind was full of speculations as to her fate.

Did the ruffianly man who sought her hand intend to slay her? or was she merely to be kept in durance till she would consent to restore him the papers?

"Never shall he lay hands on them while I have life or strength to resist."

Would death, if death were to be her fate, be bloody, swift and violent, or the slow and lingering agony of starvation?

Horrid, horrid thought was the latter, and yet, if food were given her, might it not be poisoned?

The ruffian in whose clutches she had fallen would doubtlessly take measures to prevent her from revealing her secret.

Lady Jane fell upon her knees and prayed—prayed for strength and courage to endure whatever sufferings might be her lot—for wisdom to enable her to outwit her cunning adversaries.

She then once more made the circuit of her prison walls, passing her hand along them as high up as she could reach, in hopes that she might discover a window or some other outlet from her dungeon.

At length she paused, and her heart beat high with hopes of escape.

She had discovered a kind of recess in the thickness of the wall at a considerable height above the floor.

Two iron bars guarded it, but they were so wide apart that she was able to squeeze between them without much difficulty.

There was no outlet, however, no window or grating; the place was only a niche very like those in which granite saints and marble martyrs stand doing sentinels' duty in old churches and cathedrals.

Lady Jane, however, hoped that Sir Thomas Brooke and the ruffians in his service would overlook this place when they descended to take the papers from her body. She also hoped that in their confusion and excitement on not finding her stretched lifeless upon the floor of the vault they would hurry away, and perhaps leave the door unlocked in their eagerness to prevent her escape from the building.

She forgot what a risk she ran of being locked in and left to starve.

She had scarcely ensconced herself in the hiding-place when the door was thrown open, and two men appeared.

The foremost was Sir Thomas Brooke, the other Bill the Crusher.

The two villains trembled in their shoes as they entered the vault, expecting to see their victim lying dead upon the floor.

Bill the Crusher held the candle in his shivering fingers, and by its light the two human fiends glanced around.

"She is not here!" said the servant.

"Hush! she is hiding!"

"Well, after that fall, she can't do much harm to any one."

"You forget she has the pistol."

The Crusher trembled more than ever.

He had a deep-rooted aversion to fire-arms, unless, indeed, the weapon should be his own.

Sir Thomas advanced a step or two inside the door.

No trace whatever could he behold of Lady Jane.

"You have deceived me, rascal!" cried he, turning to his servant.

"No, upon my honour, she fell through the trap."

"Liar! this is some trick of yours, by which you hope to get me in your power."

"I have you in my power now, Sir Thomas; I know quite enough."

"Your knowledge shall avail you but little. You shall never quit this vault alive!"

With these words he sprang upon the Crusher, and seized him by the throat.

A struggle ensued; and had either of the men possessed a weapon of any kind, blood would speedily have been spilt.

They grappled and wrestled, and fell upon the floor.

In the struggle the candle was extinguished, and the vault became dark as before.

Judging this a favourable opportunity for escaping, Lady Jane hastily left her place of concealment, and having previously noticed the position of the door, she made her way to it.

She passed through, closed it, and turned the key.

The two men were now as much prisoners as she had been.

"Ha! what's that? who's there?" exclaimed Sir Thomas Brooke, as he heard the noise made by the key in turning.

The struggle ceased.

Both men rose to their feet, and stood in silence.

"Villains! your evil designs are defeated!" exclaimed Lady Jane. "I am free, while you are prisoners in your own dungeon."

Sir Thomas rushed towards the spot from whence the sounds proceeded.

"Dear Lady Jane!" exclaimed he; "pray release me. I vow I intended you no injury."

"You will remain there, Sir Thomas, till such time as you are removed by the constables. Your design to entrap me shall be punished."

"But, dear lady, I swear this was done without my knowledge, and against my orders."

"It's false!" screamed Bill the Crusher; "it was he who ordered me to do it."

"You lie, rascal!" roared Sir Thomas.

There was a scuffling sound, and Lady Jane rightly judged that the combat between Sir Thomas and his servant had been renewed.

Little caring which might prove the conqueror now that she had accomplished the object of her visit to Albion Hall, the intrepid girl ran nimbly up the stairs, and speedily found her way to the room in which stood the box from which she had abstracted the papers.

After hastily glancing round to assure herself that no one was present, Lady Jane locked the door, and once more approached the box.

From its contents she selected such documents as she deemed would be of most value to her lover in aiding him to recover his property.

There were the title-deeds of the estate, a certificate of the marriage of Lord and Lady Montague, and a copy of the baptismal registry of their son Albert, dated a twelvemonth subsequent.

Lady Jane secreted all these documents, and then, with hasty steps, left the mansion of blood, mystery, and crime.

But the brave young Lady Jane's adventures were by no means terminated.

On arriving at the spot where she had left her carriage, that vehicle was nowhere to be seen.

She knew not that her father had discovered the truant coachman, and had compelled him to return to Vandeleur Park.

Many miles from home in a lonely part of the country with midnight close at hand, Lady Cleveland's prospects were anything but cheering.

She had money in her pocket and jewels about her person, but then that fact brought fear to her mind as well as self-congratulation.

If she could succeed in reaching an inn, or even a labourer's cottage, she would no doubt be able to procure shelter for the night; but, on the other hand, should she meet with robbers, her riches would prove a temptation, and an excuse for rudeness and violence.

However, having no choice, she set out boldy and rapidly, though full of regrets for the loss of her weapon.

For more than an hour she walked rapidly, and then fatigue began to assail her delicate limbs.

Hope, however, buoyed her up, and after struggling on for a short distance further, she was gladdened by the sight of a house by the roadside, from one of the windows of which streamed a ray of light illuminating the dusky road.

Lady Jane paused, and took a good glance over the exterior of the house.

It certainly had not a very prepossessing appearance.

The walls were of mud and seemed crumbling away, the thatch on the roof appeared too heavy for the rafters, the windows were patched up with pieces of paper and old rags, and the whole place had an aspect of decay and slovenliness about it.

But Lady Jane was weary, and knew not where to find another human residence.

She knocked at the door boldly.

There was no immediate response to her summons, and after waiting a short time she knocked again more loudly than before.

"Coming, coming," croaked a hoarse voice; "who's there?"

"A friend," replied Lady Jane.

A chain was unfastened on the inside, several bolts drawn, and then the door was thrown open.

A hideous-looking old woman with a candle in her hand stood looking in surprise at the beautiful and well-dressed visitor.

"What do ye please to want, ma'am?" said the old crone, trying to smile.

"I have lost my way, and should be very glad if you could give me shelter till the morning," replied Lady Jane.

"Are you by yourself?" asked the woman, glancing suspiciously up and down the road.

"Yes, quite alone. I will pay you well in the morning for any trouble or expense that I may cause."

"Walk in, my lady, walk in," said the mistress of the house, again grinning horribly, in an abortive attempt to look pleasant.

Lady Jane accepted the invitation, and found herself in a large room, the furniture of which was both scanty and coarse.

A round deal table graced the centre of the apartment, a few wooden chairs were scattered about, and along one side of the wide, open fire-place was a bench on which was stretched a man apparently asleep.

"My son. He's asleep, poor fellow, after his hard day's work," said the old woman, as she perceived Lady Jane's eye wandered towards the heavy boots and coarse features of the sleeper.

The hard day's work which had so much fatigued the man, was, if the truth must be known, a poaching excursion, which had proved very successful.

In fact part of the spoils, a rabbit and a pheasant, were at that moment simmering in the great iron pot that hung over the wood fire.

The fragrant smell reached Lady Jane's nostrils, and made her feel excessively hungry.

"You shall have some supper in a few minutes, my lady," said the old woman, "and then you shall go to sleep in my bed—the best in the house."

The son, the hard-working man, slept on all the while Lady Jane was eating her repast.

When that was finished she begged to be shown her chamber, and the hag led the way to a back room.

This was not much better furnished than the other, but Lady Jane was too fatigued to be very fastidious.

The old woman bade her good night, and left the room.

There was then heard a sound which at once roused Lady Jane's suspicions, and caused her to wish she had not been so hasty in her choice of lodgings.

The sound was as if a bolt had been placed across the door, accompanied by a low, chuckling laugh.

Lady Jane walked noiselessly across the room, and found that her suspicions were correct.

The door was bolted, and she was once more a prisoner.

The object of thus fastening her in was very easily guessed.

Her jewels and promises of money had excited the cupidity of the old hag, who had thereupon resolved to possess all.

Lady Jane then tried the window, but that, too, was fastened.

She listened, and could hear the voice of the treacherous hostess in conversation with her tired son.

"She has money—plenty of money, and lots of rings and chains."

"Then she won't have them much longer," growled the male ruffian, in hoarse tones.

"You must wait a bit till she is asleep."

"All right. She'll go where the others are when I've had my supper. There's nothing like finishing a job when you begin."

These awful words fell distinctly upon Lady Jane's ear, and she was at no loss to guess their meaning.

She was in a den of murderers, where mercy was unknown.

It was a terrible situation for a young and delicately trained girl; but Lady Jane Cleveland's spirit was fashioned in Nature's most heroic mould.

She feared not death, though she had many reasons for wishing to live.

Even in that terrible moment her lover occupied the greater part of her thoughts, and she felt a pang of regret as she thought that perhaps, after all, the papers she had dared so much to obtain would never reach his hand.

Then a thought flashed across her mind that perhaps this brutal plebian murderer might be an agent of the more aristocratic villain at Albion Hall.

She resolved to conceal the papers about her dress in a manner well calculated to escape observation, even should the ruffians strip her.

This done, she looked about for means of defence.

CHAPTER XXVIII.

MERLIN PICKS UP AN ISRAELITE—THE TRAITOR DISCOVERED—THE TRIAL—THE FATAL AXE—PREPARATIONS FOR DEFENCE.

MERLIN HAWKE, after his interview with the three witches, proceeded in a more cautious manner than he had previously done towards the Haunt of the Black Hawkes.

He had some doubts in his mind as to the dependence to be placed in his strange informants; nevertheless, he deemed it as well to be cautious.

He was now within a mile of the haunt, and as yet no signs of the enemy were visible.

He halted Fair Rosamond under a clump of trees and listened.

For a short time all was silent.

Then his steed pricked her ears and uttered a low sound.

That sound Merlin well knew was a warning that some one was approaching.

Merlin listened attentively, and in a few minutes could distinguish a dull, heavy, thumping sound.

In a few minutes more the arms and plumes of a troop of dragoons glittered in the faint light of the early morning.

The chieftain of the band of highwaymen watched the coming foe with the greatest attention.

They outnumbered his own band considerably, but then their cattle were not to be compared with the dashing steeds his friends possessed.

Besides, were not these soldiers the aggressors? and Merlin well knew that those who fight in defence of their homes have a moral advantage on their side which often enables them to achieve the victory in spite of superior numbers.

But again he reflected, and, calling to mind the fact of a traitor being within his own stronghold, perceived that, on the whole, the enemy had the greater chance of victory, and that all his influence and valour would be needed to bring the impending conflict to a satisfactory conclusion.

Merlin's eye gleamed forth fires of hatred as he perceived the form of Simeon Lazarus.

The child of Abraham was much more anxious to share the reward than to partake in the conflict, and, therefore, hung behind the soldiers as much as possible for shelter.

In fact, he was at least twenty yards behind the column of dragoons when Merlin's eye fell upon him.

The bold highwayman at once resolved to secure the Jew.

The soldiers turned aside from the main road, and it became evident that they were proceeding to the secret entrance to the haunt of the band.

"Now, Fair Rosamond, one more noble effort, my brave steed!"

He set spurs to her flanks and rushed down upon the unhappy Israelite, who still lagged behind, like an eagle pouncing upon a dove.

In an instant Simeon Lazarus was dragged from his horse and hoisted upon Merlin's saddle!

"Oh! holy Mo——"

"Not a word!" exclaimed Merlin, pressing the barrel of a pistol close to the unfortunate man's forehead.

The Jew closed his mouth abruptly, and Merlin galloped off with his prize.

So swiftly and quietly was all this accomplished that the

dragoons did not perceive that their guide was missing till the riderless horse rejoined their ranks.

The officer in command at once gave the order to pursue.

Pistols and carbines were discharged, and the bullets whistled round Merlin in a manner that was anything but pleasant to the old Jew. He would have shrieked out, but the fear of his captor was so great he dared not open his lips.

Merlin soon gained the portals of the haunt, and his pursuers lost sight of him.

They were in a state of doubt how to proceed, for they knew not how to enter the stronghold of the robbers, now that their guide was taken from them.

The commanding officer consulted with his junior, and the result was that a belt of sentries was placed, extending for a considerable distance, with strict orders to fire at any stranger who might appear.

In the meantime, Merlin had dismounted, and grasping Simeon Lazarus by the throat dragged him into the hall of the haunt.

The whole band was assembled, for they expected the instant trial of Marmaduke Greville and Captain Ashburne.

"Take those gentlemen to their cells," exclaimed Merlin. "Much more important business claims our present attention."

These words caused the most intense excitement amongst those present.

Marmaduke Greville and Henry Ashburne were removed, and all eagerly waited for the next words of their leader.

"Call the muster roll," said Merlin, addressing himself to Hal Hunter.

The names of all the band were called in succession.

All were present except Albert Montague.

But Merlin had no suspicion that he was the traitor.

"There is a traitor here," said Merlin.

Every man glanced at his neighbour with a kind of suspicious look.

"Let him stand forth and confess," continued the chief.

No one stirred.

"Let not the base villain think that silence will screen him from the arm of the justice. Bring forward the Jew."

Simeon Lazarus was dragged into the midst of the assembly.

"If you wish to save your miserable life, Jew, you will instantly point out the traitor, for you know him."

"Oh! Moshesh! Ah! ma tear shir, I knows nothink!"

"You lie! Point out the traitor instantly, or fifty daggers shall find bloody sheathes in your vile carcase."

"I shwear——"

"Don't waste time in useless talk; but point out the man who was to have opened the doors of this place to yon troop of soldiers."

The Jew made no reply, but his face indicated extreme terror of mind.

Merlin beckoned forward six of the Black Hawkes.

"If he still refuses to answer, plunge your daggers into his body to the depth of half an inch."

Every man raised his weapon.

"Now, for the last time. I ask you which member of my band is the traitor?" said Merlin, solemnly.

"Oh! spare me! This one!" screamed the Jew, laying his hand on a man whose dagger was directed to his throat.

The traitor's blow fell, and had not Simeon Lazarus stepped back he would have swiftly been gathered to his forefathers.

As it was he received a severe cut on the arm which caused the blood to flow freely.

The traitor was instantly seized and securely bound.

"Search him," said Merlin.

His pockets were speedily turned out, and amongst the contents was a letter.

"I am innocent," said the man, at the same time turning pale as death as he saw the evidence of his guilt in the hands of his captors.

Merlin at once seated himself in a great chair that stood at one end of the hall.

Hal Hunter, Will Merry, and Frank Morton stationed themselves near at hand.

"Call a jury," exclaimed Merlin.

Captain Merry then called the names of twelve members of the band.

Each man stepped forward as his name echoed through the hall.

"Bring forward the prisoner."

The wretch, whose perfidy had so nearly proved fatal to the whole party, was brought in front of the judgment seat.

A man, with drawn sword and pistol, stood on each side of him.

He was a tall, powerful-looking man, with red hair and whiskers, and freckled, sunburnt face.

"Owen Carter," said Merlin, "have you any objection to be tried by a jury of the members of this band?"

"It would be little use if I did object," responded the prisoner. "It seems that you have already decided the matter."

"If you can prove your innocence you will be released," said the judge. "Produce what evidence you have, Captain Merry."

Will Merry then read aloud the note which had been taken from the person of the prisoner.

It was from Simeon Lazarus, and appointed the hour for the treacherous act which had so nearly been accomplished.

The Jew was then called forward, and compelled to identify his own handwriting.

In fact the whole scene much resembled the interior of one of his majesty's courts of justice, excepting that the judge kept his hat on his head instead of wearing a wig, and that there were no barristers, or embarrassers, as they might more properly be called.

The evidence for the prosecution was brief, though to the point.

"Have you any defence to make?" asked the judge.

"No," was the surly reply; "I do not acknowledge your right to try me, nor will I plead before you."

"Bring forward the register," said Merlin to his attendants.

A parchment-covered book, with brass clasps, was placed in his hands.

Having opened the volume, the judge read, aloud,

"I, Owen Carter, do hereby bind myself, soul and body, to the Band of the Black Hawkes, denying the authority of any other save our chief, under penalty of a bloody death in this world, and unending torments in the next. In witness whereI have signed this book with my blood."

"You cannot, after being reminded of your vows when you joined our band, deny my authority to reward and to punish," said Merlin, when he had finished reading. "Once more, therefore, I ask, have you any defence to make?"

"No."

"Gentlemen of the jury, retire and consider well your verdict."

Amid breathless silence the twelve men selected for the occasion walked slowly from the room into an adjoining apartment.

Every eye was fixed upon the door by which they had departed.

Five minutes had not elapsed ere they returned, headed by the man who had been elected to fill the office of foreman.

They took up their position on the right hand of the judge.

Again there was the most profound silence.

Merlin then spoke after the form used in courts of law.

"Gentlemen, have you well considered your verdict?" he asked.

"We have," replied the jurymen, with one voice.

"How say you, gentlemen, is the prisoner guilty or not guilty of the crime charged against him?"

Every eye was fixed upon the twelve men in whose hands rested the fate of the prisoner.

"We find the prisoner guilty of treason against the members of this band of which he is a sworn member."

The prisoner turned ghastly pale, and his limbs trembled beneath him.

Merlin rose from his seat and uncovered his head.

"Owen Carter," said he, "you have had as fair and impartial a trial as human justice can give you, and the result is that your comrades have found you guilty of treason against them. What motives you may have had for betraying us into the hands of our enemies I know not, nor is it my present business to inquire; my duty is simply to see justice executed. The terms of your oath on entering our brotherhood can leave you in no doubt as to the punishment you have to suffer, and I have now only to pronounce sentence publicly. The sentence is that your head be severed from your body in the presence of all the members of the association, and I earnestly hope that your death may prove a warning to others. In ten minutes the executioner will be in readiness, and I should advise you to spend the remaining moments of life in preparing your soul for eternity."

"Is mercy entirely banished from your code of laws?" asked the prisoner.

"There is no mercy for traitors," replied Merlin, solemnly.

The doomed one turned suddenly, and endeavoured to wrest the sword from one of his guards, for during the trial his hands had been set free.

In this he was prevented, and a cord was once more passed round his wrists to prevent him from doing injury to himself or others.

Two men now began to prepare the hall for the solemn scene that was about to be enacted.

A large square of black cloth was spread at one end of the hall, and on the centre of this was placed a huge block of wood with a hollow in the top.

By the side of the block was a large, glittering axe.

The executioner entered, clad in garments of the deepest black, and took up a position by the side of the dreadful apparatus of death.

He alone was masked.

The prisoner spoke not, but every feature expressed agony of spirit at the sight of these preparations for the execution of the sentence.

Hal Hunter advanced and bound a handkerchief over the wretch's eyes.

The guards then led him to the block and compelled him to kneel, and, at the same time, the solemn sound of a bell reverberated through the vast apartment.

"When the clock points to the hour, strike!" exclaimed Merlin, in clear, distinct tones, addressing the headsman.

Slowly it seemed the hands moved round the face of the dial.

Every man uncovered his head as the fatal moment approached.

At length the executioner raised his deadly weapon.

A moment, it flashed like lightning, and then descended with a dull, heavy "thud" upon the block.

A headless trunk fell to the floor, spouting forth fountains of warm, steaming blood.

The executioner grasped the head of his victim by the hair and held it aloft, while the gore fell in large drops upon the floor.

"So perish all traitors!" said he, in a deep voice.

"Amen!" exclaimed every man present, in equally solemn tones.

Simeon Lazarus, the Jew, had been a spectator of the fearful tragedy, but it proved too much for his nerves.

As the axe descended Simeon fell senseless upon the floor.

When the block and axe had been removed and the hall had resumed its wonted aspect some of the band raised him, and soon restored him to consciousness.

Tradition asserts that Hal Hunter proved a most successful physician, and perfectly revived the deadened senses of the Jew by the simple means of rubbing a slice of fat bacon over his face and mouth.

Whether there is truth in this assertion or not one thing is certain—the Jew opened his eyes, and, beholding Merlin, fell upon his knees, and prayed for mercy in the most piteous accents.

"Remove him, and lock him up in your strongest cell," said Merlin. "We will take time to consider his sentence."

(To be continued.)

A LEGEND OF OLD LONDON.

(*Concluded from page* 104).

The horseman who had uttered this exclamation dismounted, and threw the bridle to one of his companions. He then pushed his way through the crowd, in which he was assisted by the begging friar, who had hitherto been looking on with folded arms, a quiet spectator of the scene; at the same moment, a shrill whistle was given, which had a magical effect upon the crowd. Instantly all was uproar and wild confusion,—fierce cries arose on all sides: the circle formed by the bill-men round the stake was broken, and the pile of fagots scattered as if by whirlwind, the larger sticks which they contained furnishing weapons to the most violent. The sheriffs were thunderstruck, and called out to the guard to stand firm. But the call was drowned in wild cries of "Rescue! rescue!" The mendicant friar, who had overturned several in the scuffle, was now by the side of the Jewess.

"My sweetest Miriam!" cried he, throwing off his disguise—"thy lover will save thee or perish."

It was Arthur; he cast aside the coarse garment in which he was clad, and appeared armed from head to foot. Miriam uttered a faint shriek, and fell into his arms. The executioner rushed forward and roughly seized his victim, but was struck to the ground by a blow from Lechmere's mailed fist.

"Arthur! Arthur!" cried Hal Pearce, whom the reader will remember in the Holly-Branch, "God ha' mercy, man! art distraught? Quick, mount or we are lost."

The tumult increased; blows, shouts, and execrations bespoke the obstinacy of the struggle. The bill-men did their best to prevent the rescue, but their weapons were of little use in the crowd, and some of the sturdy beggars had succeeded in dismounting the sheriffs, though not before one or two of them had fallen beneath the swords of those officers. Arthur's immediate friends kept as much as possible aloof from the scuffle, in order that they might be enabled the more effectually to cover his retreat, which was effected with some difficulty. The bold youth was soon on horseback, and the disarmed sheriffs had the mortification to see him ride from the field, bearing before him on his powerful steed, the object for which he had achieved so dangerous an enterprise. His friends Pearce and Lovelace followed in his rear, and struck down two or three men who attempted to stop their flight, while the executioner and his men escaped from the spot, amid the hootings and peltings of the crowd, and ran off to Castle Baynard, for a party of mounted archers to pursue the fugitives.

CHAPTER VIII.

THE LAST PANG.

On the evening preceding the morning described in the last chapter, Master Herlion had retired to his chamber at an earlier hour than usual. The old man was unprepared for the stroke which he had received. He felt that the youth who had been the sole object of his most anxious care and solicitude, was estranged from him; and he had now nothing left in the world for which life was desirable. Hideous dreams were his companions for the night. Ghastly spectres, assuming the semblance of his much loved but unworthy nephew, hovered over his couch and seemed to implore pity and forgiveness—then a huge chasm yawned at his feet and belched forth crimson flames, through which grim fiends were dragging Arthur, and the woman who had lured him, to destruction. Such were the horrors which superstition lent to "a mind diseased," and haunted the slumbers of the Alderman, until the beams of the sun breaking through the fog, gleamed on the window of his chamber. He arose, pale and enfeebled, and having made his toilet, knelt before a large crucifix which occupied a niche in the wall; scarcely, however, had his lips moved in prayer, when a hasty knocking at the door caused him to start to his feet.

"Who knocks?" inquired Master Herlion, hoping, yet doubting that some one had brought news of his nephew.

His surprise and vexation were, however, great indeed, when he learned that an aged Jew was waiting to see him, and had forced his way up stairs in spite of the opposition of the porter, whom he had overthrown in the scuffle. As the Alderman descended, his frame quivered with a thousand emotions,—hope, fear, doubt, and dread palsied the old man, and he entered the room in which the intruder was waiting, trembling like a criminal.

There stood Abraham the Jew, who immediately in a strain of piteous entreaty besought him to intercede for his daughter. Master Herlion was not unmoved at the Israelite's passionate appeal, but he felt that it was now too late.

"It is of no avail," said he, "I would not save her if I had the power; appeal to satan, who has brought her to this pass."

Big tears rose in the eyes of Abraham on hearing these words. It was well perhaps for Master Herlion that grief had rendered him weak and helpless, or he might in his despair have been tempted to revenge himself upon the Christian.

"Alderman," said Abraham, falling at his feet and catching the skirt of his furred gown. "hear me, hear me as thou wouldst be heard at that great day when the Jew and the Christian shall be summoned to the judgment. The sweet girl who has been doomed to death is innocent as thyself of sorcery. Oh! Christian! if thou ever hadst a child, think for one moment on the agony of him who kneels at your feet. Before the most High God, do I proclaim her innocent. Take my life, my wealth—thou knowest I am wealthy—but spare my poor child."

The Alderman averted his head, and drew his right hand across his eyes.

"I cannot serve you," said he, "she is beyond my power, you should have appealed to the court."

"I did, I did appeal," cried the Jew vehemently, and they bade me begone and try the hearts of those who had doomed my child. You, Master Herlion, saw her on the accursed engine. Looked she liked a witch, think ye? Can so much innocence consort with vain and wicked arts? Angels might look upon that sweet girl and claim her as their sister—and you, oh! cruelty of unjust man!—you were present when her fair limbs were given to the torture!"

Master Herlion attempted to reply, but emotion choked his utterance. He turned towards the door as if he would have escaped from the room, but the Jew anticipated him, and starting on his feet opposed his exit.

"Stay!" cried Abraham. "I read thy heart, old man; thou wouldst save her, but she is a Jewess. Lo! I discover what threats or persuasion could not have wrung from me; no not even that rack which *Christians* delight to use."

He took from his bosom a small chased and enameled locket, with a representation of the Virgin and Child, to which was appended a green silk cord.

"Behold this jewel!" cried the Jew. "Twenty years ago I took it from the neck of that dear child whom I have called my daughter."

The Alderman writhed at the sight of the trinket, as though he had been transfixed with a lance, and staggering backwards sunk into a chair, gasping like a dying man. Abraham paused for a moment, but attributing the shock to some other emotion, continued:

"Yes; twenty years ago, Alderman. It was the Fast of Kipur: the Londoners fell upon and despoiled the Jews. I was a young man, and strong of limb then. I helped my brethren to beat off the rout, that drove them through Leadenhall Street like a herd of deer. The citizens armed at last, and put down the tumult, but not before many had fallen in the fray."

"But the jewel?" said the Alderman, recovering himself.

Abraham waved his hand as if enjoining silence, and continued:

"Yes, the hellish rout slew in their fury both women and children; my Miriam and her little ones perished, and I could not revenge them then—my costly merchandise was burned, with all my goods. Now mark, Alderman, we found shelter in a large and strong place near Ald-gate, and there we remained till the wrath of our enemies was appeased."

"What of the jewel? what of the jewel?" cried Master Herlion, rising from his seat, and advancing with a threatening gesture. Horrible doubts arose in the breast of the Alderman.

"Be still," said the Israelite, in a calm but fearful tone, and thrusting his hand into his bosom he half unsheathed a long knife.

"Be still, Christian," he repeated; "be still and thou shalt hear all; but move one step, or call thy servants, and my tale is ended. Hearken! one night when all were sleeping soundly, three of my brethren came to me, 'Up, Abraham,' said they, 'arouse thee and come with us.' I followed, scarce knowing whither I went; we reached a vault; a fire burnt brightly;—but I see thou art impatient, and I will be brief; they were about to sacrifice a child to the spirit of evil, and *that child was a Christian's!*"

Master Herlion shuddered violently, but he waited without speaking, to hear what followed. Abraham continued:—

"Alderman, that child looked in my face as the lamb turns its mild eyes upon the butcher; it clung to my gaberdine for protection, it supplicated for its little life; and *although a Jew*, my heart melted. I swore by the God of my fathers that it should not be harmed."

"What then?" said the Alderman, gasping for breath.

"*It did not plead in vain!*" shouted the old Jew, in a voice of thunder. "I saved its life, but at the price of five hundred marks, and Oh, it was a life worth saving. For twenty years have I treasured up the trinket which then hung around its neck, and now my darling is torn from me for ever! for twenty years——"

He paused. The Alderman faintly ejaculating "*Christ Jesu! my child!*" had once more sunk into his chair, where he lay without sense or motion; a crimson stream issued from his mouth and dyed his venerable beard. Death had come to his relief, and severed the father and his child for ever!

CHAPTER IX.
LOVE'S LAST STRUGGLE.

ARTHUR LECHMERE'S desperate and successful enterprise was soon noised over the city, and a few minutes after his flight, a party of mounted archers and cross-bowmen dashed through Chepe in pursuit of the fugitives, whose course had been marked by the watchmen on the city wall. Arthur and his friends, as soon as they had cleared all impediments, made a diversion to the right, and in less than half an hour were on the road to Stratford-le-Bow, where he had in readiness proper disguises for himself and the partner of his flight, preparatory to their embarking in a small vessel which lay at anchor in the Thames below Greenwich. But the road they had taken was circuitous, and their pursuers were gaining on them unobserved, in their way through the city. They had scarcely arrived within sight of Bow, when the shouts of the party in pursuit struck on their ears. Arthur shuddered, and looked backed on the advancing troop; he urged forward his steed, but the noble animal was oppressed by the unusual burthen. The waters too were out, and the flat marshy country, which even at this day is subject to inundations in wet seasons, was flooded by the recent rains, so much so, indeed, that the road was rendered impassable.

"Courage, my boy! courage, Arthur!" cried Hal Pearce, observing that his friend appeared irresolute, and mistrustful of the water; "'twill reach but to your saddle-girths; haste, or we are lost!"

The water was rushing furiously across the road, and gurgled fearfully, and the tottering steeds were carried off their legs; yet it was death to hesitate. Arthur clasped his Miriam tightly, gave his horse the rein, and bade her take courage; but, alas for the lovers! the pursuers were upon them. Two or three of the archers dashed fearlessly into the water, but their horses were carried down the stream, and their companions began to pour their shafts upon the fugitives. Pearce and Lovelace soon fell, covered with arrows, but Arthur's mailed coat of proof protected him, while he shielded with his body the terrified girl whom he snatched from the stake, and still urged forward his steed, who quivered and plunged under the galling discharge of the archers. At length an arrow pierced its flank, and the poor animal, in the throes of death, rolled over, and plunged the lovers in the flood. There was a faint shriek from the unfortunate girl, as she disappeared below the surface of the waters, and a momentary struggle of her lover; but his heavy mail, which had so well protected him from the arrows of his pursuers, rendered escape impossible; the waters rolled over them, and, locked in each other's arms, they sank beneath the flood!

The archers with difficulty saved themselves from a similar fate; and having regained the land, and become satisfied that their prey was beyond their reach, collected together and proceeded back to the city, where all was astonishment and wonder. The death of old Herlion, and the sad fate of his daughter and his nephew cast a gloom over the honest folks of the Westchepe; but few pitied Abraham the Jew; he was an unbeliever; and Christians in that age could find no sympathy for an old Israelite, who had wilfully concealed the child of another. On the morrow he was seized by the officers of justice, his wealth confiscated, and he himself committed to Newgate, where he died broken hearted, a few days afterwards, exclaiming with his last breath against the cruelty of those who had destroyed his adopted child.

BLACK HAWKE, THE HIGHWAYMAN.

A DESPERATE ENCOUNTER.

CHAPTER XXVIII.—(continued.)

The Jew was dragged away, still screaming out protestations of his innocence, and vowing on the faith and honour of an Israelite, that he had not the slightest intention of harming any of "de gentlemansh."

His captors, however, were incredulous, and altogether refused to believe one word he uttered.

"Now, gentlemen," said Merlin, when some kind of order was restored, "our foes are here at our gates. Shall we ride forth and fall upon them sword in hand, or endeavour to outwit them by superior cunning?"

"A fight! a fight!" exclaimed every voice but one.

That one was Captain Will Merry.

"How many are they in number?" asked he.

"At least one third more than we."

Will shook his head.

"Captain," said he to Merlin, "you know well enough that I am no coward, but in this case I would willingly avoid fighting. Our band, as you know, has sustained several severe losses lately, and if our number is reduced much more we shall be compelled to disperse. Now, as these dragoons have been waiting outside some time, I dare say they have occupied every post of advantage, so that we should not be able to cut our way through without severe loss."

"Your words are those of a wise man," responded Merlin.

No. 15.

"However, before we come to any decision, I will go and survey their position, so that we may know all the better what course to take."

CHAPTER XXIX.

A LONELY RIDE — TWO MEN IN THE DITCH — ALBERT MONTAGUE OVERHEARS THEIR CONVERSATION, AND PREVENTS THEM FROM ROBBING A PRIEST.

ALBERT MONTAGUE, as he rode away from Vandeleur Park, felt tolerably certain that Lady Jane would be safe in her chamber long ere the duke and his dependents could return to the house.

He had not the slightest fear that she would suffer any ill-usage at the hands of her parents; for he knew her to be possessed of quick wit, and doubted not that she would be able to clear herself from all suspicion.

Therefore, with a light heart, he rode along at a sharp canter, glancing over his shoulder occasionally to see whether he was pursued or not.

The duke's servants did not pursue him, for this reason, long before they could saddle their horses and lead them from the stables Albert Montague had passed out of sight.

Albert soon discovered that he had nothing to fear from

behind, and, drawing up his steed, began to consider what should be his next move.

It would be hardly safe to venture into any of his usual haunts he fancied, while the news of his escape from the hands of justice was so fresh.

He resolved to ride away to a district which he had never before visited, and there remain for a few days, until he could see Lady Jane again in fact.

His steed was suffered to proceed at a very gentle pace, and the young highwayman soon became lost in thought.

His murdered father and his stolen inheritance formed the subject matter of his meditations ; and, as may be expected, his thoughts were not very pleasant.

He was entering a woody district where plantations and clumps of trees were scattered in an irregular fashion each side of the road.

There was no boundary to this road beyond a ditch scarcely a yard in width and about the same depth.

Albert leaped his horse over this slight obstacle on to the soft mossy turf of the common.

Everything seemed still as the grave ; even his horse's hoofs made no noise as they pressed the soft green carpet.

Suddenly a sound fell upon the young man's ear, and he at once listened in the most attentive manner.

It seemed as though a party of men were holding a conversation.

There was a group of trees about twenty yards away and that was the only shelter for some distance.

Albert headed his horse towards the grove determined to find out if possible, who the talkers were, and what was the subject of their conversation.

The voices died away as he approached the grove, though so gradually that it seemed almost as if the men were receding from him.

When he reached the trees he dismounted, and, drawing his sword, searched thoroughly.

Not a trace of any human being could he discover, though he even looked up, thinking that the invisible speakers might have concealed themselves amongst the foliage.

The bright moon rendered every branch distinctly visible, but no one was to be seen.

Full of astonishment at this most extraordinary circumstance, he again mounted his steed, and returned to the roadside.

Again he could hear voices, more distinctly than before.

A thought suddenly entered his brain.

The speakers must be concealed in the ditch ; for there were no trees nearer than those he had just searched.

Whoever they might be, the fact of their hiding in the ditch proved that they were there for no good purpose.

So thought Albert, and, acting upon the thought, he dismounted.

The well-trained animal needed no tether ; a *whisper* was sufficient to chain him to the spot till his master should return or should call him forward by voice.

Albert Montague crawled along on his hands and knees till he reached the edge of the ditch ; then, throwing himself flat upon his stomach, he peered over.

About twenty feet distant from him two men were lying in the ditch, conversing in a low tone.

Albert crept still nearer and listened.

He could plainly see that they were men of a wealthier class than the poor peasantry of the district, for they were dressed well and armed well.

"Confound the old priest, what does he mean by keeping us waiting such a time ?" muttered one, the elder of the two.

"Perhaps he has had a hint that travelling is dangerous, and means to wait till daylight," replied the other.

"I tell you what it is, Fred," cried the first speaker ; "I'm getting cold and savage ; I fear I shall do old black gown some injury when he comes."

"Take some of this, it will warm your body and cool your temper."

Fred handed his companion a square bottle, and the angry watcher immediately applied his lips to it.

The conversation then ceased for a short time.

Albert resolved to keep guard along with them after his own

fashion, and, therefore, rolled himself a couple of yards nearer to them to a spot where some of the green turf had been taken off the soil, and piled up ready for removal.

The young highwayman felt a particular wish to know more about this brace of night birds who were so suspiciously hiding in the ditch.

Who was the priest they expected ? and why did they chose such a place for an interview with the absent churchman ?

From the manner in which they spoke it appeared pretty evident to the young man that the object of his two unknown comrades was to rob the priest.

Priest !

Surely it must be a Roman Catholic churchman, then, who was expected. These fellows would never use the word priest in speaking of a member of the Protestant faith.

Albert Montague, though baptized and brought up in the latter persuasion, had a strong inclination towards the church of Rome—that is, at such times as he felt or thought of religion in any shape or form.

"Then they wish to rob a father of the Holy Catholic church !" thought Albert. "The villains ! Luckily I am here to interfere with their little game."

"Suppose he should not bring the child," said the younger of the two in the ditch.

"D——n him ! he'll find himself in a very awkward situation. Why, that child is the great object with us."

"Well, it certainly seems very queer to take the child away from one priest in order to hand it over to another."

"That's the beauty of the plan. No one will ever suspect that a youngster taken out of the hands of the Carmelites would be handed over at once to the Franciscans."

"Hush ! May I never see Heaven if I don't hear the sound of wheels ! It must be his post chaise."

"We shall know the instant it comes round the corner yonder. Old Crupper, the postmaster, keeps no colour but grey in his stables."

One of the party then raised his head above the level of the ditch, and glanced along the road.

The sound of wheels could be heard in the distance and Albert began to prepare for action.

He looked to the priming of his pistols, and loosened his sword in the scabbard.

The carriage drew nearer and nearer ; it turned a corner of the road hidden by a clump of trees.

It was drawn by two grey horses !

The men in the ditch crouched down out of sight, and whispered to each other to be ready.

The vehicle approached.

It was within ten yards of the ambush.

The two men sprang forth from their hiding-place, and gave a loud shout.

The driver at once stopped his horses while the younger of the two held a pistol to his head, and threatened him with instant death if he dared advance another step.

The other man opened the door of the vehicle and in rough tones desired the passenger to descend.

The priest seemed unwilling to do so, and the ruffian without any more ceremony dragged him out of the carriage.

"Now, you infernal old Jesuit, give me that child, and any documents you may have about you relating to its birth."

"I cannot part with the child," replied the old man, firmly.

The robber raised his pistol menacingly.

"Don't compel me to use violence. I am in rather a savage mood, and you will find it much the best plan to comply with my demands without hesitation."

"I have already given my answer."

"Then take your fate, obstinate fool !" ejaculated the ruffian.

He pulled the trigger of his pistol ; but the bullet flew high into the air.

At the moment of firing Albert Montague's sword struck the robber's wrist, throwing his hand upwards, and thus saving the priest's life.

The ruffian turned, and uttering a furious oath drew his sword.

The weapons crossed each other, and the most deadly hatred gleamed in the eye of the ruffian, who had been thus disappointed in his intention of robbing the old priest of his charge.

"Who the devil told you to interfere?" he exclaimed, making a vicious thrust at Albert's breast.

Albert made no reply with his tongue; but his blade spoke for him.

It pierced the ruffian's shoulder, causing an agony of pain to shoot through his huge frame.

He staggered back apace.

"Shoot! Fred, shoot!" he cried.

The young man who had been engaged in stopping the horses was hardly aware that their plans had been interfered with till he heard his companion's cry.

He at once changed the direction of his pistol, and pointing it towards Albert pulled the trigger.

His weapon, too, like that of his companion, was rendered ineffectual.

Just as he fired, the driver of the vehicle brought the lash of his whip down with fearful violence upon the outstretched arm that held the pistol.

Then, jumping down from his seat ere the amazed young robber had time to draw a second weapon, the post-boy grappled his foe, and prevented him from rendering any assistance to his comrade.

Albert and his adversary once more closed in combat, while the grey-haired old priest, still holding the infant cause of dispute in his arms, stood looking on in amazement, wondering from whence his gallant young ally had so suddenly sprung.

A few minutes sufficed to prove that Albert Montague's skill was more than a match for his adversary's strength.

In ten minutes, from the time their swords crossed, the weapon of the would-be priest-slayer was twisted from his grasp, and sent flying half-a-dozen yards away from him.

"Spare his life!" cried the priest, "spare his life; he has been sufficiently punished!"

"It is more than he deserves," ejaculated Albert, as he returned his sword to its scabbard. "Now, villains!" continued he, "if you wish to preserve your skin free from holes you had better make a speedy departure from this place."

The men needed no further exhortation, but springing across the ditch were soon out of sight in one of the groves.

"I sincerely hope you are not hurt, reverend sir," said Albert.

"No; many thanks to you, I have escaped unscathed, though, when you first interfered, I was in great danger; but I will now resume my journey. Will you share my carriage with me?"

"Many thanks, reverend sir; but I have my horse close at hand," and he pointed to the spot where his good steed stood.

There was a short pause, and then Albert Montague again spoke.

"May I ask, holy father, if you know the ruffians who attacked you?"

"I know not the men, though I can well guess who urged them on to such violence."

Albert looked as though he would like to hear the story, but the priest did not feel inclined to gratify the young man's curiosity.

He stepped into the postchaise, saying as he did so,

"I know not who you may be, young gentleman, nor how you managed to arrive on the spot just as my enemies had attacked me; but, from my heart, I thank you for your kind interference on my behalf. May the blessing of Heaven rest upon you, and an old man's blessing will do you no harm, even if you belong to a different creed."

Before Albert could reply the vehicle was in motion, and the old priest was out of hearing.

The young highwayman returned to his steed, and mounting continued his journey, wondering what all this might mean.

Ere long big drops of rain began to fall, and the gathering clouds announced that a heavy storm was at hand.

Albert urged his steed onwards in the hope of reaching some human habitation ere the fury of the elements could harm him.

Not a house was in sight.

He eagerly gazed round for a shelter, and discovered at a little distance from him a lime-kiln that appeared to be deserted.

Towards this he directed his course, feeling convinced that even such a poor covering as that would be preferable to meeting the fury of the storm.

The lime-kiln was situated in a hollow scooped out in the side of the hill, and looked neglected and uninviting enough.

A rough road that led to it from the main highway, though once practicable for carts, was overgrown with brambles, rough grass, weeds, and nettles.

In some places dark spots on the ground told where hordes of gipsies had made their encampment for the night, and it was just such a spot as the houseless wanderer would select for his lodgings.

Albert Montague took notice of all these things as his horse slowly picked his way along the rough track.

But what mostly excited his curiosity and caused him for a moment to forget the pelting storm was a large printed bill pasted on the front of the building.

CHAPTER XXX.

SIR THOMAS BROOKE IN THE VAULT—THE SECRET DOOR—THE PASSAGE—THE HIDDEN WINE CELLAR—A DEED OF BLOOD.

WHILE Albert Montague is busily employed in deciphering the placard on the old lime-kiln, let us return to Albion Hall and see how matters progress with Sir Thomas Brooke and his faithful servant Bill the Crusher.

When the two confederate villains found themselves caught in the trap they had prepared for Lady Jane, the first thought of each was that the other had played the traitor.

This accounts for the renewed scuffle which Lady Jane heard as she ascended the stairs to freedom.

"Rascal!" ejaculated Sir Thomas, grappling with the Crusher, "you have betrayed me, like a base hound as you are!"

The Crusher made no reply, in fact, he was unable to speak, and almost unable to draw breath, so tightly was his throat compressed by the hand of the enraged Sir Thomas.

The Crusher, however, struggled most desperately, and at length succeeded in knocking his master's head against the floor with sufficient violence to stun him.

Bill had serious thoughts of putting an end to the baronet's life, but after some consideration came to the conclusion, that, perhaps, after all, it would be better to let him live.

It would not do to be *found alone* with the corpse, and, as yet, Bill saw no means of escaping from the vault.

He retreated to the most remote part of the cellar when he had reduced his master to a state of insensibility, and sitting down upon the floor, waited with as much patience as possible for the light of morning; when, perhaps, he would be able to discover some means of making his exit from the dungeon he had prepared for another.

He dared not go to sleep, lest his master should recover and renew the attack upon him; yet the gloom of the vault, together with the brandy he had swallowed, combined to render him excessively drowsy.

As he sat crouched down in his corner, all kinds of ugly images began to float before his mind.

It seemed as though the vault was growing light, a dim shadowy figure appeared to be slowly emerging from the opposite side!

The light grew stronger, the shadow more dense and well defined; it assumed human form, and pointed with pale finger to a deep gash in its throat.

Bill the Crusher gave a loud shriek, as he recognised the features of the murdered Lord Montague.

The form slowly advanced, while Bill the Crusher trembled with fright.

It stood by his side, and glared upon him with deep sunken eyes.

Then it raised its finger to the gash in its throat, and withdrew that member covered with blood.

"Let him go forth with Cain's mark upon his forehead," a solemn voice seemed to say, and the apparition laid its gory finger upon Bill the Crusher's brow.

The unhappy man uttered another cry, for it seemed as though a hot iron had been pressed upon his flesh.

The light faded, the shadowy figure melted away, and Bill the Crusher was once more in the dark with his senseless master.

Was it all a dream, or had he really seen the spirit of his victim?

The burning pain on his forehead convinced Bill the Crusher that he had in reality been visited by a supernatural being from another world.

He rose to his feet, and with silent steps paced backwards and forwards.

Minutes passed away; those minutes seemed hours.

Hours winged their noiseless course, seeming to the imprisoned watchers like whole days.

How awful it would be if he should be compelled to remain there!

Remain! Why, then he would starve.

Bill the Crusher had much the same thoughts floating about his head as had vexed Lady Jane Cleveland's soul during her temporary imprisonment.

To remain in that vault would be to starve!

Bill the Crusher knew the pangs of hunger of old.

He had fasted a whole day—two days, and more than that.

He knew the sickening, desponding feeling which overspreads the enfeebled body when the *acute pain* of starvation has passed away, when, with desponding heart, the suffering one grows indifferent as to his fate and makes no effort to avoid the approach of death.

And he would have to undergo all this, and then to die!

Few indeed are they for whom death has no terrors—few are they who can contemplate his outstretched hand with unfaltering nerves.

True, there may be no outward sign of fear, but in the heart will be an undefined dread of the mysterious, unsolved riddle of ceasing to exist.

To such a man as Bill the Crusher a lingering death had double terrors.

Superstition drove his brain almost to madness as he contemplated the grave in which he seemed doomed to leave his bones.

The stings and arrows of an outraged conscience shot their venom into his soul till he could have howled aloud in sheer terror.

A rustling noise beside him attracted his attention.

It was a rat, and the unclean animal was soon joined by a tribe of its fellows.

Would those fierce little animals respect the life of the captives, or would the morrow only show a heap of bare bones on the floor of the vault to mark where two men had miserably perished?

Bill the Crusher made a slight noise, and the four-footed visitors quickly retreated to their dens.

"Where am I?" asked the voice of Sir Thomas Brooke, suddenly and in a faint voice, like a man who has suddenly been aroused from slumber.

"Why, don't ye recollect, Sir Thomas," replied Bill, "how we came down here and that blessed party in petticoats slipped out and locked us in?"

"Ah! and you——"

"You said as 'ow it were my fault, Sir Thomas, but I'll take my solemn oath it wasn't."

"You villain, you tried to kill me!"

"If I'd been trying to kill you, Sir Thomas, I could a done it very comfortable while you was a-lying there for two hours and couldn't help yourself."

This answer seemed to re-assure Sir Thomas Brooke of the faith of his servant.

He remained silent for some time.

"How long have we been here?" he asked after a while.

"More than two hours by the clock, though it seems like two days to me."

"How are we to get out?"

Bill the Crusher was silent.

Sir Thomas had asked a question which he was totally unprepared to answer.

"Why don't you speak?" said Sir Thomas.

"Because I don't know."

"What, then, is to be done?"

Bill hesitated.

"Wait till daylight," he said.

"And what then?"

"We may, perhaps, be able to make some of the people about the house hear us."

"How long shall we have to wait?"

"At the least three hours longer."

Sir Thomas was silent again.

"Curses on that infernal woman!" said he at length. "She has the papers in her hand which will destroy us both. Who was the muddle-headed rascal who allowed her to enter that room?"

"I don't know."

Again there was a short silence.

"Did you ever see a man die on the gallows?" asked Sir Thomas, suddenly.

"Yes—many a one."

"Is it, do you think, very painful?"

"Why do you ask?"

"Do you think we shall be hanged?"

"In the devil's name, Sir Thomas, what possesses you to ask such questions? We're in trouble enough now without making it worse by bothering our heads about Jack Ketch."

Sir Thomas began to mutter to himself, while Bill the Crusher once more seated himself in his corner.

So the time passed away.

At length a faint light began to peep through two small gratings high up in the wall of the vault, announcing that another day was close at hand.

By it the prisoners eagerly viewed their dungeon.

"There is a secret door here," said Sir Thomas Brooke, breaking silence. "If we could only find it we might manage to escape."

"Don't you know whereabouts it lies?" asked the Crusher.

"No."

"Then we had better have a good search all round."

There was sense in this proposition, and, starting from each side of the iron-cased door by which they had entered, they searched with eager eyes for anything that might betoken the situation of the hidden aperture.

They hammered the wall with their fists in order to discover it by the sound, and passed their hands over the surface of the stones to feel if any projecting spring existed.

"Hurrah! here's the door I believe!" exclaimed the Crusher.

In hammering the wall one part of it gave out a different sound from the other portions.

There seemed to be a hollow space beyond.

Sir Thomas rushed eagerly towards the spot, and satisfied himself that such was the fact.

"But how are we to open it?" he asked.

The surface of the door appeared to be huge blocks of stone uniform with the remainder of the building.

They both applied their shoulders to the place, and pushed with all their force; but the spring or bolt was strong and resisted their efforts.

After trying in vain for some minutes, the two men drew back from the wall, uttering exclamations of rage and disappointment.

"Curse it!" exclaimed Sir Thomas.

"The man as made it ought to be shut up here just as we are," growled the Crusher.

As he uttered these words he fell heavily to the ground.

"What is the matter?" asked the master of the Hall.

Bill the Crusher rose to his feet, rubbing his head, which had sustained a severe bump.

"I caught my foot in something."

Both stooped simultaneously to see what this something was.

It was a large iron ring seemingly imbedded in a flagstone forming part of the floor of the vault.

Bill the Crusher pulled with all his force, but no result followed.

"D———n!" he muttered. "I thought this was it."

"Try and turn the ring round," said his master.

The man obeyed.

It yielded to his efforts with a harsh noise.

At the same time what appeared to be a portion of the wall glided slowly backwards.

A dark passage was visible.

The two men stepped through without hesitation.

Bill the Crusher turned and gave the ponderous door a push.

He pushed harder than he intended.

The spring snapped as the chasm in the wall closed up.

Retreat was impossible.

"Fool! what have you done?" cried Sir Thomas.

The Crusher made no reply; but trembled with fear at the thoughts of the probable consequences of his rash action.

Should they be unable to find any further outlet they were still more helplessly cut off from the outer world than while they remained in the vault.

"I didn't mean to do that," sighed the servant in tones which at once convinced his master that the affair was an accident.

"Come along, come along, I am beginning to feel faint," replied the baronet.

There was no fear of their losing each other, for the passage was so narrow that two persons would have been unable to pass each other.

There was no turning, it seemed straight as an arrow.

About a hundred paces distant from the vault they again met an obstacle.

"This must be the door," said Sir Thomas."

"I wonder where we shall find ourselves if we get out?" exclaimed the Crusher.

There was no difficulty about the door.

It swung open before their push, and the two men found themselves in a much lighter and larger passage which appeared to be cut in a chalk hill.

The light appeared to proceed from a number of irregular crevices in the roof of the rude archway.

In some places roots of trees were hanging down looking in the dull light like huge snakes suspended over the heads of the two wanderers.

Rats and mice ran squeaking to their holes at the approach of Sir Thomas Brooke and his companion, huge toads crawled over the rough pathway, and bats winged their shadowy flight about the silent space.

On they walked wondering when they should reach the end of their journey, and where they should find themselves on emerging once more into the light of day.

They had travelled for half an hour or more, and there seemed to be no signs of a termination to their walk when Bill the Crusher exclaimed,

"Here's a little side-path; shall we go down that?"

The baronet assented, and they entered the narrow archway.

It was merely a little nook or recess.

There was a huge box standing in it.

Bill the Crusher laid his hand on the lid with the intention of lifting it.

"Some poor devil's coffin, most likely," said Sir Thomas. "Queer things have been done in these hidden places."

Bill the Crusher opened the chest and glanced in.

There was no skeleton, no traces of humanity in decay; but bottles packed neatly side by side.

"Well I'm blest!" he exclaimed, as he drew forth a couple of them. "If this ain't what I call a good find."

Without any more words he knocked the necks off the bottles, and handing one to Sir Thomas, carried the other to his own lips.

"Suppose it should be poisoned?" said the baronet.

Bill the Crusher paused.

But the love of good liquor was too strong upon him to turn him aside from his purpose.

"There's at least three dozen bottles in that chest; they wouldn't spoil such a lot all at once."

He once more placed the bottle to his lips, and without removing it, swallowed the contents.

It was sherry of rare flavour, mellow with age. It had most probably been placed there by a generation that had passed away.

Sir Thomas longed to drink, but the fear of poison was too great to allow him to do so.

He sat himself down on the edge of the chest, watching the countenance of his servant, to see whether the wine had any ill effect or not.

Its only effect upon Bill the Crusher was to redden his face, and make his eyes glow with the light of intoxication.

"Surely there can be no harm," thought Sir Thomas; and he too swallowed the wine.

"That's what I call jolly good stuff," exclaimed the Crusher, dashing his empty bottle against the wall. "Let's have another?"

Sir Thomas made no objection, and the dry-throated servant speedily poured the contents of a second bottle down his throat.

This was quite sufficient to overthrow the Crusher's brain, and make his body totter in a very precarious manner.

"Now, come along," said Sir Thomas.

"No, I'll have 'nother bottle."

"You have had enough;" and so in good truth had Sir Thomas himself.

"You go 'long," said the drunkard, "I'll stop as long as I like."

The baronet, almost mad with rage, ejaculated the word,

"Murderer!"

The face of the servant glowed with rage. Raising his bottle on high, he hurled it at Sir Thomas's head.

Luckily it missed its aim, or in all probability the guilty life of Sir Thomas Brooke would have come to a sudden and bloody termination.

As it was, he stooped down to avoid the blow, and as he did so, caught sight of an object lying on the ground.

It was a heavy hammer.

Grasping it before the Crusher could repeat his attempt, Sir Thomas struck his servant a heavy blow on the head.

The Crusher fell like a log, while blood streamed from his temples.

"He is dead!" murmured Sir Thomas, gazing with terrified looks upon the prostrate body.

He stooped down, and, feeling for his victim's heart, discovered that there was still a motion.

Life was not extinct.

"If he recovers he will betray me. Shall I——?"

So mused the baronet, hesitating to commit the crime he wished to perpetrate.

A low groan from the man at his feet roused Sir Thomas.

Raising the hammer with all the fury and desperation of a madman, he rained down a succession of fearful blows upon the skull of Bill the Crusher.

Bits of bone, blood, and brains were scattered all over the floor of the vaulted passage, but the murderer did not hold his hand till it was quite impossible to discern a trace of human features in the lifeless corpse before him.

Then he looked around with a fearful gaze, as though he expected to see some one standing at his elbow.

"I was compelled to do it; he would have killed me; it was in self-defence," muttered the wretched man, endeavouring with such shallow arguments to convince himself that he had done no crime.

But the load of guilt still weighed on his heart, as, after draining another bottle, he continued his journey through the archway alone.

CHAPTER XXXI.

THE HAUNT OF THE BAND OF BLACK HAWKE—A COUNCIL OF WAR—THE STRATAGEM—THE ESCAPE—THE STRANGE HORSEMAN—THE SHOT.

MERLIN HAWKE, as will be recollected, volunteered to survey the position taken up by the military around the haunt of the band.

"I will go with you," exclaimed Will Merry. "You may need a sword beside your own."

Merlin made no objection, and the two friends were speedily creeping along beneath the shadow of some thick holly bushes that concealed them from the view of the enemy.

The soldiers had dismounted, and were grouped together in small parties, while a complete chain of sentries had been established.

Looking over all these arrangements it was very easy for Merlin and his companions to guess the intention of the commander of the dragoons.

That worthy officer evidently declined to attack the lions in their den with the force he had, and was waiting for the arrival of fresh troops.

Since the moment Simeon Lazarus had been carried off he had given up all hope of entering the stronghold of the robbers by stratagem.

"Now we can see the whole position," whispered Will Merry, as he moved a yard or two further through the bushes. "Which do you consider the strongest part of their position?"

"Here, immediately facing us," replied Merlin. "They expected to enter by the secret entrance, and therefore massed their strength on this side."

"And what are we to do?"

"We must fight our way out, that is very certain, unless we wish to be starved to death or taken prisoners."

"I give up all hopes of escaping by stratagem," said Merry. "Now, how are we to make our *sortie?*"

"A feint here to draw them away from the other entrance will be the first movement, and, then, while they are looking for us this side of the haunt we ride away from the opposite side."

Captain Will Merry was silent for a few minutes.

"Is your horse in good order?" said he, at length.

"No; I must leave Fair Rosamond behind, I fear."

"What, allow your gallant mare to fall into the hands of the enemy?"

"She will be safe enough here."

"Do you think so?"

"Yes; our enemies will follow without staying to search our retreat."

Again there was a pause, and the two captains slowly retraced their steps.

"Where is our rendezvous if it should happen that we get separated?" asked Captain Merry, when they were once more in their home.

Merlin paused for a few moments.

"The old almshouses near Albion Hall. It is a neighbourhood where I am not expected, and I have a little business to do there."

"I have none, but will assist you if you need assistance."

"Thanks; but I have no doubt I shall be able to accomplish my task single-handed; if I need a friend you shall be the one I choose."

"And now—how about the ladies?" asked Captain Merry.

"True; I had nearly forgotten them in all this bustle and excitement."

"We must not leave them behind."

"Certainly not, unless you wish them to become the victims of yonder brutal dragoons. We have spare horses, and can easily take them with us."

Captain Merry's brow grew smooth once more.

"We must also take our prisoners with us," continued Merlin. "It would be a poor plan to suffer them to escape, now we have them in our hands."

"If you will entrust them to me, I will answer for their safety."

"You shall have the task of escorting them," replied Merlin; "and now summon the band, and let them be told the decision we have made."

In a very few minutes every man of the company had heard the news that they must leave their haunt. All felt sorry and down-hearted to be compelled to yield their old home up to the enemy.

"We shall return again ere long, my brave comrades," said Merlin; "but, for the present, this step is absolutely necessary. Put your trust in me, and all will go well; but, beware of treason or mutiny; reflect on the scene you have witnessed this night, for though I am slow to anger, my arm is swift to punish."

The horses were then saddled and led out, Lady Florence, and Polly, the innkeeper's daughter, being accommodated with as noble animals as ever bore ladies on their backs.

Captain Ashburne and Marmaduke Greville were then mounted, care being taken to surround them with a party of the most resolute men of the band.

"Vile wanton," said Henry Ashburne, as he caught sight of his sister, "it is you who have brought us to this captivity. Go your ways, faithless wife, dishonoured woman! Take with you a brother's curse, and may it blight upon you, and your rascally paramour."

"Silence!" thundered Merlin, as he heard the words, "silence, villain, or my sword shall silence your vile tongue."

"How boldly he threatens an unarmed man," said Marmaduke Greville, sneeringly.

Merlin whispered a word in the fair ear of Lady Florence, and she at once quitted the spot. The scene was as painful to her as it was irritating to Merlin.

"Rascal, I will be avenged on you," shouted Ashburne.

"And I, too," exclaimed Marmaduke Greville, plucking up courage from the example of his companion in captivity.

"Gag them," cried Merlin, angrily.

A party of men at once seized the captives, and speedily reduced them to a complete silence.

"Now, mark well my words," said the chieftain, "you know the rendezvous, and the road to it; our enemies do not know it, and in order to keep them in ignorance it will be necessary to scatter as soon as we are well clear of the hostile line. You who have charge of the prisoners, shoot them if you are in danger, rather than suffer them to escape."

The men who surrounded Captain Ashburne and Marmaduke Greville grasped their pistols as though they would like to do so then and there.

A small party was then detailed to make the sham attack, while the others mounted in readiness to ride off the moment they should receive the signal.

Shots were heard, and shouts and oaths.

"Forward!" cried Merlin, setting spurs to his steed, and grasping Lady Florence's bridle. "Forward, lads; our brave comrades are close behind."

The whole party dashed out into the open road, and thundered away at full speed.

Those who had given the soldiers the false alarm were but a few paces behind.

The stratagem had succeeded admirably.

The highwaymen had shown themselves to the dragoons, and so drawn the whole force to one point; then, while the soldiers were indulging in a little ball practice, they retreated, and mounting their steeds soon rejoined the band.

Before the soldiers could be got in readiness to follow, the whole party had combined, and Black Hawke's band had a start of at least three hundred yards.

The dragoons continued firing with their carbines, but without doing the least harm.

They were more heavily equipped than the highwaymen, and the distance between the two parties increased every minute.

An hour after quitting the haunt, Merlin and his companions were at least a mile and half ahead.

They reached a spot where the road was crossed by another.

Merlin spoke a few rapid words to his men, and instantly the band divided into three sections, each of which took a separate road.

Merlin kept close by Lady Florence, along with some of his trustiest followers.

While Will Merry commanded the escort, which had charge of the three prisoners, for the Jew had been brought with them from the haunt.

"You may drop him as soon as you can do so conveniently," cried Merlin, alluding to the Israelite.

"The convenient moment will be when we reach a river," responded the jovial captain. "I will drop him in the deepest part."

With many wishes of good luck the three then separated.

There was great shouting heard a long way behind; but the soldiers were not visible.

Lady Florence turned suddenly as she rode by Merlin's side, and said,

"How long is this fearful drama to last? When am I to have rest and peace once more?"

"Are you angry with me for what I have done, dear Lady Florence?" asked the highwayman, gazing tenderly on her face.

For some moments she made no reply; but at length heaving a deep sigh, she said,

"My husband is—so is my brother."

"Little care I for their frowns, if you smile on me; but you are mine now—mine for ever!"

"That cannot be, Merlin."

"Why?"

"My husband still lives."

"Your husband? You allude to Sir Andrew Greville, I suppose?"

"I do. He is my husband."

"We will find means to unloosen the tie which binds you to him."

Again Lady Florence sighed deeply; yet despite the sorrow of the sound, she did not appear displeased at the idea of being freed from her tyrant husband.

Merlin, in the midst of all this conversation, frequently glanced back over his shoulder to discover what progress his pursuers were making.

Presently he discerned a single horseman mounted on a superb steed, who was evidently rapidly overtaking them.

"Who can it be?" thought he.

He urged his party onwards; but it was useless.

He had left Fair Rosamond behind.

Presently there was a flash and a loud report.

A bullet came whistling through the air.

(*To be continued.*)

A TRUE PIRATE STORY.

THIS adventurer was mate of a sloop that sailed from Jamaica, and was taken by Captain Winter, a pirate, just before the settlement of the pirates at Providence Island. After the pirates had surrendered to his Majesty's pardon, and Providence Island was peopled by the English government, our captain sailed to Africa. There he took several vessels, particularly the "Cadogan," from Bristol, commanded by one Skinner. When he struck to the pirate, he was ordered to come on board in his boat. The person upon whom he first cast his eye proved to be his old boatswain, who stared him in the face, and accosted him in the following manner,

"Ah, Captain Skinner, is it you? The only person I wished to see; I am much in your debt, and I shall pay you all in your own coin."

The poor man trembled in every joint, and dreaded the event, as he well might. It happened that Skinner and his old boatswain, with some of his men, had quarrelled, so that he thought fit to remove them on board a man-of-war, while he refused to pay them their wages. Not long after, they found means to leave the man-of-war, and went on board a small ship in the West Indies. They were taken by a pirate, and brought to Providence; from thence they sailed as pirates along with Captain England. Thus accidentally meeting their old captain, they severely revenged the treatment which they had received.

After the rough salutation which has been related, the boatswain called to his comrades, laid hold of Skinner, tied him fast to the windlass, and pelted him with glass bottles until they cut him in a shocking manner; then whipped him about the deck until they were quite fatigued, remaining deaf to all his prayers and entreaties; and at last, in an insulting tone, observed, that as he had been a good master to his men, he should have an easy death; and upon this, shot him through the head.

Having taken such things as they stood most in need of out of the snow, she was given to captain Davis, in order to try his fortune, with a few hands.

Captain England, some time after, took a ship called the "Pearl," for which he exchanged his own sloop, fitted her up for piratical service, and called her the "Royal James." In that vessel he was very fortunate, and took several ships of different sizes and different nations. In the spring of 1719 the pirates returned to Africa, and, beginning at the River Gambia, they then sailed down the coast to Cape Corse, and captured several vessels. Some of them they pillaged, and allowed to proceed, some they fitted out for the pirate service, and others they burnt.

Leaving our pirate upon this coast, the "Revenge" and the "Flying King" sailed for the West Indies, where they took several prizes, then cleared and sailed for Brazil. There they captured some Portuguese vessels; but a large Portuguese man-of-war coming up to them, proved an unwelcome guest. The "Revenge" escaped, but was soon lost upon that coast. "Flying King" in despair run ashore. There were then seventy on board, twelve of whom were slain, and the remainder taken prisoners. The Portuguese hanged thirty-eight of them.

Captain England, whilst cruizing upon that coast, took the "Peterborough," of Bristol, and the "Victory." The former they detained, the latter they plundered and dismissed. In the course of his voyage, England met with two ships, but these taking shelter under Cape Corse Castle, he unsuccessfully attempted to set them on fire. He next sailed down to Whydah road, where Captain La Bouche had been before England, and left him no spoil. He now went into the harbour, cleaned his own ship, and fitted up the "Peterborough," which he called the "Victory." During several weeks the pirates remained in this quarter, indulging in every species of riot and debauchery, until the natives, exasperated with their conduct, came to an open rupture, when several of the negroes were slain, and one of their towns set on fire by the pirates.

Leaving that port, the pirates, when at sea, determined, by vote, to sail for the East Indies, arrived at Madagascar. After watering and taking in some provisions, they sailed for the cost of Malabar. This place is situated in the Mogul empire, and is one of its most beautiful and fertile districts. It extends from the coast of Canora to Cape Comorin. The original natives are negroes; but a mingled race of Mahometans, who are generally merchants, have been introduced in modern times. Having sailed almost round the one-half of the globe, literally seeking whom they might devour, our pirates arrived in this country.

Not long after their settlement at Madagascar, they took a cruize, in which they captured two Indian vessels and a Dutchman. They exchanged the latter for one of their own, and directed their course again to Madagascar Several of their hands were sent on shore with tents and ammunition, to kill such beasts and venison as the island afforded. They also formed the resolution to go in search of Avery's crew, which they knew had settled upon the island; but, as their residence was upon the other side of the island, their loss of time and labour were all the fruits of their search.

They tarried here but a very short time, then steered their course to Juanna, and, coming out of that harbour, fell in with two English and an Ostend ship, all Indiamen, which, after a desperate action, they captured. The particulars of this extraordinary action are related in the following letter from Captain Mackra:—

"Bombay, November 16, 1720.

"We arrived the 25th of July last, in company with the 'Greenwich,' at Juanna, an island not far from Madagascar. Putting in there to refresh our men, we found fourteen pirates that came in their canoes from the Mayotta, where the pirate ship to which they belonged, viz., 'The Indian Queen,' two hundred and fifty tons, twenty-eight guns, and ninety men, commanded by Captain Oliver de la Bouche, bound from the Guinea coast to the East Indies, had been bulged and lost. They said they left the captain and forty o their men building a new vessel, to proceed on their wicked design. Captain Kirby and I, concluding that it might be of great service to the East India Company to destroy such a nest of rogues, were ready to sail for the purpose on the 17th of August, about eight o'clock in the morning, when we discovered two pirates standing into the bay of Juanna, one of thirty-four, and the other of thirty-six guns. I immediately went on board the 'Greenwich,' where they seemed very diligent in preparations for an engagement, and I left Captain Kirby with mutual promises of standing by each other. I then unmoored, got under sail, and brought two boats a-head to row me close to the 'Greenwich;' but he, being open to a valley and a breeze, made the best of his way from me; which an Ostender, in our company, of twenty-two guns, seeing, did the same, though the captain had promised heartily to engage with us, and I believe would have been as good as his word, if Captain Kirby had kept his. About half an hour after twelve, I called several times to the 'Greenwich' to bear down to our assistance, and fired a shot at him, but to no purpose. For though we did not doubt but he would join us, because, when he got about a league from us, he brought his ship to, and looked on; yet both he and the Ostender basely deserted us, and left us engaged with barbarous and inhuman enemies, with their black and bloody flags hanging over us, without the least appearance of ever escaping, but to be cut to pieces. But God, in his good providence, determined otherwise; for, notwithstanding their superiority, we engaged them both about three hours; during which time the largest of them received some shot betwixt wind and water, which made her keep off a little to stop her leaks. The other endeavoured all she could to board us, by rowing with her oars, being within half a ship's length of us above an hour; but, by good fortune, we shot all her oars to pieces, which prevented them, and by consequence saved our lives.

"About four o'clock, most of the officers and men posted on the quarter-deck being killed and wounded, the largest ship making up to us with diligence, being still within a cable's length of us, often giving us a broadside; there being now no hopes of Captain Kirby coming to our assistance we endeavoured to run ashore, and, though we drew four feet of water more than the pirate, it pleased God that he stuck fast on a higher ground than, happily, we fell in with, so was disappointed a second time from boarding us.

"Here we had a more violent engagement than before; all my officers and most of my men behaved with unexpected courage, and, as we had a considerable advantage by having a broadside to his bow, we did him great damage; so that, had Captain Kirby come in then, I believe we should have taken both the vessels, for we had one of them sure, but the other pirate, who was still firing at us, seeing the 'Greenwich' did not offer to assist us, he supplied his consort with three boats' full of fresh men.

"About five in the evening the 'Greenwich' stood clear away to sea, leaving us struggling hard for life, in the very jaws of death, which the other pirate that was afloat seeing, got a warp out, and was hauling under our stern.

"By this time many of my men being killed and wounded, and no hopes left us of escaping being all murdered by enraged, barbarous conquerors, I ordered all that could to get into the long-boat, under the cover of the smoke of our guns, so that, with what some did in boats and others by swimming, most of us that were able got ashore by seven o'clock.

"When the pirates came aboard they cut three of our wounded men to pieces. I, with some of my people, made what haste I could to the King's-town, twenty-five miles from us, where I arrived next day, almost dead with the fatigue and loss of blood, having been sorely wounded in the head by a musket-ball.

"At this town I heard that the pirates had offered ten thousand dollars to the country people to bring me in, which many of them would have accepted, only they knew the king and all his chief people were in my interest. Meantime I caused a report to be spread that I was dead of my wounds, which much abated their fury. About ten days after, being pretty well recovered, and hoping the malice of our enemies was nigh over, I began to consider the dismal condition we were reduced to, being in a place where we had no hopes of getting a passage home, all of us in a manner naked, not having had time to get off another shirt, or a pair of shoes, than what we had on.

"Having obtained leave to go on board the pirates, and gotten a promise of safety, several of the chief of them knew me, and some of them had sailed with me, which I found to be of great advantage, because, notwithstanding their promise, some of them would have cut me, and all that would not enter with them, to pieces, had it not been for the chief captain, Edward England, and some others whom I knew.

"They talked of burning one of their ships, which we had so entirely disabled as to be no further useful to them, and to fit the 'Cassandra' in her room; but in the end I managed the affair so well that they made me a present of the said shattered ship, which was Dutch built, and called the 'Fancy,' her burden was about three-hundred tons. I procured also a hundred and twenty-nine

bales of the Company's cloth, though they would not give me a rag of my own clothes.

"They sailed the 3rd of September, and I, with jury-masts, and such old sails as they left me, made a shift to do the like on the 8th, together with forty-three of my ship's crew, including two passengers and twelve soldiers; having no more than five tons of water on board.

"After a passage of forty-eight days I arrived here on the 26th of October, almost naked and starved; having been reduced to a pint of water a day, and almost in despair of ever seeing land, by reason of the calms we met with between the coast of Arabia and Malabar.

"We had in all thirteen men killed, and twenty-four wounded; and we were told, that we destroyed about ninety or a hundred of the pirates. When they left us, there were about 300 whites and 80 blacks in both ships.

"I am persuaded, had our consort the 'Greenwich' done his duty, we had destroyed both of them, and got two hundred thousand pounds for our owners and selves; whereas the loss of the 'Cassandra' may justly be imputed to his deserting us. I have delivered all the bales that were given me into the Company's warehouse, for which the governor and council have ordered me a reward. Our governor, Mr. Boon, who is extremely kind and civil to me, had ordered me home with the packet; but Captain Harvey, who had a prior promise, being come in with the fleet, goes in my room. The governor hath promised me a country voyage to help to make up my losses, and would have me stay and accompany him to England next year."

Captain Mackra was certainly in imminent danger in trusting himself and his men on board the pirate ship; and, unquestionably, nothing but the desperate circumstances in which he was placed could have justified such a hazardous step.

The honour and influence of Captain England, however, protected him and his men from the fury of the crew, who would willingly have wreaked their vengeance upon them.

It is pleasing to discover any instance of generosity or honour among such an abandoned race, who have bid defiance to all the laws of honour, and are regardless of all laws human and divine.

Captain England was so steady to Captain Mackra, that he informed him, that it would be with no small difficulty and address, that it would be able to preserve him and his men from the fury of the crew who were greatly enraged at the resistance which had been made. He likewise acquainted him that his influence and authority among them was giving place to that of Captain Taylor, chiefly because the dispositions of the latter were more savage and brutal. They, therefore, consulted between them what was the best method to secure the favour of Taylor, and to keep him in good humour.

Mackra made the punch to flow in great abundance, and employed every artifice to sooth the mind of that ferocious villain. A singular incident was also very favourable to the unfortunate captain.

It happened that a pirate with a prodigious pair of whiskers, a wooden leg, and stuck round with pistols, came blustering and swearing upon the quarter-deck, inquiring where was Captain Mackra.

He naturally supposed that this barbarous-looking fellow would be his executioner; but, as he approached him, he took the captain by the hand, swearing that he was an honest fellow, and that he had formerly sailed with him, and would stand by him; and let him see the man that would touch him.

This terminated the dispute, and Captain Taylor's disposition was so ameliorated with punch, that he consented that the old pirate ship, and so many bales of cloth, should be given to Mackra; and then sunk into the arms of intoxication.

England now pressed Mackra to hasten away, lest the ruffian, upon his becoming sober, should not only retract his word, but give liberty to the crew to cut him and his men in pieces.

But the gentle temper of Captain England, and his generosity towards the unfortunate Mackra, proved the origin of much calamity to himself.

The crew, in general, deeming that kind of usage which Mackra had received inconsistent with piratical policy, they circulated a report that he was coming against them with the Company's force.

(*To be continued.*)

BLACK HAWKE, THE HIGHWAYMAN.

THE DEATH STRUGGLE.

CHAPTER XXXII.

THE RAGE OF THE ELEMENTS—ALBERT MONTAGUE IN THE
LIME-KILN — MUTTERED THREATS — THE CONTENTS OF
THE BAG.

"£500 *REWARD!*

" *Whereas, Lady Florence Greville, the wife of Sir Andrew
Greville, Bart., has been feloniously enticed or conveyed away
from her home by a notorious highwayman, known as Merlin
Hawke, alias Black Hawke, and divers others ; now, this is
to give notice, that the above sum will be given as a reward to
any person or persons who may capture the offenders and
bring them to justice.*

" *Information to be given to any Justice of the Peace.*"

The placard which contained this announcement was
printed in large letters, surmounted by the royal arms.

Albert Montague, sole tenant of the abandoned lime-kiln,
had no difficulty whatever in reading it, so great was the
contrast between the big black letters of the bill and the
whitened face of the old building on which it was pasted.

Just as he had finished the perusal of this interesting piece
of information, the dark clouds were torn asunder by a bright
flash of lightning.

At the same time a terrific peal of thunder shook the earth.
The young man dismounted, and led his steed into the interior of the building.

He struck a light, and, glancing round, perceived that there
was another room or recess beyond that in which he stood.

However, Albert, after satisfying himself that he was the

No. 16.

only present inhabitant of the deserted building, took up his
station near the door, and, first tying his handkerchief over
his horse's eyes to prevent the lightning from frightening the
noble animal, waited with considerable impatience for the
return of fair weather.

"Our gallant captain is a valuable article at the present
moment," he muttered to himself, his thoughts reverting to
the bill overhead. "How seldom do men really know what
they are worth! I should like, though, to know at what
price the ' divers others ' are estimated, and whether I am in-
cluded in the list——Jove ! what a crash !"

The last exclamation had reference to an ear-splitting clap
of thunder, along with which came a perfect deluge of rain.

"I was lucky to find out this spot," continued Albert, still
musing. "I should have been well-nigh drowned by this time
had I kept on the road ; the trees would be no shelter, nor
would it be safe to take refuge under them."

As he spoke, a forked flash descended upon a lofty elm that
grew by the roadside, splitting off huge branches, and leaving
the fair tree only a blackened, smoking stump.

Albert shuddered as he thought what might have been his
fate had he acted upon his first thoughts when he saw the
approaching storm, and taken refuge beneath that very tree.

The storm continued, and it seemed excessively unlikely
that any one should be abroad in such weather.

Yet, at that moment a man was seen coming towards the
lime-kiln at a swift pace.

Albert Montague at once withdrew from his position near
the door into the inner chamber before spoken of.

He had hardly done so, and given his horse the signal to remain perfectly still, when the man entered, the water dripping in torrents from his coat and hat.

The outer portion of the cave was much larger and more light, so that the occupant of the inner den could see what his unknown companion looked like without being observed himself.

It was a man with a forehead wrinkled and furrowed by deep lines, with a sallow, sickly complexion, and stooping gait.

He seemed one of those worn-out wrecks of humanity of whom an observer would say, with careless pity, that he must have been good-looking in his youth.

If the long, matted, rusty, black hair had been trimmed; if the wrinkled traces of care, sorrow, and dissipation had been smoothed away from his face; if the hard, wild expression of those dark eyes had been softened, women and children might have looked upon the wanderer without dislike or fear.

Coarsely clad as was the man in a suit of ill-made slops, heavy-nailed boots, and rough cap, a lingering air of refinement peeped through the coarse disguise.

That he was an educated person no one could doubt; the hand was too white, the fingers too delicate and taper to belong to a man who earned his bread by manual labour.

He threw on the ground a bundle, and a rough stick cut from a hedge.

Albert Montague looked on in silence and surprise.

He knew the man, and greatly wondered what he might be doing in such a place, and in such a dress.

The owner of the bundle opened it, and laid the various contents upon the floor of the lime-kiln.

There was a powder flask, part of a loaf of bread, a roll of paper, some pieces of sheet lead, and a clasp knife.

He took up the fragment of lead, and worked away with the knife at it till he had cut off eight or ten pieces the size of large peas.

These he carefully wrapped up in paper, and placed in his coat pocket.

He then took up the bread and began to eat ravenously; but his hunger was soon satisfied, or his mood changed, for he ceased eating as abruptly as he had begun.

Then he sat with tears in his eyes, rocking himself to and fro, muttering scraps of disjointed talk all the while.

"Beautiful as heaven's brightest angel!—false as hell's blackest fiend! Oh! how I loved—but he—no—she must die by my hand!"

"She must do nothing of the kind, my angry friend," thought Albert, for, knowing the man, he could well guess of whom he was speaking.

"She must die!" and the man laughed harshly, though there was no merriment in the sound.

As the mournful sound died away, the man drew a kind of bag from the inside of his dress, and opened it.

It contained about a dozen guineas, a gold ring, evidently made for a lady's wear, set with pearls and rubies, and a miniature portrait set in a gold case.

The man frowned deeply as he gazed upon the ring.

He dashed it to the ground, and, for a moment, seemed as though about to crush it to atoms beneath his heel.

But when his eyes fell upon the portrait his humour changed.

He pressed the precious trinket to his lips, and kissed it wildly, passionately, as bereaved mothers will kiss the tiny lock of hair or broken plaything that reminds them of their lost little ones.

Long and earnestly he gazed on it, while his countenance changed rapidly, now assuming an aspect of the deepest grief, and then wearing a look of ungovernable rage.

After a while he replaced the money, the ring, and the picture in the bag, tied up his bundle, and rose to his feet with the evident intention of quitting the old lime-kiln.

At that moment the blackened sky seemed torn asunder once more, a broad yellow flash lit up the whole horizon, while two seconds after came the deep-toned roll of the thunder, echoing and crashing amongst the chalk pits in which the lime-kiln was situated.

The rain dashed down in enormous flat drops, and a cold moist wind rushed howling into the cave.

The wayfarer changed his intention of continuing on his journey, and resumed his former position on the ground with the air of one who almost feared the storm raging without.

Shading his wily eyes with one thin hand, he watched the elemental war with a look of interest.

The flashes of lightning gleamed now in forked streams of dazzling light, now in sheets of flame, banked up by swarthy cloud banks.

The rain came with a hissing sound, dashing the stones around, and filling the cart-track with a foaming torrent of water. The darkness became more and more intense.

But still there was sufficient light to enable Albert Montague, as he stood in the inner chamber of the lime-kiln, to see his fellow lodger, and take note of his actions.

Albert saw a pistol clutched firmly in the wild-looking man's hand. He heard the click of the spring as he tried the lock.

He saw powder poured into the barrel, and the pieces of jagged lead dropped down the dark tube.

He saw a deadly purpose of murder gleaming in the man's eye, and resolved to save, if possible, the life of the unknown doomed one.

The storm passed away as rapidly as it had come; the thunder only growled at intervals, and all was silent save the pattering of heavy drops of water as they fell from the bushes to the soddened earth beneath.

Then, with a long-drawn sigh, the man started to his feet, exclaiming, in accents of mingled rage and sorrow,

"Florence, I loved you once; but now no passion remains but revenge. You die, or my name is not Andrew Greville."

He passed hastily from the cave, and made towards the main road.

After a pause of some minutes, Albert Montague led out his horse, and followed the baronet.

If danger menaced Lady Florence, the bold Captain Merlin was also in danger, and Albert was too deeply indebted to Black Hawke to allow any evil to threaten the chief of the band without endeavouring to avert it.

He, therefore, kept the baronet in sight, though, at the same time, he was careful to remain far enough behind to prevent the slight sound made by the hoofs of his horse upon the rain-soaked road from reaching the ears of the man he was following.

In spite of the strange events—the strange meeting which had taken place within the few hours past—Albert could not keep his thoughts from wandering back to Vandeleur Park.

He reflected the hasty manner in which he had quitted Lady Jane, and felt by no means easy in his mind when he reflected that it was not unlikely that the lady of his love would incur the suspicion, if not the severe displeasure of her father, the Duke of Cleveland.

"I was foolish to venture when I knew the duke was there; but she is a bold girl, and knows how to get out of a scrape as well as I do myself, though that is not saying much, for I am a much better hand at plunging into difficulties and dangers than extricating myself from them."

So thought the young man, as he jogged quietly along behind Sir Andrew Greville, who was quite unconscious of being watched.

CHAPTER XXXIII.

MERLIN'S ADVERSARY—THE DUKE DEMANDS HIS DAUGHTER —SUSPICIONS AND EXPLANATIONS—THE CRY FOR HELP.

MERLIN felt a sudden pang in his left arm, as though a red-hot knife had pierced it, and he knew well enough that the pistol bullet had seared the limb in its flight.

He could even feel the warm blood trickling down inside his sleeve, but the wound was not of sufficient importance to cause him to halt in his onward career.

The boldness of the attack puzzled Merlin slightly, for the horseman was not in military dress, nor were the pursuing dragoons in sight; it was hardly possible that a constable or Bow-Street runner would venture to attack a whole band of highwaymen single-handed.

A slight hill was before them, and up this the whole party rushed as swiftly as their horses could carry them.

On reaching the top Merlin glanced back over his shoulder and could plainly see that the man who had fired was alone, the soldiers being nowhere visible.

He therefore checked his steed, and suffered the stranger to approach gradually.

"Forward, my men; leave me to deal with this madman," said he.

Lady Florence then spoke.

"For Heaven's sake, dear Merlin, do not encounter him; he has another pistol in his hand."

Merlin's heart bounded at the sweet words.

They assured him that she loved him still.

"There is nothing to fear, sweet Lady Florence."

"Be cautious, for my sake."

"For your sake? For your sake, dearest, I take upon myself the task of punishing this impertinent ruffian. His shot might have struck you."

"Would to Heaven it had!"

"Forward, forward!" cried Merlin, as the stranger approached.

But Lady Florence seemed loth to obey.

Merlin made a signal to one of his band, and the man, seizing hold of the bridle of her horse, led Lady Florence beyond the sound of her lover's voice.

The horse on which the unknown was mounted was a black one of great size and strength.

The stranger's hat was drawn down in such a manner as to conceal the wearer's face, so that Merlin was unable to catch a glimpse of his adversary's features.

He could only see that a pistol was again directed towards him.

Then came the puff of white smoke and the hiss of the bullet as it winged its rapid flight past his ear.

Merlin's blood began to approach boiling heat, and, drawing his sword from the sheath, he spurred his steed towards the impetuous stranger.

"Stand aside! stand aside! it is not you I seek. Your turn is to come," shouted the man.

Merlin heeded not, and the two horses met with a shock that nearly threw both riders from their saddles.

The superior horsemanship of Black Hawke saved him from being overthrown, while at the same time it checked the furious career of his antagonist.

In an instant they both recovered, and their keen swords met with a ringing sound.

Cuts and thrusts were exchanged with the greatest fury, Merlin being compelled to use a great deal of caution to guard himself against the longer and heavier weapon of his foe.

The combat was not of long duration.

In a few moments Merlin saw an opportunity, and passed his sword through the fleshy part of his antagonist's right arm.

The man uttered a scream and an oath as he dropped his weapon.

"Now, sir, let us see your face," said Merlin, as with the point of his sword he removed the hat from his wounded foe's face.

It was the Duke of Cleveland!

Merlin made a stately bow.

"May I ask," said he, "how have I offended so as to incur the animosity of your grace?"

"Villain!" exclaimed the wounded duke; "you have stolen my daughter and disarmed me; finish your vile career by taking my life, for I have no wish to live while I see my child borne away by your minions before my eyes."

"Your daughter?"

"Aye, my daughter."

"You mistake. The lady——"

"The Lady Jane Cleveland is my only daughter, and you, base rascal, have stolen her away. You will hardly have the hardihood to deny it when I see her yonder among your ruffian comrades, one of whom holds the rein of her horse."

"You are mistaken, sir," exclaimed Merlin, "and were it not that I can make some allowance for the feelings of a father robbed of his daughter, I should not allow your uncourteous speech to pass unnoticed. That lady is not your daughter as I will prove."

So saying, he gave a shrill whistle, and the party with which Lady Florence was riding at once halted.

"Now, sir, ride forward and see if it be your daughter," continued the highwayman.

"You mean no false play?"

"I do not."

"And when I have satisfied myself of the truth of your words I shall be free to depart?"

"Certainly."

"Then I will trust to your honour."

"You may do so with perfect safety," replied Merlin, with somewhat of a sneer on his features; "though, had I met you under other circumstances, it would have been otherwise."

They then rode forward till they overtook Lady Florence and Merlin's companions.

A glance was sufficient to satisfy the duke that he had been deceived.

Lifting his hat he bowed politely to Lady Florence, and apologised for his violent conduct, adding, by way of excuse,

"I was told in the village behind us that a party of men had been seen carrying away two ladies, and as your dress resembles that worn by my daughter, I fancied that at last I had found the right track. However, I must try elsewhere."

"Have you any reason to suspect any one of enticing her away?" asked Merlin.

"Yes. A young fellow who not long since took to the highway for a profession. I believe he claims to be the son of Lord Montague who was murdered some years ago, and therefore the rightful owner of Albion Hall; but we all know that Lord Montague's son was murdered along with the unfortunate nobleman himself."

"If so, the body of the youth was never discovered," said Merlin, gravely. "I happen to be very intimately acquainted with the young man you allude to, and believe in the truth of his assertions and the justice of his claim to the property."

"Humph," muttered the duke; "if I thought so—I'd——"

"You would make no objection whatever to his marriage with Lady Jane Cleveland, your missing daughter; is it not so, my lord duke?"

"It is. He is a young rascal, though, to carry her away in this style."

"Softly, softly. What proof have you that my young friend had any hand whatever in your daughter's abduction?"

The duke was completely taken by surprise at this question, which he ought to have asked himself as soon as he discovered his daughter's absence, or, at all events, as soon as he began to suspect Albert Montague.

"I—I—have no—positive proof."

"Then, why suspect, much less accuse?"

"He was seen in my park not a very long time since."

"And does your daughter's absence date from that time?"

"No; she was at home the next day. She paid a visit to Albion Hall——"

"Alone?"

"Yes. And she never returned."

"Then, why not search Albion Hall?"

"I have been there. In fact, I was there the same evening. Sir Thomas Brooke assured me that she had not left the Hall half an hour when I arrived."

Merlin was silent for some time.

"This is a strange affair," he said, at length. "If you would pledge your word not to betray anything you might see or hear while in our company, I could perhaps aid you considerably in your search for the missing lady. I could procure you an interview with the young heir of Albion Hall for instance."

"I give you my word, as a man of honour and a peer of the realm, that I will divulge none of your secrets with which you may think proper to entrust me," replied the duke.

"Then, forward, lads, forward, or we shall have the dragoons at our heels. People would stare with astonishment when the news was heard that the Duke of Cleveland was captured in company with a party of outlaws."

"If the party of soldiers I passed are hunting for you, I fancy they will be unsuccessful. They took the road leading to Oxford, and are some miles distant by this time."

Merlin, however, determined to lose no time in reaching the spot towards which he was travelling, for his horses were all fatigued, and his men needed rest and refreshment.

Lady Florence, too, and Polly, the inn-keeper's daughter, rescued by Captain Will Merry from her father's anger, were beginning to exhibit most decided symptoms of fatigue and need of repose.

"Cheer up, sweet Florence," whispered Merlin, as he took up his place by her side. "We have not many miles to travel; our destination lies just beyond the wood you see on the hill side yonder."

"I shall be glad to reach any shelter, for in good truth both body and mind alike require rest," replied she, with a weary sigh.

The wood mentioned was quickly passed, and the whole party proceeded at a brisk pace down a rough road, near the bottom of which the thatched roof of what appeared to be a poor cottage was visible amongst the trees.

"There is our halting-place, dear love," said Merlin, pointing out the house, the only one in the neighbourhood.

"What, that hovel?" exclaimed the duke, who had overheard the words.

"We can accommodate your grace there as well as the best London hotel."

As he spoke these words a loud piercing cry came through the air,

"Help! help! for Heaven's sake!"

The cry came from the building they were gazing at.

CHAPTER XXXIV.

A NEW SCENE, THOUGH AN OLD LOCALITY—A CARD—THE WIDOW RECEIVES A NURSELING—WHOSE CHILD IS IT?

IN order that the reader may not lose sight of a small individual, who of unimportant appearance, exercises a considerable influence over our heroine, it is necessary to change the scene to London, and lead the way to one of the lowest, shabbiest streets or alleys which cluster about the Seven Dials.

Why the point where a number of streets meet should bear such a name is an unsolved question, for at the time of our story, the gorgeous gin palace which in the present day shows one dial to the British public was not in existence, and when the aborigines of the land wished to know the flight of time, they either had to enter a public house or extend their travels till they arrived in sight of St. Giles's church.

In Westmoreland Row, Seven Dials, there was a dingy underground apartment, inhabited by an old woman and her daughter, and devoted to the purposes of trade.

People called it a chandler's shop.

It was lighted by a window from which the occupants of the den could command a splendid view of the hob-nailed shoes, or more frequently the bare feet of passengers, and the wheels of an occasional vehicle, for it sometimes happened that a hackney coach strayed into Westmoreland Row.

In this window might be seen a few red herrings, a bar of coarse soap, an article for which there was little demand, a piece of bacon ditto, evil-smelling cheese, a few tobacco pipes, and a blue paper parcel, supposed to contain half a pound of sugar, along with a few other trifling sundries.

There was a little room at the back of this shop, containing a bed, a deal table, two wooden chairs, and a few cooking utensils upon the dirty untidy hearth.

The woman and her daughter called this dingy den home, and no doubt it was so to them.

Besides the articles of commerce, which, as above stated, were displayed in the window, there was a placard hanging with this inscription,

"A child wanted to nurse."

Heaven pity the poor infant who should be consigned to that dark and dreary abode, where the balmy fresh air had never been known to enter, where neither blue sky, twinkling stars, waving trees, nor even the glorious sun could ever be seen.

Would it not be better that the pining helpless atom of humanity should be buried deep in some quiet churchyard, than entombed alive in that dismal cellar?

But the poor—the poor of large towns, I mean—have no choice in these matters, they must live, and in order to do so without suffering the pangs of hunger, they must crowd together in wretched garrets and cellars, in an atmosphere which is hurtful alike to body and soul.

Mother Trot only demanded the small sum of one shilling per week for board and lodging and attendance for infants under twelve months old; but small as that sum was, her want still remained unsatisfied, for the simple reason that a shilling was a great object with the poor who lived around; and the rich surely would never think of leaving their offspring in such a wretched locality to be brought up and educated.

So that the card had grown dirty and flyblown, and the widow woman began seriously to think of taking it down.

But one evening, just as she had illuminated her shop for the evening with a couple of cotton dips stuck in old bottles, and was about to sit down to her evening meal, she was not a little surprised at the fact that a hackney coach had stopped before the door, and that some one bearing a child was standing at the top of the steps leading down to the shop.

The some one was a tall, gaunt, bony woman, who earned a livelihood by hawking tapes, needles, and such like small wares, to say nothing of doing a little business in the fortune telling line.

It was not likely that she had arrived in the coach, so therefore Mrs. Trot mechanically assumed her place behind the counter, expecting that the hawker-woman would prove a good customer.

"Nothing to night, ma'am," said the tall woman; "nothing for me. But I've brought a child for you."

"A child?"

"Yes, to nurse."

The shopkeeper looked incredulous, as well she might.

Her eyes needed but one glance to detect that the clothes of the sleeping innocent were of costly material, made up in the best style. It was evidently the child of rich parents; none of the natives of that neighbourhood could dress their offspring in such fine linen as that in which the infant was dressed.

"Whose is it?" asked Mrs Trot.

"Well, I dont know; but there's a queer old gentleman in the coach—something in the clergy, I fancy—who asked me if I knew a woman who would take a child to nurse, and so I brought him here."

"Just ask the gentleman to step down, will you?"

The hawker-woman did so, and in a few moments an elderly man, wrapped in a large cloak, was seen to descend the steps of the cellar.

Had Albert Montague seen him he would at once have recognised the priest he rescued from the hands of two ruffians.

The child, too, was the one those ruffians seemed so anxious to secure.

The priest seemed to know how to keep his own counsels, and was proof against all Mrs. Trot's little tricks to entrap him into an avowal of who were the parents of the child.

"I should require three shillings a week, sir, for the little dear," said the woman ; "and my daughter, there, will take great care of him."

"You shall be paid. Here are five guineas to begin with."

"And who am I to send word to if the darling should be ill, sir ?"

"You need not trouble. If he is ill his friends will hear of it without your telling any one."

"Yes, sir," said Mrs. Trot, growing very confused between the large sum of money she held in her hand, and the deep mystery which surrounded the little stranger.

"We may consider our bargain settled, then ?" continued the priest.

"Yes, sir."

"You will receive more money in the course of six months, and, in the meantime, don't distress yourself by endeavouring to discover the parents of this child. From this moment treat him as one of your own."

So saying, the man in the cloak turned on his heel and returned to his hackney coach, leaving Mrs. Trot in a state of mind which can hardly be described.

The hawker-woman received half-a-crown, and the vehicle which had brought such strange luck to the shopkeeper departed at a rapid pace.

"Well, well, I wonder what it all means," exclaimed the poor woman. "How on earth did that old chap become possessed of such a lovely child? It's not a bit like him ; he's not the father, I know."

So saying, the good woman took the still sleeping infant into the inner room, and entrusted him to the arms of her daughter.

But first of all she took off the velvet mantle in which the infant was enveloped, and searched all over for some mark which might give a clue to the child's parentage.

The search was in vain.

The child's clothes were, as before said, costly ; but there was nothing to show the rank or station of the owners beyond that fact.

Mrs. Trot was compelled to confess her inquisitiveness vanquished, and to acknowledge that she "had no idea whose child it could be."

There is, however, no earthly reason for leaving the reader in the same state of ignorance, so let the fact at once be avowed.

The child was the son and heir of Sir Andrew and Lady Florence Greville, and in times past had been the especial charge of the miller's daughter.

But the mill, as is well known, had perished by fire and gunpowder, and the babe had fallen into strange hands.

Who the priest was, how he came to have possession of the child, as well as his motives in leaving it with Mrs. Trot, must form the subject for another chapter.

CHAPTER XXXV.

LADY JANE CLEVELAND'S TROUBLES—A STRANGE DEBATE—A FOUL, UNNATURAL MURDER—MORNING—THE MOVABLE FIRE-PLACE.

WHEN Lady Jane Cleveland overheard the old hag and her ruffian son debating schemes for robbing if not murdering herself, her first thought and action, as before said, was to conceal the papers she had risked so much to obtain. That done, means of defence were her next consideration.

But means of defence were not to be seen at first ; so bare was the room of furniture that there was hardly anything with which she could barricade the door.

By exerting all her strength she managed to drag the bed from its position, and placed it across the entrance, and then placed the table between it and the opposite wall.

When this was done it was impossible to open the door without first smashing these articles of furniture.

She then looked about for a weapon, but could find none.

Sick at heart she laid herself down on the bed with her fair head close to the door by which the assassins would be compelled to enter.

In that position she could hear if the slightest attempt were made to force open the door.

She could also hear the conversation of the old woman and her son, if son he were, and it was not of a nature to cheer her spirits very much.

One thing, however, gave her some slight hope.

From a word dropped by the man it seemed that he and his mother were not the owners of the house, the master having been absent for a long time.

"He may return," thought Lady Jane, "and I may be saved."

From the manner in which the man and woman spoke of the absent master, it seemed that he was a man of very different disposition.

The fair Lady Jane listened earnestly, expecting each moment that her life would be assailed.

The night passed away, and she could hear the jingle of bottles and glasses on the table in the outer room.

Oaths and curses too became more frequent in their conversation, and it was apparent that the old woman and her son were indulging in a drunken quarrel.

Lady Jane was the principal topic of their conversation, as may be guessed.

Her rich dress and jewels were an immense temptation to the old hag ; but worse than that, the fair girl's soul was filled with horror and dismay, as she heard the ruffian son in maudlin speech praise her beauty of form and feature, and express a determination to make himself the possessor of so much loveliness.

"Take your knife, lad, and finish the job at once," said the old woman, in a loud whisper.

"No, no, not yet," replied her son.

"Why not? The longer we wait, the more risk we run."

"There's no risk."

"There is! Suppose the captain were to take it into his head to pay us a visit."

"He's miles away."

"Nobody ever knows where he is. You are turned coward I suppose, and can't handle the knife as you used."

"I can handle a knife as well as ever, but—I don't want to kill her."

"What then?"

"Why, she's a good-looking bit of stuff, I should like to keep her here for a time."

"Ha! ha! my boy, you don't know much about these fine ladies. Why, she would turn up her nose, and refuse you even if your knife was at her throat."

"She might refuse if she liked, I am stronger than she is."

"And pray, my dear boy, good boy, handsome boy, what would you do with your lady love when you were tired of her?"

"Now, damn it, don't go on in that way, calling me dear, and good and handsome——"

"Ha, ha, ha, you must be good and handsome, if you go to make love to this fine lady, you great fool."

"Shut up your infernal clatter, or I'll make you."

"You make me? you——"

"Yes, you old witch."

"You infernal villain, I'll kill you. I'll have your life, you good-for-nothing limb of the devil."

"If I'm a limb of the devil, you're my mother——"

In an instant there was a loud crash, as though tables, bottles, glasses had been overturned, and the oaths, though not louder, were more frequent, and uttered with more vigour and vehemence.

Mother and son were fighting, that was evident, and Lady Jane drew hopes of safety from the fact.

"D———n!" roared the man, at length, "you've killed me!"

"Ha! ha! ha! I can use the knife, you see, as well as yourself."

Lady Jane's alarms increased.

The old hag, then, had a weapon.

What if, in her drunken fury, she were to burst into the room, and plunge the blade still dripping with the man's blood into her heart!

That such a thing should happen appeared most probable, for the old woman's passions were aroused, and she was a perfect demon in her fury.

"Ha! ha! my fine boy!" Lady Jane heard her say, "how do you like the knife yourself, you who have given it to so many? Blood for blood! You would have killed me, and I have killed you!"

"Mother—you've killed—me. May all the hottest—flames —of hell burn the flesh from your—bones. My last dying curse on——"

Then there was a deep silence.

The man's guilty spirit had taken its flight.

The body of the strong man was nought but clay.

"Oh! this is terrible! this is fearful!" thought Lady Jane, as she pressed her hand over her forehead and eyes to shut out, if possible, the horrid visions that would arise to her brain. "Albert! Albert! would to heaven you were here, for then I should be in safety."

"More brandy! more brandy!" the old woman was heard to mutter. "I must drink deeply, or I shall have bad dreams. Ha! ha! ha! I should like to know what he is thinking or dreaming about now—about that fair-haired wench. Hell seize her! if she had not come here my son would be alive now! But I'll have her blood! I'll have her blood!"

With these words the old hag crossed the room, and drew the bolts of the door which confined Lady Jane.

"Heaven be merciful, and protect me!" ejaculated the noble girl. "Albert! Albert! if I die, 'tis for your sake."

The vile harridan having withdrawn the bolts, evidently expected the door to give way before her, and uttered an exclamation of surprise when she found herself unable to gain admission to the chamber occupied by her guest—her intended victim.

"How's this? What's the matter?" she muttered, at the same time giving the door a good push.

Lady Jane sprang to her feet, resolved and prepared to struggle to the utmost of her strength for life.

The door opened inward, and was prevented from opening by the bed and table, from which, as before said, Lady Jane had formed a barricade.

It was formed of strong oak planks well fitted together, and having been constructed for the express purpose of securing prisoners, did its duty so effectually in the present instance that the old hag the gaoler was unable to enter.

"Curse it! the hinges want oiling," she muttered. "Never mind, I'll get through in the morning. If I can't enter one way, I can the other."

"So, then, there is another entrance," thought Lady Jane to herself, and she looked round eagerly to discover it.

There was no sign of any door save the one by which she had entered.

If such a thing existed it was carefully and skilfully concealed.

Perhaps the old woman alluded to the window, which was secured by bars, which, in turn, were kept in their places by strong padlocks.

At all events, Lady Jane had no intention of sleeping; the fearful events of the past night had totally banished drowsiness from her eyes.

She would keep a good watch.

Foiled in her efforts to enter the chamber, the old hag stumbled and fell heavily to the floor beside her son.

She slept the sleep of drunkenness; he, the sleep from which there is no awakening.

When convinced by heavy snores that the old murderess slept soundly, Lady Jane removed her barricade, and tried the door; but it was securely fastened as before.

She replaced her defences, and, with heavy heart and aching head, lay down, but not to sleep.

How long that night seemed, how slowly it passed away.

It seemed as though the events of a lifetime had passed in rapid succession.

Lady Jane's bewildered brain was almost unable to look back to or contemplate the past.

And to what could she look forward with any certainty save a bloody and violent death?

She prayed with heart and soul as she had never prayed before.

At length the stars began to fade away, and a grey light in the east announced the approach of the lingering dawn.

Lady Jane Cleveland rose from her sleepless couch, and prepared for the threatened visit of the beldame who lay sleeping beside her dead son.

At length the old hag was heard moving, the door was once more attempted without success, and then it seemed as though she had left the house.

Lady Jane kept her eye on the window, feeling convinced that she was to be assailed from thence.

Still no enemy appeared.

A slight noise at the side of the room attracted her attention.

It appeared to proceed from the open fire-place.

Lady Jane's heart beat violently; her face was pale as death.

She saw a massive piece of brickwork at the back of the hearth give way, and the old woman appeared knife in hand.

Quick as lightning, and before the woman could emerge from the fire-place, Lady Jane flew at her, and clutched the hand which held the blood-stained knife.

They wrestled together, but the young and delicate girl was no match for the sinewy old hag.

Lady Jane found her strength give way.

She uttered a loud cry—

"*Help! help! for Heaven's sake!*"

(*To be continued.*)

A TRUE PIRATE STORY.

(*Concluded from page* 120).

The result of these invidious reports was to deprive England of his command, and to excite those cruel villains to put him on shore with three others, upon the Island of Mauritius.

If England and his small company had not been destitute of every necessary, they might have made a comfortable subsistence here, as the island abounds with deer, hogs, and other animals.

It is even said that the shores are replete with coral and ambergris; but had this been the fact the Dutch would not have abandoned such a rich treasure.

Dissatisfied with their solitary situation, Captain England and his three men exerted their industry and ingenuity, and formed a small boat, with which they sailed to Madagascar, where they subsisted upon the generosity of some more fortunate piratical companions.

Captain Taylor detained some of the officers and men belonging to Captain Mackra, and, having repaired their vessel, sailed for India. The day before they made land, they espied two ships to the eastward, and supposing them to be English, Captain Taylor ordered one of the officers of Mackra's ship to communicate to him the private signals between the Company's ships, swearing, that if he did not do so immediately, he would cut him into pound pieces. But the poor man being unable to give the information demanded, he was under the necessity of enduring their threats.

Arrived at the vessels, they found that they were two Moorish ships, laden with horses. The pirates brought the captains and merchants on board, and tortured them in a barbarous manner, to constrain them to tell where they had hid their treasure. They were, however, disappointed, and the next morning they discovered land, and at the same time a fleet on shore plying to windward. In this situation, they were at a considerable loss how to dispose of their prizes. To let them go, would lead to their discovery, and thus defeat the design of their voyage; and it was a distressing matter to sink the men and the horses, though many of them were for adopting that measure. They, however, brought them to anchor, threw all her sails overboard, and cut one of her masts half through.

While they lay at anchor, and were employed in taking in water, one of the above-mentioned fleet moved towards them with English colours, and was answered by the pirate with a red ensign, but they did not hail each other. At night they left the Muscat ships, and sailed after the fleet. About four next morning, the pirates were in the midst of the fleet, but, seeing their vast superiority, they were greatly at a loss what method to adopt.

The "Victory" was become leaky, and their hands were so few in number, that it only remained for them to deceive, if possible, the English squadron. They were unsuccessful in gaining anything out of that fleet, and only had the wretched satisfaction of burning a single galley. They, however, that day seized a galliot, loaded with cotton, and made inquiry of the men concerning the fleet. They protested that they had not seen a ship since they left Gogo, and earnestly implored their mercy; but, instead of treating them with lenity, they racked their joints, in order to extort further confession.

The day following, a fresh easterly wind blew hard, and rent the galliot's sails; upon this the pirates put her company into a boat, with nothing but a try-sail, no provisions, and only four gallons of water; and, though they were out of sight of land, left them to shift for themselves.

It may be proper to inform our readers, that one Angria an Indian prince, of considerable territory and strength, had proved a troublesome enemy to Europeans, and particularly to the English. Callaba was his principal fort, situated not many leagues from Bombay, and he possessed an island in sight of the port, from whence he molested the Company's ships. His heart in bribing the ministers of the great Mogul, and the shallowness of the water, that prevents large ships of war from approaching, are the principal causes of his safety.

The Bombay fleet, consisting of four grabs, the "London" and the "Candois," and two other ships with galliot, having an additional thousand men aboard for this enterprise, sailed to attack a fort belonging to Angria, upon the Malabar coast. Though their strength was great, yet they were totally unsuccessful in their enterprise. It was this fleet, returning home, that our pirates discovered upon the present occasion.

Upon the sight of the pirates, the commodore of the fleet intimated to Mr. Brown, the general, that as they had no orders to fight, and had gone upon a different purpose, it would be improper for them to engage. Informed of the loss of this favourable opportunity to destroy the robbers, the governor of Bombay was highly enraged, and, giving the command of the fleet to Captain Mackra, ordered him to pursue and engage them wherever they should be found.

The pirates having barbarously sent away the galliot with her men, they arrived southward, and between Goa and Carwar they heard several guns; so that they came to anchor, and sent their boat to reconnoitre, which returned next morning with the intelligence of two grabs lying at anchor in the road. They accordingly weighed, run towards the bay, and in the morning were discovered by the grabs, who had just time to run under India-Diva Castle for protection. This was the more vexatious to the pirates, as they were without water; some of them, therefore, were for making a descent upon the island, but that measure not being generally approved, they sailed towards the south, and took a small ship, which had only a Dutchman and two Portuguese on board. They sent one of these on shore to the captain, to inform him, that if he would give them some water and fresh provisions, he might have his vessel returned.

He replied, that if they would give him possession over the bar, he would comply with their request. But suspecting the integrity of his design, they sailed for Lacca Deva islands, uttering dreadful imprecations against the captain.

Disappointed in finding water at these islands they sailed to Malinda island, and sent their boats on shore to discover if there was any water, or if there were any inhabitants. They returned with the information that there was abundance of water, that the houses were only inhabited by women and children, the men having fled at the appearance of the ships. They accordingly hastened to supply themselves with water, used the defenceless women in a brutal manner, destroyed many of their fruit trees, and set some of their houses on fire.

While off this island they lost several of their anchors by the rockiness of the ground, and, one day blowing more violently than usual, they were forced to take to sea, leaving several people and most of the water casks; but when the gale was over they returned to take in their men and water. Their provisions being nearly exhausted they resolved to visit the Dutch at Cochin. After sailing three days they arrived off Tellechery, and took a small vessel belonging to Governor Adams, and brought the master on board very much intoxicated, who informed them of the expedition of Captain Mackra. This intelligence raised their utmost indignation. "A villain!" said they, "to whom we have given a ship and presents to come against us. He ought to be hanged, and, since we cannot show our resentment to him, let us hang the dogs, his people, who wish him well, and would do the same if they were clear."

"If it be in my power," says the quarter-master, "both masters and officers of ships shall be carried with us for the future only to plague them. Now, England, we may mark him for this."

They proceeded to Calicut, and attempting to cut out a ship were prevented by some guns placed on shore. One of Captain Mackra's officers was under deck at this time, and was commanded, both by the captain and quarter-master, to tend the braces on the booms in hopes that a shot would take him before they got clear.

He was about to have excused himself, but they threatened to shoot him, and, when he expostulated, and claimed their promise to put him on shore, he got an unmerciful beating from the quarter-master, Captain Taylor, to whom that duty belonged, being lame of his hands.

The day following they met a Dutch galliot loaded with limestone, bound for Calicut, on board of which they put one Captain Fawks; and, some of the crew interceding for Mackra's officer, Taylor and his party replied,

"If we let this dog go, who has overheard our designs and resolutions, he will overset all our well-advised resolutions, and particularly this supply we are seeking for at the hands of the Dutch."

When they arrived at Cochin they sent a letter on shore by a fishing boat, entered the road and anchored, each ship saluting the fort with eleven guns, and receiving the same number in return. This was the token of their welcome reception, and at night a large boat was sent deeply laden with liquors and all kinds of provisions, and in it a servant of John Trumpet, one of their friends, to inform them that it would be necessary for them to run further south where they would be supplied both with provisions and naval stores.

They had scarcely anchored at the appointed place when several canoes, with white and black inhabitants, came on board, and continued, without interruption, to perform all the good offices in their power during their stay in that place.

In particular, John Trumpet brought a large boat of arrack, and sixty bales of sugar, as a present from the governor and his daughter, the one receiving a table clock, and the other a gold watch, the spoil of Captain Mackra's vessel.

When their provisions were all on board Trumpet was rewarded with six or seven thousand pounds, was saluted with three cheers and eleven guns, and several handfuls of silver were thrown into the boat for the men to gather at pleasure.

There being little wind that night they remained at anchor, and in the morning were surprised with the return of Trumpet, bringing another boat equally well stored with provisions, with chests of piece-goods and ready-made clothes, and along with him the fiscal of the place.

At noon they espied a sail towards the south, and immediately gave chase, but she out-sailed them, and sheltered under the fort of Cochin. Informed that they would not be molested in taking her from under the castle they sailed towards her; but upon the fort firing two guns, they ran off for fear of more serious altercation, and returning anchored in their former station. They were too welcome visitants to be permitted to depart as long as John Trumpet could contrive to detain them. With this view he informed them that in a few days a rich vessel, commanded by the General of Bombay's brother was to pass that way.

That government is certainly in a wretched state, which is under the necessity of trading with pirates in order to enrich itself. Nor will such a government hesitate by what means an injury can be repaired, or a fortune gained. Neither can language describe the low and base principles of that government which can employ such miscreants as John Trumpet in its service. He was a tool in the hands of the government of Cochin, and, as the dog said in the fable, "What is done by the master's orders is the master's action."

While under the direction of Trumpet some proposed to proceed directly to Madagascar, but others were disposed to wait until they should be provided with a store-ship. The majority being of the latter opinion they steered to the south, and seeing a ship on shore they were desirous to get near her; but the wind preventing they separated, the one sailing northward and the other southward in hopes of securing her when she should come out, whatever direction she might take.

They were now, however, almost entrapped in the snare laid for them. In the morning, to their astonishment and consternation, instead of being called to give chace, five large ships were near, who made a signal for the pirates to bear down. The pirates were in the greatest dread lest it should be Captain Mackra, of whose activity and courage they had formerly sufficient proof.

The pirate ships, however, joined and fled with all speed from the fleet. In three hours' chace none of the fleet gained upon them, except one grab. The remainder of the day was calm, and, to their great consolation, the next day this fleet was entirely out of sight.

This alarm being over they resolved to spend the Christmas in feasting and mirth, in order to drown care and to banish thoughtfulness. Nor did one day suffice, but they continued their revelling for several days, and made so free with their fresh provisions that in their next cruise they were put upon short allowance, and it was entirely owing to the sugar and other provisions that were in the leaky ship that they were preserved from perishing.

In this condition they reached the island of Mauritius, refitted the "Victory," and left that place with the following inscription written upon one of the walls: "Left this place on the 5th of April to go to Madagascar for Limos." This they did lest any visit should be paid to the place during their absence.

They, however, did not sail directly for Madagascar, but to the island of Mascarius, where they fortunately fell in with a Portuguese of seventy guns lying at anchor. The greater part of her guns were thrown overboard, her masts lost, and the whole vessel disabled by a storm, therefore she became an easy prey to the pirates.

Conde de Ericeira, Viceroy of Goa, who went upon the fruitless expedition against Angria the Indian, and several passengers, were on board, besides other valuable articles and specie they found in her diamonds to the amount of four millions of dollars. Supposing that the ship was an Englishman, the viceroy came on board the next morning, was made prisoner, and obliged to pay two thousand dollars as a ransom for himself and the other prisoners. After this he was set ashore, with the express engagement to leave a ship to convey him and his companions to another port.

Meanwhile they received the intelligence that a vessel was to the leeward of the island, which they pursued and captured; but instead of performing their promise to the viceroy, which they could easily have done, they sent the Ostender along with some of their men to Madagascar to inform their friends of their success, with instructions to prepare masts for the prize, and they soon followed, carrying two thousand negroes in the Portuguese vessel.

Madagascar is an island larger than Great Britain, situated upon the eastern coast of Africa, abounding with all sorts of provisions, such as oxen, goats, sheep, poultry, fish, citrons, oranges, tamarinds, dates, cocoa-nuts, bananas, wax, honey, rice, cotton, indigo, and all the other fruits common in that quarter of the globe; ebony, of which lances are made, gums of several kinds, and many other valuable productions.

The locusts on land, and the crocodiles in the river, form the principal inconvenience that the inhabitants experience. Here, in St. Augustine's Bay, the ships sometimes stop to take in water, when they take the inner passage to India, and do not intend to stop at Johanna.

Though they are still few in number, compared to the natives, yet the Europeans, and particularly the pirates, have reared a mulatto race since the discovery of this island by the Portuguese in 1506. The natives are negroes, with short curled hair, active, and formerly malicious and revengeful; but, on account of the presents they are accustomed to receive, they are become tractable and communicative.

They live in terms of friendship with the Europeans who reside amongst them, and the latter can, on a minute's warning, muster two or three hundred. The natives find it their interest to cultivate their friendship, because they are divided into small governments, who carry on a continued war with each other; so that the pirates render the party with whom they join always victorious.

When the Portuguese ship arrived here, they received the intelligence that the Ostender had taken the advantage of an hour when the men were intoxicated, rose upon them, and carried the ship to Mozambique, from whence the governor ordered her to Goa.

The pirates now divided their plunder, receiving forty-two diamonds per man, or in smaller proportion according to their magnitude.

A foolish jocular fellow, who had received a large diamond of the value of forty-two, was highly displeased, and so went and broke it in pieces, exclaiming, that he had many more shares than either of them. Some, contented with their treasure, and unwilling to run the risk of losing what they possessed, and perhaps their lives also,

resolved to remain with their friends at Madagascar, under the stipulation, that the longest livers should enjoy all the booty.

The number of adventurers being now lessened, they burnt the "Victory," cleaned the "Cassandra," and the remainder went on board under the command of Taylor, whom we must leave for a little, to give an account of that squadron that arrived in India in 1721.

When the commodore arrived at the Cape, he received a letter that had been written by the governor of Pondicherry to the governor of Madras, informing him, that the pirates were strong in the Indian seas; that they had eleven sail and fifteen hundred men; but adding, that many of them retired about that time to Brazil and Guinea, while others fortified themselves at Madagascar, Mauritius, Johanna, and Mohilla; and that a crew under the command of Condin, in a ship called the "Dragon," had captured a vessel with thirteen lacks of rupees on board, and, having divided their plunder, they had taken up their residence with their friends at Madagascar.

Upon receiving this intelligence, Commodore Matthews sailed for these islands, as the most probable place of success. He endeavoured ineffectually to prevail on England, at St. Mary's, to communicate to him what information he could give respecting the pirates.

But the pirate declined, thinking that this would be almost to surrender at discretion. He then took up the guns of the "Jubilee" sloop that were on board, and the men-of-war made several cruizes in search of the pirates, but to no purpose. The squadron was then sent down to Bombay, was saluted by the port, and, after these exploits, returned home.

The pirate, Captain Taylor, in the "Cassandra," now fitted up the Portuguese man-of-war, and resolved upon another voyage to the Indies; but, informed that four men-of-war had been sent after the pirates in that quarter, he changed his determination, and sailed for Africa.

Arrived there, they put in at a place near the river Spirito Sancto, on the coast of Monomotapa. As there was no correspondence by land, nor any trade carried on by sea to this place, they thought that it would afford a safe retreat. To their astonishment, however, when they approached the shore, it being in the dusk of the evening, they were accosted by several shot. They immediately anchored, and in the morning saw that the shot had come from a small fort of six guns, which they attacked and destroyed.

This small fort was erected by the Dutch East India Company a few weeks before, and committed to the care of an hundred and fifty men, the one half of whom had perished by sickness or other causes. Upon their petition, sixteen of these were admitted into the society of the pirates, and the rest would also have been received, had they not been Dutchmen, to whom they had a rooted aversion.

In this place they continued during four months, refitting their vessels, and amusing themselves with all manner of diversions, until the scarcity of their provisions awakened them to industry and exertion. They, however, left several parcels of goods to the starving Dutchmen, which Mynheer joyfully exchanged for provisions with the next vessel that touched at that fort.

Leaving that place, they were divided in opinion what course to steer; some went on board the Portuguese prize, and, sailing for Madagascar, abandoned the pirate life; and others, going on board the "Cassandra," sailed for the Spanish West Indies. The "Mermaid" man-of-war, returning from a convoy, got near the pirates, and would have attacked them, but a consultation being held, it was deemed inexpedient, and thus the pirates escaped.

A sloop was, however, dispatched to Jamaica with the intelligence, and the "Lancaster" was sent after them, but they were some days too late, the pirates having, with all their riches, surrendered to the governor of Portobello.

Calming their consciences, that others would have acted a similar part, without the least remorse they took up their residence here, to spend the remainder of their days in living upon the spoil of nations.

Nor can the reflection be restrained, that if they had known what was transacting in England by South-sea directors, they would at least have had one proof to adduce, " that whatever robberies they had committed, they might be pretty sure that they were not the greatest villains then living in the world."

It is difficult to compute the injury done by this crew during five years. Whether to gratify their humour, to prevent intelligence, or from the want of men to navigate, or from the brave resistance made, or from wanton folly and barbarity, the moment the resolution was formed the vessels they captured were frequently sent to the bottom.

After their surrender to the Spaniards, several of them left that place, and it is reported that Captain Taylor accepted of a commission in the Spanish service, and commanded the man-of-war that attacked the English logwood-cutters in the Bay of Honduras.

BLACK HAWKE, THE HIGHWAYMAN.

THE ROOM ON FIRE.

CHAPTER XXXVI.

CAPTAIN MERRY'S ADVENTURES WITH SIMEON LAZARUS—
A JEW'S RANSOM — SIMEON AMONG THE HOGS — THE
ALE-HOUSE—THE STRANGE HORSEMAN—A NEAT TRICK.

CAPTAIN WILL MERRY, after parting from Merlin, rode onwards with a light heart, yet with care and caution lest he
should be followed by the military.

The three prisoners were bound to their horses and disarmed, so that there was not the slightest chance of their
escaping without assistance.

Lucky it was for Simeon Lazarus that his captors had
taken the precaution of binding him to the saddle.

Had he not been so secured he would have fallen to the
earth.

The fearful scene of the trial and execution of the traitor
which he had been compelled to witness, had filled his mind
with horrid forbodings as to his own fate.

Death he doubted not was his doom—death by lingering
tortures, for otherwise the highwaymen would have slain him
at the same time that the traitor suffered death.

In the midst of all his moody reflections Captain Will rode
up and gave him a hearty slap on the back.

"Hark ye, my friend," cried the jovial outlaw; "you are
descended from one of the twelve tribes of Israel, are you not?"

"Yesh, yer honour," replied the Jew, humbly.

"And, no doubt, you believe in the law and the prophets?"

"Oh, holy Moshesh, I'm only a poor Shew, put I keepsh
de lawsh an' lovesh everypody."

"Ha! ha! a nice way you have got—a pleasant way of
showing your love, at all events. Now, you are in my power,
and I mean to pay you out well for your attempt to hand us
over to the dragoons."

"Oh, mercy! mercy!"

"Hush! Do you value your life very much?"

"Oh, ma tear shir, I vouldn't die for all de vorld!"

"Very good, my hook-nosed friend. Then, as you value
your life so very highly, of course you won't object to pay a
good sum for it?"

"I have no moneysh; I am a poor man, and have peen
robbed."

"Lazarus, if I kill you, you will not rise from the dead like
your good name-sake. So, my worthy Israelite, just reflect
for a few moments."

"Itsh true, ma tear, itsh true. See now, this ish all the
moneysh I have."

As he uttered the words Simeon Lazarus drew forth from his breeches pocket a handful of greasy copper coins, and offered them to the captain.

"You miserable fool, do you think a handful of halfpence will save your worthless life? It's gold that I want; bright gold, and a good quantity of it too."

"Oh, holy Moshesh! an' vere am I to get gold, ma tear? Ah, let me go, Mishter Merry; let me go, and take all I have."

"I should very much like to do so. But do you see yon cottage?"

"Yesh."

"Very well; now, I happen to know that in a little out-house at the back of that cottage, there are a couple of ferocious boars. Now, unless you give me two hundred pounds before we reach that spot, I will bind you hand and foot and cast you to the swine who will eat you in less time than it has taken me to tell you this."

The Jew was too much overcome by this most awful threat to make any reply but a deep groan.

Tears ran down his cheek in torrents.

The thought was an awful one that he, one of the chosen people, should not only be thrown amongst swine but be killed by them, and entombed in the stomachs of the unclean animals!

Death never appeared in such a fearful shape before.

Captain Will watched the anguish of the Jew with great glee.

He imagined that he was performing a public duty as well as avenging private wrongs in thus working on the feelings of the Israelite.

"Come, Lazarus, you have only about five minutes left; you will be food for pork in a short time unless you suddenly discover a gold mine."

"Oh! Father Abraham! Loosen my left hand a little, captain."

"Certainly, and I'm very glad to see that you are becoming sensible of your danger."

The rope was slackened a little, and with many a mournful groan, the Jew unfastened from his body a weighty belt full of broad pieces of gold.

"Hurrah! this is something like business. By the bye, you mean to make me a present of this, don't you, Simeon?"

Again the wretched Israelite sighed.

"Say yes, before all these witnesses, or else I still throw you to the swine, and afterwards make myself your heir."

"Yesh, Captain Merry, I—I—give it."

"From the hesitating manner in which Simeon Lazarus pronounced the word 'give' it was evident that he did not bestow his blessing along with his gold.

The spectators of this extraordinary act of benevolence laughed aloud as they gazed upon the woeful countenance of the Jew, down whose face tears were rolling fast.

"Ain't yer going to let me go, captain?" said Simeon.

"Yes, in a minute. You must come on to the cottage and have a rasher of bacon with me, though, before we part."

"Vat, I eat bacon? Ha, ha, ha!"

It was a very sickly laugh that poor Simeon Lazarus uttered; he was faint at heart, and feared that the loathsome, unclean food would be forced into his mouth.

In a few minutes they reached the cottage, which was also an ale-house.

The poor Jew's fears were not much diminished when, from the back of the building, he heard a series of sonorous grunts that could only proceed from members of the porcine tribe.

Captain Will Merry dismounted, two of his men did the same, and the Jew, also, was permitted to descend from his uncomfortable seat on the back of a rather bony horse.

The other men remained on their horses guarding Captain Ashburne and Marmaduke Greville.

"Bring him along," said Will Merry, making a signal.

The two men at once laid violent hands upon Simeon Lazarus, and, lifting him from his feet, bore him through the house.

He was hoisted high in the air and fell plump upon the unclean straw which formed the bed, not of two fierce boars, but of a couple of fat porkers, who stared and grunted with surprise at their unexpected visitor.

Simeon Lazarus gave a yell of anguish as he found himself in such great danger of contamination from the touch of the unclean animals.

The pigs grunted and kept moving round and sniffing at him, apparently endeavouring to discover the difference between the Jewish visitor and ordinary pork-eating Christians.

At length one of them made a sudden rush, just as Simeon rose to his feet, and getting his head between the Jew's legs, sent him spinning in the mud and filth of the pig-stye.

Captain Merry and his companions laughed till their sides ached at the strange scene.

"Oh! murder, murder! I shall never dare go into the synagogue again!" yelled Lazarus, as he scrambled out of the enclosure, leaving a large portion of his garments behind.

He gained the road with more speed than any one would have deemed him capable of, and turning, shook his fist towards the laughing highwaymen.

"Ah! laugh on! My curse be on you—the curse of a man who can hate better than he can love. For the insults you have this day put upon me you shall all suffer. You shall hang for this as sure as my name is Simeon Lazarus. Curse you all!"

More than one pistol was levelled towards the Jew, who was now thoroughly mad with rage, and perfectly reckless of the consequences of his words.

He made no effort to avoid the bullet, but, with a look of the most ferocious hate upon his satanic countenance, stood defying his tormentors.

"Hold!" exclaimed Captain Will; "don't fire a shot. In his present humour death has no terrors for him. To horse once more, and let us be on our road before he has time to communicate with the authorities."

The band soon moved away from the little ale-house, the last sound that reached their ears being the voice of the Jew, who cursed them vehemently in the name of all the patriarchs, priests and prophets.

They quickly passed beyond hearing distance, were speedily out of sight of the Jew, and very shortly after had forgotten him.

The life led by these men was one of continued change and excitement.

Here to-day, there to-morrow; rich one week, poor the next; practising innumerable tricks and stratagems to elude the officers of justice, as well as to secure booty, it was not to be wondered that the recollection of such a circumstance as a Jew in a hog-pen should pass away from their minds.

The booty they had compelled the Jew to give them had been fairly divided, but still their pockets were not uncomfortably full, and Will Merry began to look around for some other client whom he could plunder.

The two prisoners, Captain Ashburne and Marmaduke Greville, retained their watches, purses and jewels by order of the chief, and Will Merry was too well disciplined to dream of touching their valuables until permission was given.

The road was a lonely one, as, indeed, were most of the king's highways at the period of our story, for in those good old times a journey of fifty miles was considered a great and a serious undertaking, before commencing which men made their wills, and set all their worldly affairs in order, not knowing whether they might ever return to their homes again.

The day was warm and sultry, and the whole party were beginning to feel fatigued.

A second ale-house was reached, and they dismounted for the purpose of refreshing themselves, their steeds, and their prisoners ere they pursued their journey.

The house was situated near the spot where a road branched off from the main highway, and was as pleasant a place to pass away a sultry afternoon as could be found.

The ale was good; the hostess pretty and agreeable.

The time passed, and Captain Will was just thinking of calling for his horse when an exclamation from one of his men drew his attention to the window.

Looking out he perceived, not a party of soldiers, as he had at first expected, but a solitary man on horseback.

The individual in question was mounted on a fine, powerful horse, and was coming from London at a very leisurely pace.

In two minutes Captain Will was in the saddle, and in two more he was by the stranger's side.

He was a young man, with a rather vacant face, and dressed in a shabby-genteel manner.

Under his arm he carried a small casket or box of ebony, inlaid with gold.

"Good day, my friend," said Captain Will, lifting his hat courteously.

"Good day, sir," replied the other.

"May I make so bold as to ask whither you are travelling?" continued the highwayman; "because, if our roads are the same, we may as well keep each other company."

"Oh! yes, sir; I am going to Admiral Banjemore's house."

"Oh, indeed! I am going that way myself."

"I shall be very glad of your company, sir," continued the flunkey.

"You are in the worthy admiral's employ, I presume?" said Captain Will, scrutinizing the dress of his companion.

"I am, sir."

"In what capacity?"

"I am his confidential valet."

"Indeed? I dare say you have a very comfortable place and a good salary?"

"I have. The worthy admiral, as you call him, paid me a month's wages yesterday."

"Ah! then you have been for a holiday, I presume?"

"Yes; that is, I have been to London, partly on my own business and partly on the admiral's."

"He trusts you a great deal in his private affairs, I suppose?"

"Yes; why, I am, at the present moment, carrying three thousand pounds' worth of jewels that he ordered in town; a present for a lady."

"Indeed! Then they must be valuable?"

"They are. There's a diamond necklace and ear-rings to match, besides rings and bracelets."

"Are they pure diamonds?" asked the highwayman, coolly holding out his hand for the box.

He had no fear whatever but that the foolish servant would trust him with them, having trusted him with so much information.

"Pure diamonds? Of course they are!" was the valet's indignant reply. "Why, you can see that yourself, if you ever set eyes on a diamond before."

"Yes, you are right; they are pure diamonds, and a very handsome set, too!" exclaimed Captain Will, examining the box and its contents in an attentive and critical manner.

"Who are these horsemen?" suddenly asked the valet, pointing towards a group of three equestrians that were rapidly approaching.

Captain Will gave a single glance and recognized the coats of a couple of dragoons.

The third person was in civil attire, but his appearance had a certain Bow Street air in it which the highwayman at once recognized.

A thought flashed swift as lightning through his active brain, and he handed back the box to the servant.

"Are you not afraid to carry such valuable property about with you?" he inquired.

"Bless your soul, no. Why should I?" responded the admiral's valet.

"Because you are very liable to be robbed. This part is much infested with highwaymen."

"You don't mean to say so?" exclaimed the flunkey, a little startled.

"It's a fact, I assure you."

"Then I—I think I had better make haste home."

"No, stop a minute; I'll put you up to a trick."

"Do you think they are highwaymen?" asked the trembling servant, pointing to the rapidly advancing horsemen.

"I shouldn't wonder," replied Will, uttering a great fib.

"What am I to do if any one stops me?"

"Why, in the first place," said Will, "if any one stops you, to cry 'Stand and deliver,' place your hands on his shoulder in this manner:" and Will placed the valet's paws on his own shoulders.

"But that won't stop them, will it?"

"Certainly not, unless at the same time you pull out your pistol and place it against his forehead thus—"

And, suiting the action to the word, Will Merry pressed the muzzle of his own weapon against the brow of the trembling flunkey.

"Take it away; supposing it were to go off?"

"And then," continued Captain Will, "you must cry out, 'Thieves, murder, highwaymen!'"

And then, to make his acting perfect, Captain Will bawled out the words with all the force of his powerful lungs.

In a minute the three strangers were by the side of Will and his friend.

The constable was, luckily for Captain Will, a perfect stranger.

"Ha! here is the villian!" cried he, pointing to the trembling valet, and mistaking him for the robber of whom they were in pursuit.

"Yes, that's he! seize him!" shouted Will, lending his voice to the tumult.

In an instant the two dragoons had the unfortunate flunkey by the throat, tied his hands behind him, and thrust a gag into his mouth.

"Has he robbed you of anything?" inquired the constable.

"Yes, that box," replied Captain Will.

"Are you sure?" asked the officer, in a doubting manner.

"Yes, it's my property."

"What is there inside?"

"A diamond necklace, a pair of diamond ear-drops, two rings, and two bracelets, all marked with the crest of Admiral Banjemore, whose son I am," replied Captain Will.

The officer peeped into the box and quickly satisfied himself that the contents were correctly described.

"They are yours, sir, said he," handing the casket to Will Merry. "Bring along that villain; we must make haste to catch the rest of the gang."

So saying, they rode away, dragging the unfortunate valet with them, and when they were out of sight Captain Will returned to his comrades.

CHAPTER XXXVII.

THE TRACKER—THE OPEN HEATH—PREPARATIONS FOR WAR—A DESPERATE ENCOUNTER—TIMELY RESCUE OF ALBERT.

ALBERT MONTAGUE, being mounted, had considerable difficulty in carrying out his self-appointed task of watching Sir Andrew Greville, and at the same time remain unseen himself.

When the stormy night had passed away, and the bright sunshine of another fair and beautiful morn began to gladden the earth, the husband of Lady Florence was still tramping forward with measured pace.

All his hesitation and indecision seemed to have vanished; he walked like a man who had an object in view.

He passed through a little village, and by the roadside alehouse, on the outskirts of that village, without halting.

Not so Albert.

The young man knew the landlord well, and, dismounting at his door, called for refreshment.

"Why, who on earth would have thought of seeing you here?" exclaimed the publican.

"Evidently you did not expect me," cried Albert. "But, now I am here, give me a glass of your best ale, and a crust of bread."

"Won't you walk in, sir?"

"No, I can't wait now. But, take my horse and see after him; I am going to travel on foot for a time."

"Heaven and earth! what is the matter? You pad the hoof? I can't—I won't believe it!" exclaimed the host.

He could not imagine his young guest meant what he said.

"It is true, though."

"More's the pity, then. But, look here, mister, I know

you pretty well, and you've been a good customer; if you're hard up, why, I can lend ——"

"No, no, my good friend; I have money. But I have a job in hand which compels me to dismount; so take care of my nag till I come back."

"And when will that be?" inquired the landlord, doubtfully.

"I don't know. Don't spare the oats, however; I will pay the bill."

So saying, the young man strode rapidly away from the inn, and soon was enabled to catch sight of Sir Andrew Greville again.

The disguised baronet took a road which Albert well knew.

It was the path leading to the second rendezvous of the band of which he was a member.

"What can he want there?" thought Albert. "Surely he does not expect to find any of our friends there?"

The young man was totally unaware that Merlin and his brave band had been compelled to quit their usual retreat.

Before they could reach Black Hawke's rendezvous, however, it was necessary to pass a little hovel inhabited by a lonely man, who gained a precarious subsistence by snaring song birds and wild animals.

Before this hovel the baronet paused, and rapped at the door with his stick.

In a moment it was thrown open, and Sir Andrew Greville at once entered.

Albert Montague approached as near as he could without being liable to observation, and watched the hovel attentively.

In a quarter of an hour the baronet once more appeared.

He was no longer the tattered dirty awkward tramp, however; his dress was good and becoming the station he held in society.

"What means this change?" thought Albert, as he watched the baronet's footsteps.

Sir Andrew did not appear to have relinquished his plans along with his old clothes, for he still kept onwards towards the rendezvous of Merlin's band.

"This is very extraordinary," thought Albert. "I am not aware that any of our friends have been here for some time past, and yet—he is searching for his wife here."

In order to reach the cottage to which it seemed certain that Sir Andrew was journeying, they had to cross a wide open common, whose inhospitable expanse gave no hopes of shelter or concealment.

In one spot, indeed, three trees lifted their lanky stems and threw out a few stunted branches, hardly sufficient to shelter any one from the rays of the sun.

Albert resolved to walk at a more rapid pace, so as to overtake the baronet so soon as he should reach the other side of the heath.

When Sir Andrew was half way across, however, he chanced to look back, and perceiving a man following, waited for the approach of the individual, who, as our readers are well aware, was Albert Montague.

To have stopped midway would have had a suspicious look, therefore Albert judged it best to keep straight on, and meet the angry husband face to face.

"At all events he cannot accuse me of stealing his wife," muttered the young man, as he slightly drew the hilt of his sword forward; "and if he asks me where she is, I can with truth reply that I know not."

A few seconds more sufficed to bring him within two yards of the baronet.

"One of the cursed gang. Where is my wife, villain?" cried Sir Andrew.

"I know not——"

"Liar!" exclaimed Sir Andrew, firing a pistol full at the young man's head.

One slug passed through Albert's hat, and a second grazed his ear, but no damage was received.

Hurling the pistol to the ground, the maddened baronet fired a second, one of the missiles from which struck Albert in the right shoulder.

In an instant his sword was in his hand, and—bitterly

regretting that he had left his own pistols in his holsters—the young man sprang forward to punish this unprovoked attack.

Their swords met with a ringing clang, and a desperate encounter ensued.

Good swordsman as he was, through practice with Merlin, Albert had great difficulty in guarding himself from the furious thrusts of the enraged baronet.

At length, after many fierce blows and thrusts had been delivered and parried, the weapons of both the combatants snapped a few inches from the hilts.

"Villain! you shall die, though all the fiends in hell were here to save your worthless life!" muttered Sir Andrew, as, with the remnant of his weapon firmly grasped in his hand, he closed with Albert.

"Don't be too certain about that," replied Albert. "I am a young man, and have no wish to give up the ghost yet."

They struck furious blows at each other with the fragments of their blades, and grappled at each other's throats.

It was a struggle for life.

Anger gleamed from their eyes; oaths and curses fell from their lips.

Twined in each other's embrace they fell to the ground, but still they ceased not in their endeavours to kill.

Like maniacs they writhed and rolled upon the ground.

Albert found himself almost unequal to cope with the baronet; the wound in his shoulder had drawn from his frame a quantity of blood and weakened his sinews.

He felt certain that the husband of Lady Florence was gradually getting the upper hand, and prepared to meet death, if such should be his fate, like a man.

Sir Andrew Greville raised the stump of his sword in the air, and prepared to deal a blow that should decide the combat.

Albert saw the rude fragment flashing in the sun; he saw the eyes of the baronet glaring with hate.

Then there was a strange sound like hasty footsteps; a large body passed across his own, and in another moment Sir Andrew Greville was hurled backwards and held to the earth by a huge dog.

It was a noble animal, used as watch dog at the rendezvous of the highwaymen, and, having been loosened from his collar, had arrived just in the nick of time to save Albert.

The huge animal gave two or three terrible growls as he grasped Sir Andrew Greville by the throat and shook him; then seeing that Albert had risen to his feet and stood prepared, he walked leisurely away.

Albert gazed for some seconds on his foe; but the baronet gave no signs of life.

His eyes were open, but fixed on vacancy, and his breathing was not perceptible.

The young highwayman knelt down and placed his hand on his antagonist's bosom.

He lived!—he breathed!

"I am glad of this. It is not my hand, but that of our chief, which must take the life of this maniac," said Albert to himself. "But what shall I do with him? Shall I leave him here to take his chance, or shall I call assistance for him?"

After some hesitation the young man decided on the latter course.

His own wound was growing painful and needed attention.

"I will walk on till I reach the haunt; and there I have no doubt I shall find some one. They are bound to give me shelter and assistance."

The distance he had to traverse was not great; and in a few minutes he stood before the door of the cottage.

No one appeared to be about the house, so, lifting the latch, he boldly entered.

A sight of horror met his eyes!

CHAPTER XXXVIII.

SIR THOMAS BROOKE IN THE VAULT—THE CURIOUS FLASK—MERLIN AND THE DUKE RESCUE LADY JANE—THE SECRET DOOR—ARRIVAL OF ALBERT MONTAGUE.

THE ghastly image of the man he had murdered pursued Sir Thomas Brooke on his way through the subterranean passage

Bill the Crusher's last groan seemed to echo through the lonely vault.

The wretched murderer in vain endeavoured to drown regret and stifle the pangs of conscience by trying to force himself to believe that he had done right, and that his servant would have slain him.

"It was self-defence," he muttered, wringing his hands wildly, "it was in self-defence."

Neither did the wine he had swallowed ease his sin-burdened conscience or bring oblivion to his mind. The wine was the colour of blood!

"I am alone!—alone with the dead! Oh, Heavens, how horrible!—shut up here beneath the surface of the earth with a ghastly corpse!—the corpse of the man I slew! This is fearful indeed!"

He passed on a few steps, then once more paused.

"How can I escape? What outlet is there from this vault of death? And if I escape, whither can I hide myself, for by this time all is known? Curses on that woman! May the fiends of hell blast her beauty and deform her fair shape! Curses on her!"

His fate seemed, indeed, desperate. He clenched his fists, tore his hair, and gnashed his teeth together in the madness of his despair.

"I must starve to death, or else surrender myself to—to the hands—of—" he hesitated ere he pronounced the words "the hangman! I must die here with all the agony that starvation brings its victims, or else perish miserably on the scaffold, a holiday sight for ten thousand gaping brutes, who would flock to see Sir Thomas Brooke, the master of Albion Hall, perish on the scaffold. Ah! Montague, Montague, you are avenged!"

Again he staggered forward a few paces, and again halted to chew the bitter cud of reflection.

"That boy, too, lives to torment me while my life lasts. Why was not he placed in a gory grave beside his father? It is always thus with those who employ others to strike the blow they themselves should deal. But away with regret! I must accept my fate whate'er it be. First some more wine, and then to find my way out of this cursed vault."

He retraced his steps till he reached the recess in which the dead body of Bill the Crusher was lying beside the wine bin.

Sir Thomas Brooke could not help shuddering as his eye fell once more upon his bloody handiwork.

He averted his gaze as much as possible, and advanced to the huge chest in which the liquor was stored.

Another bottle was carried to his lips and drained of its contents, and he was about to leave when a flask of peculiar shape and appearance met his eye.

He drew it from its place of concealment and held it up to the light which poured in through a crevice.

"This is a rare old flask, and, I have no doubt, contains choice liquor," he muttered. "I wonder who hid away this secret store? Some old miser, I'll warrant, who used to drain a bottle on the sly."

He thrust the flask into his pocket, and then walked on.

He was determined to find a way out of the vault by some means or other.

At length he arrived at what seemed the termination of the subterranean passage.

It was darker than any other portion of the vault, but there was just sufficient light to enable him to discern a flight of steps leading upwards.

"Here, then, is my journey's end. I wonder where I am, and what kind of reception I shall meet with on showing myself to the world?"

Sir Thomas ascended the steps, and found himself before a narrow door, which was bolted.

The huge iron fastenings had grown rusty in their sockets, and it was some minutes before he could move them.

While still engaged in so doing, he fancied he heard a scream.

"Help! help!"

The guilty man trembled, and gazed round fearfully.

"From whence came that cry? Was it the sound of a mortal voice or was it——Pshaw! I am afraid without cause; it was nothing but the wind whistling through some crevice."

At length one of the bolts slipped back with a harsh, grating noise, and in an instant another curious sound was heard.

What it was the guilty, fear-stricken baronet knew not, but it filled his soul with alarm.

A moment he paused, debating in his own mind whether he should go forward or wait awhile.

"I know not what that sound means," he thought to himself; "but if it portends danger may I not as well face that danger now as wait till hunger and fatigue have racked my frame, and rendered me incapable of resisting my enemies, if I have any to fear? I will advance."

So saying, he exerted all his strength to draw the remaining bolt.

It yielded, and the narrow door swung back upon its hinges.

The baronet then gave a loud scream, and fell senseless at the top of the steps.

* * * * * *

The cry for help which Merlin Hawke heard was that uttered by Lady Jane Cleveland as she struggled with the old hag, into whose power she had fallen.

"'Tis the cry of a woman," said the Duke of Cleveland.

"Aye, and of one in distress, too," replied Merlin. "If they have dared to take such a liberty——"

He drew his sword, and, setting spurs to his horse, pressed onward.

The duke followed, anxious to aid the man whose life he would have taken an hour before.

"Do you know the inhabitants of yon cottage?" he asked.

"They are my servants," replied Merlin.

The duke gazed at his companion inquiringly.

"This house belongs to me, though I seldom use it. A man and woman have charge of it, with strict orders to be kind and attentive to all travellers who may demand hospitality; though, from the sounds I hear, I fear they have disobeyed my commands."

"And if they have?"

"Why, I know how to punish."

In a few minutes they had reached the house, and, throwing themselves from their horses, advanced to the door.

It was fastened.

At that moment the scream was repeated in feebler tones.

"The back, the back of the house, for Heaven's sake, or we shall be too late to save the poor creature!"

Following Merlin he rushed round, and in a moment had gained the window.

The sight that met their eyes was that of a young girl, just budding into womanhood, struggling with a withered, wrinkled, toothless old hag, who held in her long, claw-like hand a knife, the blade of which was dyed crimson with blood.

"Good Heavens, my daughter!" exclaimed the duke, in tones of agony. "Off, off, vile wretch! if you dare harm one hair of her head, I swear, by all the saints above, you shall suffer the most lingering tortures that man's cruelty can devise."

"Vengeance!" shouted the woman, as, wrenching her arm free from Lady Jane's feeble grasp, she brandished the ensanguined blade in the air.

"Oh, Heaven have mercy!" groaned the duke.

There was a loud report from a pistol, and, at the same moment, the blade descended.

It fell harmlessly, though, for Merlin's bullet had passed through the old woman's body, and at the same moment she fell lifeless across the senseless form of Lady Jane Cleveland.

The duke turned and grasped Merlin by the hand.

His heart was too full to permit him to speak, but his look and his action proved that he was not ungrateful.

"We must hasten to break into the house before she revives from her swoon, and carry her away from that loathsome carcase," said Merlin.

His men soon arrived and forced an entrance.

The old woman was dead, the bullet having passed through her heart.

Lady Jane was carried into the front room, and laid upon a rough couch of cloaks.

The highwaymen did not at first notice the corpse of the old woman's son which was lying by the wide, open fire-place.

The duke, her father, knelt by her side, and sprinkled cold water on her face, calling her by name, and endeavouring to revive her.

At length she opened her eyes and sat up.

"Where am I?" she asked.

"With friends; with——"

"Father!"

"Even so, my dear girl."

"I have had a fearful dream."

"Banish it from your mind, dear; the evil is past."

"I dreamt," said Lady Jane, "that I sought refuge in a cottage in which was an old woman and her son. The old woman murdered her son, and—— Ah! see, there is his gory corpse! It was no dream, then."

The duke lifted her in his arms and bore her out into the air.

She had relapsed into her swoon.

Lady Florence Greville and Polly, the innkeeper's daughter, now approached, and proffered their assistance, while Merlin and his men prepared to clear away the traces of the foul deed.

Just as they were about to remove the corpses, having conveyed both of them to the front room of the house, a strange sound was heard by the side of the chimney.

In another moment a secret door flew open, and the pale, haggard face of Sir Thomas Brooke appeared at the opening.

As before said, he uttered a loud scream, and sank down—senseless.

At the same moment the door of the cottage was thrown open, and Albert Montague made his appearance.

"What on earth means all this?" asked the new comer, staring, with surprise, at the two corpses.

"Perhaps you can explain this mystery," said Merlin, in reply; "in the first place the Duke of Cleveland is here."

"Who brought him hither?"

"I did."

"Doubtless you had some good reason for so doing?"

"I had; my object in bringing him hither was to persuade him that you had no hand in the abduction of his daughter."

"What, in Heaven's name, do you mean! Where is Lady Jane?"

"In the field at the back. Stay, you had better not go for a few minutes."

"And what have these done?"

"How the man came by his death I know not, unless it be true, as Lady Jane says in her raving, Dark Meggie killed him."

"And the old woman?"

"I shot her just as she was about to stab Lady Jane Cleveland."

Albert looked perplexed.

"How, on earth, did Lady Jane come here? Did she accompany her father?"

"No; as I before said, her father was searching for her when I met him. I don't know how she found out this spot any more than I know how yon friend of yours has managed to penetrate the secret passage, which even I had never heard of."

Albert's eyes followed Merlin's hand, and then he beheld his rival—his foe—the murderer of his father.

The young man hastily drew his sword from his sheath, and made a step towards Sir Thomas Brooke.

"Hold!" cried Merlin; "what would you do?"

"Do? why, slay him, even as my father was killed by his minions."

"Death on the scaffold is his proper doom, therefore let him live a little while longer."

Albert played with the hilt of his sword for a moment, but at length plunged it back into the scabbard.

"It is necessary that he should live in order that you may gain possession of your title and estate. To see him hanged I think would satisfy your just hatred."

So spoke Merlin, but Albert heeded him not.

His thoughts had wandered to Lady Jane Cleveland.

"Cannot I go to see her?" he asked.

"Not yet."

"But she needs watching?"

"Lady Florence Greville is with her."

"Lady Florence? Listen! Ten minutes have hardly elapsed since I encountered her husband, and nearly lost my life. He lies senseless on the heath near the three trees."

"Ha! is it so? Go, my men, and bring him hither."

CHAPTER XXXIX.

THE LANDLORD'S LITTLE BILL—THE OFFICER IN PURSUIT—THE ENCOUNTER—WILL MERRY SEEMS DEAD—BUT IS AFTERWARDS IN GREATER DANGER OF DEATH—QUARRELLING OVER THE REWARD.

GREAT was the joy and merriment when Captain Will Merry returned and related to his companions his adventures with the admiral's servant and the constable.

"You have done admirably well, captain," said one of his band.

"Is not this valet a most honest and trustworthy fellow?" cried another. "Now, I dare swear, he will tell his old sea-dog of a master that he was set upon by at least twenty armed men."

"And the enemy will report a victory over not less than two dozen, reporting half that number killed and wounded," exclaimed a third.

"Two soldiers and a Bow Street runner! Why, I would encounter them myself hand to hand," said the first speaker, a huge swarthy fellow, whose countenance bore the mark of many a hard fight. "These dragoons are nothing but gilded gingerbread fellows, who look upon honest men like us as though they were the pure ore, and we the dross."

"Well, lads," said Captain Will, "this booty must go to the melting-pot and the diamond dealer's, and then we all share equally."

"Bravo! three cheers for Captain Merry!" shouted all the party.

"We must be off now," cried the bold captain, when he had bowed his acknowledgment of the compliment bestowed upon him. "Hullo, landlord! some more sherry, and along with it the bill."

The wine was brought, and mine host, with many bows and expressions of good will, presented the reckoning.

Three pounds ten shillings was the amount, and loud was the grumbling when Captain Will Merry announced that piece of information.

"By Bacchus, god of wine, you are the most extortionate cellarman that ever placed bad liquor before thirsty men," exclaimed Captain Will.

"Don't pay him, captain," exclaimed more than one voice.

Will Merry hesitated a moment.

"I *will* pay him," said he, after a short pause, "but I vow that ere another month has flown his cellar shall be empty, his money bags in a similar condition, and his house in ruins. And now to horse, comrades, to horse. Hullo, ostler, our steeds!"

The landlord looked at the money, and at the angry speaker, and then, thinking that perhaps after all, he had not done right, said,

"Captain, I am sorry I have offended you; but next time you come this way I promise you shall have no reason to complain of the wine or of the charges."

"The foul fiend fly away with me if I ever drink wine in your house again; but here come our horses."

Even as Captain Will spoke a trampling was heard in the inn-yard, and from the window of the parlour they beheld the stable attendants with their steeds in readiness to set out as soon as the riders should make their appearance.

In a few minutes the highwaymen and their prisoners were mounted, and rode out of the inn-yard.

"The groom, your honour—please remember the groom," said the principal attendant.

"I think your master can well spare you a crown out of the money he has robbed us of this day," replied Captain Will.

"I don't think we shall get anything out of him, though," responded the groom.

Captain Will threw the man a few coins, and, riding away, cut short all further attempt at discussion.

The disappointed groom, who had reckoned upon receiving a guinea at the least, turned sullenly away towards his stables, while Captain Will and his band, with the two prisoners in their midst, rode briskly off, pursued by the benedictions of the host and his blooming wife, who stood bowing and curtseying at the door, in gratitude, doubtless, for the receipt of an unconscionable reckoning.

In about a quarter of an hour after their departure another party drew up at the inn yard and loudly called for the landlord.

Amongst them was the unfortunate valet whom Will Merry had so dexterously robbed, and then given into custody.

The poor fellow seemed scarcely to have recovered from the effects of the astonishment caused by the events which had so recently befallen him. His manner was that of a man who had been wrestling vigorously with some imaginary foe in a dream, and had scarcely recovered from the effects of the fatiguing encounter.

Along with him rode the constable who had captured him, and the two dragoons, together with several members of a volunteer force, which had recently been embodied in the neighbourhood.

"Hullo, landlord! house!" the officer cried.

A delay of some minutes occurred before the host made his appearance.

"What the devil does this mean? I half fancy the rascal is in league with the robbers; he had best be careful, for if my suspicions prove correct he shall suffer for it."

"What is your good pleasure, gentlemen?" exclaimed the host, when at length he emerged from his private retreat.

"Have you seen anything of Will Merry, the highwayman, lately?" asked the officer.

"Yes."

"Where and when?"

"He and his men rode away from this place only an hour ago."

"His men? And how many has he with him?"

"Ten, besides two gentlemen, who appeared to be kept as prisoners."

"There, there!" exclaimed the valet, "I told you there were at least a dozen."

"Hold your tongue, fool. It was only one who robbed you, as I saw. Which way did they go, master landlord?"

"They took the western road," bawled out the groom.

"Then forward, my friends, forward, and let us capture these ruffians, and rescue Captain Ashburne and Marmaduke Greville!"

The whole party turned their horses heads about and followed the highwaymen, which they could easily do by means of the impressions of the hoofs of their steeds on the sandy road.

"The devil take you all for a lot of dry dogs who waste a man's time without tasting his liquor," exclaimed the landlord, as the constable and his gang trotted off.

"I wonder what in the name of satan could possess Tom, the ostler, that he should *speak* the truth for the only time in his life just when he should have held his tongue, or told a rattling good lie?"

The worthy constable who was doing his duty, and obeying the orders of his superiors in authority in thus hunting down the highwaymen, soon had the satisfaction of seeing the party he was in pursuit of on the road before him.

"I must charge them," thought he, "for if they once get wind of my hostile intentions I shall never be able to come up with them."

"There they are, there they are! That's the man that stole my master's jewels!" bawled the valet.

(*To be continued.*)

THE YEW OF CROISSEY.

I AM about to tell you, sir, why I come here every evening to smoke my pipe under the Yew of Croissey.

I was brought up by an old uncle, curate of a neighbouring parish, and, as it was intended I should join the spiritual hosts of the church, I for some time escaped serving in the belligerent ones of Napoleon—the conscription of 1812 having returned me as an ecclesiastic. But just at that time my uncle died; and as the good old soul had always divided his last sous with the poor around him, he had nothing to leave his nephew but the poverty he previously shared with his neighbours. Behold me, then, at the age of twenty, alone, unfettered by restraint, unencumbered with cash, full of disgust for my present station and of indecision as to what other to attain; feeling all the humiliations incidental to indigence, and the ennobling sentiments inspired by education—hoping everything, possessing nothing, and dreaming of fortune in a tattered coat! I cared for neither man or woman, but was just in that state when the mind is most open to receive impressions either of good or evil; so that chance alone was to determine whether I became a pattern of virtue or a libertine—an honest man or a rogue—a good citizen or a rebel!

My habits were pensive—they were also ambulatory. I used to saunter in the great wood which crowns yon chain of hills, to descend into the valley you have just left, and thread its miniature forest. I would cross, too, the wild moor which you see enclosed on three sides by the wood, bounded on the fourth by this precipice, which I often climbed to enjoy the lovely prospect presented from its summit—the steeple of Croissey church, that seems *driven in* to the dense abyss from which it rises—the red tops of the fishing boats glistening in the Seine —the white smoke of the lime-kilns—the long avenue of the Chateau de Montmorency—and, lastly, the immense and sombre forest of Esserds were scattered in detail, or combined in one grand panoramic view over an extent of ten or a dozen leagues. But I had contrived a plan sufficiently romantic to double the pleasure I derived from the scene.

The colossal yew that covers us and seems to grow upon this shelf of the quarry on purpose to shelter the spectator, made this my favourite place for meditation. With a warmth of romance peculiar to my disposition, I wished it were possible for me to live for ever—"sub tegmine fagi,"—to set up my everlasting rest at the root of this tree; and even went so far as to domicile half the day in its branches. You see that cluster of fibres entangled like the roots of a thicket? It was there—as pretty a locality for forgetting the world and encouraging morbid and misanthropic thoughts as one might meet with in a summer's day.

One evening, as I was as usual at my post, the moon had risen in the distance, giving light and *breadth* to the scene. The wind moaned in deep and sullen gusts, bearing to my ear varied and confused noises. The weathercock of the church steeple creaked at intervals, and, among indistinct sounds from the river, I distinguished from time to time the rattle of tackle, the shrill boatswain's pipe, or the uniform creaking of a capstan. I was just beginning to dose, when suddenly I heard beneath me a voice, or rather a sigh, which murmured,

"The last time!"

Then I heard something awfully like a kiss; and another voice, evidently that of a man, replied,

"Come, come, Louise, courage, courage!"

This was succeeded by the tones of another girl, delicate, but decided.

"No, no, *not* the last time. Listen! I will not have it."

"Ah, ah!" thought I, "a rustic love affair."

I peeped through the branches, and perceived by the light of the moon a young man in the dress of a carrier, his hat decorated with the cockade of a conscript, and exhibiting the fatal number.

On his right arm he supported a girl bathed in tears; his left arm was locked in that of another maiden, evidently younger, who did not cry, and was, without doubt, she who had exclaimed, "I will not have it."

I comprehended pretty quickly the nature of this short colloquy; it was the farewell of a conscript.

"Poor sister Christine," replied the young fellow, with a melancholy smile, "I am very sorry that, whether you will have it or no, it must be so."

"But, brother, have you not brought me up? Have we ever been severed? Have you not been my companion, my instructor—almost my parent? Think, too, of Louise, your betrothed. She—she cannot speak for the tears that choke her. You will not—cannot leave us! Go, go—tell them so—say to the cruel colonel, you will *not* leave us!"

And the lovely rebel ended her speech by crying also, her tears sparkling in the moonbeams as they fell one by one on her cheek; to hide them she gave her pretty head a toss.

Louise replied, in the midst of her sobs,

"Nay, Christine, we must submit as patiently as——"

A flood of tears prevented her from ending the sentence.

"Poor Louise! poor Christine!" exclaimed Eugene, as he drew them both closer to his breast.

"Very well, Louise," cried the sister, in a firm tone, "since he will not hear us—since he believes we can live without him—you see this precipice; it is deep, Louise, and perpendicular. Come, let us end our troubles at once; one dash, and ——"

She grasped the arm of Louise, and pulled her away from that of Eugene.

"Are ye both mad?" exclaimed the youth, restraining his headstrong companions. "Listen to me: would you not have me strike the blow for France, for you, for the Cross? I will return in eight months; what can prevent me? Shall I not have enough of your good wishes, of your love in my heart, to encounter even a lion, to make me return decorated, or at least with a pair of epaulettes? Will you not be delighted to have an officer in the family? they will make me one in good time. Come, Louise—Christine, no more words—let me away."

"Oh, 'in good time,' say you?" repeated Christine. "There was Stephen, the mechanic, who went to Russia with the others; he was 'made in good time'—made a corpse, poor fellow—left to perish in the snows of Moscow. His mother is mourning for him; and as to the others, they never have returned, and never will while that dog of an emper——"

"Will you be quiet?" interrupted Eugene, putting his hand before her pretty mouth.

"No, I will not be quiet," persisted the refractory damsel. "You have a colonel—he who enrolled you; very well; go to him—throw yourself at his feet, and say, 'Oh, sir, I cannot, will not go to be killed like Stephen, the mechanic. I have a sister and a sweetheart who cannot live without me, and who will, in my absence, certainly drown themselves. Punish me, sir—put me in prison; but do—do not send me to the wars. I am a free man, and have no right to leave my sister Christine—who, in fact, won't let me, and who has made up her mind to detest you, sir, with all her might, if you persist in depriving her of her brother!'"

"A pretty speech for one soldier to make to another," answered the conscript, trying to restrain his laughter.

Finding she could make no impression on her obstinate brother, Christine burst into tears, and fell on the neck of Louise.

There was a short silence, during which I had moved from my hiding-place, but was so absorbed with the situation of the conscript and his companions, that I quite forgot my own. Presently Christine recovered, and soothed by the solicitude of Eugene and Louise, appeared more calm.

"Ah!" she cried, "a thought strikes me. Can we not get a substitute?"

"Certainly," answered Eugene.

"Of course we can," rejoined Louise. "How silly not to think of that before!"

"But," said the conscript, "we must *buy* one, and where are we to find sufficient money by to-morrow?"

"Very easily," replied Christine. "I will give all I have—

my gold cross, my earrings, my necklace—in short, everything I possess in the world."

"All which would not amount to half the price of a man," said Eugene.

Christine reflected for a little while, and, seizing her brother's arm, exclaimed,

"I see the way—I must throw *myself* into the bargain! Yes, if any one is willing to take your place, I will say to him, 'Go for my dear brother, and I will be your wife. Look at me! I am rather pretty—at least, they tell me so—rather good tempered, and will love you very much indeed if you will but save Eugene.' Yes, I swear by this golden cross, that I will marry any man who becomes your substitute."

"Dear—dear sister!" replied Eugene, "you are a most devoted, kind, and affectionate creature; but I fear your senses have taken wing this evening. You do not seem to know that all your plans are utterly impracticable. Come, let us go home, for if we continue here much longer, your brains are so addled, I fear you will throw your dear little self over the precipice in earnest."

I did not hear his sister's reply, for I soon lost sight of all three in the shade of the trees, but my head and heart were both filled with the lovely, romantic Christine.

The same evening, as the conscript, with Christine and Louise, were gazing through their tears at their humble repast, of which neither were able to partake, a loud knock was heard at the cottage door.

"Come in!" said the youth, hastily.

An old sergeant presented himself.

"Save you!" he said; "are you the conscript, Eugene Livon?"

"Yes, sergeant."

"Then I have a letter for you," said the soldier, throwing a sealed packet on the table.

Eugene read the superscription, and, while breaking the seal, made the sergeant a bow, with an expression in which surprise and politeness were comically blended.

"That will inform you that you are superseded, and have lost the chance of having your moustachios blackened with gunpowder; some lucky rascal has been accepted in your stead. Poor fellow, I pity you; bear your loss with fortitude; but enough, I must march. Good day!"

And, giving a *congé à la militaire*, the old soldier placed his hand on the door to depart.

"Pipe of the devil!" said he, returning, "I had nearly forgotten. I have something for Christine Livon, your sister, I believe. Where is she?"

"Here," said Eugene, presenting Christine, who trembled with joy and wonder.

(*To be continued.*)

BLACK HAWKE, THE HIGHWAYMAN.

LADY ELLEN CURTIS.

CHAPTER XXXIX.—(continued).

The form of Captain Will Merry was easily recognisable by the waving plume which decked his hat. In the midst of the party could be seen the two prisoners.

"Hold your tongue, you rascal," cried the constable, rebuking the flunkey for his unseemly noise.

The officer then gathered his men together, and looked ahead for a spot suitable for the enterprise he meditated.

At length they saw a long tract of road before them leading down a gentle incline, and unvaried by the least appearance of man, beast, or human habitation. On each side of this road was a wide waste space overgrown with grass and weeds.

Keeping their horses on this, the constable and his followers increased their pace and lessened the distance between themselves and the highwaymen, till they were within twenty yards of the latter.

Fearing then that they should be overheard, the worthy officer gave the signal to charge.

At the sudden increase of their speed, and the noise with which it was attended, Captain Will Merry glanced over his shoulders, and at once saw the coming danger.

"Left wheel!" he shouted, as though commanding a troop of soldiers, and his well trained men at once obeyed the word of command.

But so sudden and furious was the onset of the pursuers, that before all his men could turn out of the road, two of them were rolling on the ground along with their horses.

Captain Merry faced his men about in an instant, and drawing his sword fell upon the attacking force ere they could check their impetuous career.

A furious encounter took place, sword thrusts and blows were aimed in every direction, and pistol balls began to hiss through the air.

At the first charge Captain Ashburne and Marmaduke Greville, whose hands had not been secured since leaving the inn, escaped from their captors, and joined the ranks of the constables' force.

They procured weapons from the two men who had been dismounted and disabled, and joined in the *mélee*.

Their aid was most valuable, and it soon became apparent that the highwaymen were over-matched.

Henry Ashburne especially was of a most fiery and

impetuous nature ; his hot blood boiled to avenge the insults to which he had been compelled to submit.

Marmaduke Greville, though not possessed of so much natural courage, had too much dread of ridicule to attempt to shun the combat.

"Courage, my lads ; one more charge !" cried Captain Will, waving his sword and dashing forward.

"It shall be your last !" cried Henry Ashburne, firing a pistol.

The gallant highwayman reeled in his saddle and fell heavily to the earth.

"Hurrah ! their leader is down ; pepper the rascals well !" shouted the officer.

Will Merry's followers made one last and desperate effort to retrieve the fortunes of the day ; but their efforts were unavailing.

"Save yourselves !" was the cry, and in an instant the men dispersed, each in a different direction.

"Follow them ! cut them down !" cried Henry Ashburne.

Now the constable, the dragoons, and the volunteers, though fighting bravely enough together, had none of them the least inclination to encounter one of the highwaymen single handed.

While they were debating *which* should be followed and cut down, all the robbers got safely away.

"At all events he's dead enough," said the constable, pointing to Will Merry. "Captain Ashburne, you earned five hundred pounds by your shot."

"Which shall be divided amongst you and your comrades. I have not the slightest wish to enrich myself by killing highwaymen."

The men gave three cheers for Captain Ashburne.

"Where are my jewels ? my master's jewels ?" exclaimed the admiral's valet, who had carefully abstained from taking any part in the conflict.

"Get down and look for them yourself," cried the constable, who had observed and was disgusted with the young man's cowardly conduct.

"Oh, lord, I dare not touch a real highwayman !"

"Why, you great fool, he's dead as a barn door."

"Yes, but then his spirit would be sure to haunt me for the rest of my life. Don't you know it is unlucky to take anything from a dead body ?"

"Well, my friend, if you don't like to take the jewels yourself, you may leave them. None of my men will touch them, if, as you say, it is unlucky."

"Oh, dear ! oh, dear ! What shall I do ?"

"Do ? Why, take the jewels, and don't make an ass of yourself."

The man dismounted from his horse and slowly approached the body of Captain Will Merry.

"I don't like to touch him, though I suppose I must."

"I'll do it if you'll give me half the jewels," said one of the dragoons.

"Half ? Why, they ain't mine."

"Well, give me five guineas, then ?" continued the soldier.

The valet hesitated, and a look of indecision crossed his face.

According to the old proverb the man who hesitates is lost.

"It's a great deal of money for a very little work," he said, with a sigh.

"I don't think five guineas is much to get back your valuable property, and make me unlucky for life."

"Very well, you shall have the money, if I have as much about me."

With a long face he drew a purse from his pocket, and poured the contents out into his hand.

It contained exactly the sum demanded by the dragoon.

"There goes the last of my wages," cried the poor valet, as he poured the money out into the soldier's palm.

"Never mind, I dare say your master will repay you. Now, then, to see whether he has the jewels or not."

So saying, the dragoon knelt down by the side of the highwayman and thrust his hand into Captain Will's coat-pocket.

Suddenly he started up.

"The devil !" he ejaculated.

"What is the matter ?" cried all the others.

The dragoon drew a pistol and levelled it at the prostrate body.

"The deuce take me, if he is dead after all !"

The instant the constable heard those words, he sprang forward and laid his hand upon the soldier's weapon.

"Hold ! there is a greater reward for taking him alive than for killing him."

"Very well, I am quite agreeable," said the soldier, lowering his pistol and slipping back a pace or two.

The constable then stooped down by the side of the senseless though still living man.

"Captain Will Merry," said he, "I apprehend you for highway robbery. You had best make no resistance."

The last words were perhaps unnecessary, but they were part of a formula which the worthy constable always used on similar occasions, and any departure from that form would have been as great a sin in his eyes as lowering the franchise is to a Tory senator.

The constable wound up his speech by producing a stout pair of handcuffs, which he fastened about poor Will Merry's wrists in a professional manner quite edifying to behold.

He then turned to the men who stood round about and said,

"Bear witness, all of you, that *I* captured the highwayman alive."

"Yes, that's true," responded several.

"Therefore, *I* alone am entitled to the reward for his apprehension."

In an instant the countenances of his friends were changed.

"D——d villain !" "Sneaking thief !" "No better than a highwayman himself." "Ought to be tarred and set fire to." Such were the complimentary expressions which were heard on every side.

"And do you mean to say that you won't share the reward with us ?" asked the dragoon who had made the discovery that Captain Will still breathed.

"I certainly mean to stick to every penny of the money."

"Then you may stick to the man yourself, and get him to prison the best way you can," replied the soldier.

"I hope the poor fellow will revive and get away," said his comrade.

"And I hope the first glass of liquor he buys with the money may blister his bowels and kill him," cried one of the volunteers.

"What, mutiny !" said the constable. "Captain Ashburne, will you be kind enough to compel these men, who belong to your regiment, to obey my orders."

There was no response to this appeal, and, in an instant the greedy Bow-Street official discovered that Captain Ashburne and Marmaduke Greville had quitted the spot and were riding away from the scene of the combat.

"Come, come, my good men, lend a hand to get this fellow comfortably housed ; perhaps I'll stand treat if you do, so bear a hand."

One by one they refused.

"Share the reward all round and we will," cried the dragoons.

"I'll be hanged if I do," replied the official, whose blood began to rise as he found himself opposed.

"Then we'll be hanged if we help you."

The officer looked at the malcontents, and then at the senseless prisoner.

At length he drew a pistol and pointed it at Will Merry's head.

"I'll just put a bullet through his brain, then none of you can claim the reward for killing him."

"If you fire at him now, while he is not resisting, it will be a case of wilful murder, and you will most certainly be sent to Tyburn," said the discontented dragoon, "so just put up your pistol."

"You villains, you shall suffer for this ; you shall be flogged before the whole regiment."

"I am not afraid," was the reply ; "our colonel will not be angry with us when he hears how *you* behaved."

They mounted their horses, and the volunteers did the same.

In a few minutes the constable was left alone by his prisoner, though the valet stood at some little distance to learn the probable fate of his master's diamonds.

"Now, how the devil shall I manage to get this fellow locked up?" muttered the officer, as he paced up and down. "Curse those fellows, they always want to rob a man of his rights."

He placed his hand upon Will Merry's bosom.

The heart still fluttered faintly, but that was the only sign of life perceptible.

"Ha! glorious," exclaimed the officer, as he heard a sound at hand, and saw an empty post-chaise approaching.

It was the work of a few seconds to stop the driver and place Will inside.

"My jewels!" cried the valet, as the vehicle drove off.

"You must claim them at Newgate," was the response.

CHAPTER XL.

THE DEATH OF OLD BADGER.

ACCORDING to the orders given by Merlin, a party of men proceeded to the spot indicated by Albert Montague for the purpose of making a prisoner of Sir Andrew Greville.

They were three in number, and deemed themselves competent to deal with half-a-dozen baronets.

The leader of the party was a raw-boned old man, with grizzled hair and moustache.

In the band he was known by the nick-name of "The Badger," and was one of Merlin's most trusty followers.

"You had better get your popguns in order, lads," said he; "there's no knowing what this precious baronet may be up to."

"I don't fancy he's up to much, now that the young lad yonder and the dog have both had a turn at him," replied one of the men.

"I'll manage the varmint myself, Master Badger, if you're afraid," cried the second.

"I'm not afraid," said Badger, coolly, "you know that, lads."

At all events the scars on the man's weather-beaten countenance, bearing witness of many a stubborn fight, ought to have told them that cowardice was not one of Badger's failings.

The man who hinted at fear as Badger's reason for pistol-loading changed his tone suddenly.

"I DO know you are not afraid of any man living, and I ask your pardon for saying anything about it. I haven't forgot how you saved my life once."

"Saved your life?" ejaculated the other man, "why, how was that?"

Didn't you ever hear the story?"

"No."

The man being one of the latest recruits Black Hawke had enlisted, knew very little of the past adventures of the band to which he belonged.

"Then, if Badger don't mind, I'll tell you all about it in two minutes," continued he who owed his life to the bravery of the old man.

"You see, four of us were out one night looking about for a chance of a prize, when we saw a party coming on horseback—two gentlemen and two ladies. Well, of course we stopped them to take toll, and, as a matter of course, the gentlemen they out with their weapons and showed fight. That was just the sort of thing to please us, you know, so in a few minutes we were beating time in a very pretty style with our swords; Badger and I against the two strangers, while our pals took care that the ladies didn't run away.

"In the very first charge my horse got a thrust which sent him at full length on the turf, but my man was a fair fighter, and as soon as he saw me down he dismounted. But he was too good a fencer for me, and in a few minutes sent my blade flying through the air, while at the same moment my foot caught in some long grass, and I fell backwards. His sword was raised to thrust through me, but then came old friend Badger here, who had just disarmed his man, and saved me. He hadn't time to ward off the thrust with his sword, but he threw out his leg and took the point in his foot.

"That's how Badger saved my life, and that's why he walks a little lame at times. And now you know the story."

"And how about the man you fought with?" asked the other.

"Why, Badger soon served him as he had served me—knocked his sword out of his hand and bade him surrender. We made a very nice little booty out of that party."

"About forty pounds each, if I don't forget," chimed in Badger.

The scene of the conflict between Albert Montague and Sir Andrew Greville was soon reached.

The three men looked around, but though there were traces of the conflict in the shape of footmarks, empty pistols, and a broken sword blade, Sir Andrew Greville was nowhere to be seen.

"He's bolted," said one.

"Like a sneak as he is," cried the second one.

"Take care of yourselves, lads; don't be too sure. He may be lurking about among some of those bushes there," said Badger.

"I'm blest if I don't think there is something or somebody moving there."

"Well, then, just spread yourselves out; you go about thirty yards this side, and you, Tom, the same distance on the right, I'll take the centre, and then if we advance at the same time there will be little danger."

Such were the directions of the old highwayman, and it took but a few seconds to do as he commanded.

The men advanced like skirmishers before a regiment, but before they could reach the bushes where they supposed the baronet had taken shelter, the report of a pistol was heard.

The men looked from one to the other to see who was hurt.

They were not long kept in suspense.

Old Badger was seen to reel about like a man under the influence of liquor, and finally to fall upon the ground.

The others at once ran up to him.

"It's no use, lads," said the old man, "it's no use; the only thing you can do is to avenge me. Make haste, or the rascal will be gone!"

They laid him back carefully on the ground, and then dashed headlong into the thicket from which the shot had been fired.

The man who had fired it was gone, and the only token of his presence was a thin wreath of white smoke which hung about the branches of the shrubs.

"This is about as queer a start as ever I saw," said one.

"Have another look round, he might be fixed in some dark corner," replied the other.

The search was renewed, but without success; Sir Andrew Greville had vanished!

"What's to be done?" was the next question asked.

"Why, go back to the captain," was the reply.

"And leave old Badger here?"

"Not if I know it," replied the man whose life had been saved by the wounded highwayman. "You can just help me to carry him back to the house."

They once more approached the wounded man, and related their want of success.

"I saw it, lads, I saw it; but it's no use moving me, I may as well die here as anywhere. Go and tell the captain it's all up with poor old Badger."

One of them ran with full speed to the house to inform Merlin, while the other knelt by the side of his dying companion, and did all he could to soothe his pain.

In a few minutes Merlin came, and along with him Frank Morton, Hal Hunter, and Albert Montague, who had all a strong liking for the dying man.

"Well, captain," said he, "you'll have to scratch my name from the book at last, though it will not be necessary to put a black cross against it."

The black cross was a mark put on the muster roll against

the names of all those who were so unfortunate as to suffer the penalty of the law.

"I hope it is not so bad as you fancy," said Merlin ; "but here comes the doctor."

The *doctor*, as he was called, was not a regular and licensed practitioner, but a youth who, after one year's study of the healing art, had renounced it for the more exciting life of a gentleman of the highway.

Still he was not altogether ignorant of medicine and surgery, and was frequently called upon to heal the hurts received by the band of Black Hawke in their numerous encounters.

The "Doctor" knelt by the side of old Badger, and with gentle fingers examined his wound.

The ball had shattered one rib, and from the direction taken, it seemed as though it had pierced the lungs.

And as soon as the doctor's fingers closed the gaping orifice in the wounded man's side, blood poured from his mouth and nose in streams, for a time completely stopping his breath.

"Nothing can save him, in my opinion," said the young medical deserter.

"I must have better advice," cried Merlin ; "ride post haste one of you and call the surgeon from the next village."

A man at once started as swiftly as his horse could carry him.

But ere he was out of sight, a shout caused the messenger to turn his head.

His companions were beckoning him to return.

When he rejoined the group, old Badger was a corpse.

"I swear to Heaven, the rascal who fired that shot shall suffer for it !" cried the man whose life had been saved by the dead. "Vengeance for Badger is my task, if you please, captain."

Merlin made no reply, but walked towards the house.

CHAPTER XLI.

WILL MERRY IN THE LOCK-UP—THE STRANGE DOCTOR—THE ESCAPE FROM THE LOCK-UP.

WHEN Will Merry recovered the use of his eyes and his brain he was considerably surprised to discover that he was the inmate of a carriage, and that opposite to him sat a stout, bull-necked gentleman, with coarse features and closely-cropped hair, whose general aspect was most unmistakably that of the thief-taking tribe.

The officer nodded and winked in a most affable and condescending manner when he saw his prisoner open his eyes.

"You see it's all right, captain ; got you safe enough at last," he said.

"How the devil is this? How came I here?" exclaimed the highwayman.

"Ha, ha, ha! Can't make it out, can you? That was a 'cute dodge of yours to get hold of the jewels, though."

Recollection began to return slowly to the bewildered brain of the highwayman.

"Ah ! but how came I here?"

"Pistol bullet knocked you out of your saddle. I thought it was all up with you for a time."

"My head !" exclaimed Captain Will, raising his hands towards his forehead ; then he dropped them down again in astonishment.

"Ironed ! Handcuffed !"

"Yes, all right. Safe bind, safe find, you know. And you are rather a slippery customer."

"It's impossible for me to get away, weak as I am. But where are the others ?"

"What others? your chaps ?"

"No ; those with you."

"Oh, curse them ! they left me because I wouldn't share the reward. You're worth a lot of money, you know, captain."

"And my comrades ?"

"All got clean away."

"Cowards, for deserting me !"

"No, they ain't ; they fought hard after you were down, but it was no go. Never mind, we'll have one or two of them to keep you company before long. *Your* two prisoners are vowing vengeance against all the lot."

Will Merry leaned back in the corner of the carriage and heaved a deep sigh.

It seemed as though his career had almost come to its conclusion, for he was alone, a prisoner, and severely wounded.

Ugly visions of the last act of life's drama began to float through his brain—the condemned cell, the road to Tyburn, and the fatal tree.

Luckily, exhausted, weakened nature befriended him, and, by a kindly fainting fit, relieved him from the horrors of imagination.

The officer, Mr. Scott by name, looked upon the prisoner with an air of deep concern and compassion, and directed the post-boy to halt at the first house they came to.

This happened to be an inn at the commencement of a populous town, and the worthy catchpole's heart rejoiced at the sight of the sign-board swinging over the door.

"Bring brandy, quickly !" he shouted, as they approached the house. "Brandy, or there'll be a life lost !"

Not that Mr. Scott had any particular wish that Captain Will Merry should live to rival old Parr ; but he certainly did wish to prolong the highwayman's days till he could be formally tried and convicted.

The reward for a dead highwayman, as before stated, was not so large as that offered for the living offender ; and Mr. Scott of Bow Street was by no means free from the love of filthy lucre.

The appearance of the post-chaise, together with the Bow Street runner's hasty words, soon collected a little crowd, consisting of all the village gossips and idlers, before the door of the "Rose and Crown."

"Is any one ill ?" exclaimed a respectably-dressed man, pushing his way forward.

"Yes," replied the officer, briefly.

"I am a surgeon," continued the stranger ; "perhaps I can be of service."

"You may, perhaps," said Scott ; "but what is your name, and where do you live ?"

The surgeon gave the required information, and appealed to the landlord of the inn to corroborate his words.

"You see I am obliged to look sharp and keep my eyes open," continued Scott, "because the pals of these chaps are always up to all kinds of dodges to rescue our prisoners. However, you can just see what is the matter with him."

The surgeon stepped into the vehicle, and quickly examined Will Merry's wounds.

He slowly shook his head, and looked at the officer with a grave face.

"He can't last half an hour if you keep him shut up in that shaking, jolting carriage."

The constable's countenance fell at this intelligence.

"Is he dangerously wounded, then ?"

"So badly that it would be murder to take him on another mile."

"It must be done, though ; he's a prisoner, and I dare not let him remain in any private house. He must go to gaol."

"Then he'll go as a corpse, unless, indeed, you put him in our lock-up."

"What sort of a place is it ?"

"Why, strong enough to hold half a dozen able-bodied burglars, to say nothing of this poor dying fellow."

"And whereabouts is it ?"

"Up in the market-place."

"Well, if you're a doctor, you may as well just come with me. I shouldn't like the fellow to die."

The last words were spoken with earnestness, and in good faith, for reasons with which the reader is already acquainted.

In a very short space of time the carriage containing the Bow Street runner, the highwayman and the surgeon arrived at the lock-up, or cage, in which Mr. Scott proposed to incarcerate his prisoner till such time as the latter might be removed to Newgate without danger of dying by the way.

"By-the-bye," said the surgeon, "who is to pay my bill for this case?"

The officer rubbed his chin thoughtfully, and gazed upwards at the roof of the coach.

"Well, it ought to be a county job; but, however, I'll settle it, and then send in my claim to the authorities," replied he, after a short reflection.

"That's right; I don't like anything to do with those big wigs. They always have some excuse for keeping a fellow waiting."

"I shall have to leave this chap in the hands of the parish authorities for a few days while I go and look after other business, so I may as well give you a trifle on account," continued the officer.

The worthy surgeon expressed himself perfectly satisfied with such an arrangement, and quietly pocketed the two guineas which Scott slid into his hand."

"But you must keep your eye on him, and see that your constable or turnkey doesn't let him get out," resumed he of Bow Street.

"All right, I'll take care of him, though he'd be perfectly safe if the door was left open. But the cell must be made a little bit comfortable; we must have a comfortable bed for our patient."

This article of comfort was soon procured, and the wounded highwayman laid thereon.

"Off with the handcuffs," continued the doctor.

"Couldn't think of it," replied Scott.

"Then its no use trying to cure the poor man."

"Why not?"

"Because he has two ribs smashed by falling, and they'll never heal while his arm is laid across them in that style."

After some hesitation Mr. Scott consented to remove the manacles, and then departed in pursuit of the other members of the band of highwaymen, all of whom he swore to bring to justice. He gave the turnkey, who had charge of the lock-up, to understand that if the prisoner escaped, he (the turnkey) would most certainly be substituted as a victim for the gallows, and the worthy country constable, knowing very little of law, fully believed the official words of the Bow Street gentleman.

A few minutes after Scott had departed Will Merry opened his eyes and looked around.

It required but a brief glance to assure him that he was in some kind of prison; the narrow windows with iron bars, the iron-bound door, with its ponderous lock, all told the tale.

The face of the surgeon, who was bending over him, seemed familiar, though the wounded highwayman could not recollect where he had seen it before.

"I think I shall have to cut this arm off," said the surgeon, addressing the turnkey, who was very intently watching his manipulations of the prisoner's limbs.

The gaoler shuddered at the thought.

"Just send your little girl to fetch my instruments," continued the doctor.

The turnkey turned away muttering something about barbarity.

"You'd better leave my arm alone," said Will Merry, speaking for the first time, "or you'll find it's strong enough to knock you down."

"Hush! you don't——"

What the surgeon would have said the highwayman was compelled to guess, for the re-appearance of the turnkey completely stopped the speech.

Then turning up the wounded man's shirt-sleeve the medical man pinched it in various places, felt the bone between his finger and thumb, and then pulled a long face.

Strange to say, in several places where the doctor's fingers had touched they left a discolouration on the skin.

The gaoler's daughter returned with a leather case, which the surgeon forthwith opened, and arranged on the floor by the patient's bedside.

"In ten minutes I shall know whether it is necessary to amputate or no," said he, assuming a look of scientific importance, and taking the highwayman's wrist between his finger and thumb.

The time passed, and then, after another examination of the arm the doctor again spoke.

"Bring me a large jug of cold water, and a basin, will you, Lockerby?"

The officer departed to obey the surgeon's directions, and while he was absent the doctor replaced his knives and saws in the black leather case.

Not all of them, however, for one long thin saw with fine file-like teeth, having received an accidental touch of his foot, remained beneath the patient's bed.

When the turnkey returned to the cell the doctor bathed the wound on Will Merry's head, applied a plaster, and left saying that he would send up some medicine, and call again in the morning.

"Would you like anything to eat, master?" asked the turnkey.

Will was beginning to revive; now that the blood had ceased flowing and the motion of the carriage had ceased, he felt rather faint and very hungry.

"Yes, I should like a beef-steak, and some wine," replied he.

The man left the cell, promising it should be brought.

"I wonder what that fellow meant by pulling my arm about and talking of cutting it off," thought Will, as he laid on his back. "I feel certain that I have seen that fellow before, though I can't recollect where."

In vain he ransacked his brain to no purpose—the surgeon's face was a mystery he could not solve.

Shortly afterwards the turnkey re-appeared, with the steak on a plate and a bottle of wine. A fork only was given the prisoner to eat his food with—the man giving as a reason the fact that Captain Will's arm was broken in two places, and that therefore a knife would be useless.

"Who told you that?" asked the prisoner.

"The doctor."

Captain Will felt inclined to intimate in decided language that the doctor was far from the truth, but suddenly, as he recollected various circumstances, he resolved to hold his tongue.

The doctor had insisted upon the removal of the handcuffs; the doctor had commenced saying something, and then had suddenly ceased at the appearance of the turnkey; and finally, the doctor had persuaded that official that his prisoner's arm was broken, when in fact it was well and sound as ever, barring weakness from loss of blood, and a trifling contusion on the elbow caused by falling from the saddle.

If the doctor was not mad he had some reason for so doing; and if he were mad, why then Captain Will resolved to make use of him in a plan which he was not long in devising.

When he had finished eating his supper the turnkey once more appeared.

He cleared the rude table which he placed upon the prisoner's bed, and placed upon it a lamp.

"The doctor said as how you were to have a light burning all night."

"I am glad of that, for I might be taken worse you know," replied Will, gravely, at the same time wondering what the doctor was thinking about.

"You might; but here's your physic, I haven't opened the paper, but you can do that. Good night, I shan't disturb you very early in the morning."

So saying, the gaoler left the cell, and carefully locked the door upon the prisoner.

As soon as he was gone, Captain Will sat up on his bed, and had a good look round his cell.

It was about ten feet square, and as many high, and, during the day, received light from two narrow windows, through one of which it struck the prisoner he *might* be able to squeeze himself if he could remove the iron bar which divided it in two parts.

He leaped from his couch, and at once tried all his strength upon the rusty metal, but it would not yield a hair's breadth to his most violent efforts.

The door he knew was of two-inch oak planks, clamped with iron, and fastened by a huge lock, so that it would not be the slightest use attempting to break through it.

The window was his only chance.

"After all, I don't know why I should remain here," he

muttered, gazing with an air of defiance at the iron bars. "That Bow Street fellow has gone, and it would be very strange indeed if I could not out-wit the country bumpkin he has left in charge of me. The doctor, too, seems a friend ——"

As he uttered the last words his eye fell upon the packet which the unsuspicious gaoler had placed upon the table.

He unrolled it, and discovered a phial and a pill-box.

On the top of the latter article was written—

"One to be taken occasionally."

"They seem very heavy pills," thought the highwayman; "let's see what they are like."

He opened the box, looked, rubbed his eyes, and looked again.

There lay in the little receptacle for pills ten bright guineas.

"Good Heavens ! What does all this mean ? Am I dreaming, or have my senses entirely left me ?"

He rubbed the guineas with his hand, sounded them upon the table, and, at length, managed to convince himself that they were real.

"Now for the draught ; that can't be liquid gold."

The label on the phial bore this inscription—

"To be applied immediately."

The cork was carefully covered over with a piece of white leather, and upon removing it some letters were visible—

"Aquafortis."

"Now, by all that's good in this evil world, I swear I'll never speak evil of a doctor again. Who on earth can this man be who aids me to escape in this style ? Ha, ha ! my friend from Bow Street, I fancy it will be some time ere you finger the reward for the apprehension of Will Merry."

The bar, which before had seemed almost too much for any human being, was now looked upon as a mere trifle.

"I'll dress myself, and then set to work with a good heart."

He looked round for his clothes, and discovered that they had been thrust beneath the bed.

He drew them forth, and along with them the file saw which the surgeon had accidentally (?) left behind him.

"Better and better. This sawbones must be a real gentleman ; if he isn't I'll soon make him one. Why, this is one of the most splendid house-breaking implements that ever a man handled ; it will cut through the iron as easily as through my arm."

He was about to commence operations with his file and aquafortis, when he heard a noise outside his door, and then he recollected that it was yet early, and that in all probability the gaoler had not retired to bed.

"Confound him for a dissipated rascal, what does he mean by sitting up till this time at night ?" muttered the impatient highwayman, as he ensconced himself in bed with his clothes on.

At length, however, the noise ceased, the fumes of the gaoler's pipe died away, and Captain Will Merry set himself seriously to the task of escaping from the lock-up.

Nor was it a very serious task.

With the file he soon made a deep cut in the iron bar, and, aided by the strong chemical, was enabled to remove the iron bar, and thrust his shoulders through the window.

How delicious the night breeze seemed as it fanned his cheeks and brow ; how calm and peaceful every thing seemed in the faint moonlight.

Not even a mouse seemed stirring.

Captain Will emptied his bottle of wine, thrust the file into his pocket, and cautiously crept through the open window.

Not knowing which path to take, he walked onwards at random, taking care to keep the darkest side of the street, so as to escape observation.

But there was little fear of his being observed, for not a being did he see, nor a voice did he hear till he reached the "Rose and Crown."

Then the head ostler was heard bullying his subordinates, and bidding them look alive.

"The coach will be here in a quarter of an hour, and them 'osses nothing like ready yet—lazy dogs."

The word coach fell with a strange sound upon Will Merry's ear.

Had he possessed anything like a steed or a weapon, he would have undertaken the task of stopping it with the greatest of pleasure. But he was on foot, and totally unarmed.

"Hang it all, I wonder which road it comes, and where is it going ?" thought he, as he took up his stand in a narrow passage nearly opposite the inn, resolved to wait till the coach had passed.

"No ; I'll be a passenger for once in my life," he muttered. "What fun if any of our people should chance to be out and find me inside."

As he spoke the coach could be heard in the distance, and Will Merry walked away, not wishing to be seen by any of the people about the inn.

One little bit of conversation he heard comforted him greatly. A voice shouted out—

"Any passengers for the London coach ?"

"No," was the reply ; "and only one parcel."

No one who saw him enter the village a wounded prisoner would see him depart with the air of an invalid gentleman.

By the time the coach had reached the inn door, Captain Will was on the high road, half a mile off.

He then halted and resolved to wait for the vehicle.

"It will look suspicious though," thought he ; "they might ask, and with good reason, too, why I did not wait at the inn. I must have a good tale ready, in case any questions are asked."

So after a few minutes' reflection he hit upon a tale which he fancied would not only avert suspicion, but enlist the sympathy of the passengers in his behalf.

As the coach drew near he threw himself on the ground, and began to crawl along on hands and knees feebly shouting for help.

As he expected, the driver of the vehicle checked his horses, and the guard dismounting inquired what was the matter.

"Oh ! help ! help !" replied Will.

"How can we help you ?"

"Lift me up. My legs are weak."

They lifted him to his feet in a second, and again asked what ailed him ?"

"I have been set upon by robbers and beaten."

"Robbers !" screamed a female voice, from the interior of the coach.

"Aye ; two ruffians."

"Which way did they go ?" asked the guard.

"Towards the town."

"Did they take anything from you ?"

"Yes ; they took my purse ; but when I saw them coming I took the precaution to hide ten guineas in my boot, so that they did not get everything."

"How long ago was that ?"

"About twenty minutes or half an hour," replied Will Merry.

"I say, Bob," cried the coachman, "Dick, up at the 'Rose and Crown,' said he heard somebody go along while he was harnessing the horses."

"Aye, that were them, no doubt," replied Bob.

"But have you got room for an inside passenger ?" asked the highwayman. "I was going to the 'Rose and Crown' to take a seat when these villains stopped me."

"Yes, room for three. We're licensed to carry six inside."

"Then I'll take the three seats, for I like to have plenty of room."

"Just as you like, sir. How far are you going ?"

"To London."

The guard nodded his head.

"What kind of people are they inside ?" asked Will.

"Stout old lady and gent, and a werry pretty-looking girl as they tries to tease and bother every way they know how."

"All right, then, open the door."

As the guard obeyed this order he thrust a large loaded pistol into Captain Will's hand, saying,

"The old cock inside is a regular old coward, and won't have nothing to do with fire-arms for fear of shooting his blessed self. Will you just take this 'ere pistol, and blaze away if anybody tries to stop us ?"

(To be continued.)

THE YEW OF CROISSEY.

(Concluded from page 136).

"Here is a letter for *you*, ma'amselle," he continued, placing another packet on the table.

"Soldier," asked Eugene, "will you not take a glass of wine?" and he overwhelmed the sergeant with questions concerning his mysterious release from military service.

Louise was so overjoyed that she chattered almost at random, kept embracing Eugene, and kissing his sister.

"But the wine," inquired the soldier, "where is it?"

Poor Louise was so bewildered that she ran round the room, but could not for a long time see the cupboard.

When she found it she brought glasses and no wine, then carried the wine to the table, and took it away again; in short the poor girl seemed to have lost her wits in excess of joy.

"Ha! ha!" exclaimed the soldier, showing his white teeth under his black moustachios, "your other sister seems——"

"Pardon," said Eugene, "she is my—my——"

"Ha! ha! your comrade for life that is to be, eh, boy? Well, well, I do not wonder at her being glad that you do not march with us, for women have no notion of military glory. Your health, *ma belle!* Yours, ma'amselle!"

The sergeant was about to drink, but when his eyes fell upon the form of Christine, the glass remained in his hand untasted.

The girl stood with the letter rumpled in her hand, pale and trembling, intently gazing upon the table, a picture of mute astonishment.

"For Heaven's sake, Christine," exclaimed her brother, "what is the matter? Ah, that letter! let us see it! Who has dared to agitate you thus?"

And he hastily took the letter, and scanned its contents.

"Oh, read aloud!" said Christine, making a desperate effort to recover her gaiety. "It is from some unknown beau who has taken me at my word. Holy mother! my prayers for dear, dear Eugene, have been heard!"

The freed conscript read as follows:—

"MADEMOISELLE,—I exact nothing; I depart unconditionally; I have become your brother's substitute. Your situation requires he should remain at home; there is no one upon earth who has need of me, and I have no home at which to remain. I love you—deeply, devotedly. Your tears have engraven an everlasting affection upon my heart. I send you a ring which belonged to my mother; if you have any compassion for me send me the golden cross which hung this evening on your neck. Suspend it in one of the crevices of the great yew; to-morrow morning I will fetch it. Expect me in two years; if the campaign leaves me alive, I will return with your cross. Remember your oath solemnly made upon the cross of gold! Adieu!"

"What is the meaning of all this?" cried Eugene, bewildered with astonishment. "How came this letter-writer to know about Christine's vow? Can you explain, sergeant?"

"All I know is that you are exempted," replied the grenadier.

"But why has he not presented himself in person?" inquired Eugene.

"Oh," answered the sergeant, "I think it is easy to account for that. It is quite evident that your friend, the voluntary conscript, must have overheard the vow Ma'amselle Christine seems to have made, and, as ambuscading is sometimes against the articles of war, he was in doubt as to what sort of a reception he may have met with."

"Soldier," exclaimed Eugene, after some consideration, "my mind is made up; my sister shall not be sacrificed for my sake! I am ready to join the regiment; let us go."

Eugene moved towards the door with great precipitation, but his sister stopped him.

"You shall not leave us!" she exclaimed; "my unknown lover has done well. Who but a brave and honourable person would have acted as he has? I *will* carry my cross to the yew-tree. Pray, sergeant, have you seen him?" continued the maiden, vivaciously.

"For a moment," was the answer.

"He is not very ugly, or—or—hump-backed, is he?"

"Hump-backed!" repeated the soldier, indignantly. "I would have you to know, ma'amselle, that the imperial army is not composed of the 'ugly' or the 'hump-backed,' but boasts of individuals without blemish or reproach, either physical or moral."

The last word was accompanied with an oath, to give it force.

"It is well, Monsieur Soldat," said Christine, removing from her pretty neck the black ribbon to which the cross was suspended; "tell the generous stranger that I have, and will continue to preserve my oath most religiously. Take this cross, and, on your way to quarters, put it in the crevice of the great yew. Be his companion, his friend; do not leave him, so that when you both return you may be able to say, 'All is well; he has been worthy of my care; he is an honourable man, and has become a brave soldier.'"

Eugene and Louise looked at her without being able to speak.

The grenadier took off his cap, received the cross, and, dashing away a tear, could only say,

"Enough!"

Christine turned to her brother and future sister, and, looking towards heaven, said, in the deep tones of irrevocable determination,

"I am affianced! My gage is in the hands of a soldier of the guard!"

The next morning I found the golden cross in the crevice of the yew, and thought I observed among the branches of a neighbouring thicket the uniform and red epaulettes of a sergeant by whom I was probably watched.

A year after, the campaign of Saxony ended, and that of France began. Eugene was married to Louise. The terrible requisition of 1813 reached him, with every one in ten who were fit for service; but this time he escaped. The whole nation foresaw that one determined blow would be decisive; and even the pupils of the various colleges armed themselves, and marched to the frontiers. All, whom health and circumstances permitted, hastened to join the emperor; among others, Eugene left his wife and sister for the army.

During this short war, the bridge of Monterau was, for a long time, most obstinately contested. Eugene fought with bravery, and, at one time, having expended all his ammunition was obliged to defend himself with his small infantry-sabre against five grenadiers; but a lieutenant of carabineers galloped forward to his assistance, crying,

"Conscript! go back to your sister and wife! Leave death to those who have neither kith nor kin!"

And the officer rushed upon the whitecoats, and cut two of the down, but his horse received a bayonet-wound, and fell. A french fusillade struck the three remaining adversaries, and Eugene, having fallen also, was carried with the lieutenant to a neighbouring cottage, where both were partially recovered.

Eugene could not account for the disinterested devotion of his companion, neither could he comprehend the words by which it was accompanied. The soldier was sorely puzzled to know how he could possibly pay the debt of gratitude he owed. At length, when the forces were about to be disbanded, Eugene said to the officer, who had become his friend and brother-in-arms,

"My lieutenant! you say you have no kindred, no domestic ties—that you are alone. Come and live with me; though I am but a young husbandman, I have a pretty wife, and a sister not very ill-looking. You will not disdain my offer the more for them, as they shall do everything to make you happy; nay, do not refuse. Remain with us until you are tired—at all events, until your country has again need of your service."

The officer was unable to resist the homely and sincere gratitude of the conscript, and thanked him with fervency. Eight days after Eugene returned in the arms of Louise and and Christine, to whom he presented Monsieur Charles, his deliverer.

"Behold," said he, "a brave man, who preserved my life at

the risk of his own, who, having no sister, no wife to lament his loss, has saved you the tears you would, but for him, have shed over my grave. He has said he will not disdain our humble home, which in future shall be his. One day, perhaps, our circumstances may improve, when our house shall be made more worthy the residence of a lieutenant !"

"A lieutenant !" exclaimed Christine.

"Yes," answered Eugene, "and, although so much my superior in rank, scorned not to become my brother-in-arms. A day might arrive," he continued, casting a sly glance at his sister, "when I shall have to regard him as my brother in reality."

Christine blushed, and as her glances fell to the ground they stole in their descent a furtive look at the defendant. Alas! I fear he was not the most ill-looking man in his regiment, and his epaulettes—the wounds he had received in defending her much-loved brother, added to a design he had previously formed of making himself excessively agreeable—lost not their effect on the handsome peasant, who, at the end of two months, was unable to withstand his expressive looks withot emotion. Her manner became reserved—her remarks were less frequent and *piquant* than formerly. Eugene marked this change in his sister with secret satisfaction; he attributed it to her increasing admiration for his guest.

One evening Charles and Christine were walking in the garden, when Eugene suddenly came behind them, and withdrawing his sister's arm from Charles's support, drew it under his own, and, taking his preserver's arm, said, with a vivacity somewhat abrupt,

"Charles, do you love my sister?"

Although the lieutenant was not a little confounded, he did not fail to reply, with energy,

"With all my soul !"

Christine trembled violently.

The inexorable Eugene hardly gave time for Charles's answer, ere he turned to his sister, saying,

"Christine, do you love Charles?"

The artless girl struggled desperately to overcome her agitation.

"Love him?" said she. "Of course I do. Did he not save you from——"

"Yes, yes," interrupted the impatient brother; "but that is not what I mean. I want to know whether you—that is to say, if you are in—a—or—you know what I mean well enough. Do not you think she does, Charles?"

"*I* understand what you would say," answered the soldier, with some embarrassment, "though I dare not express it."

"In one word," repeated Eugene, "do you love him?"

"I do," answered the maiden, and the next moment she was folded in my arms.

Yes, sir, in *my* arms; for in me you behold the Lieutenant Charles, who, rather than compel the affections of her whom I had loved from the time of my adventure in the branches of this tree, determined to gain her heart voluntarily, and without constraint. This blessing I had attained, and leave you to judge of my happiness. But it was decreed that my joy should be interrupted.

"This is well! excellent!" continued Eugene, gleefully; "the wedding I have so long wished for will take place, and Charles will be my brother, after all."

"Never !" exclaimed Christine, sorrowfully, but firmly.

"Never? How do you make that out?" asked her brother.

"I am," she answered, "promised to another—affianced !"

"What folly is this?" cried Eugene. "Why, it is not common sense! What! marry a man you have never seen? who is, possibly, ugly, old, and poor; a man who is ashamed to own himself. Besides, by this time he is, very likely, dead."

"Dead, Eugene, to preserve your life! Oh, my brother! can you ungratefully forget you owe him a debt, of which *I* am the price? My oath is binding, and I will keep it religiously. If he be dead my cross will come back to me without him, and I shall mourn for him as for a husband. If he be alive I will wait his return."

"But the two years agreed upon have not yet elapsed?"

"And even had they passed, I would not break my oath.

Suppose he should return poor, wounded, and without a home? Oh, no! no! I cannot be false to him. But when he does come, if without regret or hesitation he will release me from my oath, then, and not till then, shall I be free."

Eugene began to be angry, but I interrupted him.

"Christine," said I, "it is time you should know all. *I* am the person to whom you are affianced. I overheard the parting of Eugene with yourself and Louise, while concealed in the great yew. I enlisted instead of your brother, and here, on my knees, I claim my mother's ring, and my own—my own Christine."

"You?" cried both brother and sister, in amazement.

Christine took the ring and letter, in which it was wrapped, from her bosom, and was about to give it to me, when suddenly she stopped.

"But the cross of gold—where is it?"

"Oh," said I, "believing at the battle of Leipsic I could not survive, I parted with it."

"Brother," said Christine, thoughtfully, "I see it all. You would deceive me; you have told Monsieur Charles the secret of my oath, that there might be no obstacle to our union."

"What !" I ejaculated, "does my dear Christine refuse to believe the word of a man of honour—a soldier?"

"But the cross! the cross!" she repeated.

"That I gave to an old sergeant of the guard, on the field of Leipsic."

"Where is he?"

"Killed," I answered.

"Thunder and bombs !" cried a voice behind us, "killed, eh? Not a bit of it! I have enough life left, you see, to hobble here. Ah, my lieutenant, is that you?"

"Why, how did you come to life again?" I exclaimed, receiving the sergeant in my arms.

"Oh, I had the luck to be conveyed to the hospital at Leipsic, where they have taken all this time to patch me up—*sacre bleu!* But, enough; we will speak of that presently. Ma'am'selle Christine, your most obedient! I am the sergeant who brought you the letter and wring, and here—here is the gentleman who sent them, of whom I am enabled to say what you wished me—that he is as brave a soldier as he is an honourable man. Witness his rapid promotion, which his superior education and unflinching courage procured him. At Dresden he was made sub-lieutenant; at Liepsic he often went into the thickest of the fight, as if he had been going to a dance. There was a desperate struggle to gain the bridge, and enter the barracks. Monsieur Charles fought like a lion; but his valour did not prevent a white-coated villain from wounding him. He fell by my side. 'Sergeant,' said he, 'I have a *gage d'amour*—the cross—carry it to Croissey. If I recover I will return without it, and, if possible, gain the affections of Christine without imposing the constraint of her oath.' We were now separated, and the dogs of Austrians afterwards left me for dead on the field. Some good comrade, however, took pity on me, and I was taken to the hospital, where I remained for eleven months, and they so physicked and plastered my poor old carcass, that 'twas a miracle I escaped the death our enemies intended for me; and here I am ready to perform the promise I made on the bridge at Leipsic, and doubly happy to find my lieutenant here before me."

"Can you believe me now, Christine?" I asked.

"Oh, pardon me !" she exclaimed, as we embraced, "pardon me for doubting your fidelity."

"But the cross! the cross!" shouted Eugene, mimicking his sister's voice.

"Is here !" said the sergeant.

Christine took it in a transport, and, pressing it to her lips, whispered to me,

"We are now affianced for ever."

We were, sir, soon married, and all the happiness I anticipated has been mine.

The sergeant, poor fellow, was killed at Waterloo.

Eugene and I have prospered in the world, for, although a lieutenant in the imperial army, I have not been too proud to turn my sword into a ploughshare.

We live in that little white house which you see among the trees yonder; and every evening I come and smoke my pipe under THE YEW OF CROISSEY.

BLACK HAWKE, THE HIGHWAYMAN.

THE DUKE OF CLEVELAND.

No offer could have been more acceptible to Captain Will, though he was cautious not to betray the joy he felt at once more having a weapon in his hand.

If molested by the dragoons he would, at all events, have a chance of defending himself.

He jumped into the coach quite briskly, and the coachman having cracked his whip, the vehicle was again in rapid motion.

CHAPTER XLII.

WHEN Albert Montague had finished the relation of his adventures with Sir Andrew Greville, Merlin approached the door expecting to see his men returning bringing with them the baronet as a prisoner.

As he did so the shot was fired which deprived old Badger of his life.

"Ah, my brave fellows have found him, though it seems as if he is capable of making some resistance still," murmured the chief.

"What shall we do with this fellow, captain?" asked one of the men, pointing to the prostrate, senseless form of Sir Thomas Brooke.

"Bring him hither. Restore him to consiousness if you can ; but guard him well."

The men dragged the lord of Albion Manor into the midst of the apartment with as little ceremony as though he had been a brute beast.

"Why, what's this he has in his pocket?" said one of them.

"Search him," said Merlin.

The man obeyed the command.

"What's in this bottle?" asked the first.

"It looks like brandy," was the reply.

At that moment the prisoner opened his eyes and heaved a deep sigh.

"Where is the brandy? Give me some," said he.

The men looked towards their chief to know his will, and Merlin made a gesture of assent.

The bottle was uncorked, and the neck of it placed to his lips.

The wretched man drank eagerly, and would have swallowed the whole of the liquor had it not been forcibly taken from him.

In another moment he began to fill the air with piercing shrieks.

"Water, water, for Heaven's sake! Curses on your souls, it is poison!"

"Poison?" ejaculated the man who held the bottle, dropping it in his excitement.

"Aye, poison! It burns me! it gnaws at my heart! I am on fire!—the fires of hell!—water! water!"

A large bowl of the crystal fluid was given him, and the wretched sufferer drained it to the bottom.

But the draught, instead of allaying his pain, seemed only to aggravate it.

He moaned, and cursed, and writhed about; his limbs and features undergoing the most fearful contortions.

"Hell's curses on your heads, all of you! paltry, cowardly murderers that you are! Where is that boy? Let me strangle him before I die!" he shrieked, while large drops of foam fell from his blackened lips to the floor.

At that moment Albert Montague and the Duke of Cleveland returned to the apartment.

The sight rendered the poisoned man mad with fury.

He sprang towards the son of his murdered kinsman, and, in all probability, would have done the young man some serious injury had he not been seized and bound.

Such was the strength which frenzy imparted to his limbs that it required the utmost efforts of four strong men to secure his arms and prevent him from doing mischief to himself or others.

He kicked, struggled, and snapped with his teeth like a rabid dog, all the while howling and yelling the most awful curses and imprecations.

"Lord Montague died in a ditch with a gash across his throat; his son, the highwayman, shall perish on the scaffold to the delight of a crowd of ruffians! and may the hotest flames of hell scorch him! Keep that murdered man away! I did not kill him! Ha! ha! ha! he's gone now—I can the fiend?"

Thus raved the delirious Sir Thomas Brooke, striking awe defy into the bosoms of all those who heard his words.

Presently his eyes fell upon the Duke of Cleveland.

"What, my worthy father-in-law that should have been, here! And where is the bride—where is the sweet Lady Jane?"

"Ruffian, villain, you shall never set eyes on her again!" exclaimed the peer.

"Ha, ha! then my dream is true. She is to be the bride of this foundling—this highwayman, who claims the titles and estate of Montague! May you be happy, fair young sir, with your wife—your *chaste* wife—who scrupled not to pay a midnight visit to Albion Hall *alone!*"

"Accursed scoundrel!" cried Albert, unsheathing his sword, "your worthless life shall repay this infamous libel."

"Hold!" cried Merlin, again arresting Albert's arm, "the rascal is not worthy of your sword. Let the poison work its course, for nothing on earth can save him; his death is close at hand."

"Death! Where is death? I dare not face the ghastly king of terrors. Save me! save me! for even now I feel his keen arrows entering my heart."

"This is fearful!" muttered the Duke of Cleveland. "Is there no clergyman near at hand whose prayers might lead this wretched man to penitence, and sooth his dying moments?"

"There is," exclaimed a voice, and a venerable man, clothed in a clerical garb, appeared in the midst of the group.

Albert Montague at once recognised him as the priest whom he had saved from the two robbers.

"Hasten to relieve his sin-burdened conscience," continued the duke. "His curses are fearful when he is so near death."

"The prayers of all the blessed saints in Heaven would be powerless to save his guilty soul," replied the priest, crossing himself. "He is beyond hope of redemption."

"May your lying tongue rot in your mouth, false, lying priest! What do you know about the soul of man? Where is the hell of which you speak? It is here! here! here!"

"Pray Heaven his sufferings may be short," murmured the duke.

"Pray the devil your torments may be everlasting!" roared the wretched dying sinner, who had overheard the words.

At this moment there was a noise heard without, and the men who had been ordered to pursue and capture Sir Andrew Greville entered the apartment, dragging their prisoner with them.

The husband of Lady Florence was pale as death, and blood streamed down his face from a wound on his head.

The sight caused Sir Thomas Brooke to redouble his yells and curses.

"Keep him off! Keep him off! *He is come for the paper,* but he shall not have it. Why should my crimes be brought to light, and he be enabled to destroy the evidence of his misdeeds? Keep him off! Don't let him touch my breast pocket."

No sooner did Sir Andrew Greville hear these words, than, with a sudden bound, he burst from his captors and sprang towards the prostrate form of Sir Thomas Brooke.

The latter managed to free one hand from the cords that bound him and grappled his antagonist with a more than maniac fury.

The object of Sir Andrew Greville was evidently to force his hand into the pocket spoken of by Sir Thomas, as though he expected to discover the paper.

"Help! help! help!" shrieked Sir Andrew, suddenly; "he is killing me—he has his teeth in my throat!"

These awful words were perfectly true.

The madman had fixed upon the neck of Lady Florence's husband with all the tenacity of a bull-dog, nor could the united strength of all present cause him to relax his grip.

Blows were struck on his head by the bystanders, but the madman took not the slightest heed of them.

Sir Andrew, in his fearful struggles to free himself, totally forgot the object for which he first attacked the maniac.

"He is dead at last," said the priest, as Sir Thomas Brooke lay motionless.

CHAPTER XLIII.

AN UNEXPECTED MEETING AND ITS RESULT.

THE coach in which Captain Will Merry departed from the scene of his temporary incarceration was emphatically a fast one; not one of those crawling stages, whose utmost speed never exceeded eight miles an hour, but one of the rattling mail coaches, the drivers of which were as smart and thoroughbred as the animals whose fiery energies they controlled.

Will gave a long, inquisitive stare at the fat lady and gentleman, hardly knowing whether to set them down as quakers out for a spree, or provincial tradespeople taking a business trip to London.

At all events they looked comfortable and well-to-do in the world, so Will resolved to recruit his own finances at their expense.

He then turned his gaze towards the young lady, not, however, with any idea of depriving her of anything she might possess, but with the intention of amusing himself with a little quiet flirtation while he carried out his designs against the stout people.

"You are travelling by yourself, madam?" said he, interrogatively.

"I am, sir," replied the young lady, breathing a deep sigh.

The blood thrilled in Will Merry's veins, so familiar did that voice seem to him.

But weak and confused as he was from the effects of his wound, he could not recall to mind where, when, or under what circumstances he had heard those silvery accents.

"Humph! I told you so, Joshua," said the stout female, shaking her husband's arm.

A low, hog-like grunt was the only response Joshua Wilson, draper and hosier, vouchsafed to his wife's remark.

"From your manner I should fancy that this journey is

not one of pleasure so far as you are concerned?" continued Captain Will, taking no heed of the interruption.

"It is not, indeed, sir."

"Pardon me, madam, but is it possible that we can have met before? Your voice seems strangely familiar."

"We have met before, Captain Delmore."

Will Merry started.

"Then you are ——"

The youthful stranger slowly raised her veil, revealing her beautiful features to the gaze of Captain Merry *alias* Delmore.

"Good heavens! Lady Ellen Curtis!"

"The same."

Captain Will leaned over, and passing his arm round her waist printed a warm kiss upon her lips.

"Humph! didn't I tell you so, Joshua? Them as travels alone are never no better than they ought to be," moaned Mrs. Joshua Wilson.

"Do you intend that remark to apply to this young lady?" demanded Captain Will, while his eyes sparkled with anger.

"Humph!"

"Because, if so, I shall thank you to retract your words and apologise instantly."

"Yah! would you strike a lady?" screamed Mrs. Joshua, who perceived that her travelling companion was in a fearful passion.

"You great, fat, female fool!—excuse me, dear Ellen, for using such language—I never strike women! But if you insult this young lady, I shall be compelled to have a very serious quarrel with your husband."

"Now, then, Jemima, you're always a getting me into a bother," said Mr. Joshua Wilson, speaking up for his own safety. "What did you say anything to the young lady for, when you knowed well enough there was one o' them milingtary gents along with her. I'm blowed if I'm a going to be massacreed just 'cause you likes to find fault with every body except yourself."

"You ugly, good-for-nothing wretch! Why, didn't I see you a winking at the young woman yourself?" screamed Mrs. Wilson, at the same time showering down blow after blow upon her husband's face and neck.

The good man in vain endeavoured to avoid the tempest of words and blows, but without any good results.

Mrs. Wilson continued the castigation till she was compelled to cease from lack of breath.

While this matrimonial war was raging, Captain Will, keeping one arm round the waist of his lady-love, quietly inserted his disengaged hand into the pocket of the enraged matron.

After wandering about the immense pouch for some seconds, he managed to extract from thence a purse, which, from its weight, he judged to be of value.

This he transferred to a hole in the cushion of the seat, not doubting that the old lady would discover her loss ere they reached the end of their journey.

He then turned his attention to Mr. Joshua Wilson, whom he took by the throat.

"Sir, is this true that I hear? Had you the insolence and presumption to make overtures to this lady?"

"No, no, no!—it's—oh! don't choke me—it's—oh! murder! It's all her lies! Oh! let me go, sir, and I'll never do it any more!"

Captain Will having extracted a bulky memorandum-book from the pocket of the draper, released his victim, saying,

"I feel inclined to believe you, sir, but let me caution you against committing any impropriety of that kind."

At this moment the coach stopped.

"Hullo! what's the matter here?" cried the guard, opening the door.

"Oh, let me out! let me out!" exclaimed Mr. Joshua Wilson.

"What for?"

"I can't stay along with that she-devil; she'll kill me."

"Well, you can get out if you like."

Mr. Joshua, minus his pocket-book, alighted from the coach with more agility than one would have expected to see in a man of his years and bulk.

"Take my luggage on, guard. I'll call for it at the 'White Horse' cellar."

"All right."

And the guard gave the signal to proceed.

"Stop! stop!" screamed Mrs. Wilson.

"Well, what *is* the matter?"

"Let me out, guard."

"With pleasure, madam; hop down. Depend on it, I am precious glad to get rid of you and your old man."

"I couldn't disgrace myself by riding with *a creature!*" exclaimed the stout party, indicating, by a scornful toss of her head, that she alluded to Lady Ellen Curtis.

Before the happy fat couple had time to change their minds the guard had sprung to his seat, the horses had set off at a sharp trot, and Mr. and Mrs. Wilson were left alone, just as day was beginning to break, in a lonely road, with no possible means of procuring a conveyance, unless they walked on for eight miles, a feat which they were physically incapable of performing.

"Thank Heaven, we have got rid of those snobs," cried Captain Merry, as the coach rolled rapidly onwards.

"They have been tormenting me during the whole of the journey," said Lady Ellen.

"But why, dearest?"

"They said that I must be a—a woman of bad character, or else I should have some one to take care of me."

"So you have, dearest, now."

"And then the man tormented me while his fat wife was asleep by making all kinds of base propositions, and trying to take liberties with me. I was so glad when the coach stopped and you entered."

"But how does it happen that you are travelling alone, darling?"

"You recollect our last interview?"

"Well."

"After that dreadful quarrel my father took me to his country residence, where I remained locked up till last night, he vowing that I should never have my liberty till I had married Lord Belmont. However, last night I managed to procure duplicate keys of all the doors in the house, having bribed the housekeeper to get them for me. When all was quiet I silently stole out, by good fortune, just as the coach was about to pass. I stopped it, and found myself opposite those horrid people who have just left us."

"You were going to London, dearest?"

"I was."

"With what object?"

Lady Ellen Curtis blushed, and hung down her pretty head.

Will Merry pressed the question.

"I had hopes of—of—meeting you there, dearest," she replied, her blushes increasing.

In an instant she was clasped in her lover's arms, and their lips met in a long, loving kiss.

"Then, dearest," said the gallant highwayman, after fondling her till her cheeks were the colour of a peony, "there is at length no obstacle to our union."

"No," she whispered, hiding her face on his shoulder, "unless——"

"Unless what?"

"Unless my father and Lord Belmont should overtake us."

"They must have a large force at their backs even then to separate us."

"But, dearest, you must not injure my father, for though he has behaved harshly I love him."

"I have no desire to quarrel with him, dearest Nell; but no power shall drag you from my arms."

"I will never leave you."

"You shall not, my darling girl. When we reach London a clergyman will quickly be found to unite us so firmly that all the fathers and Belmonts in the universe shall be powerless to sunder us. Ah! Ellen dearest, you little know what a strong and fearless man has been made captive by your bright eyes, beautiful form and warm-loving heart."

"But, dearest," replied Lady Ellen, looking up in her lover's pale but handsome face, "there *must* be some delay. The license and other forms——"

"Can be procured, and the ceremomy finished within an hour after we alight from this vehicle."

Lady Ellen made no objection to this hasty arrangement, and the remainder of the journey passed over in silence only broken by an occasional whisper.

At length the coach stopped near Charing Cross, and the two inside passengers alighted.

Captain Will made his fair companion enter the inn, and partake of some food and wine, in order, as he said, to keep her spirits up to the proper pitch.

During the repast the gallant highwayman intently studied the newspaper, and one scrap of advertisement which seemed to interest him he cut out of the broad sheet and conveyed to his pocket-book.

When the repast was finished he called a hackney coach, in which he placed the fair lady, and ordered the driver to proceed towards the city.

The worthy Jarvey nodded in a knowing manner, and whipped his horses slowly along the Strand, which, in that time differed considerably from the thoroughfare of that name which we of the present time are acquainted with.

They passed through Temple Bar, which was then surmounted by a row of spikes, every one of which bore on its summit a ghastly human head, some merely bleached skulls whitened with long exposure to the sun and wind, others from which flakes of putrid flesh had dropped under the influence of decay, while others were fresh in appearance as though they had not long been severed from the bodies of the unfortunate victims whose crimes they were intended to keep in remembrance.

Many obstructions existed in Fleet Street, such as narrow pavements, open drains, an overturned cart, so that the vehicle was compelled to proceed at a very slow pace.

Lady Ellen Curtis, whose attention had been attracted by a quarrel between two drunken porters, was suddenly startled by a voice at the coach window—

"Do you wish to be married, sir?"

Turning hastily she perceived that the question had been put by a man dressed in black with a white tie, but otherwise of a very uncanonical appearance, having a face spotted with pimples, and a nose whose ruby hue put to shame the blushes on the fair lady's cheek.

Captain Will Merry returned no answer to this point blank question, but drew from his pocket the slip he had cut from the newspaper.

Our readers may as well know the contents of this scrap, which was worded as follows :—

"Marriages with a license, a certificate, and a crown stamp, for one guinea, at the new chapel, next door to the China shop, near the Fleet Bridge, London, by a regular-bred clergyman, and not a Fleet parson, as is insinuated in some of the daily papers ; and, that the town may be freed from mistakes, no clergyman being a prisoner in the Rules of the Fleet, dare marry ; but by a gentleman who was lately chaplain on board one of His Majesty's men-of-war, and likewise has gloriously distinguished himself in defence of king and country, and is above committing the mean actions that some men impose on people, being determined to have every thing conducted with decency and regularity, such as shall be supported in law and equity." *

At this moment a printed card was thrown into the coach.†

G. R.
At the True Chapel,
At the Old Red Hand and Mitre, three doors from Fleet Lane, and next door to the White Swan,
Marriages are performed by Authority, by the Reverend Mr. Symson, of the University of Cambridge,
Late Chaplain to Earl Rothes.
N.B.—No imposition.

"You want a parson, sir? I am clerk and registrar of the Fleet," bawled another seedy man in black.

"Come with me, sir ; that fellow will take you to a peddling ale-house," shouted another.

* Verbatim from "Daily Advertiser," 1749.
† Copied from hand bill in British Museum.

"Go with me, good lady, that rascal will carry you to a brandy-shop," cried another, out of breath with running.

"Stand clear !" thundered Captain Will, presenting the pistol which he had forgotten to return to the guard of the coach.

Lady Ellen was so bewildered that she almost fancied she had arrived at another world, the only occupation of which was marrying, or being married, and where every one was either victim or priest at the altar of Hymen.

Captain Merry led his fair blushing companion to the "new chapel next to the China shop."

The chapel itself was an eating-house, with nothing ecclesiastical in its look excepting an arched doorway, over which was the following inscription :—

"Weddings Performed Cheap Here.
"The Old and True Register."

And over many of the other houses were to be seen inscriptions of a similar purport.

The gallant highwayman led his bride elect into a room at the back of the eating-house where another rusty-looking individual was seated enjoying a pipe and a tankard of ale.

This worthy, instinctively divining what was wanted, at once rose to his feet, laid down his pipe, and opened a dirty, dog-eared volume on which the pewter tankard had been resting.

"The fee is one guinea, with half-a-crown for each of the witnesses," he exclaimed.

The bridegroom threw down two guineas on the table, bidding the minister keep the change ; the proprietor of the eating-house and his spouse were called in, and, in a few minutes, the ceremony was complete.

Lady Ellen Curtis was the wife of Will Merry, the highwayman !

The parson wrote out a certificate of the affair, and then entered the marriage in his book.

As Will Merry glanced over the shoulder of the holy man he could hardly refrain from laughing at the absurd entry which immediately preceded his own name :—

"George Grant, bachelor ; Ann Gordon, spinster ; marrd. on tick ; stole my silver shoe buckles, and tried to run away with the ring lent by the landlady."

Such was the usual character of the parties who contracted matrimony at the Fleet, and so things continued for a few years when this fearful abuse of holy orders was swept clean away by a special Act of Parliament ; after which run-away couples were compelled to seek refuge on Scottish territory if they would evade the usual formalities attendent on matrimony.

The happy couple departed, carrying with them the drunken blessings of the parson and the witnesses.

Lady Ellen's ears were shocked by the blasphemy and obscene language which surrounded her on every side ; but her husband speedily hailed another hackney coach and drove her to a small though respectable inn on the Surrey side of the water, far away from his usual haunts, where he proposed to remain till he could communicate his adventures and altered state of life to Captain Merlin.

There we must leave them to enjoy the pleasures of each other's society while we hurry back the reader to the presence of the other characters of our tale, and follow the fortunes of Merlin Hawke and his companions.

CHAPTER XLIV.

DEATH OF SIR ANDREW GREVILLE, AND HAPPY UNION OF MERLIN HAWKE WITH LADY FLORENCE.

THE witnesses of the struggle between Sir Thomas Brooke and Sir Andrew Greville looked on with horror till the fearful end of the combat recalled them once more to motion.

Sir Andrew, whose throat was bleeding from the effects of his antagonist's teeth, was once more secured by Merlin's men, and then the chieftain himself plunged his hand into the dead man's pocket to secure the paper which had been the cause of contention.

His eyes glared and sparkled as they fell upon the document.

"Villain!" he thundered, regarding Sir Andrew Greville with a look of the most intense hatred, "all your schemes are at length unmasked."

The baronet replied with a smile of contempt and disdain.

Now that concealment was useless he little cared what might be the consequence of his guilt.

"Call hither the Lady Florence," continued Merlin, addressing one of his followers.

In a few moments she entered the apartment; her cheek flushed crimson as she beheld Sir Andrew, and she would have retreated.

"Nay, lady, stay; I wish you to know how you have been deceived and cheated by yon pale-faced, black-hearted villain who *calls himself* your husband!"

Lady Florence looked up in Merlin's face in astonishment.

"Listen!" continued he, beginning to read from the paper,

"My dear Sir Thomas,—I have to thank you most sincerely for the *loan of your butler*, who performed the marriage ceremony between myself and Florence Ashburne with as much ease and self-possession as though he had been in reality a member of the church. The bird is caught, and confined with fetters, which she could easily break asunder did she know that our marriage was one of the greatest pieces of deceit and sham on record. I hope sometime or other to be enabled to do as much for you.

"Sincerely yours,
"A. GREVILLE."

Before he had well finished reading the damning evidence of the baronet's fraud Merlin saw his beloved Lady Florence sink senseless to the earth.

"Carry her away," said the highwayman; "it is not fit that she should see the end of this affair."

They bore her gently away, and handed her over to the tender care of the innkeeper's daughter, who had accompanied them in their journey.

"Secure the doors and windows!" cried Merlin, when this was done.

His orders were instantly obeyed.

"Unbind the rascal!"

In a moment the hands and feet of Sir Andrew Greville were at liberty.

The caitiff gazed round him with astonishment as did those who attended upon Black Hawke's commands.

But Merlin's intentions soon became evident.

"Now give the rascal a sword, and let him defend himself if he can," was the command, and, at the same moment, the highwayman unsheathed his own weapon, standing as though waiting for his foe to attack.

For some moments not one of the band would lend the vile baronet his weapon.

"Quick! quick, my men. Find him a blade. I am anxious to finish this."

Sir Andrew Greville knew by the look of stern resolution on the brow of Black Hawke that his last hour had arrived.

"Here is a sword," at length said one of the men; "it's a pity to stop a fight for want of weapons."

The sword was placed in the hands of Sir Andrew Greville, who tried its point and temper.

He was determined to do his utmost to slay his adversary.

"Now, Sir Andrew, if you have any request to make before you die, speak out, for in five minutes you will be a lifeless corpse. Your last wishes shall be paid every attention."

"I have no request to make, rascal!" replied the baronet.

"Then defend yourself," cried Merlin, raising his weapon.

Sir Andrew Greville stepped forward a pace, and their weapons crossed.

That Merlin meant death was evident in his blazing eyes and angry features.

The baronet knew that his only hope of safety was in keeping cool, and fighting with the utmost caution and wariness.

Merlin was too angry to exercise all the caution he usually displayed in fencing, he was eager to avenge the terrible wrong which had been done to Lady Florence.

At length a slight wound from Sir Andrew Greville's sword

recalled him from his angry mood, and he began the fight anew.

Lunge for lunge, and thrust for thrust, their weapons glided along each other.

Inspirited by his partial success, Sir Andrew Greville began to have hopes of conquering his adversary.

But he was deceived.

He made a lunge which Merlin parried, and answered by a feint at the baronet's breast.

As Sir Andrew endeavoured to guard, the highwayman's sword was drawn back, and in another instant had entered the baronet's body just below the shoulder.

So quickly was that fatal thrust delivered, that it was not till the baronet dropped his weapon, and staggered backwards, that the bystanders were aware that he had been wounded.

"I am wounded!" he screamed, falling to the floor. "I am——"

"Dead!" exclaimed Merlin, finishing the sentence which his antagonist did not live to complete.

"Remove that lump of carrion," he continued, spurning the dead body with his foot.

The men obeyed; but, as they opened the door to do so, two new arrivals were seen upon the threshold.

These were Captain Ashburne and Marmaduke Greville.

"Ha! villain!" exclaimed the latter, "then you have slain my brother!"

With these words he drew a pistol, and fired it point blank at Merlin's breast.

The bullet rebounded from him, as though he had been made of iron. It had struck against a purse full of guineas, which Black Hawke had inside his coat.

Ere Marmaduke could repeat the shot, Albert Montague sprang forward and passed his weapon through the body of the would-be assassin.

With a loud groan Marmaduke Greville fell dead beside his brother.

"Wretched man, how many more murders will you lay upon your guilty soul?" cried Henry Ashburne.

"Murders? Call not the death of the wretch you looked upon as your sister's husband a murder. Here, read this letter, Captain Ashburne, and see how basely he deceived both you and Lady Florence."

Captain Ashburne read in silence, though the frown on his brow, and the lurid glare in his eyes, betrayed the agitation of his soul.

"I am sorry you killed him; my own sword should have avenged this insult to our family."

"Fire! fire!" exclaimed several voices at this moment.

"Where—where is she?"

"This way, this way."

It was impossible to reach the back room in which Lady Jane Cleveland and Lady Florence were, for a barrier of fire had suddenly sprung up.

Lady Jane, snatching a blanket from the rude bed, indeed managed to rush through the flames without injury, after she had wrapped herself in the woollen covering.

But Lady Florence was too timid for such daring exploits.

The fire gained upon her; all hope of retreat was cut off, and it seemed as if nothing could possibly preserve her from falling a victim to the raging flames.

She stood and shrieked aloud for help.

It came suddenly.

Swift as the bird whose name he bore, Merlin dashed through the flames and caught his beloved one in his arms.

She clung to him in an agony of fear as he wrapped her in his thick cloak, covering her face and arms from the raging element.

Then one more bold rush, and Merlin stood without the house unharmed, with the exception of one or two trifling scorches and bruises.

Henry Ashburne, who had witnessed this act of daring, now approached the highwayman.

"You have saved my sister's life," he said; "from henceforth I vow to do you no injury; nay, more, wed her if you will, for I verily believe she loves you."

"Where is my husband!" asked Lady Florence, faintly.

"If you mean Sir Andrew Greville he is dead; but that base man was never your husband. Dearest Florence, will you accept me, your most devoted adorer, and become my wife?"

"I will; but——"

"But what?"

"While I fancied myself the wife of Sir Andrew Greville I had a son."

At this moment the priest, who had, as before stated, joined the party, approached, and whispered in Merlin's ear.

"Is it so?" exclaimed the latter, gazing with a look of extreme compassion.

"It is the truth."

"Your words and looks tell me that some evil has befallen the babe. Speak out, I implore you, let me know all!"

"It has pleased Heaven to take your child to its bosom. At the place where I concealed him to preserve his life from the plots of his father, he sickened, and is now in a far happier world."

Tears fell fast from Lady Florence's eyes as she heard the news, and Merlin was unequal to the task of restraining them.

"We must away now," said he, as the sun began to approach the west.

"Whither do you intend to hide?" asked the Duke of Cleveland.

"Every cottage in the country will be open to receive me."

"Then instead of entering them come to Vandeleur Park, and see how your young friend behaves himself while he is being married."

Albert Montague's face flushed, and so did that of Lady Jane Cleveland, as they heard the duke's words.

The invitation was accepted, and Merlin, after he had dismissed his band, rode with the duke and Henry Ashburne towards the mansion.

The journey was long, and it was late ere they finished it; but, in spite of their fatigue, few of the inmates of the ducal dwelling slept much that night.

The next day a gay party assembled in the chapel of the mansion.

The chaplain stood within the altar railings; Albert Montague and Lady Jane knelt before him.

The vows were pronounced, the blessing invoked upon them, and the happy young couple were united for life.

And immediately afterwards the lawyers were set to work to prove the young man's right to the title and estates he claimed.

The claimant was identified by a peculiar mark on his heel, which the woman who nursed him as an infant well remembered. The documents for which Lady Jane placed her life in danger proved how the late lord met with his death, and after some forms had been gone through, and fees paid, Albert became Lord Montague, and took up his abode with his blushing bride at Albion Hall.

Hal Hunter, hearing of Will Merry's marriage, managed to persuade pretty Bella Claremont to elope with him, and the Fleet parsons soon made them one flesh.

The worthy judge, seeing that there was no help for it, settled a very handsome income upon the young couple, and took them under his special protection.

Of course, under such circumstances, Hal's exploits on the road were soon forgotten.

His friend, Frank Morton, was not so fortunate, for he was killed the day after Albert Montague's wedding by a party of dragoons, who recognised him as he was riding towards London.

Now, what shall we say of Merlin and Lady Florence? That they married, and were happy?—Certainly.

Lady Florence grieved sincerely for the death of her infant son, but after a short space of time she lent a willing ear to Merlin's suggestions that the time for their union had arrived.

The death of Sir Andrew Greville and his brother had partly removed the obstacles which lay in the way of his possession of the property which was rightfully his.

Gold soon set everything straight, and even hid his past faults from the eyes of justice.

At length Lady Florence became his bride, and their happiness was complete.

Three lovely boys blessed their union, each more beautiful than the one she had lost.

The only event which occurred to grieve her heart was the death of her brother, who fell at the head of his regiment in a desperate and successful charge against an unequal number of French troops.

And now, dear reader, farewell.

You have, perchance, been amused with some of our pages, while others have caused you to yawn and close the book.

In it, however, you must have seen that evil deeds are always punished in the end.

Even Merlin himself was not blameless, nor did he escape scathless; but while we regret his misdeeds as an outlaw, let us remember that he was outraged and wronged by that society against which he waged war under the name of

BLACK HAWKE, THE HIGHWAYMAN!

THE END.